JOSHUA THEN—Joshua Shapiro may have been the streetwise brawling kid of a former prize-fighter dandy and an outrageously scandalous sometime-stripper (particularly at Joshua's Bar Mitzvah). But that was all in the poorer sections of Montreal. That was Joshua then.

JOSHUA NOW—He's in the limelight. A highly successful TV personality and writer with a socialite wife who loves him. Now nothing about him goes unnoticed.

And the scandals that start landing in his fashionable backyard make his tough, raunchy background look like the stuff dreams are made of . . .

JOSHUA THEN AND NOW

"As ever, Richler's targets are dead on. But he is not only gifted with a fine eye and a sense of truthfulness. Richler is a *real* writer, which is rare, and even a *good* writer, which is rarer still. In fact, one is tempted to call him a *great* writer . . ."

—*Maclean's*

"A book brimming with characters and intrigues, comic and serious . . . that a more parsimonious novelist might have spread over several novels . . . A thoroughly enjoyable, exhilarating read."
—David Lodge, *Times Literary Supplement* (London)

"Funny or sad, cruel or compassionate, it's the enormous zest of the book that makes it so life-enhancing."

—Martyn Goff, *London Daily Telegraph*

Joshua
Then
and Now

Mordecai Richler

SEAL BOOKS
McClelland and Stewart-Bantam Limited
Toronto

JOSHUA THEN AND NOW

*A Seal Book / published by arrangement with
McClelland & Stewart, Limited*

PRINTING HISTORY

*McClelland & Stewart edition published May 1980
2 printings through November 1980
A Selection of Book-of-the-Month Club
Seal edition / May 1981*

PRINTED IN THE UNITED STATES OF AMERICA

0 9 8 7 6 5 4 3 2 1

For old Ted Kotcheff,
young Ted Allan,
and Miss Nina Bourne

Lay your sleeping head, my love,
Human on my faithless arm;
Time and fevers burn away
Individual beauty from
Thoughtful children, and the grave
Proves the child ephemeral:
But in my arms till break of day
Let the living creature lie,
Mortal, guilty, but to me
The entirely beautiful.

W. H. AUDEN

ONE

Look at me now, Joshua thought.

His right leg was no longer suspended by pulleys from a hospital ceiling, but it was still held in a cast, multiple fractures healing slowly at his age. There were no more tubes unwinding out of his nostrils or feeding him intravenously or draining his lungs. Lungs bubbling with blood whenever he took a breath. Yet he continued to brood about all the blood they had pumped into him. Twelve alien pints. It flooded his dreams, it polluted his waking hours. The odds were that some of the blood had been peddled to the hospital by winos or junkies. I'm bound to come down with hepatitis, he thought. Worse, maybe.

Although his cracked ribs were on the mend, or so they assured him, it was still excruciating for him to cough. The cast wouldn't come off his right arm until Thursday, but he could already wiggle the fingers of his right hand. There were places where he was free to scratch. If a magazine was mounted on his reading stand, he could turn the pages himself. But *Time*, no longer an abomination (excoriating Adlai, clapping hands for Senator Joseph McCarthy of blessed memory), wasn't much fun any more either, now that it was informed by decency. More liberal pieties. Neither were there any more gratifyingly unjust wars to read about, where you could at least root for the downtrodden. Screw the downtrodden—muggers, the lot. The Khmer Rouge, the Vietnamese, were interchangeable enigmas to him, and he didn't much care who won that one. Or, come to think of it, which National Liberation Front came out on top in Botswana, or whatever they were calling that chunk of uppity Africa this week. Good news: Bob Hope, he read, has announced that he wants to do a TV special in China. After the Long March, following the years of deprivation, the ultimate Great Leap Forward. The William Morris Agency, Swifty Lazar, Sue Mengers, or whoever represented hope with a capital *H*, would soon be out there in the Middle Kingdom, negotiating points with Teng Hsiao-p'ing, proffering serendipity in living color for once-recalcitrant chinks. Imagine, in the absence of Virginia Mayo, this year's Miss America disco-dancing out of the mouth of a cave in Yenan clad in a Halston original.

Next year maybe Sonny and Cher would come to us direct from Auschwitz, singing "The Way We Were" before the open doors of a reconstructed crematorium.

The bandages had been peeled from his shaven skull, cracks having knitted together again. Doctors no longer surrounded his bed with solicitude, their expressions grave, whispering to each other, frowning over charts, even as they asked him his name, what day of the week it was, or the ages of his children. Alex, eighteen; Susy, fourteen; Teddy, ten. I will be no more of a dolt, he thought, than I was before. Small satisfaction. But at least he was through with the bedpan. If he was helped out of bed, taking it *poco a poco*, he was now able to go to the toilet himself.

Only last Tuesday, Joshua's bed had been wheeled surreptitiously into an elevator; he was loaded into an ambulance idling at a rear door of the Montreal General and sped across the Champlain Bridge, down the familiar Route 10, *autoroute des cantons de l'est*, to their cottage on Lake Memphremagog. Bliss. Cranked into a sitting position, he could now actually see the lake through the window, rather than sour septuagenarians shuffling down a hospital hall to file a good bowel movement, as if that were proof against a carcinoma. Although the ice had broken up only a week earlier, swollen sails were already skittering across the bay. There were also men in small boats anchored off the far point—most of them bona fide fishermen casting for perch, but others equipped with telephoto lenses, casting for Joshua Shapiro, Esquire. A few had come from as far as Fleet Street to wait him out at the Hatley Inn, where they insisted on smoked salmon for breakfast, complaining loudly about its stringiness, having already stuffed hotel bath towels into the bottoms of their suitcases.

The birds were back. In the early morning hours, before

2

anybody else in the cottage had risen, he watched the lake's sole surviving loon wheeling over the water, diving for sunfish and smelts. Once he saw an early golden finch swooping between the budding birch trees. In the evening, there were the robins feeding on water spiders. He couldn't see Susy and Teddy on the dock below—even if he strained, they were beyond his line of vision—but he could hear Susy squealing each time Teddy hooked a perch, and he blessed them.

He was getting better. No doubt about it. One morning, with Reuben's support, he even managed to hobble as far as his upstairs study, fighting dizziness, trying to gather reassurance from the familiar artifacts. The framed boxing, hockey, and baseball photographs. Cassius Clay, as he was then, gloating over a prone Sonny Liston. Al Weill sitting with a puffy-eyed, bandaged Rocky Marciano after the Walcott fight. A beetle-browed Maurice "The Rocket" Richard in full flight. Koufax throwing. And then, in the place of honor, his most cherished possession. The poster.

MADRID WILL BE THE TOMB OF FASCISM
¡No pasarán!
Every house a fortress, every street a trench, every neighborhood a wall of iron and combatants . . .

Emulate Petrograd! 7 November on the Manzanares must be as glorious as on the Neva!

WIVES-
TOMORROW PREPARE TO TAKE YOUR HUSBAND'S LUNCH TO THE TRENCHES, NOT THE FACTORY

VIVA MADRID
WITHOUT A GOVERNMENT

From his study window, he had a clear view of the Trimble estate across the bay. The shuttered boathouse, with the Grew 212 secured inside; the Tanzer bobbing at anchor, its sails still stored in the padlocked cabin. Because of the sheltering pines he couldn't quite make out the incomparable tennis court or the rock garden which used to be floodlit at night, but there was the mansion itself, its windows hooded. He knew the French-Canadian pine antiques, the outsized custom-built sofas with the down pillows, the snooker table with the claw legs; everything lay temporarily under sheets. What he didn't know was whether Trimble was going to put

3

the estate up for sale—his act of contrition—or, more likely, would defiantly reopen the house on Victoria Day weekend, obliging Jane to confront the old bunch. . . . The hell with the Trimbles, he had enough problems of his own.

Two old men, Reuben and the senator, guarded against intruders. The senator enjoyed rocking on the front porch, reading the latest Travis McGee, a fly swatter on one side, a bottle of Chablis riding in an ice bucket on the other. A shotgun resting on his lap. Reuben—wizened now, his hands flecked with liver spots, but still sporting a straw boater at a jaunty angle—was here, there, and everywhere when he wasn't contemplating the morning line in the *Daily Racing Form*. Reuben watched over the children on the lake and read to them from his dog-eared Bible before tucking them in at night. He scoured the woods for interlopers and patrolled the dirt road that led to the cottage.

The day before yesterday two men in a red Mustang, a reporter and a photographer, had stopped Reuben on the road, mistaking him for a handyman. "Je m'excuse," the reporter said, "je cherche la maison de Joshua Shapiro."

Reuben, letting his wrists hang limp, said, "You don't look the type."

The reporter chuckled, appreciative, and explained that he represented the Montreal *Gazette*.

"Well, son, it's a good thing you stopped me," Reuben said, pausing to take a sip of V.O. out if his hip flask before passing it on to the reporter.

The reporter, determined to prove a good fellow, drank from the flask without wiping the neck. Retrieving it with a shaky hand, Reuben contrived to spill rye over his jacket. "Whoops. Sorry," he said.

"Oh, that's O.K.," the reporter replied tightly.

"You're on the wrong road."

"But we were told—" the photographer began.

"Which is the right road?" the reporter asked.

"I figure that's worth ten bucks."

The reporter dug into his pocket for a ten-dollar bill, making a mental note to claim twenty from the office.

"The Shapiro place is like a mile further down the main road. First right, and then take the turn-off second left right after the 'Patates Frites.' It's a dirt road and you keep bearing left. Eventually you come to a sign that says 'Road Closed, Bridge Under Repair,' but they're just trying to jew you. Remove the barrier and plow right through. Got that?"

"Oh, is he ever bullshitting us," the photographer said.

4

"I know."

"That's the house up there through the trees. I was here once before to photograph the senator."

Reuben unzipped his windbreaker to show that he was wearing a gun. "If you don't turn around right now," he said, "I'm going to shoot out your tires. Ping ping ping."

"We'll be back with the police."

"Officer Orville Moon is the fella you want."

They found Moon flipping through a copy of *Penthouse* in Lapointe's General Store.

"Yessir," Moon said, listening to the reporter's story, "yes," and he strolled back with them to the Mustang, waiting for the reporter to slip behind the wheel. "You the one who's driving?"

"Yes. Why?"

"Because you stink to high heaven of alcoholic spirits," he said, "and I'm going to have to book you."

The senator was waiting for Reuben on the porch, arthritic hand outstretched. "My share, please, partner."

"He was only good for a fiver," Reuben said, handing him two-fifty.

Reuben Shapiro was Joshua's father and the senator, Stephen Andrew Hornby, his father-in-law. At night, after the children had gone to bed, Reuben strolled down to the gate, locked it, put out his BEWARE OF THE DOG/ CHIEN MÉCHANT sign, and set his trip wires on the way back to the cottage. Then he and the senator played gin rummy in the living room or had a Bible discussion or watched the Expos lose again on television. Every now and then Reuben took a turn round the property, checking out his wires. The first night they had been set too low and a raccoon had started all the pots and pans jingling, Reuben diving for his flashlight, the senator leaping for his shotgun.

The reporters didn't get anywhere asking questions in the village either, because the cottage had been in the senator's family since he had been a boy himself and everybody for miles around remembered Pauline as a child. "Trout" they used to call her, because her fair skin was speckled with freckles. Now they felt sorry for Pauline and resented Joshua. I hardly blame them, Joshua thought.

Joshua was allowed to read his mail now, although he suspected certain letters were still being withheld. Yesterday a real zinger had slipped through Reuben's net. It was from the David and Jonathan Society, a newly formed group of young, caring, Jewish faggots. They wished him well, "Shalom, coming out is easier with friends," and invited him to be a guest of honor at their Purim ball. To each his own Queen Esther. He was also now considered well enough to see the newspapers and magazines. On the whole, his colleagues had not dealt viciously with his case, delivering no more than he deserved, but he realized there was no way his TV contract could be renewed for next season. The hell with it. Meanwhile, as might have been expected, gay publications everywhere had sprung to his defense. *The Body Politic*, Canada's very own journal for homophiles, had put him on its cover. A martyr. The Glad Day Bookshop, in Toronto, was moving the old paperback edition of his badly dated *The Volunteers*—an appreciation of the men who had fought with the International Brigades in Spain—faster than the latest Gore Vidal. *Mandate, The International Magazine of Entertainment & Eros*, had managed to get an interview with his mother, or, more likely, she had sought them out. Esther Shapiro, née Leventhal, but best known as Esty Blossom.

Oh my God, but his loopy mother—who had been unearthed in Winnipeg, where she was now managing a massage parlor called ORAL IS BEAUTIFUL—allowed that she had been surprised to read that he was gay, and that at first she had felt very sad for him, because there was such prejudice on this matter within the straight Jewish community. "And not only here. I mean, take Israel," she said. "There is a kibbutz for this and a kibbutz for that. You name it, you got it. But if there's a kibbutz anywhere out there for gays, it's still in the closet. Or maybe the Gaza Strip isn't what I think. Ha, ha, ha." His mother said she had been shocked when his now notorious correspondence with Murdoch had surfaced. "After all, he was always a bit of a prig," and, to illustrate her point, she told them what had happened at his bar-mitzvah. "But I'm in enough trouble with him already, so you spell that right. P-r-i-g. Ha, ha, ha." She regretted that she and her son were now estranged, but this, she assured the interviewer, had nothing to do with his coming out. "Don't quote me on this, but he married up and I never cared for his wife. On the other hand, who knows what Pauline has been through? Maybe she blames me." Esther was not only active in women's lib, but she was now also on the executive board of Parents of Gays in Canada, which group, she was at pains to point out, was no branch-plant organization, but entirely independent of the similarly named American society. "We, for instance, are also bilingual. Ha, ha, ha."

6

The Advocate, a more intellectual publication, in considering his collected pieces on sports, ventured that they were necessarily oblique, even deviously straight (which was understandable, the writer allowed, given the context of those pinched years), in contrast to the refreshingly new and flourishing gay book world. "An important fact about ADVOCATE readers at least, and possibly gay people in general, is that we are readers." Quoting some of the available snippets from the correspondence, it evoked Auden's relationship with Chester Kallman. But *Christopher Street* had, somehow or other, actually got its hot hands on some of the letters. Obviously one of their correspondents had penetrated the purportedly secure Rare Manuscripts Collection at Rocky Mountain University, or its curator, Colin Fraser. Or, possibly both.

Rereading some of the salacious letters for the first time in more than twenty years, Joshua laughed aloud at outrageous passages until the sharp pain in his ribs made him wince. On balance, he felt that his end of the correspondence was the more inventive, which pleased him enormously. A full-page photograph of the two of them, the way they were—London, circa 1955—introduced the letters. A much more recent photograph, the one that had become famous, showed them kissing at a Beverly Hills poolside. Markham's poolside. There followed three full pages of the correspondence and, for the rest, more letters ran down one column in the back pages of the magazine, squeezed between advertisements that he found mind-boggling.

Also available, from the same firm, were a salve called Jac-Up ("The name says it all") and something called Black-Jac. The entire set, the incomparable Jac-Combo, was offered for

$19.90, with a free catalogue of adult toys, featuring Jack Wrangler in full color. Canadians, however, would have to add ten percent to the cost of each order.

Oh God.

Only three weeks earlier, when tubes had been curling in and out of him everywhere like surgical spaghetti, Dr. Morty Zipper had gently pressed his hand and asked, "Can you hear me, Josh?"

In response, Joshua had blinked his eyes.

"You're lucky to be alive."

I'll be the judge of that, Joshua thought.

2

Charlie McCarthy was made of wood. A dummy. The capital of their country was called Ottawa, its prime minister Mackenzie King. Lux was the soap of the stars. The No. 45 streetcar would get him downtown, the 29 take him to Outremont. Girls, even Jewish girls, would grow a bush, just like he would one day, although they had nothing to hide there. He knew, he'd asked around. Howie Morenz was dead and there would never be another hockey player like him. "Before they made him," Uncle Oscar said, grieving, "they broke the mold."

When Joshua was six years old, he also knew the names of the top ten lightweights, his father's old division, as they were rated in Mr. Fleischer's *Ring* magazine, but he had no idea what his father did to earn a living now that his fighting days were finished. He did know that his father never opened the front door to a stranger, but instead sent his mother, sometimes even him, hanging back himself, a length of lead pipe in his curled fist. So when his mother registered him for school, he was surprised to hear her smartly respond "Bill collector" when asked for "father's occupation."

Bill collector? "What does Daddy do, really?" he asked.

"He's an undercover man for the RCMP."

"Aw, come on. What does he do, but?"

"Well, you could say that these days he's in insurance, sort of."

The only insurance man he knew, Finkleman, his drifting eyes milky with cataracts, shuffled round once a week to complain about his aching feet and collect fifty cents from his mother, lick his pencil and tick off the payment in his big ledger. "Like from Prudential?" he asked.

"You know what killed the cat?"

"Curiosity."

"Right. Now for the sixty-four-dollar question. Who did Max Baer, that reckless looter in Lovers' Land, the magnificent swashbuckler, beat for the heavyweight crown?"

"Primo Carnera. New York. June fourteenth, nineteen thirty-four. An eleventh-round K.O."

"And who was counting for knockdowns, if you're so smart?"

"Judge Artie Idella."

"Ladies and gentlemen," his mother announced, "we are proud to present tonight's stellar attraction, for the light-weight championship of the world . . . weighing one hundred and thirty-six pounds and wearing white trunks, the challenger from Montreal, Canada . . . RUBY SHAPIRO! . . . and his opponent . . . weighing one hundred and thirty-five pounds and wearing purple trunks . . . the lightweight champion of the world . . . from New York City . . . SAMMY ANGOTT!"

His mother was utterly unlike the other mothers on the street, even then. She was indifferent to his report cards and she did not oh and ah over his crayon drawings. His mother didn't care how late he came home from school, or where he hung around. She was not determined that he would be the one to grow up and discover the cure for cancer. Or, failing that, marry Outremont money.

In those days his mother was uncommonly beautiful, with thick black hair, a high girlish bosom, delicate white skin, and a laugh that reminded him of honey. But it was his father who could evoke her laughter, not he. Joshua could do nothing to please her. She did not even appreciate that he had to defend her good name with his fists against the other boys on the street. Their striving mothers, grown fat and sour with the years, bitterly resented his. Her marriage had not been arranged between families, as was only proper, but had been a scandal in its time, a love-match. His mother, actually born into Outremont affluence, a Leventhal, had defied her cultivated family, descending to their grubby street and marrying into a family of thugs out of Odessa, taking a struggling club fighter, lucky to get a semi-final in Albany, for her husband. Worse news. After a turbulent six years of marriage it was abundantly clear that she was still smitten with him. She could be seen leaning on his shoulder, obviously embar-

9

rassing him, all through a double feature at the Regent. She did not send his white-on-white shirts to the Chinese laundry, but ironed them herself, doing the collars just so. With money saved from her household allowance, or a good run at poker, she bought him hand-painted ties and once a fourteen-carat gold stickpin with his initials, RS. His mother kept herself indecently perfumed, her hair touched with henna, a girl, just for him. Or so it seemed. She had not yet begun to drink heavily. Or demonstrate. But so far as the other mothers on the street were concerned, she was already wanton.

Joshua could still remember the Saturday morning he first did something to please his mother. He was eleven, it was autumn, and only two months had passed since his father had been obliged to hit the road again, leaving them abruptly. His mother had grown increasingly anxious, roaming their cold-water flat at all hours of the day and night, unable to sleep, chewing 217's, playing Duke Ellington records on the gramophone, the blinds pulled down so that she could practice her routines. She consumed one lending-library book after another. *Anthony Adverse, Trader Horn,* an endless spill of Ellery Queens, anything by Edna Ferber. Every Friday morning she grudgingly marched him over to Fletcher's Field, shot a roll of film of him with her Kodak Brownie, and walked to the corner of Jeanne-Mance, where a man waited in a car. He would extract the roll of film, hand back the camera, grunt, and drive off. Then one Saturday morning, after they had just returned from a shopping expedition to Rachel Market, they discovered their front door ajar, the glass broken, the wood round the lock splintered. His mother cursed and set down her parcels in the hall. "You wait here," she said.

But unwilling to be left alone, he trailed after her all the same. The mattresses in her bedroom and his had been razored open, bleeding ticking. The same was true of all the sofa cushions in the living room. His father's favorite easy chair had been slashed. Every dresser drawer in the house had been overturned, clothes strewn all over the place. His father's white-on-white shirts. His spats. His black silk socks. His father's clothes closet, the one he had put his own cedar lining into, had also been ransacked. Somebody had put his foot through his straw boater. He had also defecated on his father's ice-cream suit. The worn kitchen linoleum had been rolled back, and some of the floorboards had been lifted.

"Should I call the police?" he asked.

His mother opened her purse, fished out a Pall Mall, and lighted it. "You mustn't be afraid."

"I'm not," he lied.

"They wouldn't dare come if we were here."

"Who?"

"Whoever."

"What do they want with us?"

"The gas ration coupon business, you know, is very competitive. It's no bowl of cherries."

"I see," he said, baffled.

"Good. Now Josh, I think Daddy left something with you. A key, maybe."

He hesitated.

"And I suppose you hid it somewhere in the house here?"

"No. I carry it with me all the time."

He showed his mother the key and she laughed and actually hugged him. "I'm going to take you to a restaurant, just you and me."

His mother slipped into her green shirtwaist dress, pinned a straw hat into her hair, and touched her mouth with ruby-red lipstick. She didn't take him to a poky neighborhood delicatessen, but to a real restaurant, on St. Catherine Street. Dinty Moore's. Where the manager kissed her on the cheek, his mother, and a waiter immediately brought a Dewar's and a splash to their table.

It didn't work out. Emboldened by the sweet memory of his mother's embrace, he chattered on mindlessly about school and his life on the street until, whatever her good intentions, he sensed her eyes glazing over, bored. Later he would realize that she was more frightened than she allowed, and that if not for his unwanted presence she could have been with his father, who was hunkering down in a fishing lodge in Irish Hills, Michigan, always remembering to check out the trip wires he had set on the property before turning in for the night. But for him, his mother could have joined him there, making sure nobody else was cooking corned beef and cabbage for him or ironing his shirt collars just so.

Even as Joshua struggled to hold her interest, they were joined by a man who he later learned was a city councillor named Ed Ryan. Mr. Ryan, a beefy man with joyful blue eyes, his nose a network of burst capillaries, was smoking a Havana. He slid into his mother's side of the booth uninvited and flicked his fingers for the waiter, directing him to bring her another Dewar's and a splash, as well as the usual for him, and a banana split for the lad.

11

"What a pleasure it is to see you here, Esther," he said.

"You'll get over it," his mother said, flushing.

"And how are you managing these days?"

"Better than Billy Conn. Not as good as J. Edgar Hoover."

"Ah, isn't it a sad business," Mr. Ryan said, his voice soothing, "a most lamentable state of affairs, but everything that can be done is being done."

"Please don't do that," his mother said, moving tighter to the wall. "You're trespassing on somebody else's property."

He didn't know what Mr. Ryan was doing, but Ryan guffawed, bringing a hairy hand up from under the table, and recited:

> "There was a young lady named Riddle
> Who had an untouchable middle.
>   She had many friends
>   Because of her ends,
> Since it isn't the middle you diddle."

His mother snickered nervously and indicated Joshua's presence. Mr. Ryan edged closer to his mother even as he winked at Joshua. "Did anyone ever tell you," he asked, "that you have your mother's haunting brown eyes and her delicate complexion?"

Fuck you.

"And how would you like to go to Belmont Park this afternoon and try all the new rides?"

"Why not?" he said, misunderstanding, assuming he meant all three of them.

"Euclid," Mr. Ryan called out, still smiling directly at Joshua.

A small, peppery French Canadian hurried over to their booth.

"How would you like to take the charming young Mr. Shapiro here to Belmont Park this afternoon?"

Confused, he appealed to his mother, who was squeezed even tighter to the wall, Mr. Ryan crowding her. "What should I do?"

"Go. Stay," his mother said in a thick voice.

Euclid was already tugging him by the elbow. "Come on, sonny, we're going to have lots of fun."

He didn't remember much about his afternoon in the amusement park, but he did recall that it had already turned dark when he let himself in the front door. His mother was on the phone, hollering at somebody. "I'm going to tell him everything you did to me, you son of a bitch." Slamming the receiver back into the cradle, she saw him standing there. "Why did you go?" she demanded.

"You said I should."

"I didn't want you to go."

The room stank of cigar smoke. His mother's feathery pink fans lay on the carpet. But there was only one purple balloon. The other had been burst.

"What happened?" he asked.

"What happened happened."

His mother was wearing a flowery housecoat over her costume. "And will you please stop staring at me," she said.

"I'm not staring at you."

"I should be with your father. I shouldn't be stuck here alone."

"I'm here."

"Wowee," she said.

Recognizing her mood, grittily determined not to be left behind again, he surprised himself by speaking harshly to her. "If you leave me with Aunt Fanny again, I'm going to run away."

"Where would you go?" she asked, interested.

"I'd manage."

"I wonder."

Now he was really scared. "If I ran away, Daddy wouldn't like it."

They stared at each other, a moment of recognition, and then, frightened, they both retreated.

"What would you like for supper?" she asked.

"I'm not hungry."

"Oh no you don't," she said fiercely. "You are not going to eat, you're going to stuff yourself. So when we go out to take your picture on Fletcher's Field this Friday, I don't want a message back that his precious one looks thin."

When he wakened the next morning he found his mother on her hands and knees with a bucket and brush, scrubbing the hall floor. "He should have left the key with me," she said. "I'm his wife."

"I didn't ask for it, but."

"Some bigshot. You're not even a man yet, if you know what I mean?"

Lying in bed in his Lower Westmount townhouse one morning, two weeks before his accident, before the letters had surfaced or anyone had accused him of being a closet

13

queer, sifting through the conundrums of a childhood that still bewildered him, Joshua was suddenly jolted awake by the front doorbell. Damn it, he had not even had his breakfast yet, and when he peeked out of his bedroom window he saw a police car parked in the drifting snow. Relieved that the kids had already left for school, he hurried into his dressing gown and raced downstairs to open the front door, in such a rush that he totally forgot what he was still wearing underneath. He beckoned the two cops inside, determined to have them state their business—especially if it was what he feared—without benefit of onlookers.

"What can I do for you?" he asked warily.

"It's what we can do for you, sir."

Aha.

"We found your car parked downtown with the keys still in the ignition."

"Outside The King's Arms?" Joshua asked, his head pounding.

"It's a tow zone."

Immensely relieved but still suspicious, Joshua said, "I had too much to drink last night and decided to take a taxi home." But the truth was, he had forgotten all about the car. "I'm sorry to have caused you any trouble."

The older of the two cops, the plainclothesman in charge, plunked down Joshua's car keys on a table and introduced himself: Detective Sergeant Stuart Donald McMaster.

McMaster was a chubby man with icy blue eyes, pudgy cheeks, a sly tiny mouth, and a chin receding into wobbly fat, the price paid for too many submarine sandwiches on the fly. "Why, it's our pleasure, Mr. Shapiro," he said. "I happen to be a great admirer of your column." And sending the younger cop back to the car, he wandered into the living room and sat down, uninvited. Immediately putting the furniture under surveillance. "You'll find your car parked across the street, incidentally."

McMaster, Joshua noticed for the first time, was carrying what appeared to be a bound manuscript, and now he revealed what Joshua took to be the real reason for his visit. McMaster was taking a night course at Concordia University, creative writing; he had been working on a novel for ten years. "I want you to know it's not one of your little one-character jobs. Shit, no. It has ten major characters and I've written the biographies of each one of them." He paused, watching Joshua closely. "Now I suppose you want to know why ten?"

14

"Only," Joshua said, beginning to enjoy himself, "if you have already copyrighted the idea."

McMaster didn't answer at once. Savoring the moment, he lit a cigarette, his face flushed with hatred. "You don't know what an honor it is just to be sitting with you, a man of your stature. We never miss you on TV. Wait till I tell my grandson. Wow."

"Please, McMaster."

"Stu."

"Stu."

"I used to know your father in the old days."

"There isn't a cop in town who didn't."

"Hey, did you know big Ed Ryan back when?"

"Never heard of him."

"Well, I got my own theories about his accident." McMaster ground his gleaming dentures together. "I read somewhere that you liked hockey better than any other sport."

"Don't we all?"

"Affirmative. But you've got a season pass, maybe even a couple in the reds, and you get to booze with all the players. Me, I only get to take my grandson to a game when the legendary Washington Caps are in town. Ginsberg of Upper Belmont lays the tickets on me. And I'm supposed to faint with gratitude and maybe cruise past his house one more time while they're in Florida. Specially these days. With all the robberies."

In as casual a voice as he could manage, Joshua asked, "Are we having an unusual number of robberies in Westmount these days?"

"Not so much an unusual number as unusual robberies. Crazy."

"How do you mean, crazy?"

"I was going to tell you why ten characters." McMaster sucked in a mighty puff of his cigarette, his cunning eyes belying his quick smile. "There's one major character from each province of Canada."

Joshua whistled, impressed. "No one from the Northwest Territories or the Yukon?"

"Minor."

"If Quebec separates, will you have to revise?"

McMaster's smile lapsed. "One of the major characters," he said, his voice filled with reproach, "is a Jew. And I'm not saying that to flatter you. I don't give a sweet fuck about anybody. Ask around."

"I don't have to. I believe you."

15

"Nobody speaks for guys like me any more. We just hacked this country out of the wilderness, that's all. But these days, you want to inherit the earth you better be a gay-libber or a jigaboo or a Jew. You're a faggot today, and you want it written in the bill of rights that you got the right to teach gym in elementary school and soap the boys down in the shower room. A Jew elbows ahead of you in a line-up outside a movie and you shove him back a little, just to keep him honest, and right off he's hollering about the six million." McMaster leaped to his surprisingly dainty little feet. "What I'm trying to say is, don't make the mistake of taking me for a fool. I may be nothing but a *goy*," he said, enormously pleased with himself, "crazy enough to be an honest cop, but I've still got all my marbles."

"I can see that you weren't born yesterday, McMaster."

"Aw, come on. *Stu.*"

"Stu."

"Don't get pissed off with me. More power to you, I say. I wish my people had your savvy. If we did, the French Canadians wouldn't be dumping on us today. Here, give me your hand. Put it there."

Feeling foolish, Joshua shook hands with him. McMaster's palm was moist.

"I get home tonight, I'm going to tell Irma I shook hands with Joshua Shapiro and that he has agreed to read my novel and give his frank opinion of it." Instead of letting go, he squeezed. "Sorry about your wife."

"What, exactly, do you mean about my wife?"

"Hey, hello there. Geez. Better ask me what I *don't* know about Westmount, this has been my turf for better than thirty years now. You must know the Trimbles. You know, Belvedere Road. The corner house."

"Yes," Joshua said wearily, "I know the Trimbles."

"Have you ever wondered why such a la-de-da Englishman served in the Canadian army?"

"His mother came from the west. Edmonton, I think."

"Calgary," McMaster said, his smile small. "Remember his Guy Fawkes parties? Everybody used to come. Too bad, isn't it?"

"Jack Trimble can walk in here any time he feels like it."

"Spoken like a born gentleman."

Joshua smiled.

"But if it's not presuming too much, Mr. Shapiro, how would your good wife feel about that?"

16

"The short answer is that you *are* presuming too much. And now, if you don't mind, I've got work to do."

"Right." McMaster wiped his brow with his sleeve. Thin gray hair was brushed back to reveal a deep running scar. "Hey, look, I still carry a steel plate in there. A souvenir of the battle of Falaise. I call it my *goy's yarmulka*."

Joshua didn't react.

"Doesn't that deserve a little hee-haw?"

"You're a live one, Stu."

"The things I know about Westmount, holy shit, I'll never sell the serial rights to the *Digest*. This classy cesspool makes Peyton Place look like the Waltons. Ah well, you know what pleases me? To cruise by here and hear you typing away. Clickety-click, clickety-click. I really am grateful that you're going to read my novel."

Leaping up to see him to the door, Joshua didn't realize that his loosely belted dressing gown had fallen open briefly, but one look at McMaster's startled face was sufficient to remind him that having tumbled into bed drunk last night, he was still wearing that ridiculous pair of black satin panties with the delicate lace trim.

"Well, I do declare," McMaster said, genuinely surprised.

"They're not mine," Joshua protested in a rush, his cheeks hot. "They're Seymour's," he added, as if that explained it.

"Seymour's," McMaster said. "Well, see you around."

Having disposed of McMaster with a rash promise to read his stuff, Joshua was unaccountably apprehensive. A conditioned reflex, possibly; after all, he was still Reuben Shapiro's boy, and a cop in the house was no way to start his day. But now he was more than apprehensive, he was frightened. He had begun to sweat. Today was Teddy's hockey day at school. A stray skate could catch him in the throat, slicing it open. When he had finally got round to sorting out the laundry for Mrs. Zwibock yesterday, he had found a bookmatch in Alex's jeans. He didn't smoke, it had to be pot. Or possibly he needs the matches to heat the substance in the spoon. He never should have had children, they scared him. Joshua felt inadequate. Lonely. If Pauline had been there, a coffee shared with her would have calmed him down and propelled him into his study to write his bloody column. But she was no longer there and she might never be back. Face it, Joshua. No, I won't face it. She's going to recover. O Pauline, Pauline, my love.

Stepping out of those black satin panties, Joshua dressed

17

quickly, gulped down a coffee, and retreated to his study to confront his Underwood 450. Immediately he saw that the ribbon was faint, and was relieved to think he could now (without cheating, without really avoiding work) go out to buy a new one. Playing by the rules, however, he had to try the top drawer of his desk first and there, as luck would have it, lay an unused ribbon. Grudgingly he changed ribbons, consuming only ten minutes, and then he scrubbed the keys with an old toothbrush. Then he went to the window and watched until a car passed with a license plate ending in a seven, always a good omen. Then he moved to the wall where his father's old boxing gloves hung, and he laid his cheek against them for luck.

One punishingly hot summer afternoon when Joshua was a snotty eleven-year-old, still too incredibly stupid to comprehend how his father really earned his living, Reuben summoned him into the kitchen. In those days it was his mother's affection he yearned for. God forgive him, but in those days he found his father's very presence an embarrassment. Snoring away with his mouth open while his mother listened to "Big Town" on the radio, Edward G. Robinson hollering, "Stop the presses, Lorelei!" His father clipping his toenails at the kitchen table. Or beginning his breakfast with a bottle of Labatt's. And now, typically, calling him into the kitchen, where he stood clad only in his initialed shorts and diamond socks, slipping into trousers with a faultless crease even as he talked to him, pausing now and then to sip V.O. out of a shot glass. Which was not the way fathers behaved in G. A. Henty novels. Or in *Boy's Own Annual*. Or even in neighboring Outremont, beautiful Outremont, where his respectable relatives lived. The Leventhals. Who would have nothing to do with them.

Because of him.

Reuben Shapiro, hitching up his trousers and then fishing into his initialed cotton shorts to sort out his genitals. Whistling through that misshapen nose, broken more times than Joshua could count, as he knotted his hand-painted tie: sunset comes to Waikiki Beach. His father, his black curly hair heavy with Vitalis, his eyebrows disappearing into scarred bumpy tissue, smiled down tenderly at him. "Hey, Josh, how's school?"

His mother was in the bedroom, sobbing, the door closed behind her.

"You doing good there?"

"I'm doing well," he countered in his prissiest manner.

18

His father smiled and moved to the window that looked out on the back lane. There was nothing there. "What's your favorite subject," he asked, "grammar?"

"Literature," Joshua said, too dim to grasp that he was being teased. "What have you done to Mother?"

He no longer said "Maw," which he had come to consider crude.

"Now listen here, Josh. You ever heard of a town called Cornwall?"

"It's just across the border in Ontario. Why is she crying like that?"

"Now in this town of Cornwall on the main street there is, like, a bank." His father glanced out of the window, cracking his knuckles. "It's called the Royal Bank of Canada. Repeat that, please."

"The Royal Bank of Canada."

"In the Royal Bank of Canada which is on the main street of Cornwall just across the Ontario border they have, well, kinda boxes there. You know what I mean?"

"Safety deposit boxes."

"Hey, yeah. Right. Well, well." His father dug a long thin key out of his pocket. "This key fits one of those boxes in the Royal Bank of Canada which is on the main street of Cornwall just across the Ontario border. The number of the box is on the key."

"So?"

"Take it. Hide it for me."

"Why?"

A car slid to a stop in the lane. A man got out, put two fingers to his mouth and whistled. His father held up five fingers. "Well, yeah. Why? I've got to take a trip. Unexpected."

"Again?"

His packed kitbag stood in the corner. Years before, he had used to lug that bag with him to Brockton, Three Rivers, Quebec City, Portland, and a couple of times even to Madison Square Garden.

"I won't be able to write. If I'm gone long and you run short here you are to go to Cornwall and open that box, but you mustn't take, um, Mother with you."

"Why not?"

Outside, the man whistled again.

"People are nosey. They might be following her."

The man in the lane blew sharply on his horn. His father went to the window and held up one finger. And then, his eyes wet, anguished, he grabbed Joshua without warning and pressed his son to him. Joshua went rigid, resisting his embrace, flinching from a kiss that reeked of V.O. and Aqua Velva. "Yeah, right. Well, well. Goodbye, *yingele*," and reaching for his kitbag, he retreated into the coal shed and down the winding stairs into the lane.

The car his father rode off in had Michigan license plates. He didn't sit beside the driver, but instead folded his jacket neatly and then climbed into the trunk.

When the detectives arrived, only five minutes later, his mother wailed and pulled her hair. She denounced his father to them, saying he had deserted her, the drunken bastard, running off to Baltimore with another woman, leaving her without a penny. "I only hope you catch him," she said cursing him again, "and teach him a good lesson this time."

Joshua watched. Bug-eyed. Amazed. He had never heard her say a bad word about his father before. But the detectives were unmoved by his mother's plight. Perreault even shook his head, laughing. "You ought to go on the stage, Esther."

"Really?" she said, enthused, and she shot Joshua a dreamy look as if to say, "Didn't I tell you?"

And he knew, once the detectives had gone, what was coming. She would draw the living room blinds, switch off all the lights, and screw the red bulb into the lamp that had been adjusted to throb on and off, like a Christmas tree light. Then, while he rolled up the rug and cleared the center of the room of furniture, she would disappear into her bedroom to dig out her props. When she signaled with a rap on the door that she was ready, he would put on the record—Fats Waller playing "Snake Hips"—and he would whistle and stamp his feet.

Joshua mounted his exercise bike, sprinting for five minutes. Then he got up to piss so he wouldn't have to break off later in the middle of a thought, should he receive one. He cut his fingernails. He trimmed his nasal hairs. Then he descended into the kitchen to make himself a pot of tea. He wandered into the living room, where he scanned the *TV Guide* to see what the afternoon movie was, not that he was going to watch, no matter what was playing, but just in case he developed a headache and couldn't work. Fair is fair. While he waited for the water to boil, he willed the phone to ring, summoning him somewhere. Picking up the phone himself, initiating an interruption, was strictly against the house rules.

Maybe Sheldon would call again this morning, his cousin Sheldon Leventhal.

When they had been kids he had seldom seen Sheldon, especially after the time he had been stashed with his unwilling family for a two-week stay. Sheldon's family was both rich and respectable; Joshua had been determined to ingratiate himself, but events had conspired against him. Aunt Fanny, appalled to be lumbered with Joshua, had fixed a cot for him in the attic. Next to the maid's room. "Hey," he demanded, "what are you putting down a rubber sheet for?"

Averting her eyes, Aunt Fanny said, "Little boys have been known to weewee in bed by mistake."

"I'm no baby, but. I'm eight years old. I wanna piss, I go to the can."

Aunt Fanny grabbed him, frog-marching him into the second-floor bathroom. An astonishing place. Shaggy white rugs everywhere, even on the toilet-seat cover. Do they walk on toilets in Outremont? And then Aunt Fanny washed his mouth out with soap. Lifebuoy. "And now you say, 'I'm sorry for using such bad language, Aunt Fanny.'"

He found plump, rosy-cheeked Sheldon curled over his electric train set on the floor of the furnished basement. "Can I play?" he asked.

"There's only one switch."

"We could take turns, fuck-face."

"I don't want to."

Joshua reared back and gave the approaching Lionel train engine a swift kick, sending it crashing against the wall. Sheldon leaped up. Joshua feinted with his left and caught him coming in with a right cross, bloodying his nose, before Aunt Fanny could intervene.

He was sent to bed without his supper, but the following evening he ate with the family. What a bunch. With all their money, the fruit in the bowl on the dining room table was made out of glass. Nibble it and you'd shit splinters. And the maid, for all her airs, didn't even know how to set a table properly. He was given two of everything: knives, forks, large spoons. . . .

Joshua had rarely seen Sheldon since he was a child, but he did remember that when he was twelve and got caught shoplifting at Eaton's it was Sheldon's father, not his, who came round to smooth his way out of there. Uncle Harvey had amazed Joshua, saying he hadn't had a fortunate upbringing, but that things would change now, the Leventhals would take a hand. Sheldon was waiting in the back of the

21

car, smirking, his flute case on his lap, and they were left alone together while his father went to speak to the plumbing contractor on one of his building sites, a sheaf of bills in his hand. "Hey, guess what," Joshua said, giving him an elbow, "I just got nabbed stealing."

Sheldon looked resolutely out the window.

"And now your old man is taking me back to your joint for a lecture, like, and after he's finished straightening me out I'm going upstairs to screw the ass off your maid."

"You're not invited to my bar-mitzvah when I have it. My mother said."

"I'll bet you can't even shoot jism yet."

Back in the house, Uncle Harvey led him into his study. He was about to speak when a flushed Aunt Fanny summoned him out into the hall. Joshua could hear them through the closed door.

"Last time he stayed here, he went through every drawer in the house when we were out."

"He's not staying here."

"I didn't dare take a bath without stuffing the keyhole with Kleenex."

Uncle Harvey joined Joshua in the study again. His manner solemn, he asked, "What would you like to be when you grow up?"

"Rich and famous and popular with girls."

"And do you think you can achieve such ambitions by stealing or through hard work?"

"Hard work."

"I would like you to go to high school. And when you're finished, provided you keep out of trouble, I will pay to send you to a good trade school."

"Geez. Would fur-trapping be considered like a trade?"

"I was thinking of plumbing, maybe. It's a very good business," he said, sighing. "Meanwhile, you might just see more of Sheldon. I want him to be an example to you."

"I don't want to get him into trouble, but when I stayed here that time he used to go through all his mother's drawers when you were out, trying on things. Yeah, now I remember, and when I told him he shouldn't do that he called me very bad names I can't repeat, and now," Joshua said, summoning up tears, "he says I can't come to his bar-mitzvah when he has it."

"Why, of course you can."

Hotch hotcha.

"I would like you to think of me as your friend," Uncle Harvey said.

Joshua grinned, appreciative. "And, listen here," he said, "you can count on me too."

"Life is a river we poor mortals sail on. Now you can drift with the current, ending up in the weeds of malcontent with the rest of the flotsam. Or, my dear Joshua, you can paddle your own canoe right through the storms of temptation into the ocean of plenty."

"Outremont," he ventured.

"Well, possibly," Uncle Harvey said, far from displeased. "But that would mean hard work. It means avoiding the undertow. It means that you've got to start paddling right now. Stroke, stroke, stroke. Do you understand?"

"Yeah, sure. May I ask a question?"

"Surely."

"When you said I would be invited to the bar-mitzvah, did you mean just for the *kiddush* in the synagogue or for the sit-down dinner as well?"

"Both."

If there was a family quarrel, Uncle Harvey lost. Joshua was not invited to Sheldon's bar-mitzvah. But he used to be sent his old clothes, which his mother altered for him, and when they were both teenagers he ran into Sheldon one day in the old Classic Bookshop and discovered that his cousin was not allowed to buy second-hand books. Because of germs. By that time Joshua was deep into books about the Spanish Civil War. Anything, absolutely anything, about the struggle.

"Don't tell me you're reading Koestler?" Sheldon asked, sneaking a glance at his Penguin.

"If I have any trouble with the big words, I'll give you a buzz."

Joshua saw him again at a McGill dance. Then, only five years ago, Sheldon had phoned out of nowhere to say how closely he had followed his surprising career, how he had tried to phone him in London once, how proud the Leventhals were, never mind what some people said—and to ask Pauline and him out to dinner. They were, Joshua insisted to Pauline, obliged to go.

"We are most certainly not obliged to go," she said, "but you're still enough of a boy to want to stick it to him."

"You should have heard his voice on the phone. Oozing envy. I love it."

"Vengeance is the Lord's, not yours, Joshua."

"Dress classy. I want your breeding to show."

23

Sheldon had invited them to a restaurant in one of the new hotels, a restaurant oppressively elegant, where the waiters came dressed like eighteenth-century *voyageurs*. Snowshoes and muskets and stretched beaver skins were mounted on the walls. Tassels dangled from the twelve-page menu. When they turned up, maybe twenty minutes later, Sheldon and his formidable wife, Bertha, were already ensconced at a table, nursing frothy drinks. Sheldon had grown into a fleshy man with melancholy eyes, long sideburns, and a vandyke beard that obviously called for a daily trimming and was certainly combed out with a *soupçon* of Grecian Formula. Bertha was both mountainous and bejeweled, her black eyes fierce, and her fuzzy cheeks streaked by the application of too much pancake. Pauline, Joshua sensed, loathed her on sight. "I wonder," she asked Bertha, before sitting down, "if you could tell me where I could find the ladies' room?"

"I only go at home," Bertha shot right back, and from that moment on, Joshua could not meet Pauline's eye without the two of them erupting in giggles.

Matters weren't helped any when the waiter, bewigged of course, his manner officious, asked Pauline for her order. "I'll have a hamburger," she sang out, "with french fries and a Coke. And don't forget the ketchup, please."

Still waiting for the kettle to boil, Joshua opened the fridge in search of a lemon and noticed vegetables everywhere. Unless he did something with them immediately, they would wizen and waste. Mind you, these were ordinary vegetables. Store-bought vegetables.

The vegetables Pauline had put in at their cottage on Lake Memphremagog had long since been consumed. He had turned the soil, she had planted the seeds, the kids had banged in the tomato stakes, and they had all plunged into the still piercingly cold lake for a swim. The old, sinking white house with the green-gabled windows and tilting wraparound porch had been in the Hornby family for generations. It was now Pauline's. She had been raised there. She knew the overgrown mountain meadow where the wild blueberries grew and the place where edible mushrooms could be found. She could also lead the children over what had once been an Indian trail and to the shaft of the old abandoned lead mine, and him to the dark waters where the smallmouth bass ran in early June. She knew where the beaver dams were, and how to amaze the children by rooting out a beaver to make a repair. She led all of them to the brook where the smelt ran af-

24

ter the ice broke up. On the lake, they were dependent on Pauline for almost everything and she thrived on it. Pauline, his love.

In the village on the lake, once a burgeoning mill town, founded by United Empire Loyalists, nobody asked Pauline if she were married to *the* Joshua Shapiro. They didn't forget her first name. And they certainly didn't tell her what she had missed, poor soul, having been deprived of a Jewish childhood. In the village, they had known and adored the senator's daughter since she had been a spunky tomboy, and it was Joshua who was taken for an interloper. A tall, loping, bushy-haired stranger, obviously street-wise; a lean, middle-aged hawk with a hooked nose, a pockmarked face, who, practicing God knows what necromancy in depraved Europe years ago, had seduced their Trout and might yet poison the wells or abscond with one of their babes, its blood required for his Passover rituals. Beware.

For years a wary Joshua had avoided anything more than the occasional long weekend at the cottage on the lake, her territory, and had argued instead for summers spent elsewhere. Combining magazine or TV assignments with family trips to Yellowknife, for the only golf he could tolerate, the Tournament of the Midnight Sun; Toronto, for the Queen's Plate; the Gaspé, while he did a documentary on salmon fishing. Then, one evening in the spring of 1972, nine years after they had returned to Montreal from London, a determined Pauline had set the coffee tray down in the living room, told the kids to scoot, and announced, "You're working too damn hard and you're forty-one years old and you've never had a real vacation."

"But we're going to Cape Cod in July. I've already arranged to do a piece on the fans in Fenway Park for the CBC."

It was his appearances on television, not anything he thought of as real writing, that had made him a household name in Canada. But he disliked TV. He especially disliked anybody who was good at it.

"Oh, sure, and while we lie on the beach you'll be dashing to and from the ball park, and when we get back you'll be up editing at all hours, trying to meet your deadline. And all that time I'll be renting out the cottage to people who will do even more damage to it. I want you to take the summer off. We'll go to the cottage, and to hell with Jane Trimble. We don't have to see her. She's certainly not keeping me away from the lake any more."

In 1963, the year they had returned to Montreal, Jane Trimble had been the first person Pauline heard from. Only a week after their arrival, the very day they had moved into their new house—a modest but sufficiently comfortable place, badly in need of a paint job, on a street of terraced houses in Lower Westmount—an enormous, gift-wrapped rubber plant had arrived, addressed to both of them. "You open it," he said.

"Not now. We haven't even put up the beds yet."

"Maybe it's from an old boyfriend."

"It's from Jane Trimble."

Late the following morning the doorbell rang as Joshua, unshaven, and stripped down to an old pair of shorts, was jimmying open a packing case; Alex was blissfully seated on a toilet somewhere, chanting that there was no paper; and a pregnant Pauline, in a loose blouse and ballooning skirt, was busy sorting dishes. Reconciled to yet another delivery, Joshua opened the door to find a slender, very fetching lady with raven-black hair smiling sweetly at him. She wore a silk blouse and a green skirt. "You could only be Joshua. I'm Jane," she said, as if she were bestowing a blessing on the house.

"Darling," he called, hastily wiping the dripping sweat from his face, "it's for you."

The two old friends embraced, they shed tears, and Jane offered her cheek to be kissed. "Welcome home," she sang out, proffering a bottle of Dom Perignon tied with a red ribbon. "You look absolutely wonderful!"

The Trimbles, Joshua was to discover, lived in an enormous stone mansion in Upper Westmount, on one of those streets of the very rich that loomed above them, hewn out of the mountainside. The champagne that Jane had descended the mountain with was chilled, but Pauline—rather rudely, Joshua thought at the time—didn't offer to open it immediately. Instead, she set it down on the floor.

"What do I wipe my bottom with?" Alex hollered.

Pauline groped for a cigarette.

"Now look here," Jane said, "I've been through this kind of chaos. I know exactly what it's like."

"Do you?" Pauline asked, impassive.

"I absolutely insist you drop everything at six o'clock, and then Jack and I will pick you up and take you out for a proper dinner."

"That would be impossible," Pauline protested.

"But I've already booked a table at the Ritz."

26

"Alex isn't used to the house yet. We can't leave him."

"Nonsense, dear, of course you can."

Alex was heard from again.

"Haven't you got any toilet paper in the house?" Jane demanded.

"Yes," Pauline snapped back, her eyes welling with tears, "we do have toilet paper."

"If you need any shopping done," Jane said, "just make me a list."

"We're doing just fine," Joshua said, sensing danger. "Honestly."

"See you at six, then."

"But we haven't even got a sitter," Joshua pointed out.

"I've arranged for our maid to sit for you. She adores children."

"No," Pauline called out sharply. "No, no," she said, leading Jane abruptly to the door. "Another night, perhaps."

Pauline did go out to lunch with Jane the following week, returning home in a vile mood, but she adroitly sidestepped further dinner invitations not only from the Trimbles, but from any of her old crowd, until they gradually dropped off altogether. When Joshua protested, she said, "We came back here so that you could finish the research for your book, not so that I could get involved with that lot again."

But now, some nine years later, there had been an understandable and, he thought, healthy sea-change in Pauline. Approaching forty herself, she longed once more for the scenes and even the foolish faces of her childhood, and they were actually going to spend a summer on the lake.

Pauline's lake. Jane's lake.

In 1972, their first summer on the lake, a defiant Pauline sometimes dragged him out to nights at the golf and country club, where he was not so much introduced to as flaunted at the crowd she had once sailed with, the boys matured into problem-solvers, hard-drinking brokers, lawyers, and advertising men, the girls graduated from A. A. Milne through Dr. Spock to Julia Child (gourmet cooks, the lot), as well as tending organic gardens and raising money for the Knowlton Pony Club. The girls seemed delighted to have their prodigal sister, however spiky her mood, among them again. They took Joshua for an exotic: a Jew, a sportswriter, a TV presence. They appeared to be stirred by his snarling hirsute presence, the incessant clatter of his typewriter as they passed the Hornby cottage, and the rumor, fed by a calculating Pauline, of a constant flow of important phone calls from editors in New York. The Jewy network. The men, testing him, plied him with drinks, and were chastened to discover that he could outlast any of them at the bar, although, sufficiently fueled, he could become something of a menace. And then, inevitably, they were invited to the Trimbles for a dinner party. The guest of honor was a visiting German industrialist looking for investment opportunities.

"Tattoo credit cards," Joshua said, grinning.

"I beg your pardon?"

"The big problem with credit cards, as I understand it, is that people lose them or they are stolen. Think of what you could do to cut down overhead if you were to tattoo the serial number on a client's arm."

Pauline was about to laugh when she noticed Jane positively glowing with understanding.

"Of course," Joshua continued, encouraged, "it would be necessary to test such an idea in the field. Germany, I think, would be ideal. You already have so many of the required technicians."

Riding home in the old outboard, an annoyed Pauline said, "You obviously set out to impress Jane tonight."

"Did I now?" he shot back sharply, but far from innocent.

"Yes, my darling."

Although they attended the occasional Sunday barbecue at the Trimbles, a ritual on the lake, they avoided further dinner invitations, Joshua cultivating a reputation for being not only difficult but also something of a recluse. For more often than not he preferred horsing around with the kids at home to generously offered invitations to dinner at the country club or to the other cottages to bend an elbow, try a hair of the hound that bit him, or hoist a few after the sun had gone down over the yardarm (and it's always below the yardarm somewhere, isn't it, Joshua? Har har har). Drinks at the other cottages, he discovered, were unfailingly followed by a cookout and the remembrance of summers past. Hey, what about the night Dickie Abbott tied Jane's bra to the top of the flagpole? Or that afternoon Tim Hickey got smashed and took out old Jack Trimble's new Tanzer and ran it into Gibraltar Point? Or, Jane would add compulsively, watching Pauline, remember the night Kevin Hornby actually drove his MG up the clubhouse stairs, through the French doors, and right into the bar? It wasn't an MG, it was an Austin-Healey. It was an MG, I was there.

At the mention of Kevin's name, Joshua noticed that the women would peer into their drinks and the men grin sheepishly at him, as if he knew, he understood. What he did know was that Pauline, bristling, changed the subject whenever Kevin's name came up. Her name and Kevin's were entwined on a tennis trophy that was kept in a glass case in the clubhouse: Mixed Doubles Champions, Eastern Quebec Region, 1952. Kevin, whom Joshua had yet to meet, was her younger brother, the family black sheep. He had dropped out of McGill law school right in the middle of his final exams. For some years now he had been rooted in Bermuda, where he ran a fishing boat.

Late one evening the following March, the kids looking pasty, Pauline also in need of some sun, Joshua suggested a holiday. "What about Bermuda?"

No, she said, looking directly at him. "My father used to take us there every winter. I'm not going back."

On a blowy afternoon only two weeks later, drinking in the Maritime Bar at the Ritz-Carlton, he looked up to see a portly man in a beaver coat standing at his table, smiling tentatively down at him, as if he expected to be dismissed. The face was not one of those slack, disappointed, boozy faces he immediately associated with the golf and country club. It was jowly, the small eyes hard, the mouth surprisingly sensual. A cupid's mouth. Jack Trimble.

By this time Joshua knew that Trimble, a good ten years older than the others in the country club set, had served in World War II—not in the RCN or the RCAF, as the others would have, but in the army ordnance corps, a captain when he was demobilized in England. He went on from there to become something in the City, first with Warburg's and then with Lloyd's, before he appeared in Montreal in the early fifties, fond of saying, "I've seen the future, and it doesn't work." He didn't fancy Attlee's welfare state and he particularly disliked Sir Stafford Cripps, whom he pronounced absolutely bonkers. On the other hand, Trimble made no attempt to conceal what he described as his own humble but genteel origins, striking just the right note. "We weren't exactly tinkers over there, you know. Or on the dole. My father was with the L.C.C. A building inspector."

To begin with, Trimble settled into a modest basement flat on Tupper Street, joining the brokerage firm of McKay, Pitman & Routledge, where he complained loudly about the unhealthiness of central heating and turned up at the office in shirts with detachable collars and, of course, with a furled umbrella. He was not liked. He was considered calculating. A striver. He had bad breath. He suffered from dandruff. Nobody invited him to lunch at the Café Martin or took him to a hockey game. But he was soon taken very seriously indeed. Trimble turned out to be most astute, his rise to a junior partnership breathtakingly swift. He had only been in Montreal for seven years when he acquired his own seat on the stock exchange, as well as a reputation for having the Midas touch. He was also, in principle, a most desirable bachelor, with what he called a "flat" in the Château, then the most exclusive apartment building in town. But his appeal was largely confined to Westmount's matrons, never their most glittering progeny. He was not an amusing man, jowly even then, his brown hair thin, his flesh pink and flaky. Then he met the dashing Jane Mitchell at a cocktail party at the British Trade Commissioner's residence and, to everyone's amazement, they were married six months later. Trimble's associates were surprised because Jane Mitchell had no money, not any more, and Pauline, when she heard about the marriage, was taken aback because the Trimble she dimly remembered had seemed such a stodgy man, middle-aged before his time, certainly too dull for a girl as sassy as Jane.

Jane and Pauline had been to McGill together. If Pauline was a senator's daughter, Jane, though her profligate father had squandered the family fortune, was not without her own cherished connections. A great-uncle had been a premier of New Brunswick. The two girls were inseparable on campus. Jane, in those days, had been the reckless leader, provoking the more naturally timorous Pauline, a loyal though resentful follower, into what passed for outrageous behavior in their set. Competition between them became fierce. So if it was Pauline who got to date Oscar Peterson, it was Jane who captivated Dylan Thomas, after he had floated on campus to read, and got to take him to Rockhead's and, she allowed, into her bed as well. Then, if it was Pauline who absconded to Europe after the family scandal—Europe, where she was to marry a decidedly well-born but avowed Communist—it was Jane who really shook everybody up four years later. Marrying Jack Trimble, of all people. Two children, a boy and a girl, came out of their marriage: Charles and Margaret Rose. Jane remained stunningly slender, her darkly ruined air heightened, if anything, by the startling streak of gray that now ran through her raven-black hair and the casual, frankly sexy manner in which she wore her expensive clothes. In 1972, she still filled the defiant and attention-getting office of the set's shocker. She had been the first one on the lake to read Kate Millett, subscribe to *Rolling Stone,* and see *Deep*

Throat. She was something else, the men said. But, after all, she was married to a broker. A bore. And now Pauline, her one-time acolyte, was back on the lake, and in her annoyingly quiet manner had finally outstripped her. She was married to a Jew. A prizefighter's son. Jane didn't care for it, not one bit.

Ostensibly, Pauline was touched by what she understood to be her old mentor's submission to a marriage of convenience, but her concern was tainted by satisfaction. Jane, on her side, infuriated Pauline by making it a point to be flutteringly attentive to Joshua, popping up unannounced on their lawn, inviting herself for drinks, engaging him with her sometimes malicious wit or by borrowing books that had shaped him, like Isaac Babel's collected short stories. A book she had never returned—mislaying it somewhere, she said. Jack Trimble muddied the two women's relationship even further. His manner with Pauline was courtly, although she shrank to see him bearing down on her, his cloying smile made all the more hideous by his recently capped teeth. Trimble's flirting would have been tolerated by Jane, a more-than-acceptable convention—but not his deference.

From the beginning, Jack Trimble had eschewed the less fashionable, book-reading crowd on the lake, largely academics, a retiring lot ensconced in modest cabins, and had elected to run with the country club set. He didn't water-ski or sail, leaving that to Jane and the children, but he was an adequate golfer, and for his sake the club subscribed to *Punch,* even as he did to *Country Life,* and kept a tin of Earl Grey tea on a kitchen shelf. But Trimble didn't understand Westmount's progeny at play. He failed to grasp that if the Hornby cottage had perhaps the most cachet on the lake, it was precisely because its dilapidated boathouse tilted further than the others, its wraparound porch sank lower, and what was laughingly known as its powerboat was actually a leaky wooden tub, its outboard unreliable at best. Trimble, seemingly British to the core, surprisingly enjoyed display. He had torn down the drafty old Mitchell cottage with its haphazard additions, slapped on over the years as children had made them necessary, and now presided over a mansion of his own—an architect-designed, ranch-style house, commanding more than a thousand feet of choice lake frontage, its picture windows enormous and its teak deck larger than anybody else's, just as his tennis court was in a state of better repair, his workshop equipped to suit the most exacting professional, and his Grew 212 easily the most imposing boat on the water. His rock

31

garden was floodlit at night. The croquet lawn could have served as the surface for a snooker table. The fattest goldfish in the Townships slumbered under the water lilies in his pond. Indoors, there was a cathedral ceiling, a billiards room, and a library. "Trimble's Folly" Jane herself dubbed it, squelching any possible criticism from the others, and the first time Joshua had been invited there to dinner, Trimble had grasped his hand, indicated the bronzed young man scraping the dock, and said, "I want you to meet a future prime minister of Canada."

Charlie dipped his head, blushed, and said, "P-p-pleased to meet you, Mr. Sh-sh-shapiro."

Another day, seated with Joshua on the sun deck at one of his Sunday barbecues, Trimble observed, "You know, there's only one thing wrong with all this. I earned the lolly to pay for all of it myself and that's unforgivable, as far as this lot's concerned," he said, gesturing at his guests gathered at the bar. "Just like your marrying Pauline."

"Oh, really," Joshua said tightly. "Why?"

"Now come on there, old son," Trimble said, and before Joshua could reply, he had darted off to fetch Jane's beach robe.

Jane had just emerged from the water, climbing onto the deck, deeply tanned, black hair clinging, nipples showing bold and hard through her bikini, everybody turning to watch as she bounced on one long leg, trying to shake the water out of her ear.

"There you are, Mother," Trimble said, enveloping her in the towel robe, and then he sat down beside Joshua again. "She has no idea how dishy she still is."

Trimble (on Jane's insistence, Joshua suspected) entertained often, dutifully serving up thick steaks from his built-in brick barbecue, his smile forced, his Bermuda shorts biting into rolls of overlying fat. Although he himself liked nothing better than a bottle of Guinness at lunchtime, there was often champagne for the others. Lobster, hideously expensive, was not unusual. But then, driving to the post office at the cocktail hour, he might see eight cars parked in the Hickey driveway, among them Jane's Volvo, or taking his Grew out for a spin in the evening, all the familiar boats collected at the McTeer dock, laughter washing across the water. He didn't complain. He resolutely continued to court the country club set.

Trimble, with his ordnance corps tie, his yachtsman's cap, his brass-buttoned blazer, his British slang, was tolerated not only for Jane's sake, or the even more opulent parties he threw in his Westmount mansion, but also because he seemed to be awfully good with money and helped the others untangle their tax and estate problems, often doubling the yield of their portfolios by enlisting them into a fund he managed, its membership limited to one hundred. Ironically, even as they condescended to him, it was evident to Joshua that he was more intelligent than any of them. It was also clear that he was a liar, an outrageous liar; not at all what he pretended to be.

And now Joshua invited him to sit down, Trimble ordering a Glenlivet, straight up, no ice please, and setting right in to chat compulsively about Kevin. Kevin, he told Joshua, his manner mocking, had twice been Quebec amateur golf champion. He had once tried to acquire a PGA tour card but couldn't qualify, poor sod. "You should have been there," Trimble recited, his small eyes watchful, "the night he drove his MG up the clubhouse stairs and right into the bar."

"Yes. I'm sorry to have missed that."

"You know, we have something in common, old son. We're both married to smashing girls. Does that worry you?"

"Should it?"

"I once returned from a trip to Zurich and found a bookmatch from Les Halles in Jane's bag. I never eat there."

During the summer of '73, their second summer on the lake, Pauline, though she continued to mock the old crowd, was increasingly drawn to the country club, if only for the tennis. She allowed that Joshua was an inhibiting presence at the club, a Jewy thundercloud, casting a pall on her admittedly nostalgic fun; and just as she was declared redundant on his Mackenzie King Memorial Society poker nights, so it was agreed that he could, if he chose, confine his appearances at the club to the annual dinner dance and, of course, the closing-day sailing race. The latter ritual was also followed by a dinner dance. Crazed couplings in the parking lot. Illicit unzippings at the ninth hole. A disheveled, obviously zonked Liz Harper hoisting her skirt and kicking off her shoes to dance on the bar. Repeated expressions of regret from Jane Trimble that Kevin couldn't be there. Good old Kevin. A savage row between the Friars. The sodden stragglers refusing to depart until good old Gavin McTeer had been cajoled into going home to fetch his bagpipes and kilts and play out the summer on the dewy lawn. And then there would be a perplexed but still ingratiating Jack Trimble wandering out there

33

in his Bermuda shorts, his knees dimply, imploring, "Anybody seen Jane?"

Nobody saying.

"I'm afraid she may have passed out somewhere." Trimble cupping his hands to his mouth, calling, "Jane! HALLO! Time to go."

And even as the stragglers were departing, drifting across the deliciously wet grass and fallen leaves to their cars, the giggly ladies carrying their shoes, the men nudging each other, the ladies shushing them, saying oh you're terrible, oh you're simply awful, boys, even then, they could still hear him calling into the wind, "Jane! Party's over. HALLO!"

In succeeding summers on the lake, there continued to be what Joshua, trying to lighten matters for Pauline, airily dismissed as "Trimble trouble."

Jane, whom he had yet to see in the same outfit twice, continued to appear unannounced on their lawn, usually at their private cocktail hour. Late one afternoon she came striding across the grass, pausing at the one flower bed that was in need of weeding, just as a somewhat forlorn, clearly exhausted Pauline emerged from their vegetable garden.

The vegetable garden, Joshua understood, was Pauline's pride. It was also her sanctuary, her downtown bar, where she retired to ruminate, away from his problems and temporarily liberated from the demands of the children. He adored watching her, unsuspected, from a window as she stooped so intently there in her sloppy straw hat, unaware of just how charming she appeared. Cutting back the tomato plants, thinning carrots, pondering over the peas, or simply weeding. And, in August, bounding rosy-cheeked onto the porch, bearing a basketful of the season's hard-won bounty, Joshua and the kids lining up to whistle and applaud, shouting, "Let's hear it for Ma Shapiro." Pauline handing out gnarled, delicious rose tomatoes, big as potatoes, for them to feel. Showing them the cucumbers that she would be pickling. The green peppers that would be stuffed for dinner. Cabbages. Brussels sprouts. Beets. Carrots that could be wiped off on your trousers and eaten on the spot.

But that summer there had been far too much rain. Bugs had infested the garden. Slugs devoured the cabbages. Cutworms attacked the tomatoes. And now, as she stepped onto the porch, her porch, lugging a basket of skimpy, blighted produce, there sat her husband, laughing at something, and there stood a smiling Jane, drink in hand, looking as if she had just skipped out of the pages of *Vogue*. "Damn it, Pauline, I do admire your energy," she said, peering into the basket, "but why bother any more? I certainly don't. Local produce is so cheap and plentiful this time of year. I can't imagine that it's worth the effort."

In succeeding summers on the lake, Joshua also took to a ritual of his own. After work, say around four o'clock, if he knew Pauline was playing tennis, he would load the kids into the old Hornby Jeep, drive out to the club, and settle with them on the grass overlooking the tennis courts. Oh, but his heart leaped to watch Pauline at play. Her honey-colored hair drawn back with a bauble, her fine arms tense, her long bronzed legs ready to spring. Chaste white shirt and shorts notwithstanding, she struck him as incredibly sexy. Pure joy, his Pauline.

All of which led to the incident and his becoming, albeit belatedly, a most unwilling part of the country club lore. "Remember the night Shapiro stormed into the clubhouse . . ."

Occasionally, after her game was done, he would wander out onto the court with the kids and Pauline would try to entice him into volleying with her.

"I'd only embarrass you, Pauline. I probably couldn't even hit the ball."

"You could never embarrass me, and if you'd only try we could play together."

"Yes, yes," the kids cried, bouncing up and down.

Joshua was tempted more than once, and then one day last summer he had finally yielded. Had he or Pauline been more observant that splendidly sunny Wednesday afternoon in August, a taste of autumn already in the crisp air, the leaves running to gold here and scarlet there, they might have noticed the small seaplane moored at the club dock. Mind you, there had been other seaplanes, other Wednesday afternoons.

Pauline lofted the ball at him, a lazy serve, and hello, hello, he caught it with his own racket, sending it back over the net. He was still riding that unexpected triumph when he badly flubbed her return shot. Now he tried to serve, murderously of course, his racket swooshing through the air, utterly failing to connect with the ball. Pauline, calling out encouragement, served another ball and he took a chop at it, smashing it into the net. She tried again, he returned the ball, took her next shot and sent it back again, missing the shot that followed. Pauline served once more, imploring him not to rush the ball, and he managed another return. They were having fun, the children squealing at his every pratfall, and he did not notice that they had acquired an audience. An audience of one. A tall lean man, wearing a floppy straw hat, a gold necklace with a medallion attached, white silken trousers cut jaggedly below the knees, and espadrilles. He was seated on a bench, brooding, his skin stained dark as walnut by the sun. Joshua didn't notice him. He was also unaware of his audience's audience. The ladies drinking on the terrace had stopped talking, the more intrepid ones drawing closer to the courts. Joshua didn't notice because at that moment nothing meant more to him than connecting with the ball, earning a satisfying thunk. Alas, the greater his ambition, the more inept he became. Even more baffling, Pauline didn't seem to be having fun any more. She was flushed, agitated, and the next time he flubbed badly she suddenly snapped, "Had enough?"

"No, not yet," he said, stupidly missing her distress signal as well as her next service, a surprisingly swift one.

"Oh, for God's sake," she cried out, "it wasn't that difficult to hit."

Startled, he rushed toward the net. "Pauline, what in the hell's wrong with you?"

"Damn" was all she said. "Damn damn damn. And here he comes."

The tall lean man with the straw-colored hair and twinkly blue eyes was striding toward him, his smile captivating, but a little too fully aware of its own charm. "Hi, there," he sang out. "You must be Joshua." Shaking Joshua's hand with immense warmth, as if his search for him had been long and arduous and the pleasures of this meeting indescribable, he also eased the tennis racket away from him, his manner benevolent but firm, much as Joshua had once relieved Alex of a hatchet he was then too young to handle. "I'm awfully pleased to meet you at last."

Before Joshua could respond, he had scooped up the ball, bounced it once, twice, slid away, and sent it booming over the net with a sudden leap and a deft thrust of his racket. Pauline, swooping low after it, returned the ball with more anger than grace.

Seething, Joshua backed out of the court, only to discover that most of the ladies had now gathered round, rapt.

"Hey, why'd you let that guy take the racket away from you?" Alex asked, with his infuriating gift for reaching him.

"I think," Joshua said as calmly as he could manage, "that that man just happens to be your uncle."

Joshua couldn't take his eyes off Pauline, who was now playing with more rage than skill, fiercely intent on winning. Charging the ball, attempting vicious serves, she was easily outplayed by a tolerant, seemingly bemused Kevin, who did not once need to extend himself. And then, without warning, the game took a poignant turn, settling into a kind of intimacy, the ball flowing between brother and sister, both of them playing superbly. The ladies, shedding years even as he watched, Westmount debutantes once more, oohed and ahhed to see such casually brilliant play from Kevin and such spirited moves from an aroused Pauline. Once or twice, they even clapped hands. Joshua, his cheeks hot, his stomach churning, grasped that he had reached a new plateau in his life among the gentiles. Something was clearly expected of him.

Then, all at once, the mood of the game shifted again, and once more Pauline tried to knock Kevin literally out of the court. This time, however, he did not respond with tolerance. He absorbed Pauline's wickedest shots, coaxed her out of position with hanging returns, and then slammed the ball into undefended corners. A breathless Pauline, lunging, obviously flustered, was caught looking bad again and again. She was not being beaten, she was being punished. The ladies, who had been pressing against the fence, began to retreat from the court. Joshua desperately wanted to intervene, but had no idea how to manage it without further humiliating Pauline. Finally, mercifully, it was over, and Pauline and Kevin were strolling out to confront each other at the net. Brother and sister didn't embrace, didn't even touch each other. "Come on, Trout," he said, laughing easily, "one more set."

"God damn it, Kevin, what are you doing here?" he heard her demand sharply.

"I'm only here overnight. I'm flying to Georgian Bay in the morning to meet with some of the Argos people there. It's big stuff this time, Trout. Awfully big."

"Isn't it always," Pauline said, as Joshua joined them at the net, the children hanging back, bewildered.

"They're thinking of putting together an offshore fund, and they need a good man out there. I took them out fishing. They talked to me about it in the boat. I told you that would be a good investment."

"Kevin, you're incorrigible."

"I'm throwing a dinner party for some of the old gang here tonight," he said, including Joshua in his appealing smile.

37

"Tim Hickey, Dickie Abbott, and some of the others are driving in from town. Even Jane's husband is coming out."

"Now you've gone and done it. You really have. Would you please not tell any of them about your big deal?"

Ignoring her, he asked Joshua, "Don't I even get to meet the kids?"

The children were brought forward and introduced.

"I'd be absolutely miserable," Kevin said, "if the two of you didn't join us for dinner."

Pauline looked to Joshua for a response.

"The kids must be starving," he said evenly.

But before they could get away, Kevin said, "Champers at seven. And if you don't mind, Joshua, I've brought one of your books along for you to sign for me. You have no greater fan in Bermuda."

Pauline and Joshua didn't talk on the bumpy ride home, but the children wouldn't let go.

"I think he's yucky," Susy said, clinging to Joshua.

But Teddy was impressed. "He sure can play tennis."

"Possibly," Pauline said, "because he hardly does anything else."

Joshua fixed drinks for both of them. Pauline boiled sweet corn for the children. "Gee, golly," he said, once they dispersed, "my biggest fan in Bermuda. What does he take me for?"

"He's leaving in the morning. We might as well go."

"He's your brother, you go. I'm going to stay here and watch the ball game with the kids."

"I can't go without you."

"What is he, a year younger than you are?"

"Fourteen months."

"Jesus, a man of his age dressing like Tom Sawyer. No, Peter Pan. He's fucking pathetic."

"But he wasn't, once."

That stung.

"Did you buy him his boat?"

"I lent him enough money for a down payment."

"And he's in such dire need he turns up here in a seaplane?"

"Returning here after all these years scared him. He had to make a splash. So he rented a plane."

"We are a stiff-necked people," Joshua said, pouring himself another drink. "That's what we come from. Yessiree. A stiff-necked people. You should have seen yourself out there on that tennis court. Watching was indecent."

Her cheeks burned.

"I thought," he said, rounding on her, "that I could do nothing to embarrass you. You yelled at me out there."

She stared at him, startled. Clearly, she didn't even remember.

"With the kids out there, O.K., never mind, but right in front of the Westmount Pre-menopausal Hot Pants and Bigots Bend-an-Elbow Club."

"I'm sorry. I apologize."

"Champers with Peter Pan," he muttered. "And what's all that crap about meeting with the Argos people and offshore funds?"

"Another pipe dream, that's what. Some of them probably got drunk on his boat, and when he turns up at Georgian Bay they won't even remember that they invited him there."

"Does he really live off fishing trips?"

"He lives off women, if you must know."

"Why, that's reprehensible."

"Oh, you can be such a prick sometimes, darling."

"We are a stiff-necked people."

"They have reason to resent him, Josh, and if I don't turn up tonight they are going to skewer him, and they will certainly gloat for the rest of the summer if *you* fail to show."

"I'm not going to that little fart of a club, with its commodore in commodities, to have them watching and waiting for me to do something."

"You don't have to do anything. Whatever are you talking about? He's no threat to you. He's no threat to anybody any more. But don't make it impossible for me. I don't want to go there alone."

"Go, Tinkerbell. Enjoy. I really don't mind."

"Take me, Josh."

"No."

When Pauline finally emerged from her dressing room, showered and scented, touched with just a hint of eye make-up, her honey-colored hair freed of its restraining bauble, his Pauline, looking achingly beautiful in a white linen shift calculated to enhance her tan, he was consumed with regret. "I don't mind driving you," he said ruefully.

"I've already ordered a taxi," she replied, her voice also subdued.

He trailed after her onto the front lawn. "Stay. I'm beginning to feel horny."

"Stop it. Please, Josh," and she ran into the oncoming taxi lights, gesturing for old Orville Moon to stop.

39

Wizened, mottled old Moon, with his lizardy eyes and yellow teeth, did not care for Joshua. Once he had stopped him in the village post office and asked, "Will you be needing a hunting license this autumn?"

"No."

"I figured."

Joshua lingered on the lawn for a while, watching the ancient, battered taxi clatter off into the night. Fallen apples, soft, rotting, were everywhere. The trees needed spraying and pruning. The lawn smelled sweetly of cut grass, decay, and Pauline's perfume. She would have dabbed herself behind the ears, on the backs of her knees, and between her breasts. I married a whore.

The children, sensing his filthy mood, retreated to the safety of their beds. Except for Alex, naturally. Alex flicked on the TV set to watch the Expos. Joshua freshened his drink and started out for the porch. "Hey, Dad, I want to quit school."

"Everybody's demented today. You're only seventeen, Alex."

"So were you when you quit."

"We'll talk about it in the morning."

If Reuben had still been there, Joshua knew what he'd say. His father had actually lasted ten days with them this summer before he began to itch for the streets again. Once, during his visit, Joshua had wandered out after work to discover his father and Alex on the grounds, just this side of the tilting boathouse, with their boxing gloves and helmets on. Reuben Shapiro, once rated "Prospect of the Month" by the exacting Mr. Nat Fleischer, was instructing his grandson, even as he had once coached Joshua, in the fine art of jabbing, attended by Susy and Teddy, the cornermen, ready with towels and pails of water; and by a giggly Pauline, serving as referee.

"Now you try that once more," Reuben said. "Only remember: my chin's not here, it's another foot away. So when you jab at it you're still gathering speed, get it, you're not slowing down, anticipating bone, but still coming at me. And then, kid, it's stick, stick, and away you go. O.K., Pauline, let's hear it."

"Ding-a-ling," Pauline called out. "Ding-a-ling." And Joshua, filled with delight, thought, Hey, we're some family. We really are some family.

Drinking out on the porch, glaring at the country club lights across the lake, Joshua realized that he was eventually going to have to get out the Jeep and fetch her. Hell. And then, suddenly, there was a resounding crack of thunder, a rumbling across the water, and the lake was leaping with lightning. He was being pelted. But before retreating into the house, he did notice the clubhouse lights fail. A moment later, even as the lightning struck again, their own lights went out and he was bumping into things, cursing, hunting for a flashlight. O.K., he was going to fetch her, but should he take a knife? Like that other time on Ibiza.

Ibiza, my God, he reflected, dashing for the Jeep, he hadn't thought about Ibiza in months.

• Joshua decided to make a soup. That was constructive. It wasn't avoiding work. Soup was nourishing for the kids, his responsibility these days. He poured the boiling water into a pot. He cubed six carrots and plunged them into the water. Oh shit, he forgot to peel them. The hell with it. He chopped some cabbage, discarding the moldy bits, diced some celery limp with age, adding salt, pepper, six Knorr chicken cubes, a handful of frozen peas, and last night's corncobs retrieved from the garbage pail. Never mind, they add taste. He also found some mushrooms, a little slippery, somewhat fuzzy here and there, and wiped them with a dishtowel before adding them to the pot. Then he discovered some abandoned baked potatoes in the bottom tray and scooped them out, mashing vigorously, as they say, before dumping them into the pot for thickening. Waste not, want not. Slicing onions, he sneaked a glance at his wristwatch and noted that it was only 9:30. His rule was that only if he honestly didn't get anything done before 11 a.m. could he write off the rest of the day. Even opening a tin of tomatoes and chopping parsley, even counting time to stir for taste, he would still be done before ten, when Mrs. Zwibock arrived for the day. Mrs. Zwibock, with her mindless chatter.

The phone rang.

"Hello, Joshua, I hope I'm not disturbing you."

"No. No. That's O.K."

It was a call he feared. His bank manager, Gibson of the Royal. Would he like him to extend his $10,000 note, his overdraft, for another month? No sweat, mind you.

"Now that's not a bad idea," Joshua said, trying to sound casual, adding that as soon as it was convenient he would bring in sterling to cover the note. "You can count on it, Hugh."

Joshua was now late with his school fees, and he had nothing set aside against this year's taxes. Chargex's computer was

41

unhappy, and American Express was disappointed in him. No wonder he couldn't work. What's the point? If, he argued with himself, he could take the rest of the day off, tomorrow was bound to be good. He would make a clean start on that column. With his pretty new typewriter ribbon already in place, the keys freshly scrubbed and twinkly.

Yes yes.

Which was when the phone rang again. Jane Trimble, he thought, breaking into a sweat. *Tell her we're not to blame.* But it was long distance. Peabody at *Playboy*, outlining an assignment which appealed to him but meant going to London. "I can't do it," he said, and he told Peabody about Pauline. Not everything, but enough. "I can't fly anywhere now. I can't leave the kids."

Even as he said that, he sensed Peabody tuning out, scratching his name off a list on his pad. "Wait. Don't hang up. How are you?"

"Hanging in there. Nothing terminal yet."

"And Janet?"

"She's had her consciousness raised. We separated last month."

"I'm sorry."

"Bless you. I couldn't be more pleased." There were two kids. They had, Peabody assured him in his most astringent manner, adjusted marvelously. "I mean, I used to see them every night, but I'd come home whacked and all I'd wanted to do was booze or watch football on TV. Now I see them only on the weekends, but as darling Janet has explained, I spend quality time with them. Are you sure you can't go, or is it just that you want more money?"

"Think of something I can do from here."

"From Canada? Are you out of your mind? You never should have gone home, Josh."

"Neither of us should have come back," Joshua said, startling himself.

"Maybe. Just maybe. *À la prochaine fois, mon vieux.* Hey, wait." There was a pause. And suddenly Peabody laughed a reckless laugh, full-hearted, and Joshua found himself suffused with warmth, responding to the old charm. "Say there, Josh," he said, "why don't we clean out the old *deux-chevaux* and drive to Arles tonight? Or maybe Amsterdam?"

"If only we could."

"God damn it," Peabody said, his voice cracking, "what happened to everybody?"

42

"Come on now," Joshua replied without conviction, "it's not that bad."

"Markham passed through Chicago last week. He invited me to his suite in the Ambassador East. Took me to lunch and whenever I mentioned a writer, he jotted down his name in a thin little Gucci pad. He offered me an annual retainer, a fucking *pourboire*, to put things his way."

"Markham's rotten to the core."

"Yeah. Sure. Only I'm no better. I'm screwing my secretary. She's twenty-two years old and has read *Trout Fishing in America* three times. She's never heard of Saroyan. Never mind Saroyan—she thinks Henry James is the guy who wrote the script for a Montgomery Clift film we saw on the late show. And I'm so scared of being unable to satisfy her I drown her in gifts. I've had my hair styled. We listen to Elton John records together. Elton John. I'm going to be forty-nine."

Peabody, Markham, and Joshua had met in Paris in the fifties. In those days Markham was going to be a novelist—as who wasn't, Joshua thought, grieving.

Oh I remember Markham. Yes sir. Joshua once found out where Samuel Beckett lived and used to wait across the street from his flat, shivering in the rain for hours in the hope of seeing him venture forth. He never spoke to Beckett, but he would watch him pass and smile. Hey, there goes big Sam Beckett, a man who used to shoot the breeze with Jimmy Joyce.

"Why don't you introduce yourself, ask for an interview?" Markham asked. "I'm sure you could sell it somewhere."

"Bill, your presence alone would have been sufficient to taint the Sermon on the Mount."

No more ambitious than the rest of them really, Markham made the mistake of letting it show. If there was a New York publisher in town, he found out which hotel he was staying at and lay in wait for him in the bar. But, to be fair, he was also obliging. If you were without hashish, Markham, an abstainer himself, would provide. He was there to help when you had to move. He never made a pass at anybody else's girlfriend. But possibly because he seemed to incorporate all these virtues in one restless, yearning body, just about everybody felt ill at ease in his presence. They used Markham, but they never trusted him, and Peabody was gratuitously insulting. "Tell me, Bill, do you set yourself a number of words to write each day?"

Joshua had first met Peabody at 1 a.m. on an enchanting

spring night outside the Café Royal, now Le Drugstore, on Place St.-Germain. 1951 it was. Elegant, spare, jauntily dressed, favoring a snap-brim fedora, Peabody was already a legend in the *quartier*, drinking his way through an inheritance, zooming from St.-Germain to Montparnasse and back again in a battered *deux-chevaux,* merrily denouncing everybody he met in the cafés as resoundingly third-rate. Energy and pushy Jewish mothers were not quite enough, he delighted in warning them. Talent would also be required. Marcel Proust made them look sickly. Jane Austen knew more than they did.

Joshua espied Peabody often enough striding down the boulevard, not only the last of the family railroad money, but the world itself his inheritance. One night, soft with slanting rain and the smell of roasting chestnuts, he would pluck a schoolteacher at random, the most innocent of American girls, from a table at the Mabillon, and sweep her off for a week in an *auberge* only he knew of on the banks of the Loire, rendering the husband she had yet to meet inadequate forevermore. Another night, after having painstakingly arranged an assignation at the Café de Flore with the visiting aunt of an old Exeter classmate, he would sit across the boulevard at the Café Royal well past the appointed hour, watching out of the corner of his eye as his quarry, alone at her table, increasingly distraught, turned back one scruffy importuning stranger after another until, all hope abandoned, she rose to depart. Only then would Peabody dash gaily across the boulevard, zigzagging through the oncoming traffic, to carry her off without apology or dinner to the seediest hotel in the *quartier,* a fleabag, where he would coolly strip her of what remained of her dignity, thrust her into a taxi when he was finished, and be back at the Café Royal within the hour to rage against the depravity of the times.

Peabody was bankrolling and editing a little magazine, a typically snobbish and quixotic venture, with stories and poems in French, Spanish, and Italian as well as English, lavishing the last of his inheritance on his favored writers. He had never spoken to Joshua, he did not even acknowledge him on the street, so Joshua was delighted to catch the fastidious Peabody early one morning in the Café Royal, saddled with the embarrassing, complaining Melrose—Melrose, the banished Hollywood scriptwriter. Joshua, who had enjoyed a winning afternoon at Maison Lafitte for once, was in rare high spirits. He stood at the bar, rocking drunkenly, shamelessly eavesdropping on their conversation. Then he buttonholed Melrose as they stepped outside.

"I wonder if you know," he said, "that on this very square, in front of that church, in the spring of 1557, the gentry of this charming *quartier* gathered in their thousands for a burning. Two Huguenots, who refused under torture to deny their faith, were dragged right out here and offered mercy: if they renounced their heresy, they would be strangled before they were roasted—*à point,* it goes without saying. If not, their tongues would be ripped out of their mouths. They didn't take the Fifth," Joshua said, leering. "They had the natural dignity to say no, without equivocation, and out came their tongues, the crowd roaring more, more. Afterwards they were tied to stakes, hoisted high, so that their loins might be reduced to ashes while the other half of their bodies remained intact. And so, my friend, Senator McCarthy should be looked on as comic relief. A puerile American variation on a European theme. And before he came along, your only heresy was to grovel to producers and write banal scripts for which you were most assuredly overpaid."

"Why, you creep," Melrose began, "you crypto-fascist—"

But Peabody was guffawing, delighted. "Why don't you send me a story, Mr. Shapiro? I can't promise to publish, but I will read it myself."

"Well now, I don't write stories. I am a reporter. And what makes you think I'd want to be published in your pretentious little rich boy's magazine in the first place?"

One night much later, long after they had become friends and Joshua had become a regular at Peabody's table in The Old Navy, joining him in jeering at the passing parade, he told him about his need to get to Spain. Peabody was charged with concern. He smiled his tender smile and said, "Try Ibiza."

"Ibiza?"

"Ibiza," he said.

As Joshua recalled it, he yawned.

Imagine.

The lights had failed everywhere. Driving through the blackened village, the rain belting down, the streets awash, Joshua glanced at his dashboard clock. It was nearly 2 a.m. Shit, they can only be up to no good there. Those horny brokers and ad agency men with the slack, boozy faces, weekend John Waynes, utterly transmogrified once they held Canada Tire power saws in their hands. Or stood tall as Mr. Christian

45

behind the masts of their Lasers. And their saucy, newly liberated wives running around braless, those steamy compost heaps they called vaginas sprayed with Misty or Oo La La!, taking themselves for sophisticates because they could now compare fucking notes as freely as their mothers had once compared strawberry shortcake recipes. What were they up to in the dark, those yahoos, and what did they want with Pauline?

Parked outside the clubhouse, Joshua lighted a cigarette and counted nine other cars in the lot the next time lightning rocked the lake. Group grope, that's what they were into. Westmount's summer saturnalia. But the clubhouse was not in total darkness. Obviously, they had set out paraffin lamps here and there. Should I propel the Jeep right up the clubhouse stairs, bashing through the French doors? "Hey, remember the night that crazy Jew . . ."

Bolting up the clubhouse stairs, Joshua opened the front door softly, slipping quietly inside, fully expecting to trip over copulating couples. Gentile jogger nuts mounting Geritol-fed harridans. From the bar, he heard the sound of music and clapping hands. Somebody must have had a transistor radio. Or maybe a cassette player. But as his eyes adjusted to the dim light, he grasped that only Mr. Harry James was blowing. "The Four O'Clock Jump." Everybody was gathered round the swirling couple. Yes, yes, the Mixed Doubles Champions, Eastern Quebec Region, 1952. The wrong side of forty, both of them, and jitterbugging. His wife, his brother-in-law. Even as Joshua stood there, feverishly jealous, he could see that his barefoot wife, her hair flying, her long legs flashing, looked simply splendid. He also had to allow that Peter Pan, Esquire, could certainly cut a rug, as they used to say. Oh how graceful he appeared!

Joshua slid behind the bar, which was unattended, and poured himself a walloping cognac. A voice came from behind, startling him. "Crack his nuts for him."

It was Trimble, his ordnance corps tie askew, his little eyes floating in malice.

"You're out of your gourd, Jack."

"Don't count on it, old son," he said thickly.

Now, unfortunately, Joshua was cast in the light of one of the paraffin lamps and so his presence was no longer undetected, though Pauline was still unaware of it. And that's when Kevin did the unforgivable. Something Joshua took for an act of defiance. What he did, catching sight of Joshua, was to twirl Pauline around so that she could receive, startled, the full benefit of his grim, disapproving face.

Impulsively, Joshua walked around to the other side of the bar and clicked off the cassette player. Silence. Consternation. Rabbi Shapiro has pronounced. No more cakes, no more ale.

Pauline, never one to be caught off balance in any social situation, strode into his arms, hugged him, and said, "I knew you'd come to pick me up."

Moist hair stuck to the back of her neck. "I began to worry once the power went," he said.

Kevin joined them, his smile revealing dimples Joshua had not noticed before. "Now that you've finally honored us with your presence," he said, "I'm not going to let you go until you sign that book for me."

Joshua eased Pauline back from the bar so that there was nobody between him and Kevin. Remember: stick, stick, and away you go. "I was just saying to Pauline that you not only play boy's—" it nearly came out "goy's"—"games surpassingly well, but you also dance divinely."

"Joshua, please."

Jane Trimble sashayed up to the bar, glistening with excitement. Tim Hickey, the McTeers, and a few more, equally sodden, were now also drawn to the bar, anticipating an incident. Only Dickie Abbott, whom Joshua liked, was intent on keeping the peace. "Good to see you, Joshua," he said.

But Joshua ignored him. He picked off a strand of honey-colored hair from Kevin's shoulder. "Hey," he said, "now I know where I've seen you before. Didn't you model underwear for *Esquire*'s nineteen-fifty-five back-to-college issue?"

"Oh, shit, let's go home."

"My wife wants to go home, but I haven't finished my drink yet."

"That wasn't me," Kevin said, seemingly not the least offended, "but you could have seen me in *Thunderball*. You know, the Bond film."

"Holy cow. Were you really in that?"

"I was one of the scuba divers."

"There is absolutely no reason for you to be angry," Pauline said, thrusting herself against him.

"I'm not angry."

"We're going to be friends," Kevin said reassuringly.

Trimble, disgusted, retreated from the bar, but not Jane. The rain had settled into a soft, steady drizzle. First one couple and then another moved off. Maybe there wasn't going to be a fight after all. "Don't tell me the party's ending just when I get here," Joshua complained.

"It's not ending," Jane said, her voice soft and sympathetic, "we were just waiting for the rain to ease up before going in for a skinny-dip."

Joshua went rigid. "My wife," he said, "doesn't skinny-dip with anybody but me."

"Would you please stop calling me 'my wife.' I do have a name."

"I beg your pardon. Mrs. Shapiro doesn't skinny-dip with anybody but me."

"It's just something we used to do together when we were kids," Kevin said. "It's innocent, it doesn't mean a thing."

Remembering what his father had taught him about bar brawls, Joshua didn't intend to jab, he was going to let go a short fast one. But it was Pauline's face. Weaker. The eyes inclined to waver. But her face. He couldn't bring himself to strike it.

"You're looking at one of your admirers," Kevin was pleading, his smile enchanting. "Really you are. She wanted to leave long ago, I kept her here."

"We're leaving right now," Pauline said, taking his arm.

They drove in silence until they reached the main road.

"Would you have gone skinny-dipping with them if I hadn't turned up?"

"When we were kids, Kevin and I used to be tossed into the same bathtub here every night."

"But you're not kids any more, and you haven't answered my question."

"No, I guess not."

"Why?"

"Because you wouldn't have liked it, I'm forty-two years old, I've had three kids, and my breasts aren't what they once were."

"I wonder what I could get for you as a trade-in."

Back at the cottage, they found a bottle of Chablis in the fridge and drank it together on the dock, their feet dangling in the water.

"I don't want to grow any older," she said.

But he wasn't listening.

"Josh?"

"I want to go back to Spain," he announced out of nowhere.

"What are you talking about?"

"Ibiza."

"Why?"

"Because I behaved badly there once."

"Oh, come now. You didn't behave *that* badly. And that, as they say, was long ago and in another country. There's nothing you can do about it now."

"I could find out what happened to everybody after I fled."

"Forget it."

"What if I can't?"

"I don't really think you care that much about Spain any more. Or what happened to everybody on Ibiza. I think there's just a part of you that craves to be twenty-one again."

"You don't understand. I hated being twenty-one."

"Then, maybe, but now now."

Pauline scribbled a note for the children, left it on the kitchen table, and they retreated to their bedroom, Joshua collapsing gratefully on the bed, letting his clothes fall anywhere. But then the sight of Pauline, in the flimsiest of bras and pink satin halfslip, struck him as so provocative, even after all their years together, that he now felt more aroused than weary. He pulled her down to the bed with him. It didn't work. Pauline felt as if she were being rather brusquely reclaimed, a territory of doubtful ownership, and she was not pleased. And Joshua, finding her unresponsive, was resentful. He slept badly. He dreamed about Ibiza again. Mueller. Monique. Mariano.

They didn't come out of their bedroom again until early afternoon. Pauline made scrambled eggs and coffee and carried it out to the porch overlooking the lake.

"His seaplane's still docked at the club," Joshua said.

"I should hope so. He hasn't even said goodbye yet."

Fumbling for his binoculars, scanning the bay, Joshua soon added, "Wait. Further intelligence. Guess who's taken him out water-skiing?"

"Jane Trimble."

"Why yes," he replied, impressed, "you're right. And wait for it. The Grew's headed right for our dock. "I think we are about to have guesties."

But, at the last moment, the Grew, its nose prodding the air, veered sharply away.

Nineteen thirty-nine, a bad time for most, was a vintage year for the Shapiros. Joshua's father, after an absence of two years—an absence that was not satisfactorily explained to him—was living at home again, laboring in the family scrap yard. Joshua was only eight years old, and he had no idea why his father had to work for Uncle Oscar; neither did he suspect how much he hated it. Reuben Shapiro was not the most forthcoming of men.

"Daddy, weren't you in the liquor business once? Before I was born?"

"Yeah, well. Right."

"What did you do?"

"You could say I was in deliveries, sort of."

Although they lived in Montreal, his father used to bring home the New York newspapers after his long days in the junkyard, the pages stained with chopped egg and onion, hasty notations on the morning line at Belmont scrawled in the margins. The *News,* the *Mirror.* And always something for Joshua. *Action Comics,* an Oh Henry bar, or, if one of his horses had come in, a model airplane kit. Once a week his father also brought home *Life* magazine. Lying on the living room carpet one evening in the spring of 1939, idly flipping the pages, Joshua came on a picture of Franco leading his troops into a stricken Madrid. Franco triumphant, ending a siege that had begun more than two years earlier, on November 6, 1936.

Their massive, walnut-finished radio was tuned to "Fibber McGee and Molly." Uncle Oscar, visiting with them, pronouncing over a Johnson's Wax commercial, assured his father that aluminum, aluminum was the stuff, it was going to be needed for airplanes, but, he cautioned, even if war came the Germans were bound to collapse after six months. The Maginot Line was impregnable. Take it from me, Ruby.

His father bobbed his head, agreeing, rather than argue with Uncle Oscar, who considered himself the ultimate authority on all matters. He knew, for instance, that GM had developed an engine that could run for sixty miles on an eyedropper full of paraffin, but the oil interests had had it suppressed. He was also aware that Hitler was down to two doubles, the third having already been assassinated. Hardly a baseball fan, he was still able to assure Joshua that Hank Greenberg wore a special steel jockstrap, because when he slid into second base they tried to tag him you-know-where, the bastards, just because he was born a Hebe. "And hey there, Denny Dimwit, if you were my son you wouldn't sit there with your head buried in the sports pages."

"He's not your son," his father said.

"Sports is for dummies. Look where it got your dad."

Joshua, bright-eyed, turned expectantly to his father. *Hit him. Smash him one, please.* But all his father said was, "Yeah, well. Right."

Reuben watched his son, his only son, flee the living room.

Uncle Oscar, the most wintry of men, knew only one mood: outrage. Outrage against the stacked deck this world had dealt him. Busted flushes. Heartburn. Bunions. Blocked sinuses. Constipation. Foul-tempered, constantly on the boil, he would stomp through his yard, urging on the men as they sledge-hammered brass bedsteads, worth twenty-five cents a pound, smashed Franklin stoves for the cast iron, cannibalized twenty-year-old Gray-Dort sport roadsters and Frontenac coupes, anything those crazy farmers brought in, realizing only a frustratingly small profit after the metals had been separated. He trekked through his shit-pile of spittoons, prehistoric sewing machines, ridiculous old barber chairs, marble sinks that were being gutted to get at the brass taps, scales and other fixtures from country general stores equipped during the ice age, everybody's dreck dumped on him, wracking his head for the money-making idea that would lift him out of his dreaded yard and into Outremont with all its splendors.

Once, summoned by his jangling phone, Reuben stumbled into the hall in the early morning hours only to have Oscar bellow at him, "Advertising on hotel ceilings."

"What?"

"There's all this wasted space, see? A drummer checks in, he's lonely, he lies down on the bed, and there it is on the ceiling for him. Restaurants, nightclubs, strip joints, list of movies. Everything all laid out. What do you think?"

Though younger than his father, Uncle Oscar wore a business suit and held forth in the scrap yard office. This was no more than a glorified shack, but he was behind a desk all the same, sucking on a House of Lords, ruminating over penny mining stocks, while his father drove the truck or spun out his days wading through the muck of the small yard with the French Canadians, sorting out metals. A dandy born,

51

Reuben came home dirty as a miner to be served supper by his watchful wife.

"It's only another fourteen months there, Ruby, and then you'll be free to leave."

"Yeah, well. Right."

Afterwards his father usually settled into his easy chair, nodding off over a copy of *Black Mask* or, if it was a Friday night, calling him in to listen to the fights, Don Dunphy reaching out to them through their walnut-finished RCA radio. Whenever any of Colucci's people came to call, his mother filled the doorway, hands on her hips, and said he was out.

Joshua's father drove home in the truck. But Uncle Oscar, who had graduated from Commercial High, owned a car, he was on the executive of the synagogue and played golf with gentile customers from time to time, if only on a municipal course. "Hey, Heeney, what if you could defrost the St. Lawrence in January, keeping the harbor open all year round?"

Boy, these Jews. Clever. "How?" Heeney asked.

"Warming it with underwater cables."

Uncle Oscar was taking a correspondence course in engineering, he kept a set of the *Encyclopedia Britannica* in a glass-enclosed case in his living room. When things were slack in the yard, he composed letters to the editor of the *Star* on world conditions, the possibility of life on Mars, and the plight of the Jews in Europe. Once he had conceived a new form of crossword puzzle, but couldn't get anywhere in New York, no syndicate would handle it. Of course not, he was merely a Canadian. He hurried to Ottawa to offer his war plan to the Ministry of Defence, unavailingly. He invented one ingenious radio game after another, and took his ideas to Toronto, but would the CBC buy from a Jew? No. But in 1940 he was still in there. Scheming, fulminating. "What if you could get off the train in Washington," Joshua once heard him speculate, "walk right into a government office, and patent the fucking alphabet. Imagine, only twenty-five letters, but they'd have to be worth a fortune."

One afternoon when Joshua had just turned ten, the secretary in the scrap yard's outer office, a neighborhood girl, was home sick. Joshua happened to be hanging around, out of school, and was enormously flattered to be asked to take care of the phone calls. Handling the first one, he said, "One moment, please," and turned the receiver over to his father. "Yes," his father said, nodding, apologizing to the caller, and

52

passed the receiver to Uncle Oscar. Uncle Oscar talked at some length as usual—going into the only proper method for curing tobacco, and how only a few important people knew that Mussolini was suffering from the syph—before he got to the price of zinc. When he finally hung up, he turned to Joshua, his eyes taunting. "Who did they ask for?"

"Mr. Shapiro," Joshua replied hotly.

"If they ask for Mr. Shapiro in this office, it's for me. If they want to speak to your father, they ask, 'Is Ruby around?' "

His father, the scar tissue round his eyebrows drained white, didn't say a word.

"Fuck you, Uncle Oscar."

Uncle Oscar whacked him one. His father, springing with a speed that terrified Joshua, lunged at Uncle Oscar, driving him against the wall.

"Don't, Ruby. For your sake," he pleaded, even as he sank to the floor, whimpering.

His father backed away from him, striding out of the office without a word. Uncle Oscar removed his steel-rimmed spectacles and wiped his eyes. He stood up, dusting off his trousers, and turned to Joshua. "You're nothing but a little fart," he said, "and if he walks off this job, it's you who are to blame, not me. Now get the hell out of here, Denny Dimwit," he added, already dialing his mother's number on the phone.

To Joshua's astonishment, his mother didn't reproach him when he got home. Neither was his father's truck parked outside. Ignoring him, his mother waited by the window. His father didn't come back for supper, he didn't return until long after Joshua had gone to bed, and the next morning, when he got up to get ready for school, Joshua was surprised to discover that his father was still at home. Furthermore, he wasn't dressed in the workclothes that smelled sharply of axle grease. Reuben was wearing his Adam hat, a white-on-white shirt, a hand-painted tie, a checked sports jacket, neatly creased brown trousers, diamond socks, and patent leather shoes.

"I'm sorry if I did something wrong," Joshua said.

"You did me a favor," his father said.

"Some favor," his mother said, glowering at Joshua. "This means the end of his parole."

Joshua didn't yet know what "parole" meant, but he didn't dare ask.

"Don't worry," his father said, "Colucci is taking care of everything."

His father never went back to the scrap yard. Instead, he drifted into the insurance business again, a field where Sonny Colucci still had need of his expertise. Less than three months later, his father was obliged to leave town again, suddenly. Esther, disobeying strict instructions, followed after, and Joshua was dumped with his Aunt Fanny once more.

Things ended badly for Reuben. There was a trial.

The problem was Pinsky's Jubilee Outfitting, on Jean-Talon, which had burned to the ground late on a Saturday night. An act of God, Pinsky said—mind you, a friendly one for a change, because at the time Pinsky was just one breathless step ahead of his many creditors. The fire inspector, a sour type, suspected arson, but was unable to find any hard evidence. All the same, the insurance company refused to pay Pinsky's claim and he was forced to sue. At the trial, the insurance company's lawyers made many a sarcastic reference to Pinsky's books, which strongly suggested that Jubilee was teetering on the edge of bankruptcy. They also tried to make a good deal out of the fact that Pinsky had withdrawn $1,500 in cash from his account only a week before the fire. The withdrawal seemed inexplicable, possibly even compromising, until Reuben Shapiro took the stand.

Occupation, he was asked.

"Metal merchant and like, you know, boxing instructor."

"Boxing instructor?"

It was explained that Mr. Shapiro, a former lightweight boxing champion of Canada, now saw it as his civic duty to instruct underprivileged youngsters, who might otherwise turn to crime, in the manly art of self-defense at the Neighbourhood House A.C. He did this work voluntarily, without recompense.

Reuben's tangled tale, as it emerged piece by piece, was that he just happened to be in Pinsky's office, shooting the breeze, a week before the fire. That very morning, he said, he had seen an absolute dream of a fur coat in Ogilvy's window, just the number for his wife, and Pinsky had lent him the $1,500 so that he could pick it up. Members of the jury exchanged knowing glances and smirked. Reuben, grinning, blinking, playing it goofy, exactly as he had been instructed by the lawyer, explained that Pinsky was an avid boxing fan, a longtime admirer of his ring feats. And to this Pinsky added, his manner defiantly sincere, that he had felt sorry for Shapiro, who had obviously answered the bell once too often, and no matter how bad it looked in court he would never regret having lent him a helping hand. Furthermore, given the choice he would do it again, because that's the sort of fellow he was. But Mr. Justice Boyer was not impressed. Summing up for the jury, he said, "Like me, you may find Mr. Shapiro's tale incredible. Obviously, if Mr. Shapiro was going to buy a fur coat he would, true to his kind, not shop at Ogilvy's. He would get it wholesale."

The jury found in favor of the insurance company, Pinsky's claim being disallowed. But Pinsky's outraged lawyers put in an immediate appeal, on the grounds that Mr. Justice Boyer had misdirected the jury with a blatant and inexcusable racial slander. The appeal was granted and, after many delays, the insurance company, rather than go to court again and risk offending its Jewish clientele, settled Pinsky's claim.

Pinsky, exultant, talked too much, and his boy, a classmate of Joshua's, carried the tale to school. "If you need maybe a fire, my father says Shapiro's the man. What a *yold!*"

Joshua fell on Pinsky's boy in the schoolyard, knocking him down, sitting on his stomach, and beating him about the face, until Seymour Kaplan and Morty Zipper managed to tie him up, Pinsky's boy squirming free.

Reuben, it was decided, ought to absent himself from the insurance business for a while. And so, with Colucci's help, he went into the printing business, sort of.

Gas ration coupons.

4

It was only 10:30 a.m., nothing accomplished, when Joshua decided what the hell, he could bend his own work rules if he felt like it. He went out for a walk.

Their street of terraced houses, in Lower Westmount, was now a thicket of A VENDRE/FOR SALE signs, slush everywhere, crumbling frozen dog shit lying on the snow. Joshua lived in a failing city, a wasting place, many of its shiny new office towers crying out for tenants, the construction hammers silenced, the stock exchange mute. Almost everybody he knew was jittery, drinking more, inclined to stumble out of bed at 3 a.m. to jot down a list of redeemable assets on the back of an envelope. Or study French verbs. Many English-speaking natives were packing their bags, making ready to run. Safety deposit boxes had been emptied, bank accounts

55

cleaned out. Lawyers, twenty years out of school, were eschewing noonday squash to bone up on the bar requirements of the other provinces. Doctors were brooding over real estate portfolios suddenly stricken with malignancy, involved with ill health at last, if only their own.

The Canadian dollar continued to sink. There were rumors it wouldn't bottom out until it reached eighty cents American. A disaster for many, but not for Izzy Singers. Izzy had added to his fortune, speculating on the international exchange. But Izzy, who had considerable holdings in La Belle Province, was not in good shape. He had broken out in shingles, his skinny little body girdled in scabs. Becky rubbed him down nightly with an ointment of atropine, a cocaine-type drug which exacerbated the ailment, only because Izzy was secretly fearful that the salve might be habit-forming. Keenly aware of the Italian syndrome, he was also scared of being kidnapped and now varied the time of his daily departure from his office, cunningly driving home by a different route each night. He wouldn't open thick envelopes or ride in an elevator with a Japanese in it. He carried a doctor's letter with him at all times, properly notarized and addressed "To Whom It May Concern," saying he was allergic to down pillows, must be kept on a salt-free diet, and responded poorly to physical pain; attached to it were Japanese, French, and Arabic translations. Izzy triple-locked his doors and there were double bolts on his windows. He had had his alarm systems renewed and bought a new pair of Alsatians. So now he tiptoed about his own house, not only itching everywhere, but also terrified of being torn apart. Coming home from his office, he slid out of his Cadillac already in a crouch, proffering gifts, minced steak or calf's liver from Dionne's, doing his utmost to ingratiate himself with his new hounds. "Here, boy. Here. Easy does it now. It's me, only me. Izzy."

In this city, Joshua's Montreal, nobody he knew was redecorating. Or planting. Everybody was thinking hard. The more cultivated were buying sterling silver, diamonds, jade, gold, and other movables; the coarser, Saturday night specials.

There were many who feared that the city was teetering over an abyss.

Certainly standards weren't what they had once been. Take the Ritz-Carlton, for instance, the most opulent of their hotels.

The Ritz, desecrated.

The incomparable Ritz. Where once impeccably schooled

brokers could conspire over malt whiskies and dishes of smoked almonds to send a dubious mining stock soaring. Where, after a morning of trying on dresses in neighboring Holt Renfrew, matrons of good family could meet for a lunch of cold Gaspé salmon and tossed salad in the garden café. Where, in halcyon days, even the doorman, an appraiser born, could make him feel Jewy. The Ritz had fallen on such hard times that it now admitted visiting hockey players to its gilt bedrooms—even the players from expansion teams. The Café de Paris, the Maritime Bar, would never be the same. This winter, the sweetly scented ladies in their mink wraps and the gentlemen in the beaver coats, drifting in after a hockey game, were obliged to actually mingle with the players. Youngsters with angry boils on their necks, only a season out of northern mining towns, whooping it up at the bar, attended by groupies reeking of cheap perfume. Taut-sweatered girls who favored bikini panties, DYNAMITE embossed on the crotch. O God, Joshua thought, where once only the very best Westmount had to offer met for discreet assignations, now one groupie working a floor could service the power play, obliging the penalty-killing squad in overtime.

Joshua had come to adore Montreal as never before.

In this city, his Montreal, a few weeks after the Parti Québécois had bounded into office, surprising themselves more than anybody else, their newly elected premier, René Lévesque, was in a car accident. Sweeping down Côte-des-Neiges Road, on the flank of Mount Royal, at 4 a.m., he inadvertently hit a derelict, who was snoozing on the street, and killed him. Montreal's intrepid police, who used to gleefully crack Separatist skulls with riot sticks in the days when they were still demonstrating in the streets, quickly adjusted to the new power structure. On the spot almost instantly, they assessed the situation and grasped where their duty lay. They tenderly escorted the distressed premier and his mistress from the scene, out of sight of obnoxious reporters, and booked the offending corpse, removing it to the hospital for a blood test, to establish whether or not it had been drunk.

On Joshua's daily stroll to a favored downtown bar, where he met informally for late-afternoon drinks with cronies, sometimes including visiting members of The William Lyon Mackenzie King Memorial Society, he had taken to counting the moving vans, which seemed to be here, there, and everywhere. The bar he frequented was ensconced in a veritable Victorian pile, a hotel that had once been grand but was now dilapidated. It was still known to its habitués as The King's Arms, but in deference to unfavorable vibrations, it now boasted a garish new sign, "Armes du Roi." One of the regulars, sour Robbie MacIntyre, a hefty man in his early sixties, his blue eyes truculent, churned out a monthly newsletter for an insurance company. A sedentary type, Robbie was filled with such scorn for all physical-fitness freaks that he kept a scrapbook on them, a doomsday book, entering the obituaries of those who had died an untimely death. When Lloyd Percival, the head of Canada's Physical Fitness College, was struck down by a heart attack while out jogging one morning, the usually parsimonious MacIntyre bought drinks all around, literally hopping about with glee.

Another regular, the gentle Roger Goyer, a cherished chum, was back with them after an absence of more than a week; his hands trembling, having outlasted an Antabuse course, even as he had once triumphed over two weeks in a clinic, sent there to dry out. Roger, a desk man in the *Star*'s city room, confronted the world that confounded him on a diet of ale, the first one consumed at a late breakfast in Toe Blake's Tavern. Once, invited out to lunch by him, Joshua noticed a mutual acquaintance bent into the sleet on the other side of St. James Street. "Hey, there's Finley," he said. "Should we ask him to join us?"

Roger regarded Joshua with a look of utter distaste. "He eats," he said.

Among the regular clientele at The King's Arms, there were also many upwardly mobile corporation lawyers, advertising men, and brokers, many of whom had sported digital wristwatches long before they were generally available in Canada. Their chatter, largely about stereo equipment or commodity futures, baffled Joshua. "Dylan" meant Bob, not Thomas, to them. They were too young to remember Maurice Richard cutting in over the blue line or to have heard Oscar Peterson play at the Alberta Lounge. But it was their bustling presence that flushed out liberated young secretaries from the surrounding office towers, especially during The Happy Hour. A number of these nifty girls, The Flopper assured Joshua, provided nookie free, though never for the likes of MacIntyre, Goyer, or the rest of their bunch, who they appreciated were going nowhere. It was the beer-bellied Flopper, of course, who drew the sporting crowd to The King's Arms.

The legendary Flopper, so-called because of the inimitable manner in which he had once minded the nets for the Boston

58

Bruins, was a child of prairie penury. Pug-nosed, his gray eyes hard as pebbles, his impudent moon-face scored with more than a hundred stitches, he still wore his steely gray hair brush-cut, a memento of the day when he had been sent down to Springfield to play for the great Eddie Shore. The Flopper, born in a sod hut, the fifth of seven children, had worn a flour sack, holes scissored out for his arms, until he was nine years old. He was pulling carrots for ten cents an hour before he learned how to read, and even now his English was enriched by felicities all his own. Once, flipping through a book about the Holocaust that Joshua had just bought, The Flopper was startled to come across photographs of Dachau's survivors. "They sure as shit didn't get much to eat," he said. "I mean, lookit how emancipated they look."

A hard-nosed conservative, The Flopper was vehemently opposed to abortion-on-demand, spearing on ice, or an independent Quebec. "I condone it," he had said again and again. "I absolutely condone that kinda shit."

The bartender, an otherwise amiable Griffintown boy, was also a firm advocate of Canadian unity. He had taken to keeping a baseball bat, a Louisville Slugger, in full view of the clientele. It lay on his rear counter, intimidating, underneath a framed photograph of Queen Elizabeth. George, who called his bat "my Pepsi-tamer," had also developed a line of jokes about French Canadians. "Hey, did you hear that the Berkowitz boy, you know, Son of Sam, has got himself a Pepsi lawyer?"

"Is that so?"

"Yeah, he's going to plead guilty to the six murders, but fight the parking ticket."

But when Joshua was standing at the bar, George restrained himself for his sake. Pauline, on her mother's side, was a de Gaspé Benoit. The blood of seigneurs coursed through her exquisite veins. George, like all the regulars in The King's Arms, was fond of Pauline, and inquired after her daily, now that she was resting in the psychiatric ward of the Royal Victoria Hospital.

Wasting.

Bolstered on Scotch—usually two quick ones, sometimes more—Joshua visited Pauline every afternoon. He read to her. Treading carefully, he talked to her about the children. Their love, their happiness. The seemingly impregnable fortress they had made for themselves, before her brother's intrusion. But Pauline, once so fastidious, better than beautiful, an excitement, no longer even combed her soft honey-colored hair. It was tangled, dirty. He combed it out for her. Then he noticed that her once faultless fingernails were broken here, bitten there. There were foodstains on her negligee. Joshua protested to the nurses, but he knew there was nothing they could do. She didn't care. His wife languished in bed, selfishly adrift on Valium, her blue eyes listless, her face a sickly white. Staring at him. Once, he had angrily tried to shock her out of her comatose state. "She insists on coming to see you. She won't let go."

Pauline didn't even stir.

"I'll bring her tomorrow."

Nothing.

"She wants to explain everything to you."

Still, she didn't ask who.

"Jane Trimble."

Pauline began to weep without sound, her lips quivering, and he leaped up to take her surprisingly cold hand and say, "Oh, I'm sorry. I'm so sorry, my darling."

Only a week after Pauline had been admitted to the Royal Victoria, Joshua was summoned to the psychiatrist's office.

The esteemed Dr. Jonathan Cole, author of *My Kind, Your Kind, Mankind,* a rotund man, brown eyes mournful, turned out to be Yossel Kugelman, of all people. When they had been kids together on St. Urbain Street, Yossel had already catalogued his library of Big Little Books. If you borrowed one, you signed for it. To be fair, they had all collected salvage door-to-door for the war effort, but only Yossel hadn't carted his junk to Debrofsky's yard on St. Dominique, selling it there. No sir, that fink was no warprofiteer, he actually turned in his take at school. And now, Joshua could see Yossel was still a collector. From salvage he had graduated to art. Canadiana. A Pellan hung on one wall, a William Ronald on another.

Cole (or Kugelman) acknowledged Joshua's sly grin of recognition with an awkward offering of pleasantries. But Joshua wasn't listening. He was trying to remember if Yossel had been the one to turn up at Bea Rosen's sweet-sixteen wearing a fedora, when he was suddenly startled by a direct question. "Has she any reason to resent you?" Yossel inquired in a soothing voice.

Affronted, Joshua snapped back, "I leave a rim round the bathtub. No matter how hard I wipe, there are stains on my underwear."

Yossel, obviously unshockable, continued, "Now tell me, what was your sex life like before—"

"None of your fucking business, Kugelman."

Yossel flung his pen on the desk. "You're not taking this seriously. I'm trying to help."

"You're full of shit, you always were. You turned up at Bea Rosen's sweet-sixteen wearing a fedora. Ha, ha. Prick."

Yossel sighed wearily, slicked back his hair with a plump hand, and asked Joshua what his feelings were about electric shock treatment.

Lunging, Joshua grabbed him by his tie, yanking hard. "You just come near her with those electrodes, you even think of it, and I'll kill you."

Breaking free, his face stinging red, Yossel demanded, "Are you crazy?"

"What's crazy these days? You tell me, Dr. *Cole*."

"It wasn't me who changed the name. It was my mother. My son has reverted to Kugelman."

"He has?"

"He's studying piano. He's at Juilliard. And while we're at it, it wasn't me with the fedora at Bea's sweet-sixteen. It was Izzy."

Izzy Singer, who was then already into the stock market, using his war savings certificates as collateral.

"And please," Yossel continued, "if we are going to get anywhere here, you must stop being so hostile."

Joshua thought he could explain. "I saw you once at the airport," he said. "Waiting by the carousel. When your suitcase came, it had little wheels underneath and a handle. You pulled it like a wagon."

"So what?" Yossel asked, baffled.

"So you're a twit."

"I've got a bad back," he protested. "I mustn't carry."

"Look here, Yossel, I want my wife back. I want her well. I don't want any electrodes or primal scream therapy or any other shit you fakers are into. And you can take her off those drugs starting right now."

"I tell you what. We'll put her on yogurt every morning. You think that will do the trick?"

"You sure it was Izzy with the fedora?"

"Yes, I'm sure. And did you know that Bea Rosen's dead?"

No, he didn't.

"Cancer of the uterus. Last May. She left three children. The youngest's autistic."

"Hey, Yossel, you're a real barrel of fun, aren't you? How old are you now?"

"Forty-seven. Same as you."

"What's wrong with your back?"

"Nothing. A disc."

"I've got stretch marks on my ass now. I thought that only happened to women."

"Oy vey, Joshua, what a wreck you are. Do you always drink like this?"

"We've got to start taking care, Yossel. These are dangerous times for our old bunch. Forty-seven. Shit. I don't care for what's happening to us."

A perplexed Yossel suddenly regarded Joshua with something like real alarm. *"What did he tell you, that blabbermouth?"*

"Who?"

"Moish."

Moish had to be Morty Zipper, who had sat two rows away from him in Room 42 and was now his physician. "I didn't even know you were one of his patients."

Yossel rubbed his tired eyes.

"I thought you said it was only a disc."

Sighing, he allowed, "Recently I also suffer from shortness of breath after I have enjoyed intercourse."

Joshua couldn't help himself. He giggled.

"Laugh," Yossel said. "Feel free."

"With everybody or only with your wife?"

"Oh, clever! Witty! Noel Coward must be spinning with envy in his grave. I'll have you know that Bessie and I," he said tightly, "have always had a one-on-one relationship."

Now Joshua was laughing out loud. Without restraint. "Oh, my God," he said, "don't tell me that you married Bessie Orbach?"

"I am happy to be able to answer that in the affirmative."

Quaking again, scooping tears out of the corners of his eyes, Joshua said, "I took her out once. Outremont. Her father was a dentist. A poor loser. Her mother used to cover the sofas with plastic. You necked with her, it stuck to your back."

"Big talker, you never touched her."

"Aw, come on, Yossel, everybody in the Maccabees had their innings with Bessie."

"The hell they did, and anyway you struck out at the plate. Looking."

"Oh yeah?"

"You think you're really something, don't you, Joshua, and that the rest of us are fools? You, and the others in that idiotic Mackenzie King Memorial Society. Well, let me enlighten you. Your spurious articles may have won you some kind of reputation outside of the country, but we know who you are. I remember your father's picture on the front page of the *Herald*—wearing handcuffs. I was at your bar-mitzvah, and I still remember what happened there. We know you and what you come from. And I've got news for you. Bessie told me about her *one* date with the great Mr. Shapiro. Pretending to be a McGill student. Calling yourself Robert Jordan. She thought you were pathetic, that's what."

Remembering, Joshua blushed.

"She dines out on that one to this day," Yossel continued.

"I remember," Joshua said in a faltering voice, "that her mother also left cellophane on the lampshades. As a matter of interest, does Bessie—"

"My Bessie is an exemplary homemaker."

"But a wanton, eh, Yossel? I mean, she leaves you breathless," he said, erupting in laughter again. Forced laughter this time.

"My marriage works wonderfully well. But your wife is in the hospital, isn't she?"

Joshua didn't say a word.

"I'm sorry," Yossel said, retreating.

Joshua took out a pack of cigarettes and broke the cellophane. Then he fished into one pocket after another for a match, refusing the lighter Yossel held out to him. Finally he lighted up, dropping the spent match on the carpet. Then he shot Yossel his most pitying look. "I didn't want to say anything, but Moish is worried about your heart."

"You're lying through your teeth."

"I wish I were."

"Sit here and I'll phone him."

"But you don't understand. He won't say a word to you."

"Liar, liar, liar."

"Overexcitement's bad for you. He won't say anything because he doesn't want you popping right in the middle of a one-on-one with Bessie. See you around, Yossel."

That was in February, only a week after Pauline had entered the hospital.

Disgruntled, agitated, but absolutely unable to contend with his bunch at The King's Arms, Joshua wandered all the way down to St. Denis Street after quitting Yossel's office. The first bar he came to was called Chez O'Neil. Chrome everywhere. Plastic plants, the leaves dusty. Above crossed Québécois flags, a poster of René Lévesque. *Un vrai chef.*

The imitation-brick walls were plastered with posters of local *vedettes*. Pauline Julien, Gilles Vigneault, Yvan Deschamps. The new Trinity. Joshua found some solace in a double Scotch, he ordered another, and then he phoned Morty Zipper's office. "Shame on you. I hear you talk about your patients outside of office hours."

"Sure. But only the juicier cases. I tell everybody I'm treating you for syph."

"Did you know that Yossel Kugelman was at the Royal Vic?"

"Yes. Certainly. He's called me twice in the last hour."

"Of course he has. You're worried about his heart."

"I am?"

"Yes indeed. Now tell me how good he is at his suspect trade."

"There are patients who swear by him."

"He wears elevator heels. There's a fucking golf trophy in his office. And he's married to Bessie Orbach. Remember Bessie?"

"Hubba hubba."

"Would you trust him to take care of your wife?"

"Yes. No. Maybe."

"I want you to tell me if there's anything wrong with me that I don't know about."

"The way you carry on, your liver should be bloated to twice its normal size. But so far, so good. Now, if you don't mind—"

"Wait. Hold it. Remember Bea Rosen's sweet-sixteen party? We were all there. Pratt Avenue."

"Her father kept zipping down to the basement to make sure we hadn't dimmed the lights."

"Yeah. Right."

"O.K. I was there."

"Now I want you to think carefully. This is important. Didn't Yossel turn up wearing a fedora?"

"I've got a patient waiting, Josh."

"There was a sort of brush nipped into the band. Multi-colored. Like a fishing fly."

"Call me at home tonight. Goodbye, Josh."

5

"Well, yeah. Right. You know what these days are?"

"Cold."

"No, no. Anybody knows that. If you're Jewish, but."

"Colder."

"Oh, very funny. Ha ha."

"What then, Daddy?"

"These are the Days of Awe. Tomorrow is Rosh Hashonna, our new year, and like a week later it's Yom Kippur, when if you shit on anybody during the year you got a legal right to repent. And God forgives you. We're going to the synagogue in the morning, you know."

"Aw, Daddy."

"Aw, Daddy, nothing. We're going for once. It's only proper, Josh. We're Hebes, you and me, and don't you forget it."

Joshua and his father were sitting together in the backyard. On a clammy October morning in 1946, the sky a shimmering blue, the swirling leaves already slick with frost. His father had asked him to help put up the double windows. But once Joshua had followed him into the rotting gray shed to help sort them out, he produced a quart of Labatt's ale and two glasses and invited him to continue out into the yard. They settled down together on a squishy old sofa, long abandoned, bleeding stuffing where it had once been slashed with razors or where the rats had gnawed into it.

"How old are you now?"

"Fifteen."

"Already? Well, yeah. Right. It's certainly time we talked."

"About what?" Joshua asked.

Reuben shot him his most solemn look. "About fucking, and the Jewish tradition."

"In that order?"

"Don't get smart with me or I'll land you a good one."

"Aw, Daddy, you never hit me once."

"Well, I shoulda, maybe. You shouldn't be talking about quitting school, it's a shame."

His father was fidgety, embarrassed, and in his hand, Joshua saw, he now held a Bible. The real thing. The King James Version. His copy had markers sticking out here, there, and everywhere.

"Hey, Daddy, don't tell me you've been reading *that*."

"Why not?" he replied, indignant.

Joshua slapped his cheek and whistled.

"Listen here," his father said, "let's not get excited. There's no need for you to lose your temper. Tell me, you really want to be a newspaperman, or is it just that, you know, like you once thought you'd be a ball player?"

"Well, yeah. I dunno. A sportswriter, maybe."

"Sportswriters are drunks. They're bums, every one of them," Reuben said, remembering old grievances.

"I could be different, but."

"Let me tell you something," his father said, brandishing his Bible with enthusiasm, "this thing here is just filled with book titles and savvy sayings. I mean, I used to think, you were a writer you had to make things up out of your own head, but you'd be surprised how many of their titles and sayings were swiped out of this one here, and there's plenty left, so you could do a lot worse than—"

"Why don't we talk about fucking first?"

"What did you have in mind?"

"Me? Nothing. You're the one who brought it up."

"Yeah, well. Right. You know how it's done?"

"Yeah."

"You do?"

"You're goddamn right I do."

"Have you done it with anybody yet?"

"No."

"O.K., that's it."

"What do you mean, *that's it?*"

"If you know how, eventually you'll get some. It figures. What more do you want me to say?"

"Don't I get any useful instructions?"

"We're not going to talk dirty out here, you understand?"

"Don't shout at me. I didn't bring up the subject."

"You don't do it the night before a fight, it drains you, that's what Al Weill always used to say."

"I'm not going to be a fighter."

"Look, there are more important things in the world than fucking." His father cracked his knuckles. "I shoulda seen that you had a stricter upbringing."

"How do I get some?"

"I'm not a pimp, for Christsake." His father topped up their glasses with more Labatt's. "You see all those pimples you got on your face?"

"Yeah. So?"

66

"Don't worry. They're going to clear up. You'll be left with little holes in your cheeks here and there, but what the hell."

"You mean fucking drains you, but it's good for pimples?"

"Goddamn it, Josh, I don't know how we got into this!"

"You started it."

Lowering his voice to a whisper, his father said, "You are invited into a lady's boudoir, well, if you're a gentleman the first thing you do is take off your hat."

"Is that how you get it going?"

"You fold your trousers neat, see, and you're wearing clean socks, that's important, and if you got your wallet with you, you keep it under your pillow. You got that?"

Joshua nodded.

"And I want you to be wearing fresh underwear. No skid marks. But even so you wash up good first, if only as an example to her, because sometimes they can be real smelly down there."

"Down where?"

"*We're not going to talk dirty.*"

"*You* said 'down there,' not me."

"I want to teach you about the etiquette of the matter, not the actual doing of it."

"Some help."

"All right. O.K. You know what it is?" he asked, blushing a little as he thrust a three-pack of Sheiks at him.

"Yeah," Joshua said, smirking.

"As soon as your dick gets stiff, you roll one on. Don't forget that."

"And then what?"

"Why don't you read a book on the subject and leave me alone?"

"You're my father, but."

"Yeah, right. Well afterwards—"

"Afterwards?"

"Yeah, afterwards, you remember to wash up, using soap and hot water. But if, say, a couple of weeks later it hurts you to piss or it's coming out the wrong color you go right to the doctor, you don't wait. Got that?"

"Right."

"Well, that's it. Good luck."

"Aw, come on, Daddy."

Grudgingly, his father came to a decision. He dipped into his inside jacket pocket and unfolded a sheet obviously torn from a medical book. "I've been to the library on your behalf," he said, shoving the page at him. "That's what it looks like close up."

"What?"

"Her *thing,* that's what! The snatch."

Joshua groaned; it looked so uninviting.

"You must understand," his father said with some tenderness, "that this is merely a scientific diagram. A map, like."

"Uh huh."

"Look, if I showed you a relief map of the Rockies, in black and white, you think you'd be impressed?"

His father had once fought in Calgary. Another time at a smoker in the Banff Springs Hotel. He adored the mountains.

"Well," Joshua began.

"You see this little thing right here?"

He nodded.

"You diddle it with your finger, they really like it, they begin to purr."

"No shit?"

"You'd be surprised," he said, grinning fondly. "But afterwards," he added, turning solemn again, "you wash your hands with soap and hot water before you touch your face."

"There seems to be an awful lot of washing up involved, Daddy."

"You can't be too careful these days." Then he sighed, relieved, and turned to the Bible. "How many commandments are there?"

"Ten."

"Yeah, well. Right, right. Now, can you recite them to me?"

"Aw, come on, Daddy."

"But you could the batting order of the Royals. Or the Dodgers. With the averages."

"Yeah."

"We've got to have these educational talks more often, or you'll grow up a jerk like me."

"I don't think you're a jerk," Joshua said, appalled.

"Well, yeah," his father said, pleased, "but what do you know?"

"I'd certainly like to know more about fucking."

"Well, it's a big subject and it's best to pace yourself, taking it round by round. I mean, we've made a good start, right?"

"Right."

"Good. Now listen to this," he said, opening the Bible at one of his markers. "Quote, And God spake all these words,

68

saying, I am the Lord thy God, which have brought thee out of the land of Egypt, out of the house of bondage, unquote. Now when you read the whole book, which I fully expect you to do, you will understand that the Hebes were in Egypt like for generations. In those olden times they were not yet into the needle trade or scrap or bootlegging or prizefighting or whatever. They were mostly in construction. Bricks. They were working like niggers and they were not being paid a dime. They were like slaves, *in bondage*. Got that?"

"Right."

"Quote, Thou shalt have no other gods before me, unquote. You see there were lots of contenders, other gods, mostly no-account idols, bums-of-the-month, before our God, Jehovah, took the title outright, and made a covenant with our forefathers who he had helped bust out of Egypt. A covenant is a contract. Now, where was I? Oh yeah, quote, Thou shalt not make unto thee any graven image . . ." He got as far as "Thou shalt not commit adultery," stumbling a little, and then, with a burst of speed, went on to: "Quote, Thou shalt not steal. Thou shalt not bear false witness—"

"Can I stop you anywhere?"

"Sure."

" 'Thou shalt not steal'?"

"Listen here," his father said, "there are ten commandments. Right? Well, it's like an exam. I mean, you get eight out of ten, you're just about top of the class, aren't you? And don't forget, God was no horse's ass, and there's a kicker in the covenant. Like, these are the Days of Awe and all you got to do is repent, even adultery, *sincerely, but*, and you start with a clean slate in his book of records. God doesn't keep a sheet on you."

"And how does God know if you're sincere?"

"Look, I'm no fucking rabbi, you know. I don't pretend to know everything. You repent, you repent sincere. Got it?"

"Right."

Following the tenth commandment, his father said, "And these being modern times, I would add an eleventh. You interested?"

"Sure."

"Thou shalt pay thy gambling debts."

Especially, Joshua thought, if Mr. Colucci was sending Reuben Shapiro round to collect.

His father, gentle as he was at home, had another life, one Joshua learned about from time to time, but always accidentally. He filled many offices in that life away from home, and in all of them he was not only respected, he was also feared. Among other ventures, his father collected from recalcitrant gamblers on behalf of Sonny Colucci, and it was this, only two weeks earlier, that had inadvertently led to the undoing of Joshua's first date with an Outremont girl. At fifteen, he was already a washout in the Golden Gloves qualifying bouts but a better-than-average snooker player and, taking his father as his model, a spiffy dresser. The girl's name was Bessie Orbach and he met her at a "Y" dance. He asked her if she would like to go to a movie on Saturday night, she accepted, and, tricked out in his one-button roll, a hand-painted tie he had borrowed from his father (a full moon shines over Miami Beach, its beams caressing the palms and dappling the water), and trousers that were more than somewhat zoot, he went round to her fieldstone house on Pratt Avenue, only to be greeted by a sniveling, red-eyed Bessie. "I can't go with you," she said.

"Why not?"

"I can't. Go away."

All at once, her father was there. Dr. Orbach. A big, swarthy man with a reddening face. His right hand was in a cast. He wore a sling. "How dare you come to this house," he said.

"Why?"

"Aren't you the criminal's son?"

"Hey, there. You talking about my father?"

"You come around here again and I'll break your head open, and you can tell your father that I'm not finished with him. I'll soon see him back behind bars where he belongs. Now beat it, you little street arab."

He did not run into Bessie again for a couple of years, and only then did he find out what had happened.

Dr. Orbach, it seemed, was not only a gifted dentist but also a reckless gambler. Horses, baseball, and Sonny Colucci's barbotte tables. He had run up a debt, a big debt, and not only had fallen behind with his monthly payments, but had taken his account elsewhere, running up markers there as well. Sonny Colucci was offended, and sent his father to see Dr. Orbach in his office after the last patient had gone. "Dr. Orbach," Reuben said, "I'm surprised at you. You are a very respectable man."

"I'm not paying out another penny to you."

"But Doctor, you still owe us eleven thousand dollars, not counting interest."

"You've had as much money as you're going to get from me."

"But you agreed to terms with Mr. Colucci. You shook hands with him."

"I'm broke. The well is dry."

"Possibly you would prefer to settle on somewhat easier terms."

"The matter is closed. Finished. You'll get more joy pulling your mutt than bargaining with me."

"You are referring, I suppose," Reuben said with dignity, "to the sin of Onan?"

"Oh, a Bible reader, are you?" he asked, amused.

"Say, seven-fifty a month. We could live with that."

Dr. Orbach mistook Reuben's offer for a show of weakness. "Your activities are absolutely illegal," he said. "You can't take your claim to any court."

"What we are suggesting is that you make some effort to settle. Say, six hundred a month."

"You know how much money that bloodsucker has had from me over the years?"

"Didn't you ever win?"

Dr. Orbach made no reply.

"And then did Mr. Colucci say the well is dry or you have no proof, no witnesses, only a phone call, or did he send a runner round with an envelope the next morning?"

"Colucci belongs in jail, and that's exactly where Pax Plante is going to put him now that this town is being cleaned up at last."

"My instructions are not to leave this office without any money. Please be reasonable, Doctor. Even five hundred dollars a—"

"Fuck you and your instructions," Dr. Orbach said, emboldened. "And now you get the hell out of here, you little creep, before I call the police."

"Well, yeah. Right. Dr. Orbach, please understand, I really hate doing this."

"Doing what, you little prick?"

"My job."

"I don't blame you. A Bible-reading Jew collecting for *goyishe* mobsters. Shame on you, Shapiro."

"I have no education, but."

"Bernard Gursky could have said the same, and just look at him today."

"You think I wouldn't have liked to make millions out of bootlegging?"

"You haven't got the brains."

"I wouldn't even mind being a dentist."

"And what in the hell do you mean by that?"

"It's good, steady work, isn't it?"

Orbach had to laugh. "Look, I'd like to sit here and shoot the breeze with you, but I'm a busy man."

"I appreciate that, Dr. Orbach. But I can't go just yet. First I have to break the fingers on your right hand. It's my job."

"Idle threats will get you absolutely nowhere."

"Yeah, I know."

Orbach, finally grasping what was about to happen, turned chalky.

"Are you serious?"

"I'm sorry. I have to."

"Oh, please," Dr. Orbach said. "Please give me a chance."

"I'm sorry," his father said, "really I am," and he reached across the desk, seized the screaming Orbach's right hand, and began to squeeze.

His father, to be fair, was indebted to Colucci. He had been working for him on and off ever since he had been a boy, beginning as a runner. Colucci had bankrolled Reuben when he turned pro, and taken him in again when his fighting days were finished.

Joshua had never seen his father fight—he had been only three years old when Reuben had had to quit; but there were photographs of him in his ring days that he had come to cherish. In one of them, taken for one of the few advertising endorsements that Reuben ever got, he was portrayed in his ring stance, a Star of David sewn into his Everlast trunks. Superimposed, in a corner of the photograph, there was a head shot of Reuben wearing a fedora, with the tag line " 'For every round of the day, I wear an ADAM HAT.' Ruby Shapiro, Lightweight Champion of Canada." Another photograph, taken in Stillman's gym, showed his father grinning shyly in the company of Lou Ambers, Henry Armstrong, and Whitey Bimstein. And Joshua owned a snapshot of him, taken at the Tic Toc, where the group at the table included Al Weill, Frankie Carbo, the young Johnny Greco, and a couple of showgirls.

Joshua also kept an album of newspaper clippings that dated back to his father's so-called amateur days. "So-called" because when he was still only seventeen, his father was already fighting professionally, under assumed names, in northern Ontario mining towns, as well as Peoria and Albany, for $20 a bout. His first important amateur fight, a title fight, was at the Griffintown A.C. "For once, the Emerald Isle barracking brigade will have to choose between the lesser of 'two evils,' when Ruby Shapiro and Solly 'The Ghetto Kid' Bergman, a pair of Hebes, slug it out for Canada's Amateur Featherweight Title at the . . ." He went on to fight Mick Sullivan for the Canadian Amateur Lightweight Title in Toronto. "A grudge fight between a Son of Moses and a Son of Erin is a promoter's dream of heaven! And Pete 'Side-Door' O'Hara put on a real corker of a grudge fight at the Arena Gardens last night between Mick Sullivan and Ruby Shapiro, both of whom are being groomed for the pro ranks. One glance at Shapiro's schnozz and you didn't have to ask which one was the Hebe! Anyway, there were 4,952 delirious fans at the fight, 4,620 of whom talked turkey at the box office. . . . It was a fiercely fought contest from the first bell. Right off Shapiro sent over a haymaker with the Celt's name on it and nearly had Sullivan crying for his momma. But when he raced in to finish him, the Celt countered with a left-hander that had the aggressive little Jewboy dreaming of chicken soup. . . ."

His father, pulling another marker free of his Bible, told him about Abraham's near-sacrifice of his only son, Isaac, to God, which apparently pleased Jehovah enormously. "Quote, for because thou hast done this thing, and hast not withheld thy son, thine only son: That in blessing I will bless thee, and in multiplying I will multiply thy seed as the stars of the heaven, and as the sand which is upon the sea shore, blah blah blah, unquote. Now we've got this covenant with God, time-honored, and going on forever and ever. Those are the terms and they're very stiff, I don't mind telling you. But— and not a word to your Uncle Harvey about this, you understand—but if I had to sign on the dotted line today, I don't know that I would. God's always needling, testing, his wrath waxing hot. He's a real blowhard. Back in Egypt, for instance, when we were in bondage, he could've got the Hebes paroled with only one plague, but no, after each one he hardened Pharaoh's heart so he could display his whole bag of tricks. And afterwards, once we were sprung, he never once talks to Moses that he doesn't remind him"—and here is father sought out another marker—"quote, I am the Lord thy God, which have brought thee out of the land of Egypt, out of the house of bondage, unquote. Now in your life if hard times come and you have to borrow money, never take it

73

from anybody like that, they drive you crazy reminding you every day what they did for you. I don't care for such types."

His father also preferred Esau to Jacob.

"Esau was one fine fella, a hunter, and he used to bring his dad venison to eat. But his brother Jacob was a cunning little bastard, a momma's boy, a jealous type. Anyway, one day Esau comes in from the hunt, fainting with hunger, and asks his brother for something to eat. And Jacob, a real Outremont kid, always looking for angles, a way to get ahead, he says you want to nosh, sell me your birthright. And poor Esau, on the point of dying, sells him his birthright for some bread and soup. And later Jacob does even worse, the tricky bastard, with the help of his bitch of a mother. The old man is dying, he still prefers Esau, a hairy man, to Mr. Peaches-and-Cream. And Jacob comes to him, the old man is blind, and lies, pretending to be Esau, in order to steal his blessing. But, what the hell, Jacob's one of our holy fathers and not Esau, and he's tricked in turn by this guy Laban, a real con, when he comes sniffing around, looking for a wife. In those days, incidentally, a Hebe could have more than one wife, and concubines, those are whores, and if one of the wives couldn't give him kids, they would offer him the maid to screw, just like that."

"And did they have to wash up before and after?" Joshua asked.

"Now you cut that out. We're into serious stuff here. Like, these are the Days of Awe." He cracked open another quart of Labatt's. "I guess we could leave the windows until tomorrow."

"Aren't we going to the synagogue tomorrow?"

"Oh, yeah. Right. Well, the day after, then."

"Sure."

"This edition, you know, it also includes the New Testament, the guy on the stick, and I must say he had a sweeter nature than most of the old prophets. But not a word about this to your Uncle Harvey, for Christsake."

In the morning, Reuben wakened Joshua early; they both got into their best suits and shined their shoes until they gleamed. Then they started out for the B'nai Jacob synagogue on Fairmount Street. The closer they got, the slower his father walked, his manner increasingly agitated.

"Hold it. We get in there, and they'll give you this sort of scarf to wear, a tallis. You watch me closely. I'll show you how to put it on."

"I remember, but. From my bar-mitzvah."

At the mention of his bar-mitzvah, more legend than scandal now, his father paled. "If anybody in there asks you about it, you deny it ever happened. Your mother never did it. Right?"

"Right."

"Oh, and listen, you stand up for certain prayers, you sit down for others. I give you the elbow once, you stand up, twice, you sit down. Got that?"

"Yeah."

Outside the synagogue, many of the faithful were gathered together in the sun. Smoking, gossiping.

"You think there's no more room inside?" Joshua asked hopefully.

His father fiddled with the brim of his Adam hat. "I'll tell you what, we'll cross to the other side of the street and walk up and down a couple of times, just to get the feel of things."

They crossed the street.

"There's Dr. Orbach," Joshua said.

"Where?"

Joshua pointed to a group of men, all of them wearing prayer shawls, standing on the synagogue steps. Dr. Orbach's right arm was held in a cast, his fingers encased. He wore a sling. "Right there," he said.

"I'll tell you what," his father said, quickening his pace. "I'm going to let you off today."

"Oh yeah?"

"But, shit, your mother isn't expecting us home until one."

It was now only ten o'clock.

"Have you seen *Union Pacific* yet?" his father asked.

"No."

"It's playing at the Palace. I'll take you."

"During the Days of Awe?"

"Yeah. Right."

6

The seaplane took off the next afternoon, wheeling over the lake again and again, fading into the sun, seemingly gone. Then, catching Joshua by surprise, it came roaring up from behind to swoop low over the Hornby cottage, wings wiggling, before it settled on the lake, making for the Trimble dock rather than the country club. Joshua watched from his study window, his mind elsewhere.

With Murdoch.

Murdoch's seventh novel, its contents sour, its jacket elegant, sat before him on his desk. It was a mechanical book, shallow, written with a fine writer's remembered skills. Joshua longed to go for a swim. He could see the kids and Pauline horsing around in the water below. Instead, he slipped paper into his typewriter, plucked a can of Bras d'Or out of his small fridge (a Christmas gift from Pauline), and sat down to write Murdoch, determined to lie.

Even before he started his letter, long overdue, Joshua imagined him tottering down the stairs to the door of his Lonsdale Road flat. He would be snorting, coughing up phlegm, a Gauloise drooping from his purply lips, his big hairy belly bouncing, breaking wind as he stooped to retrieve Joshua's letter with the rest of his morning bumpf. Murdoch huffing as he climbed the stairs once more, settling down to his long dining room table, sweeping last night's dishes aside, lifting the kettle from the gas stove, its bottom badly charred, to make himself a cup of instant, stirring Courvoisier rather than sugar into it, and washing it down with a couple of After Eights or a chocolate digestive, whichever was handy. Trying to remember the name of the bird who was surely resting in his bed, and wondering if he would have to make it clear yet again that a shared breakfast was not part of the Murdoch deal. Skat, ducks.

"One of them," he once told Joshua, outraged, "actually gave me the clap. A Rodean girl at that. I tell you, there are no bloody standards any more. My daughter, Jessica, she's seventeen now, brought round one of those frightful Fulbrights the other morning. A New York Jew. Depressingly earnest. He said he was *like, you know, man, a writer,* and so I offered him drinkees and he said no thanks, the little twit, but coffee and chocolate cake would do nicely. He was wearing denims. Bell-bottom trousers. Platform shoes. Joshua, what sort of people do you come from?"

The last time Joshua had been in London and seen the remodeled flat, bespeaking Murdoch's all-too-temporary affluence, it was filled with black leather furniture from Heal's, long on nickel tubing. A Hockney drawing, a gift from Angela, hung over the fireplace that now served as a catch-all for empty Smartie boxes, champagne corks, dial-a-chicken bones, and wads of Kleenex he had masturbated into. Built-in bookshelves, rather than old boards and bricks, were everywhere. A long, glass-topped coffee table, all jutting angles, good for nothing but painful knee-banging, came from Casa

Pupo. There was a Sansui hi-fi, any knob beyond volume an enigma to him. And central heating, which he also hated. Clippings from Durrant's, copies of *Beano* and *Dandy*, book proofs and mugs, rode every available surface. Moldy coffee in one mug, soggy Gauloise butts adrift in another. For there was not a char in NW1 who would service Murdoch's flat any longer.

In his mind's eye, Joshua saw Murdoch, scratching absently at his groin, opening his morning newspapers (the *Times*, the *Guardian*, the *Daily Mail*), hungrily searching the gossip columns for a passing salute. Digging into his mail, he shakes out check-size envelopes and then hunts for intimidating invitations to mount on his mantelpiece. Shoving the bills and fan mail and income tax demands aside, he finally comes to Joshua's thick envelope. Filled with glee, Joshua hoped.

Once profiled in the *Guardian*, Murdoch was asked, "Are you married?"

"Sometimes," he replied.

There was a spare bedroom in the flat, available for the issue of his several marriages, should any of them dare to visit.

"Ralph came to see me last week. The little snot's at St. Paul's now. Do you know what that costs? Never mind. He actually wanted advice. A father-and-son chat. Good Lord, I'm still a child myself. I like nothing better than to suck a girl's titties and have her read *Winnie the Pooh* aloud to me before I go tuckybyes. Do you give your children advice? I expect you do. The years have made you pompous, my dear. Ah well, I suppose nothing compensates for the loss of talent. Both our brains have been addled by alcohol and the young have no mercy."

Yes, yes indeed, Joshua thought, giving up on the letter and racing down the hill barefoot to join his family in the lake.

"Hey, look," Susy squealed, "it's Daddy!"

Everybody smiled or waved. Even Alex. They were happy to see him. Me, Joshua Shapiro. My family. Who would have guessed, he thought, his heart thumping with pleasure as he allowed himself to be splashed, pulled, and ducked.

But that night Joshua turned over in bed to find Pauline standing by the bedroom window, watching the seaplane by moonlight. "Why doesn't he leave here?" she implored. "Why doesn't he just fly off?"

"Maybe you underestimate Jane's charms?"

"It's not Jane that's keeping him here. I can assure you of that."

"What, then?"

"Money."

The seaplane did not take off the next morning, or the morning after, and neither did Kevin appear at their place. Then, late in the afternoon, the phone rang. "That will be Lady Jane," Pauline said.

Joshua scooped up the phone, nodded at Pauline to indicate that she was absolutely right, and then, covering the mouthpiece, said, "Dinner tonight."

"Damn," Pauline said.

Yes, Joshua thought, damn, damn, recalling an encounter he had never told Pauline about, something that had happened some five years earlier, during the winter that had followed their first summer on the lake. It was three weeks before Christmas, Pauline and the children were in Ottawa visiting the senator, and he was on his own, drinking late most nights at The King's Arms, only staying in if there was a hockey game to watch on TV.

Then one stingingly cold, windblown morning, his column completed, Joshua was obliged to hurry down to St. James Street to cable it to Toronto. His battered old Toyota wouldn't start, the battery dead again, and he was going to need a taxi. But Montreal's taxi drivers preferred retreating to the nearest tavern when a fine, powdery snow was blowing over icy roads. Westmount Taxi brought a busy signal, their phone obviously off the hook. Diamond answered, but the snotty girl on the line couldn't promise anything for half an hour; Joshua offered a fiver over the meter reading to the first taxi to show within ten minutes. Only five minutes later a taxi came slithering down the street, braking softly against a snowbank in front of his door. "Hey," the driver said, "aren't you Joshua Shapiro?"

As they drove off, wheels spinning on ice and blue salt, the driver continued to watch Joshua intently in his rear-view mirror. "My father, you know, he watches you on TV, he says all you do is shit on people."

The taxi reeked of Joy. Somebody had left behind a Hermès cowhide tote bag. Joshua zipped it open: A tube of vaginal jelly. A plunger in a white rubber case. A tiny flask of vaginal cologne. Obviously, before rushing off to her assignation, the lady had sprayed herself down there. His father would have approved.

"Where did you drop your last fare?"

"The Ritz."

"She forgot this," Joshua said, holding up the tote bag,

"and I have a feeling she'd be most grateful if you hurried right back with it."

His column delivered, Joshua stopped for a drink at The King's Arms, and continued on to the Ritz, having decided that a half-bottle of Chablis and a mushroom omelet would not be self-indulgence, but his just reward. Considering the inclement weather, he was not surprised to find the Maritime Bar all but empty. Only two of the tables were occupied. And a lady, elegantly dressed, long-legged, her black hair streaked with just a hint of gray, sat at the bar. A cowhide tote bag rested on the stool to the left of her. The stool on the other side was occupied by a tall man with thin sandy hair and a reddening neck. He was pleading with her, while she swished the olive round in her martini, shaking her head haughtily. He whispered something, and reached for her hand on the bar, which she promptly withdrew. The color rising in his cheeks, he slid irresolutely off his stool. Now she turned to him, her voice steely, and said, "Yes, right here. Do it."

"I can't."

"*Do it.*"

The people at the other two tables were caught up in their conversation, and Joshua pretended to be absorbed by his *Gazette*. The man, obviously intimidated, gave the pack of cigarettes that rested on the bar an intentional shove, dropping it to the floor, and then stooped to retrieve it. As he managed that, his face bleeding red, he shakily grasped her swinging foot by the ankle and brushed the toe of her shoe with his lips. Simultaneously, she emptied her martini glass over his sandy-haired head.

As the man fled the bar, wiping his face with a handkerchief, his eyes appalled, she already had her back to the room. It was all over so quickly that Joshua immediately doubted that it had ever happened. But then Jane turned on her bar stool and said, "Why, hello there."

"Hello," Joshua said.

"I'm Jane Trimble, remember?"

"Of course I remember," he said, leaping up. "Um, would you care to join me for a drink?"

"And what would Pauline say to that?" she asked, her eyes taunting.

"I'll phone her," he replied in a rush. "Possibly she can join us."

"But isn't she in Ottawa?"

"Yes," Joshua allowed in a faltering voice. "So she is."

"I'd love to join you, honestly, but I only came in out of

79

the cold for a quickie. I'm supposed to meet Prissie Hooper here. We're going to Holt's." She paused. "I don't think it would be a good idea for her to see us together."

Why the hell not, he thought.

"I'll catch her upstairs," she said, touching his hand lightly. "Oh, and Happy Holiday."

Holiday?

"Isn't it Chanuka this week?"

She pronounced it like the western wind, the chinook, with an "a" added.

"Yes, I suppose it is."

"Well then," she said, and gathering up her cowhide tote bag she was gone, leaving him with a stirring in the groin, torn between anger and admiration, wondering how she had managed to twist things so that it seemed as if he had tried to pick her up and failed.

Dark clouds were scudding across the lake, obscuring the surrounding mountaintops, as they set out in the boat for the Trimbles', docking just as a wall of heavy rain began to blow across the water, catching them on the lawn. "Now repeat after me," Joshua said. "Jane Trimble is a first-class bitch, but she can do nothing to upset me."

"Yes, certainly," Pauline said, already churning.

The first thing that Joshua noticed, as he and an equally drenched Pauline came tumbling through the French doors into the living room, was that Kevin—wearing a blazer with a Royal Bermuda Yacht Club crest, canvas ducks and sandals—was confidently ensconced in what Joshua knew was Jack Trimble's favorite wing chair.

> My name is George Nathaniel Curzon,
> I am a most superior person,
> My face is pink, my hair is sleek,
> I dine at Blenheim twice a week.

Joshua smiled sympathetically at Trimble, but his host, cheeks flushed, eyes bright, refused to acknowledge it. Something had happened. The air was crackling. Trimble, those dreadful tartan Bermuda shorts cutting into his ballooning belly, ending just shy of his apple-pie knees, seemed to be in good spirits, which was rare that summer, a season Joshua would always remember as the one where he, incredibly dense, failed to pick up the signals that might have saved everybody.

The season had begun as usual, with Trimble plunging into the still shatteringly cold lake long before anybody else. Compared to the water at Blackpool, where he claimed his father used to take him on Bank Holiday, "this," he was fond of saying, "is a bloody sauna bath." He entertained the old bunch as often on his sun deck, but with a distracted air, not even remembering to proffer his forced smile. Once their needs had been attended to, he would either retreat into the house, leaving them to amuse themselves, or stay on to drink more than was his habit. Not Guinness, either, but Canadian Club with ice and ginger ale, a colonial concoction he usually affected to despise. And Trimble, not the most engaging of men sober, proved even more unapproachable drunk. He stared blankly at people. Or surprised the men with lewd suggestions about the ladies present.

Joshua and Pauline, who sometimes took to their boat at midnight, sipping Scotch together as they drifted over the still, silent water—totting up impending school fees against a free-lance income he never projected correctly, speculating about his wandering mother's present whereabouts, Susy's problems with Teddy, and what to do about Alex—noticed something else. Something passingly odd. Often there would be a light burning in Trimble's study as late as 2 a.m. And, voices carrying as they did across the water at that hour, they might hear him shouting into the phone. Only then did it occur to them that this summer he seemed to be perpetually flying off to Zurich or London, and that he was also spending a good deal of time closeted in board rooms in New York. They weren't the only ones to notice these things, but as there wasn't a soul on the lake who really cared that much for Trimble, nobody sought him out to ask if anything was wrong or if he could be of any help. Like Joshua and Pauline, they shrugged and got on with more important matters. Repairing boathouses. Painting rings around birch trees. Cutting and stacking wood for the winter.

But tonight, Joshua noticed, Trimble seemed positively jolly, and Jane, demurely dressed, was uncharacteristically affectionate with him, stroking the back of his pleated neck or touching his knee. Kevin, also charged with high spirits, set out to captivate Joshua with anecdotes, one more self-deprecating than another, about the days when he had tried to win a card for the PGA tour. He also revealed that somebody had once left behind a collection of Isaac Babel's short stories on his boat in Bermuda, and that he had thereafter become an addict.

81

"Every winter," Trimble lamented, "I tell Jane that this year it's going to be Bermuda, she used to love it out there, but then there's never time. Isn't that so, Mother?"

Once more Joshua had to admire Jane's poise. Ladling soup into bowls, she didn't miss a beat.

"Mn. Marvelous," Kevin moaned.

Joshua tried a spoonful and blanched. Holy shit, it was a variation of Pauline's very own fish soup, a delicious brew she had developed herself, but only after years of trial and error. She would never have given the recipe to Jane.

"Would you mind terribly," Pauline asked, "if I asked for the pepper mill?"

Trimble leaped up and fetched the pepper mill and once Pauline had literally blackened the surface of her soup, she thrust the mill at Joshua, her smile menacing, and sang out, "Darling?"

Grabbing the pepper mill and grinding away, Joshua thought: I'm giving up women. I'm going to become a monk.

Then Charlie was standing at the dining room door, eyes lowered, his manner tentative. "S-s-sorry to interrupt, b-b-but everybody's meeting at the p-p-pub in Knowlton tonight."

Without even bothering to look up, Jane replied, "Everybody, as you put it, meets at the pub in Knowlton every night. We have guests, Charlie."

"Can I take the V-v-volvo?"

Jane's nod was perfunctory.

"Hold it, son," Trimble said, and digging into his pocket, he came up with a twenty-dollar bill. Startled, Charlie reached for it and prepared to flee.

"Good night, everybody," Jane admonished him.

"G-g-good night," he said, hurrying out of the dining room.

"You're spoiling him," Jane said.

"What do you think, Pauline?" Jack asked. "Wait till you get to know *her* children, Kevin."

"If he can find the time," Pauline put in.

"They are simply the brightest and best-behaved bunch on the lake. Well, Pauline, do you think I'm spoiling Charlie?"

"I think it's none of my affair."

"Spoken like a real lady, wouldn't you say, darling?"

Jane began to collect the soup bowls.

"I asked you a question."

"Yes. Certainly. Like a real lady."

The soup was followed by Brome Lake ducklings, a little bouncy to the fork. Pauline waited until it was clear that everybody else was struggling and then she said, "This *is* good. Usually, you know, people tend to overcook duck. It's such a mistake."

But she left half of her portion on the plate, and Joshua followed suit.

"Joshua," Jane said, "you're hardly eating a thing."

"Nobody's eating," Trimble said, pouncing.

Jane reached over for Joshua to light her cigarette, holding his hand longer than was strictly necessary.

"Everybody thinks the duck's too tough, but they're too well brought up to mention it."

Kevin leaped in to joke ingratiatingly about his initial encounter with Joshua on the tennis court and asked, if it wasn't presuming too much, would he care for a lesson or two while he was on the lake?

Before Joshua could answer, Trimble said, "And maybe you could help me with my table manners as well."

"Please, darling."

Pauline turned to Kevin. "And now, perhaps, you might tell me what you are still doing here, if you were only planning to stop overnight?"

"Why do we all love Trout?" Kevin asked rhetorically. "Because she has always been so direct. Just like our father," he added, his eyes searching.

"I haven't told him that you're back."

"Now I understand why he hasn't rushed down from Ottawa to embrace me."

"Will you please tell me what happened to your big deal with the Argos people in Georgian Bay?"

"Other matters more appealing," he replied, his chin dimpling, "have obliged me to put that on the back burner for the moment."

"And quite right too," Trimble pitched in, winking.

"What matters?"

"Please, darling," Jane said, indicating that the wineglasses ought to be refilled.

But Trimble didn't leap up. "You know, Joshua," he said thickly, "there is a difference between us and them. In a snazzy restaurant, for instance, it never bothers any of them to tip a maître d' much older than they are."

Jane indicated the wineglasses again, but Trimble didn't budge. Instead he said, "You're quite capable of filling the glasses yourself. The wine is right behind you on the sideboard. It is open. *Breathing*, as you say."

Jane smiled tightly and refilled the wineglasses and the next thing Joshua knew, an impassioned Trimble exploded, rising to the defense of Richard Nixon, whose name had not once come up at the table.

"The poor bastard never did anything that Kennedy or Roosevelt didn't do before him, but he was not a patrician, he lacked their style. FDR could try to stack the Supreme Court. So what? Kennedy's father was a bootlegger. His brother Bobby worked for Joe McCarthy. Forget it. Kennedy himself was fucking actresses and plain ordinary tarts black and blue in the White House. How risqué! What a devil! But if Tricky Dick had so much as peeked down a lady's cleavage, you would all have been moaning, 'How utterly coarse.' Oh, what a sordid little man! You didn't hate Nixon for what he stood for, but for what he came from. He came out of nowhere and everything he got he scratched and scrambled for. Unforgivable! Remember Alger Hiss? What a proper gent! Right schools. Right ideas. How dare that sewer rat call him a lying Communist bastard! But the sewer rat was telling the truth and the gentleman was lying through his fucking teeth and you've never forgiven Nixon that. After all, Dick didn't invite Casals to the White House to play. No, he had Bob Hope instead. How terribly lower-class. What bad taste! Then there were the tapes. Scandalous. Nixon was actually caught out saying, 'I don't give a fuck about the Italian lira.' Oh dear, weren't we horrified. But if Kennedy had said the same, how very droll, how clever. Good old Jack," he said, trailing off, panting, his eyes big, shocked by the resounding silence round the table. Trimble turned chalky. "Excuse me," he said, fleeing.

Jane asked Pauline if she knew of a good carpenter.

"No," she replied, her voice small.

Talk turned to tree-pruning and the difficulty of finding decent help on the lake these days. Finally, Jane announced, "We're going to have dessert in the sun room."

Trimble was already there, smiling. "I'm sorry. I apologize, Pauline. I don't know what got into me."

A glowing Mrs. Jack Trimble, of Westmount and Georgeville, doled raspberries out of an enormous crystal bowl. Trimble struggled with the cork of a champagne bottle. Dom Perignon.

"Give it here," Kevin said.

"Is this a celebration of some sort?" Pauline asked.

"Kevin is joining my firm."

"He's what?"

"But aren't you pleased?" Trimble asked, baffled.

84

"Now, now, darling. You're a big boy now. You don't need Pauline's blessing for everything you do."

"But I was sure," he said, looking at Jane with a hint of reproach, "that you'd be ever so pleased."

"Of course I am. Cheers," Pauline said, raising her glass.

"He's going to run an investment fund for me—"

"Trout doesn't think I'm up to it."

"—something new, and if Joshua is smart he'll buy in on day one."

"He's smart, Jack, smarter than any of us, except when it comes to horses, but he's also broke." And looking directly at Kevin, she asked, "Does this mean you'll be staying on in Montreal for the winter?"

"If not," a revived Trimble said, "he'll jolly well have me to answer to."

A playful Kevin leaped out of his chair to salute Trimble smartly, "Yes, sir," he said.

"Stand easy, Hornby," Trimble said, and sweeping up the fireplace poker, he was all in a fever again. Using the poker as a swagger stick, he began to strut around the towering Kevin, making deprecating remarks about the length of his styled hair, the lack of polish on his blazer buttons, and his sandals. "You're a sodding disgrace!"

"Yes, sir!"

"You're not a man, you're a fucking disaster!"

"Sir!"

He dug the poker under his chin, lifting it. "You're a lump of shit."

"Sir!"

"Say it. 'I'm a lump of shit.'"

The blood was sucked out of Pauline's cheeks. Her eyes were moist.

"That's enough," Joshua called out, snatching the poker away from Trimble.

"What's that?"

"Joshua thinks you've gone too far," Jane said, "and so do I."

Recalled from a plateau all his own, Trimble grinned. He laughed, his eyes sly. "It was all in fun. Old army guff. Sorry, everybody, this just isn't my night. What would you all say to another bottle of the bubbly?"

"We're going home now," Joshua said. "I'm whacked. So is Pauline."

Fortunately, though the racing clouds had yet to clear, the rain had stopped. They ducked under the wings of the little seaplane to climb into the boat, Pauline bailing. Once they were well out onto the lake, Joshua cut the engine. "Well, I think that dinner party will do me for a while. Jesus."

"I thought I was going to be sick. I actually felt dizzy."

"I don't quite understand what's going on there. The other night Jack wanted me to crack Kevin's nuts for him, and now . . ."

"Will you be going to Spain?"

"Possibly," he replied, surprised.

"Then you're off on a fool's errand," she said with surprising sharpness. Joshua stared at her, astonished.

"I don't want to be left alone," she said. "I hear every creak in the house. I dream I'm in my coffin."

"But if I go, I want you to come with me."

"Oh, Josh, how could I?"

He knew, without asking, what the problem was. The children. She wouldn't leave them alone. "They're devouring you," he said.

"Or keeping me sane. Or both."

"Do you think I'm an inadequate father?"

"I think you're splendid with them when they're Teddy's age, and all that's called for is horsing around, but once they've grown big and troublesome, like Alex, it's off to The King's Arms and let Pauline handle it."

"Alex doesn't like me any more."

"He doesn't want to be corrected or upstaged by you any more, is more like it. Don't go back to Ibiza, Josh."

But I have to, he thought. "I've begun to dream about him again."

"Mueller?"

"I want to settle with him. I'd also like to see if I can find the Freibergs."

"Stay here with us. I'll make *latkas*. I'll iron your shirt collars just so. I'll give head."

He laughed.

"Isn't that what they call it now?"

They docked the boat, and then Joshua, who still felt jumpy but not the least bit high any longer, fixed drinks for them on the porch. "Darling, I don't know how many times we've compared childhoods over the years. I haven't held anything back. Not even Ed Ryan. But there's always been a bit of a gap on your end."

"Kevin?"

"Yes."

"I don't want him here."

86

"Why?"

"Trimble frightens me. So does Jane. And then there's my father. It could kill him."

"Why, darling?"

"Why," she asked, laughing, "why?" And she began to tell him, falteringly at first, more than a little weepy, then in full flow, and they were still sitting on the porch, talking, when the sun came up.

7

He remembered Uncle Oscar, his dull brown eyes obscured behind steel-rimmed glasses, droning on and on about the prospects of war as Joshua continued to stare at the photograph of Franco, a paunchy man with a jaunty little moustache, strolling down an avenue of shelled buildings. In 1939 Joshua was more committed to perfecting his bolo game than to politics, and so he couldn't pretend he was choked with anger or that he grasped the photograph's real importance, but for reasons unfathomable to him it stuck in his memory unlike any other.

Joshua once mentioned the photograph to Sidney Murdoch, whose uncle had actually served with the Attlee Battalion of the International Brigades. Sidney did not recall ever seeing it. Possibly, it had never appeared in *Picture Post.*

In London, during the fifties, Murdoch and Joshua sometimes sought out his Uncle Willy in a pub in Cold Harbour Lane. A grizzled old man, somewhat sly, he would submit to Joshua's breathless questions about the Spanish Civil War, obliging him with lies, but only to keep the bitter flowing and maybe touch him for a couple of quid in parting. Uncle Willy's memories of Spain were dim; he was clearly sorry he had ever gone. And now he wasn't interested in Nye Bevan, Eden's Suez obloquy, their marches to Aldermaston, or all that codswallop. What agitated him were the bleeding blacks who seemed to be dropping like monkeys out of every tree in Brixton. A lazy lot, as far as he was concerned, most of them on the fiddle or national assistance or, more likely, both. All the same, Murdoch revered the old man, he was uncommonly gentle with him, and quickly reverted to his working-class accent in his presence. Joshua accompanied Murdoch to the funeral, a thinly attended affair. Murdoch, his eyes moist, read from Auden over the graveside.

"They clung like burrs to the long expresses that lurch
through the unjust lands, through the night, through the alpine
tunnel;
They walked the passes: they had come to present their lives."

1939.
"Joe DiMaggio, baseball's most sensational big league star,
starts what should be his best year so far," Noel F. Busch
wrote in *Life* a week after Madrid fell.

The previous season, DiMaggio, a holdout, had been
booed by the fans in Yankee Stadium. DiMaggio had held
out on the advice of his brother Tom, who was vice-president
of the San Francisco Fisherman's Union. When Tom learned
that his brother was being forced to sign a contract for
$25,000, a picayune percentage of the money he brought into
the box office, he considered it an outrage and urged Joe to
take action. Joe's strike was a failure. "Unfortunately for the
DiMaggios," Busch wrote, "the U.S. national game is run according to strictly Fascist lines. Its dictator is Judge Kenesaw
Mountain Landis. Solidarity among baseball players is impossible since, in the nature of the sport, rival teams are supposed
to hate each other bitterly and any co-operation between them
would remove their reason for existence."

Madrid fell in April, intruding on his enjoyment of Fibber
McGee. Fat Franco and his four columns claiming an emaciated city; his fifth column, as he liked to boast, already established there. Franco, he learned from *Life*, was a simple
man, an ordinary fellow, who read little, but enjoyed his
food. He was unable to stage his victory parade immediately,
the background inappropriate, Madrileños continuing to wander through the pocked streets of a ruined city, rioting for
bread. Finally, on May 19, 1939, before an arch proclaiming
Victoria once and *Franco* six times, "Spain's victorious Gen-
eralissimo reviewed the greatest Spanish army since the conquistadores of Philip II." At the head of the parade were ten
thousand Italians. Near the end were five thousand German
air-force men under Baron von Richtofen, cousin of the late
great wartime ace.

Madrid fell in April, Barcelona even earlier, on January
25. In the flight from Barcelona, some 300,000 Loyalist refugees entered France through a pass in the Pyrenees, Le Per-
thus—a pass through which Napoleon had once ridden, and
before him Hannibal and Charlemagne.

Squatting on the floor of his father's tiny den, with stacks

88

of *Life*, a razor, and a gluepot, Joshua cut out pictures for his scrap album.

"A piece of tire is used by this legless veteran to protect his stump as he drags over the ground."

"A man dies, just short of France, attended by his daughter. The long hike and the cold killed many refugees."

"The children of war have lost their legs. On crutches, they hitch slowly along past the olive groves toward France."

At Perpignan, the men of Guadalajara, of Belchite and the Ebro, exhausted Spaniards, shivering survivors of the International Brigades, were given a traditional French welcome. Under the watchful eye of the Prefect of Perpignan, they were abruptly relieved of their rifles and haversacks, their underclothes and bits of food scattered in the ditch. The parsimonious French herded them into cold, filthy camps, and all they had to cover themselves with at night were their blanket capes. Some survived on the flesh of dead mules, others were done in by dysentery or unattended wounds.

Six months later World War II, source material for *Hogan's Heroes, The Dirty Dozen, SS Sex Kitten,* and other delights, had begun.

Spike Jones sang:

> "Ven de fuhrer sagt,
> vé are ze master race,
> sieg heil (spit), heil (spit)
> right in ze fuhrer's face."

And Uncle Oscar was right for once. Aluminum, that was the stuff. And zinc. And cast iron. And brass. The scrap yard, started by Joshua's grandfather after Prohibition had ended, his services as a wheelman on the back roads leading into Vermont no longer needed, had finally begun to make what the Shapiros considered big money. Uncle Oscar, ever-aspiring Oscar, started in earnest to shop around for opportunities. WE INVEST IN INVENTIONS, his *Star* advertisement ran, a license for loonies to besiege his ramshackle office on King Street. Uncle Oscar was intrigued by, though he finally turned down, a plan to freeze clouds over Dover, clouds laden with bombs that would sail across the Channel and explode after the clouds had dissolved over Berlin. He detected the flaw at once and hollered at the inventor, "You've overlooked one thing, you prick."

"Oh, yeah. What?"

"Wind changes."

"Oh no I haven't," he shot right back. "The clouds would be propeller-driven."

"Propeller-driven. What do you take me for? A horse's ass? Let's say I'm in charge of Berlin's air defenses," Uncle Oscar said, "and I got up on a Thursday morning to see every fucking cloud in the sky racing for the North Sea, away from me. But then I look up again and see four crazy clouds blowing right at me. Well, what do I do? I quickly realize these are enemy clouds and I send up planes with hot-water bombs to dissolve them before they reach the city. Or, still better, you little shmock, I drop grappling hooks from the planes and tow them back to England."

In 1943, Uncle Oscar, prospering in the yard, took a wife, Lou Springer's daughter Hetty, and became the first Shapiro to move into a house in Outremont. The move saddened Joshua, because as much as he disliked Uncle Oscar, he had loved wandering through his St. Dominique Street flat, which was filled with junk retrieved from the yard. A spiked German army helmet from World War I. Shoeboxes overflowing with medals and pocket watches. A malfunctioning but nevertheless real Colt Peacemaker, its butt decorated with gold inlay. The confessional from an old church in the Gaspé. Stacks and stacks of paintings, which Uncle Oscar held onto for the elaborate gold frames. Inlaid Chinese screens. Lampshades of multicolored tinted glass, which he swore came from a really classy whorehouse. A player piano. A box crammed with old canes and sabres. Stained-glass windows he could never find a market for, potential customers complaining they not only kept out the light but would be a real headache to clean. A sturdy old captain's sea trunk filled with intricately uniformed grenadiers, toy soldiers, which he eventually had melted down for the lead. A shelf lined with irons that weren't even electrical, but had to be filled with boiling water before they could be used. A wind-up gramophone that played music on metal rolls. Two wooden rocking horses and a pine baby crib made by French Canadians who couldn't afford the real stuff. Grandfather clocks he never found the time to repair. A cupboard full of old telephones and typewriters. An ancient cash register. Pissy old crazy-quilts made by *yentas* in the Maritimes to get them through the long winters. Crocheted tablecloths from the old country which were no damn good because you could see the table through the holes.

Hetty, far from impractical and blessed with a real flair for decoration, rummaged through the crap, salvaging what she could. She had the Colt Peacemaker soldered onto a silver plate, which made for an interesting ashtray. Colored glass squares were worked out of the leaded lampshades to make a "really cute" coffee tabletop that could also be used as a checkerboard. An inlaid Chinese screen was chopped into squares and framed with bamboo to make a set of coasters. The confessional was gutted, painted white, and converted into a neat little garden shed. The sturdy old captain's trunk became a planter. Even the stained-glass windows were put to good use: broken up, they were cemented upright into the top of the backyard brick fence to discourage burglars as well as neighborhood kids. The rest, she insisted, was certainly not moving with her into Outremont. Which was when Uncle Oscar, chortling, told her that he had actually found a *goy*, a fairy, who had given him fifteen hundred smackers for all the remaining dreck and, furthermore, had agreed to cart it away at his own expense. With the money, Hetty bought some really lovely things at Eaton's, including a fireplace log that glowed *and* gave off heat when you turned a switch. No ashes to clean.

Only a month before the wedding, Joshua surprised Oscar at the dining-room table, biting into a peach, his manner fervent, even as he made notes on a book he was reading. The moment Joshua barged into the room, Uncle Oscar slapped the book shut, swept it off the table, and sat on it, glaring. He remembered to take the book with him when Joshua's mother called him to the phone, but, surprisingly, he left his notes behind. Alas, he hadn't gotten very far. All Joshua could make out in a quick glance at his notebook was:

Foreplay
a.
b.
c.
d.
Recommended time allowed each step
1.
2.
3.
4.

• • •

"Who," his mother said, "was the toughest opponent ever to trade blows with the Alabama Assassin?"

"Billy The Kid Conn. Polo Grounds, June eighteenth, nineteen forty-one. A thirteenth-round K.O. for the Brown Bomber. Attendance, fifty-four thousand, four hundred eighty-seven. Referee, Eddie Joseph."

Mort Cooper pitched a one-hitter over the Dodgers, and the same day Charlie Keller drove in seven Yankee runs with two homers. In the National League race, Brooklyn led the Cards by three-and-a-half games and the boys were betting they would meet the Yankees in the World Series.

The boys, the boys. Bless them, please.

Seymour Kaplan, Max Birenbaum, Morty Zipper, Grepsy Segal, Yossel Kugelman, Eli Seligson, Al Roth, Lennie Fisher, Bobby Gross, Benny Zucker, Larry Cohen, and the rest.

Out of Fairmount and Bancroft schools or the Talmud Torah, into FFHS. Room 42. Class song, "Men of Harlech." Becoming the boys of the Fletcher's Field High Cadet Corps.

> Here come the Fletcher's Cadets,
> smoking cigarettes,
> the cigarettes are lousy
> and so are the Fletcher's Cadets.

The boys, the boys. He remembered them loping down *their* Boulevard on a Friday afternoon in spring, exploring, puffing Turrets, itchy in their Grover Knit-to-Fit sweaters, brash voices hushed for once, their manner subdued, because they were in Westmount. Where, according to Morty, everyone had a maid, some even a butler as well, and there was a buzzer under the dining-room table to bring them coming on the trot. Where, Izzy swore, property values couldn't be beat. And what about the snatchola, Seymour wanted to know.

Sssh. Not for you, *bubbele*. This is Westmount. Mothers didn't bargain here, or fathers cheat at pinochle. The daughters were blonde and leggy, they were taught horseback-riding early, if only to break their cherries with impunity, and the sons didn't collect butcher bills on Sunday mornings to earn enough to buy their own two-wheel bikes, but instead were given sports cars. British. The best.

The boys stood in front of Selwyn House amazed, as cars, some of them chauffeured, came to collect the students. "If they actually had to *walk* home," Joshua ventured, "they'd only get dusty, like."

Rosy-cheeked they were, wearing navy-blue blazers and gray flannel trousers, and they didn't give St. Urbain's interlopers so much as a glance.

"Have you ever seen such pricks?" Joshua asked. "I mean, would you get into that sissy suit every morning?"

"It's not your problem," Max replied. "They don't want Jews here."

Not in Westmount, with a cricket pitch, and its own police force. Where the snow was cleared instantly, and if even a crack, never mind a real pothole, opened on the streets a French Canadian came running with a shovel of hot tar—"Yes, sir. Right away, boss." But where, on the other hand, nobody had a bar-mitzvah.

Eli's father, a hot Zionist, showed a documentary on life on the kibbutz for the boys' party at his bar-mitzvah. They showed Charlie Chaplin two-reelers at Max's party. For Seymour's, his father shoveled them all into his fruit-and-vegetable truck that stank of rotting cabbages and drove them to a doubleheader at Delorimier Downs. They laid on a Bud Abbott and Lou Costello movie for Izzy's bar-mitzvah, and a day later he was peddling the gifts he didn't want. Everybody was treated to a party at Levitt's Delicatessen for Morty Zipper's celebration. Yet, surprisingly, the bar-mitzvah that none of them would ever forget was Joshua Shapiro's.

Yessir.

Nineteen forty-four it was.

R.A.F. HITS HARD AT COLOGNE AND HAMBURG
2,000 Tons of Bombs
Rained on Rhine City

And, on St. Urbain, corner of Ontario, Vic "The Torch" Rizutto was gunned down.

"Hey, wasn't he a friend of yours, Daddy?"

"Well, yeah. Right. But there was a family quarrel."

In a frenzy, the cops padlocked bookies and barbotte and whorehouses everywhere. Colucci was charged with dealing in black market sugar, of all things, and Joshua's father, whose testimony was being sought, couldn't be found anywhere.

"I have no idea where he is," his mother told Perreault.

"Aw, Esther, you're a peach."

With his father in hiding again, his mother quickly sank into her customary stupor. Chewing 217's, consuming novels and movie magazines and sipping Dewar's and a splash as she listened to "Ma Perkins" and "Pepper Young's Family" on their walnut-finished RCA radio. She seldom bothered to dress any more, stalking through the flat in a shimmering black slip, a Pall Mall dangling from her lips. Beds were left unmade, sheets unchanged. If she bestirred herself at all, it was to practice her act. One afternoon Joshua came home to find the living room carpet rolled up, the blinds drawn, and the winking red bulb screwed into the lamp; and another afternoon he opened the front door to a surprise.

"Well," she said. "Rinky-dinky-doo."

"Wow!"

"What do you think?"

His mother was wearing a top hat, glittering tights, tails, and long black mesh stockings. Twirling a cane, wiggling her ass, she danced away from him into the living room as Jack Teagarden croaked "Anybody Seen My Baby?" on the gramophone.

Dishes and pans accumulated in the kitchen. Empty milk bottles collected in the hall. The basin under the icebox overflowed again and again, and the box itself yielded no delights. A heel of hard salami. Some moldy cottage cheese. A slushy lettuce. To begin with, Joshua was given fifty cents each evening and sent out to eat his supper; she didn't seem to mind, she was probably grateful, if he didn't return for hours. Then a routine of sorts was established. She left the money out for him on the kitchen table in the morning and he took to leaving the house at eight and not returning until eleven at night.

Then, one afternoon in June, feeling feverish, he came home directly from school, only to find himself locked out of the house. Across the street, Euclid was simonizing Mr. Ryan's black Buick.

"Hey, kid, how would you like to go for a drive?"

"Why, sure," Joshua said, his smile ingratiating, slipping close enough to heave a rock, shattering the Buick's windshield, a startled Euclid taking off after him.

Drawing him into the lane, losing him easily, Joshua scrambled over the Zippers' rotting backyard fence, landing in the old man's tomato patch. He bolted up their rear stairs to the shed, grabbing a hammer and nails, and darted through the unlocked empty house, emerging on St. Urbain again, where he began to drive nails into the Buick's tires. He was working on the third one when he looked up to see a winded Euclid running toward him. Dodging him, Joshua took off again, running as far as Fletcher's Field, collapsing on the grass, his heart pounding. He declined an offer to join a pick-up softball game and crossed the street to the "Y," settling down in the gym to watch a basketball game. When he came home again, the Buick was gone. His front door was unlocked. "This isn't a house," Joshua shouted at his mother

94

without warning, "it's a fucken stable. Why don't you clean up around here any more?"

His mother didn't slap his face. Instead, she stared at him, astonished.

"It's only a month to my bar-mitzvah," he continued, emboldened, "and nothing's been done. Am I going to have one or not?"

"Why is it so important to you to have a bar-mitzvah?" she asked in a small voice.

"Well, you've got to if you're Jewish. Don't you believe in God and all that stuff?"

"Feh."

"What does that mean?"

"I could have made a better world myself."

"I'm going to have a bar-mitzvah."

"O.K., O.K., if it's that important to you, you can have one," she said, getting up to confront the stack of dishes in the sink.

"Well, yeah. Right. And there's going to be a party for my friends."

"Who would come here?" she asked, amused.

"The boys."

"Oh, yeah, their mothers wouldn't let."

"Why not?"

"Because my tits don't hang down to my ankles and your father doesn't work at a regular job."

The other mothers wouldn't speak to her any more, clutching their children by the hand as she passed. Some even crossed the street if they saw her approaching. Mrs. Sivak from downstairs complained to the landlord about her tap-dancing at 2 a.m., Louis Armstrong blasting away on the gramophone, but when old Dworkin shuffled round to the flat Esther sent him flying with a flow of obscenities. She had also very promptly dispatched the social worker sent by the Baron de Hirsch Society to inquire about Joshua's welfare. And the more she was socially scorned, the greater was her defiance, the backyard laundry line serving as her banner of rebellion. While immense cotton bloomers and outsized bras flapped worthily in the wind on other clotheslines, sassy little black bras and lacy black panties with unbelievably narrow waist-lines danced wickedly on theirs. Right out there in the back lane, where husbands setting out the garbage could look up and swallow hard. Where growing children could see.

Joshua told her about the other parties. The movies. The

double-header at Delorimier Downs. "What are you going to do for mine?" he asked.

"I'll fly in Mr. Teagarden. And I'll bake a marble cake."

Shit.

"Don't worry, kiddo. You're going to have a party. Oh boy, are you ever going to have a party!"

8

Are you a man or a mouse, Mueller demanded, biting into that ivory cigarette holder. *A man or a mouse*, he taunted. *Man, mouse*. And Joshua, wakening, discovered that he was sliding in sweat.

Ibiza, Ibiza.

But he wasn't back on the island again, he was on an airplane. Air Canada flight 274. Flying home from yet another television assignment on a June morning in 1976.

"Isn't that Joshua Shapiro?" a passenger asked his wife.

"Everybody looks sick in this light," she replied.

Joshua began to order double Scotches from the stewardess, wondering how, once a promising thief sprung out of St. Urbain, he had ever become a television personality, a husband and a father of three, charged with contradictions. He sent his children to private schools and complained in other people's houses about being the father of children who attended private schools. Anybody good on camera was an abomination to him, yet he owed his reputation to television.

Ibiza.

Monique didn't matter. He certainly didn't want to see her again. But, increasingly, he felt a need to confront Mueller one more time and to make a final effort to find the Freibergs. The mousy Freibergs, whom he had most assuredly ruined.

One night in London, 1953 it must have been, maybe a year after he had been obliged to flee the island, he had worked up sufficient courage to put through a long-distance call to the Hotel Casa del Sol in San Antonio. "I would like to speak with Mr. Freiberg, please," he had said, his heart thudding.

A pause. Crackling. "We have no Mr. Freiberg registered here."

"He's not a guest," Joshua had cried, outraged. "He owns the hotel."

"You must be mistaken. The proprietor here is a Señor Delgado."

"Then where in the hell can I reach the Freibergs?"

"I know of no Freibergs."

From the airport, Joshua hurried right out to Selwyn House, late for the graduation ceremonies. Teddy, only eight years old then, was certainly not graduating, but he was to be presented with a certificate of distinction for his work in grade two, and Joshua edged into a folding chair beside Pauline just in time to watch him climb up to the platform, his curly-topped head bobbing. *I ran once*, Joshua thought. *Me, your father. Leaving a couple of mice behind.*

The gym was already choked with parents. Mostly stockbrokers, corporation lawyers, or accountants who specialized in tax work. The news they were getting from the platform was bad. Should the Parti Québécois ever come to power, nobody could say with any certainty what would be the future of private English-language schools in the province; but diminishing subsidies, and a consequently hefty hike in fees, were most likely. Then the speaker was before them. Stout, clear-eyed, ruddy-faced. A trust company executive who had served with a good regiment during World War II and now sat on the board of a hospital, a charitable foundation, and McGill University. Stitching bromides deftly together, he finally turned to the graduating class, offering solemn advice born of the school of experience. In these days of rampaging trade unions, he told them, learn to be handy about the house, to paint and do carpentry work, because it will serve you well once you venture into the wide world. Beyond Westmount. Where kids still wear itchy sweaters from Knit-to-Fit.

What in the hell am I doing here? Joshua thought.

Once, he had obliged Alex, Susy, and Teddy to watch a TV documentary about World War II, and as Hitler did his notorious victory jig in the Compiègne forest after accepting the French surrender, they began to fall about, giggling. Unforgivably, Joshua lost his temper. "It isn't funny. Now you be quiet and watch."

He burdened the kids boorishly with his own past, he felt. He couldn't help himself. So when Alex, once a model airplane enthusiast, innocently brought home a Messerschmitt to construct, he made him take it back to the shop at once. He wouldn't have it in the house. Embarrassed because he had made Alex cry, he sat down with him afterwards and told him what he could remember about Guernica. About the famous oak tree before which the parliament of Basque senators had used to convene. About the air raid on April 26, 1937, when the small town was crowded with refugees and retreating soldiers. He tried to explain that at their age he had sat in a St. Urbain Street flat, his father fiddling with the shortwave band of their radio until they caught Hitler addressing the Reichstag, Hitler in a rage, cresting waves of *sieg heil*'s and static. He told them how the war in Spain had begun, and about Dr. Norman Bethune of the International Brigades, and the unit he had formed, Servicio Canadiensi de Transfusion de Sangre, which introduced transfusions to the actual battlefront.

If he still worshipped any heroes whatever, he explained, they were the men who served in the International Brigades. Spain.

> On that arid square, that fragment nipped off from hot
> Africa, soldered so crudely to inventive Europe,
>   On that tableland scored by rivers,
> Our fever's menacing shapes are precise and alive.

His education, begun in the pages of *Life*, continued through high school, his obligatory stint at The Boys' Farm after he had been nabbed for stealing a car, and all the jobs of his adolescence. He applied himself to learning a political alphabet, acquiring an ideological Dr. Seuss kit for Beginning Left-wingers. Combing through second-hand bookshops for anything on the Spanish Civil War. Reading Alvah Bessie, the Duchess of Atholl, Barea, Orwell, Gustav Regler, Malraux, and Geoffrey Cox. A map of Guadalajara, with the March 1937 battle lines, was pinned to a wall of his room, some lines by Charles Donnelly, an Irish volunteer, penciled in underneath.

> There's a valley in Spain called Jarama
> It's a place that we all know too well,
> For 'tis there that we wasted our manhood.
> And most of our old age as well.

In *Casablanca*, which he saw three times, it was a veritable guarantee of Bogart's integrity and eventual redemption that he had once run guns for the republicans. Devouring Hemingway, especially *For Whom the Bell Tolls*, he never necked with a girl without wondering, if never daring to ask, O Riva Mandelbaum, O Hanna Steinberg, *"But did thee feel the earth move?"*

> *"Yes. As I died. Put thy arm around me, please."*
> *"No. I have thy hand. Thy hand is enough."*

Like Seymour Kaplan, who shared his obsession with Spain, Joshua drifted to sleep dreaming not, as James Thurber once suggested, of striking out the batting order of the New York Yankees, but of Gary Cooper as Robert Jordan, his leg smashed, taking his place behind a machine gun to cover the retreat of Ingrid Bergman, Akim Tamiroff, and the other partisans.

> *"Roberto, what hast thou?"*
> *"The leg is broken,* guapa."

Seymour and Max, Izzy, Al and Eli were all at McGill now wearing red-and-white sweaters, but Joshua, without so much as a high school leaving certificate, already determined to get to Spain, disappeared into a mining camp in the northern bush for a season, emerging with his neck riddled with black-fly bites but his bankroll fat. At the time, Reuben had already walked out on Esther. He was roistering in Havana with Colucci, and she was bumping-and-grinding her way through a circuit in New Jersey. Joshua rented a room on Dorchester Boulevard. Teaching himself Pitman's shorthand at night, he also began to attend a number of McGill lectures on the sly, slipping into a Spanish-language course and another on the history of Iberia. McGill was, as far as he could make out, an incredible scene. Lanky boys on an allowance, at ease with themselves, wearing white cardigans and tooting the horns of their convertibles as they geared down to pass through the Roddick Gates. Golden girls in cashmere twin sets, pleated tartan skirts, bobbysox, and scuffed loafers. He made the mistake of crashing something called the Harvest Moon Dance and picking up one of the girls. Fat Sheldon espied him on the dance floor.

"Hey, Joshua, what are you doing here?"

He tried to thrust the girl toward the far end of the crowded floor, but Sheldon was already in malicious pursuit.

"You're not supposed to be here unless you're a student."

Suddenly, it seemed that everybody was grinning at him, the interloper. Westmount faces. Outremont faces. He abandoned the girl, fleeing. Humiliated. And the next morning, charged with rage, he smashed open a locker, found a hockey uniform that fit him, and bluffed his way onto the ice to practice with candidates for the university hockey team. The better-bred boys were justifiably startled by his manner with a stick. Flying into corners, he was all elbows and spear. In crazed pursuit of faster skaters with the puck, he slipped his stick between their skates, upending them. Between times, he lined up innocent wingers, trailing the play, and sent them bouncing into the boards. The other players were not amused by his loutish behavior. In the dressing room, they began to whisper among themselves, and finally one of them challenged him. "Who in the hell are you?" he asked.

Joshua, elated, replied, "Well, I'm not sure yet. I'm working on it." And, brandishing his stick, he retreated from the dressing room.

In the afternoon, he acquired his first white-collar job, one that came with a title: field worker. And early the next morning he was out banging on doors. "Hello, hello. I'm an interviewer with CMC Limited, a national opinion organization, and you have been carefully selected to—"

"No," the lady said, slamming the door.

He was no more successful with his second bell or the third, but the fourth time out he managed to squeeze into the apartment of a Mrs. Burns and told her that he was conducting a bread survey. "Why do you use bread?" he asked.

"To fill out a meal."

"Why don't you use something else instead?"

"What would *you* use instead?"

"When you use bread at a meal," he asked, "how is it served?"

"I put it on the table and everybody grabs a slice."

"I'd like you to think back to the last time you bought bread. Think about it for a while, and tell me exactly what happened from the time you approached the bread counter. Ready. Steady. Go."

"I walked into the store, bought a loaf, and walked out."

"Right. Now I have one more question for you. It's sort of a game question. Mind association."

"I'm a high school graduate," she allowed.

"Good. Now when I say 'staff of life,' what do you think of?"

"If you don't get out of here this minute," Mrs. Burns said, sweeping a heavy glass ashtray off the table, "I'm going to call the police."

Joshua shot out of his chair and made for the door.

"I'm writing down the name of your firm," she called after him, "and you'll be hearing from my husband."

"I love you," he called back, blowing her a kiss.

"Filth!"

A news photograph of El Campesino was tacked over his sink. There were also some lines by the murdered García Lorca.

¿Qué sientes en tu boca
roja y sedienta?
El sabor de los huesos
de mi gran calavera.

Although it had never occurred to him that he might be able to write, really write, he figured out that if he was going to get to Spain he would need a craft to sustain him, and he settled on journalism. But he grasped that his grammar was shaky, his prose trite. So he acquired a Fowler, a thesaurus, other books on style, and he studied them in bed at night until the print danced before his eyes. He bought the *New York Times*, the *Post, Collier's*, and taking the stories apart, he made notes on structure. He picked up a rickety but still functional portable typewriter in a pawnshop on Craig Street. With a card pinched from a student locker, he gained access to the McGill library. He read Mencken, all the journalism anthologies available, the *New Statesman*, and, above all, A. J. Liebling. Then, applying himself to Montreal newspapers, he realized that he had taken the wrong models. He turned to the New York tabloids, the *News* and the *Mirror*; he subscribed to *Reader's Digest*. Six months later, Joshua wrote a hard-hitting first-person exposé of the market research business, and how it manipulated the minds of innocent housewives for profit. He took the article to the managing editor of the city's only tabloid, the Montreal *Herald*. Fortunately, CMC was not an advertiser, and the editor, a gruff-spoken man, was willing to buy it at five cents a printed column line, if the details checked out. But Joshua, swallowing hard, said no, if he wanted the article, he had to hire him.

Had Joshua any experience?

Damn right, he said, with the Sudbury *Nugget*, and he produced a letter of reference from the editor typewritten on a letterhead that he had swiped from the old boozer.

"How old are you, kid?"

"Nineteen."

"Like fuck. But I'll give you a trial."

"What will you pay me?"

"Twenty-five dollars a week to start."

"I speak Spanish. I know French. I'm an expert on boxing lore."

"Take it or leave it."

1949 that was, and, living frugally, he began to set aside money for his trip to Spain. Madrid. The Ebro. Teruel. Guernica. But he would visit Paris first.

Paris, France.

Where Hemingway had gone.

Where one Josip Broz, later known as Marshal Tito, had once been ensconced in a Left Bank hotel organizing a flow of recruits through his so-called "secret railway." The first contingent of volunteers for the International Brigades, some five hundred men, had arrived in Albacete on October 14, 1936. Their leader was "General" Emilio Kléber, a Romanian whose real name was Lazar, and who was described in propaganda releases as "a soldier of fortune of naturalized Canadian nationality." And, Joshua remembered, grinning, they were already saying that Yiddish was the Internationals' *lingua franca*.

Once in Paris, Joshua brought his scrapbook of clippings to the *Herald-Tribune*, and the managing editor sighed and asked him to please fill out a form.

"I thought you might be interested in a series on Spain now. I majored in Spanish history at McGill. I speak the language fluently."

"So does the guy we've got in Madrid."

Joshua rented a room in a small hotel on rue Mouffetard, not far from the outdoor food market, and most afternoons he read in the garden of the Church of St.-Ménard, where Jean Valjean had once accidentally encountered Javert. Where, in 1727, the Jansenist François Pâris was buried, young girls flocking to eat the dirt off his grave. Flogging themselves there, having their tongues pierced, or their breasts and thighs trampled on until they passed out. Five years later the government was obliged to have the cemetery walled and guarded, a rhyme mysteriously appearing on the locked gate:

> *De par le roi, défense à Dieu*
> *De faire miracle en ce lieu*

Spain was close, achingly close, but, overwhelmed by Paris, he was unable to budge. He met Markham, he picked up with Peabody. Then, one afternoon in the autumn of 1951, he found himself sitting out there with Peabody on the terrace of The Old Navy.

"Try Ibiza."

"Ibiza?"

"Ibiza."

He yawned.

"You cross the Pyrenees," Peabody said, "and you're leaving Europe behind you. Those mountains are a time machine. On the other side, it's a hundred years ago. Much more in some places."

Spain beckoned. Yes. But by this time he had already blown most of his stake, some of it on the horses at Longchamps and Maison Lafitte, the biggest chunk in one wild drunken night with Peabody at the roulette tables in a club near l'Opéra. So he set out for London instead, where he would at least be able to find work without a labor permit. Clippings in hand, he made the rounds. Reuters, UP, AP, CP. He filled in on somebody's vacation on a desk here, subbed somewhere else for a fortnight, and served as a stringer for a number of Canadian newspapers, filing the obligatory crap. If, for instance, a dumpy Canadian actress had a walk-on part in a play on Shaftesbury Avenue, he would write TORONTO BEAUTY DAZZLES WEST END. He also turned to plagiarism. Ripping a short story with a twist in its tail from *Collier's*, he rewrote it, setting it in Calgary, and sent it off to the Toronto *Star Weekly* with a covering letter saying he was a struggling Canadian artist, who simply refused to sell his proud heritage for a fistful of Yankee dollars. The enclosed story had been accepted by the *Saturday Evening Post*, if only he agreed to make the place-names American. This, he wrote, would be a violation of his integrity; he would rather accept less money from a Canadian publication. And, to his surprise, the story earned him a check for $300, and a request for more. Then he was asked by a Montreal editor to go to Cambridge and send them 750 words on Canadian students for an educational supplement.

Cambridge. Everywhere he looked, bats on bicycles. Rotten teeth. But there, on a wet misty Saturday morning in the Market Square, he first encountered Murdoch, literally bumping into him as they were both riffling David's Bookstall for early Penguins, ancient Everymans, costing no more than sixpence each. In those days the yet-to-be-published Murdoch still read other people's novels in anticipation of pleasure, and Joshua did not yet take them as fodder for his scabrous reviews, outbidding everybody in invective. Joshua picked up a hardback, a novel published in 1934, and the reviewers' quotes on the faded jacket were dazzling. "Not

103

to be missed." "A minor masterpiece." "Brilliant." He had never heard of the author.

Murdoch, with his gift for anticipating what others thought, grinned at him. "It's a mug's game," he said.

Joshua read the first paragraph aloud, they both guffawed, and repaired to Morley's for a pint.

Soul-mates.

Murdoch was still wiry then, National Health steel-rims riding his fussy nose, mop of greasy black hair, brown eyes amazed, his tweed jacket the standard utility wear. Already pumping wild-eyed energy and malice out of every pore. "Now tell me, who is this Adlai Badly chap they are all talking about so much over there?"

A council school boy from Bradford, a scholarship lad, Murdoch was to earn a double first at King's. Once, when they stopped there to collect his mail, he asked Joshua to wait outside the porter's gate. "Sorry," he said. "But you're not a member of the college. Indeed, you are my social inferior in every respect."

"A rare advantage for you, that, Sidney."

"If you only knew," he replied, grinning.

But later he retreated into melancholy. "Do you think there'll be a place for us?" he asked.

"Where?"

"In this world, is where. I won't stand in queues. I am not going to eat in restaurants that accept luncheon vouchers. Or keep a post office account. I want everything."

"We're going to have it, Sidney."

"You don't understand this wretched country. It's not enough to win a double first. It's pushy."

"We're special."

"Bless you. But you don't understand. If I won a Nobel Prize, the *Times* headline would read, 'Newsagent's Boy Wins . . .' And where, in God's name," he asked, rounding on Joshua, "do you get your confidence?"

Joshua unbuttoned his shirt to reveal a long thin key hanging from a silvery chain.

"What's that?"

"It's the key to a box which is in the Royal Bank of Canada on the main street of Cornwall just across the Ontario border."

"Seriously, Joshua, how come you're so sure of yourself?"

Me, sure of myself. He had to laugh. "Well," he said, "I'll tell you. When I was a kid, my father used to take me out walking downtown, and whenever we ran into somebody he

104

knew, he'd stop him and say, 'I'd like you to meet my son, Joshua. This is my boy.' And when I was old enough, he took me to meet Colucci in the La Scala Barbershop, and he said, 'Your days are numbered, Sonny.' 'How come?' Colucci asked. 'This is my boy, Joshua, now you just feel that muscle.' My father wasn't in town for my bar-mitzvah, he had business elsewhere, but when he got back he took me into his poolroom, marched me over to the rack, handed me a key, and said, 'This will unlock our cue. It's yours. Nobody else can use it.' Then he turned to the boss and said, 'Off your ass, Stash, and rack 'em up for me and my son here.' "

"What do you want, Joshua, really want?"

"Well, my father brought me up to believe I would only be making one trip round. So I want a good life, available on terms that do not offend me. I also intend to enjoy myself."

Joanna, a fetching Girton girl, smelling of old money and country houses, came between them. She failed to grasp that Murdoch's insults were a desperate form of courtship and so did Joshua, at the time. He hit it off with Joanna and called at Murdoch's rooms to ask if he might have the run of the place for the afternoon. "Certainly," Murdoch said stiffly, and when Joshua returned with Joanna he found that he had left them a bottle of Australian sherry and an envelope with Joshua's name on it. Inside there was a nasty note. Murdoch had also contrived to disconnect the gas fire, something Joshua reproached him for when he caught up with him later at Morley's.

"Never mind that. What did you do?" Murdoch demanded, flushed. "How does one go about it?"

"About what, my dear?"

"You know, the funny stuff."

Joshua ordered another pint, wincing when somebody accidentally brushed against his back at the bar.

"What's wrong?" Murdoch asked.

Lowering his voice, Joshua said, "Scratches."

"Good God, really?"

"Mn."

"Was she wearing garters? I'm absolutely bonkers about suspender belts. Well?"

"That," Joshua said, "would be indiscreet."

Sodden, reduced to a child again, Murdoch confessed that he had yearned for Joanna for months, but hadn't known how or if she would ever . . . "How do you start it?"

Unwilling to admit that they had done no more than grope at each other, both of them goosepimply and shivering in

Murdoch's subarctic room, Joshua said, "Well, it began with her sucking my toes. It's an old Orthodox Jewish custom, don't you know?"

"Go to hell."

"Just how much," Joshua asked slyly, "do you know about what *really* goes on at a bar-mitzvah ceremony?"

Early the next morning a flustered Joanna was pounding on Murdoch's door. With his help, she turned over pillows, rolled back carpets, and moved furniture, hunting everywhere, even behind bookcases, for her pearl necklace. It wasn't to be found anywhere. Murdoch, when Joshua ran into him later in the day, was most distressed. "They weren't fake, you know," he said. "They came from Asprey's."

"The strand probably broke," Joshua said, "and she lost them cycling back to Girton."

Joanna placed an ad in the evening paper. It ran for three days, but nothing came of it. Joshua returned to Paris, consulted with Peabody about Ibiza, and bought a third-class rail ticket to Seville.

He had to see Seville. On July 18, 1936, there had been an amazing *coup de main*. General Queipi de Llano, commander of the carbineers, accompanied by his ADC, with only three other officers and fifteen Falangists at his disposal, audaciously arrested officers loyal to the Republic and took over the infantry barracks. This put a regiment of a mere hundred and thirty soldiers under his command, a city of a quarter-of-a-million yet to be subdued. Fortunately for Llano, the artillery barracks agreed to support the uprising, the airport fell, and then only the working-class suburbs resisted the insurrection.

The stars are dead; the animals will not look:
We are left alone with our day, and the time is short and History
   to the defeated
May say Alas but cannot help or pardon.

From Seville, he hitchhiked to Granada. Coming out of the Sierras at Motril, Joshua joined the main road from Malaga, and now, just as he had planned, he was following the route of the retreating republican army. On January 17, 1937, he remembered, the nationalist attack on Malaga had been spearheaded by mechanized Italian units. Two German cruisers shelled the coastal city daily and, on February 6, as the pride of the Canadiens, Howie Morenz, lay in a hospital bed and Joe Louis signed to meet Tommy Farr, the civilian population was ordered to evacuate, following the road to Almeria. In Ronda, republican zealots threw several hundred of the local bourgeoisie over a clifftop to their deaths. Meanwhile, pursuing nationalist troops, supported by tanks and aircraft, massacred stragglers in the retreating republican column. On this road, Joshua, this very road. The men were killed, but the women spared, if only to add to the Republic's food crisis. Dr. Norman Bethune was there. For three days and three nights, he and three other men ferried survivors to Almeria.

> . . . the further we went the more pitiful the sights became. Thousands of children—we counted five thousand under ten years of age—and at least one thousand of them barefoot and many of them clad only in a single garment. They were slung over their mother's shoulders or clung to her hands. Here a father staggered along with two children of one and two years of age on his back in addition to carrying pots and pans or some treasured possession. . . .

A few evenings later, when Almeria was choked with refugees, some forty thousand people having reached what they believed to be a haven, the city was heavily bombed by German and Italian airplanes. The airplanes made no attempt to hit the government battleship in the harbor or bomb the barracks, but deliberately dropped bombs in the very center of the town, where the exhausted refugees were gathered. While I, Joshua thought, was learning to play bolo and cheering on Boston's Kraut Line: Milt Schmidt, Bobby Bauer, Woody Dumart.

Tourists, Joshua discovered, were rare in Spain in 1952, especially footloose young Canadians, and he was amazed, after having endured the grasping French, to find himself treated as a guest everywhere he wandered in Almeria, even bartenders standing him to drinks. *Como su casa.*

Barcelona.

There seemed, at first glance, to be a few of the very, very rich in Barcelona, many who were unspeakably poor, but hardly any middle class to speak of. The rich, he discovered, were for the most part vastly entertaining fellows who had never done a day's work in their lives and were offended by the very notion of it. Oblomovs abounded. Among them, the engaging but mindless Antonio, who wore a Savile Row suit and drove a sparkling white Austin-Healey. "Given the benefit of a couple of drinks," Antonio said, "we're all republicans here. A few more stiff ones, and we're Communists. But come four o'clock in the morning, man, every self-respecting

Spaniard is an anarchist. So we need Franco, don't you see?"

Yes. Certainly. And the next evening Joshua sailed for Ibiza.

9

Until Pauline was confined to a bed in the Royal Vic, adrift on Valium, Joshua had been able to enjoy himself in Montreal even in the pit of winter, out tramping the streets at night, the snow heaped everywhere, the black trees bare. Ears stinging, squeaking powdery snow underfoot, he would ascend the mountain into Upper Westmount, pausing here and there to peer boldly into living room windows, watching families gathered round their crackling fireplaces, proof against icy blasts, playing back the day's events to each other or maybe perusing spring seed catalogues, planning a better garden. But what he enjoyed most of all was seeking out old classmates to bait. St. Urbain urchins who had struck it rich. Especially Pinsky. Irving Pinsky. "If you need maybe a fire," Pinsky used to say in the schoolyard, "my father says Shapiro's the man. What a *yold*." Pinsky, now a dentist, lived on Summit Circle and could be found there most nights out walking his Russian wolfhound.

"Joshua, what are you doing here?"

"I come up here for the fresh air, Irving. You have no idea how it stinks down below. We even have niggers on our street."

"You're supposed to say 'blacks' now. How would you like to be called a kike?"

"I'm a Jew, Irving, you're a kike."

"Well, you haven't changed."

Which was more than he could say for Pinsky. Pimply, scrawny Pinsky had matured into a slender man with curly gray hair. Whiskey-ad distinguished. He wore his Persian lamb hat at a perky angle, a black cashmere overcoat, a silk scarf, kid gloves, suede fur-lined boots. A world traveler now, he knew what to order for breakfast at Brennan's in New Orleans, just the right fellow to deal with at Davidoff's in Geneva, the first day forced Kent asparagus became available at the Guinea in London. He also considered himself something of a lady's man. And only a month after Joshua and Pauline moved into their house, Pinsky, who had been introduced to Pauline at a concert, saw her waiting by a bus stop. He pulled up in his Mercedes 450SL and offered her a lift downtown. Pauline accepted, joking with Joshua about it. Encouraged, Pinsky phoned the following week to invite them to dinner on Tuesday.

"And how," Pinsky asked Joshua, the moment he had served drinks, "did a guy like you manage to catch such a lovely wife?"

"Why, thank you," Pauline said, driving her elbow into Joshua's ribs.

Pinsky belonged to a gourmet club. He collected vintage wines. And so it was first-rate fare they ate with him and his striving wife, Gilda, off a Belgian lace tablecloth. Irving Pinsky, once celebrated for the sneakers he let rip in Room 42, FFHS, now resplendent in a burgundy velvet dinner jacket worn over a black turtleneck sweater, Gilda's slack plump arms clattering with gold bands and bracelets. Their faces reflected in the dancing light of silver candlesticks, they drank wine served up in tinted goblets, twenty-five-year-old cognac coming in birdbath-size snifters. But before they even sat down to dinner, Pinsky took them down to inspect his wine cellar, brushing unnecessarily against Pauline on the stairs. They passed through a laundry room, with its twin tubs, into the sanctuary, its up-to-date thermostat set at 13° Celsius. And here a glowing Pinsky allowed a fulminating Joshua to fondle, warning him not to shake unduly, his cherished bottles of Château Mouton-Rothschild '61 and Château Lafite '66. A leatherbound ledger stood open on a bible stand which had been retrieved from a Lisbon antique shop, and here every bottle was entered, the date of its removal noted, as well as a few pertinent remarks about its body and texture. For future reference. Proffering a bottle of Forster Kirchenstuck '67, Pinsky asked, "Guess what this baby's worth on today's market?"

"Why, I'd say at least twenty-five bucks."

"More like a hundred," Pinsky said, quivering with delight. "Ask your absolutely enchanting wife, she'd know."

After they got home, an amused Pauline told him, "When you went to the toilet, he asked me if I'd like to have lunch with him."

The next time Joshua encountered Pinsky, out walking his Russian wolfhound, it was the day after Pinsky had returned from his winter retreat at an exquisite little hotel on a remote and as-yet-undiscovered West Indian isle. Fear and trembling showed beneath his taut tanned flesh. "Haven't you heard?" he asked.

"No. What?"

"It's terrible. Unspeakable. I've been burglarized."

"What did they take?"

"Nothing."

"Nothing?"

"Worse. Come," he said, grieving.

Pinsky led him back to the house and right down to the wine cellar. "Look at this," he said. "And this. And this," thrusting one precious bottle after another at him.

All Joshua could think to say was, "They're not as dusty as they were the last time I was here."

"Prick. *Look at this.*"

"Oh, my God, there's no label."

"Some snake, some pervert, has washed the fucking label off every fucking bottle. The bastard has also moved the bottles around in the racks."

"I hope you're insured, Irving."

"Of course I'm insured. But what can I claim? The police—they sent some jerk of a detective called McMaster here—say nothing's been stolen. Imagine anybody doing such a thing to me. Why, I keep asking myself."

"Fortunately, a man with your educated palate could open any one of these bottles and tell not only the vineyard, but the vintage."

"Certainly. But how would I know which one to open?"

"Red with meat. White for fish."

"I wish I had your simple tastes."

Walking was Joshua's only exercise. Even on the coldest nights, the streets abandoned but the lights glowing everywhere, it used to please him to stroll downtown, past the Forum, as far as the International News Store, to fetch a batch of magazines for him and Pauline to read in bed. But with Pauline in the hospital, things were no longer the same. The children were understandably upset, and when he returned from his walk it was to confront homework problems that confounded him, or to settle squabbles, something he lacked the patience for.

One afternoon he returned from The King's Arms to find a tearful, pale Susy adrift on the study carpet in a confusion of encyclopedias and other reference books, her own essay pages blank.

"What's your problem?" Joshua asked.

"It's my project. I don't know where to begin."

"I'll help," he said, aware of Alex watching.

"Tell him what you're into," Alex said.

"High school education in modern China."

"How could they ask you to write about that?"

"It was high school education anywhere. I picked China." Joshua moaned.

"You told us we should show more interest in other societies," Alex reminded him.

"When does it have to be in?"

"Tomorrow morning. Should I make you a Scotch?"

"No. Yes. I'll give you a note," he said, avoiding Alex's eyes.

The pizza Joshua had ordered arrived and they sat down to dinner. Tears rolled down Teddy's cheeks. "What's wrong?" Joshua asked.

"She's looking at me."

"He says you're looking at him."

"Because he shouldn't eat with his elbows on the table."

"Why not? I do."

Teddy glowed.

"You always take his side," Susy said, fleeing the kitchen.

Joshua turned on Teddy and asked him to stop grinning like a smart-ass.

"I hate her," he said, running off.

"Well," Joshua said, smiling at Alex, "haven't you got anything to say?"

"Sure. But you'd only say no."

"Try me."

"Can I register for driving lessons?"

Joshua reached for his Scotch.

"I'd be able to help with the shopping. I could take Teddy to his swimming lessons."

"O.K. Why not?"

"Oh, yeah. I mean, really?"

"Yeah. Really. I mean, what's a red-blooded kid your age without wheels?"

"But you didn't have a car until you were thirty, and at my age you'd read all of Dostoevsky."

"Yes, but such immortal works as *Fear of Flying* had yet to be written."

"I didn't buy the book. Carol lent it to me."

"Is she that touchingly sensitive gamin with the chewed-out fingernails who's getting her shit together, as they say?"

"That's Penny."

"Then Carol must be the long smelly one with the frizzy hair and the green nail polish."

Alex laughed, appreciative, and Joshua grinned back, won-

111

dering what would happen if he got up to hug him. "Once," he said, "when I was eleven, my father tried to kiss me and I flinched from him. If he had stayed behind to talk to me for only another five minutes, the cops would have had him."

Alex waited, hoping for more. But all Joshua said was, "Run upstairs and see what you can do with them, O.K.?"

"Sure," he said, touching Joshua on the shoulder in passing, "and you know . . ."

"What?" Joshua asked hungrily.

"I miss Grandpaw. I really do. When's he coming back from Florida?"

After everyone had gone to bed, Joshua poured himself another Scotch and flicked on the TV, catching the last period of the hockey game.

He was half asleep on the sofa when the phone rang, jolting him. Not the hospital, he thought. Please, no.

"Do you know where I'm calling from?"

"No," he replied, sinking.

"The King's Arms," Jane Trimble said thickly. "Why aren't you here?"

"Because it's one a.m. and I intend to be up at seven to see that my loved ones get a proper breakfast."

"I only came here hoping to run into you. Now I've been picked up by a young man in computers. He reeks of Old Spice. I'll bet he wears Jockey briefs," she giggled. "Multicolored. He put my hand on his thing and asked me if I had ever felt such a big one."

"Little did he know whom he was dealing with."

"Oh, thank you. Thank you very much. He says older women turn him on. I'm only forty-two, Joshua," and then she began to cry.

"Go home to bed, Jane."

"He frightens me. If I go, he'll follow."

"Call Jack, then."

"Oh, sure, call Jack. He frightens me even more. Come and get me."

"I'm not even dressed."

"I'll wait."

"No."

"I want to see Pauline."

"You so much as go near the hospital and I'll break your arm. And that goes for Jack too."

"Please come and get me out of this. Please, Joshua. *I have to hang up now. He's coming.*"

Joshua phoned the bar immediately and spoke to George the bartender. "I think you've got a lady there."

"Yeah, she's been asking for you."

"Is she in trouble?"

"Well, she's been necking with this yo-yo, but really leading him on, and now she's crying and he's calling her a cock-teaser."

"Do you think you could get him out of there and send her home in a taxi?"

"Sure," he said.

Settled, Joshua thought. But he should have known better. A half-hour later the front doorbell rang. "Well," she said, "Sir Galahad at home." Sweeping past him into the study, relieving him of his Scotch in passing, she added, "I thought you'd be undressed. How disappointing!"

Skipping from here to there, circling warily, knives certainly drawn, they went into everything. The night of the astonishing dinner party on the lake. Her version of the events that had preceded it. Kevin. Jack. Pauline. The unfortunate timing of his trip to Spain. His fool's errand. An hour later, inevitably, it ended badly.

With the back of his hand, he was driven to cuff her hard against the cheek, bouncing her off the open front door, sending her sprawling.

Jane sat down in the snow, blood leaking from her nose.

"I'll get you a towel," he said wearily.

"Oh no you won't," she said, stumbling upright, losing a shoe, as she ran for her approaching taxi.

A week later he learned that she hadn't gone home, but had continued on to Dickie and Wendy Abbott's house, drinking out the remainder of the night with them. One shoe missing. Lying with her head back to stanch her bleeding nose.

Where were you?

Joshua's.

Yossel Kugelman, sole begetter of *Your Kind, My Kind, Mankind*, was no longer on the case. But the new doctor, a cheerful young man Joshua suspected of being an oaf, wasn't making any progress either.

Pauline, Pauline.

Why hadn't he caught the signals early? Appreciated that Kevin's return had tipped the balance. Her delicate balance. So that, suddenly, there she was again, tidying everywhere, cleaning out crammed cupboards, dusting books, and compulsively making lists of chores to be done. Lists and lists of lists. Instead of recognizing the demon and helping her to expel it, he had yielded to exasperation, shuffling out of his study at five, written out, discovering her surly, and charging, "You're in a bad mood."

"Am I?"

"How come we don't have drinks together before dinner any more?"

"Do you want to hear about my day?"

"Sure," he said warily.

"I spent an hour on the phone with Eaton's, trying to get them to correct an error in last month's statement. I was switched from department to department to department and each time I had to repeat the story from the beginning and they've still got it wrong. Then I went to buy Teddy new skates. I had to double-park outside Mr. Tony's and when I came out I had a ticket. Then I drove all the way out to Ville St. Laurent to get a new blade for the garburator, but they don't make that model any more. They wanted to sell me a new one. So I drove back to the Swiss Repair Shop and talked them into soldering and sharpening the old blade. I went to pick up your shirts at Troy and stepped into the street just in time to have a passing car shoot slush and blue salt all over my suede coat which will now have to be cleaned. That, and the parking ticket, will take care of most of the money I saved on the garburator blade. I stopped at Miss Westmount for a coffee. Why not, I deserve it, I thought. A fat greasy man sat down next to me at the counter and told me I had terrific tits. I went to Steinberg's for the food order and that took another hour. Then I remembered the toaster in the back of the car and I went back to the Swiss Repair Shop and stood in line again and left it to be fixed. I registered Teddy for the spring swimming class at the 'Y.' I bought Alex the new Frank Zappa record he asked me to look out for. I went to Howarth's to buy Susy three pair of school panties. The panties are not the right shade. Alex already has the Zappa record. Teddy doesn't like the skates, they're not what the other boys at school are wearing now. Then the order came from Steinberg's and some ass had put the yogurt in upside down, and it was all over everything, and I have just finished washing all the cans before putting them away. Now it's five o'clock and you expect me to be sweet and sexy and then you will want your dinner. Well, I haven't done a thing about it yet."

"Let's go out for dinner. The kids can eat pizza."

"The kids eat enough junk food without my ordering pizza. Susy needs help with her history tonight and Alex is going out with that awful Sally again and he's bound to come home upset and want to talk to me in the kitchen. I haven't been able to read a book in more than a month. I feel stupid. My hair's greasy. You have that pained look which means 'There she goes again.' I'm a drudge. Well, you've all made me into a drudge. I'm sorry I had the children, really I am. I wish I were a cashier or a call girl with regular hours and men who brought me roses rather than split trousers to sew or skates to exchange. I don't want to go out."

"All right then, I'm going out," he said.

The Flopper, his eyes adrift, was ensconced at the bar of The King's Arms.

"Joshua, there are three things that worry me in this world. Terrorism. All those nutty Ay-rabs hijacking planes left and right. And inflation. You know what they are asking for tomatoes today?"

"You said three things."

"Right. Yeah. And Effie."

Effie was his wife.

"What's wrong with Effie?"

"I promised her I'd be home at two o'clock this afternoon. What time is it now?"

"Seven-twenty."

"Shit. I figured. Buy me a drink."

Pauline was waiting up for him in bed, reading the morning newspaper at last.

"I'm sorry," she said. "I didn't mean a word of it."

"I love you," he said.

"I didn't tell you everything."

He waited.

"I ran into Jane on Greene Avenue and we had a drink together in the Jockey Club. She's going back to work," Pauline said, biting back tears.

"Doing what? Poisoning wells? Snipping the balls off passing men and beading them into a necklace? Tell me. I'm fascinated."

"Crombie and McTeer. The copywriting department. She used to work there and now they're taking her back."

"Why should that upset you?"

"You should have seen her. She had just had her hair done. She was wearing a new outfit. She told me she was going back to work because her children were growing up and soon wouldn't need her any more and she wasn't going to be-

come a household drudge. She said we were crazy, demented, allowing our husbands to turn us into a combination of mothers, maids, and cooks, draining the life out of us, and then they would look at us one morning and tell us that we had become boring, and that they found other women more exciting. She said she certainly wasn't going to let that happen to her."

"God damn it. Son of a bitch. Jane never had time for her children or her husband or cooked a proper meal in her life. I would not find you more interesting if you had some dreary job in an ad agency or did social work. The children need you here. I need you here. I could rent an office somewhere. I work at home because I enjoy being with you."

"Jane is more interesting than I am. She has more spirit."

Joshua sat down on the bed and stroked her hair. "You and I come from very different Montreals, so I imagine the name 'Tony Vitto' means nothing to you."

"No."

"Tony was shot dead in a restaurant in Brooklyn a while back, following the killing of Crazy Joe Gallo. I met him when he was still a young hood and I asked my father, 'What does he do?' 'Well,' my father said, 'Colucci, you know, has his problems. Yeah, with his shoes.' 'His shoes?' 'Yeah, he gets stones in his shoes, see, and Tony gets them out for him. He has a problem downtown, say, and he shouts at Tony, "Livarsi na patra di la scarpa!—Take this stone out of my shoe!" And that's what he does.' Well, Jane is the stone in your shoe and I wish I could get her out. Stop seeing her."

"But we've known each other since we were Susy's age. We have fun when we're together."

"You do?" he asked, surprised.

"When you aren't there, or other men, she's different. Honestly, she can be wickedly amusing. She makes me laugh."

"I don't understand women and their relationships, I really don't. But I don't want her interfering in our lives."

After Detective Sergeant Stuart Donald McMaster had got his day off to a far-from-rousing start, and he had bent his work rules, going out for a walk at 10:30 'a.m., he had intended to stop at the Royal Vic to look in on Pauline, but as he got closer to the hospital he found himself making clever little detours, anything to delay the inevitable. Pauline was not only abysmally depressed, she was also depressing, and these daily visits to her room were beginning to get at him.

Professing great and enduring love, Joshua was astonished

at the resentments he had been able to nourish over eighteen years of happy marriage, a stock of pettiness he was able to feed on during her hour of need. Pauline had made no effort to be civil to Seymour's wife, which was hurtful to an old friend. She hadn't worn the dress he had bought her for her last birthday more than once. "It won't do. My waist is going. Or haven't you noticed?" They never went on a trip, she protested, unless he needed a break. Her needs never entered into it. Furthermore, in social matters large and small, it was his taste that always prevailed. So, no matter how much wheedling he had to do on the phone, he never failed to surface with tickets for at least one game of the Stanley Cup Finals, but he had never once taken her to Stratford.

True, true.

Pauline, the senator's daughter, had been raised on the arts, while he had been brought up on the rough justice of Mr. Nat Fleischer's *Ring* ratings. Look at it this way: While she was learning how to curtsy in the presence of the Governor-General, his father was teaching him how to jab, keeping his chin tucked in at the same time.

But that's all beside the point now, isn't it, Joshua? If not for your unnecessary return to Spain—that stupid, self-indulgent trip that was to settle nothing, absolutely nothing—she wouldn't be lying in the hospital now and he, come to think of it, might still be alive. You should have stayed home during her hour of need. Instead, you took off for bloody Ibiza, proving yourself an idiot twice.

A fool's errand, she had called it, and she had been right.

When he finally arrived at the Royal Vic, late in the afternoon, he discovered Pauline asleep. In repose, her face without strain or reproach, she looked fine, just fine, and he was sorely tempted to undress and curl into bed against her. Instead, he sat in the chair by the window for better than an hour, Pauline breathing deeply, evenly, until, in a sudden panic, he rushed out into the hall to confront her nurse. "You promised me you wouldn't let her stockpile any of those bloody pills."

"But I haven't, Mr. Shapiro."

"I told you you were to wait by her bedside and make absolutely sure she swallowed them each time."

"We're not fools here."

"Then why is she in such a deep sleep now?"

"Because she had a very restless night. She hardly slept at all. And Miss Hodges gave her something to help her rest about an hour ago."

"Well," he said, retreating, "all I ask is that you be careful."

"We are careful with all our patients, Mr. Shapiro, even those who can't afford private rooms."

"What the fuck is that supposed to mean?"

"You are being exceedingly rude."

"I'm sorry," Joshua said, fleeing down the hall.

But he certainly wasn't going to leave the hospital until she wakened. He phoned Susy to say he would be home late.

"Where are you, Daddy?"

"At the hospital. Is Teddy there?"

"He's feeding his fish."

"Alex?" he asked.

"He's not home yet. A policeman phoned three times."

Alex picked up with a nickel bag. "What did he want?"

"He wouldn't say. But he left his name. McMaster."

"Did he leave a number?"

She gave it to him.

"Is anything wrong?" she asked.

"No. Nothing, Susy. But I'd better call him right away."

Joshua called the station and got McMaster on the phone. "Why," he demanded, "did you call my house three times?"

"You sound irritated, Mr. Shapiro."

"Shouldn't I be?"

"We could have towed your car away."

"I owe you."

"I was wondering if you'd had a chance to take even a little peekie at my manuscript yet?"

Joshua began to laugh.

"Did I make a funny?"

He couldn't stop laughing.

"Mr. Shapiro?"

"You wouldn't understand," he replied.

"Well, have you looked at it yet?"

"It's a treat I'm saving for my weekend. Goodbye now."

Later it would come out that no sooner did McMaster hang up than he dug into his desk drawer for a White Owl and bit off the tip. "Hey, Henri, I want to look at some files."

"What kind?"

"Lists of stolen furniture. But going back some. And, oh yeah, let's feed Reuben Shapiro's name into the computer and see what we come up with."

It was 9 p.m. before a moaning Pauline came awake, agitated, her hands fluttering. Sitting bolt upright, she stared directly at Joshua. "The worms must be crawling in his mouth now," she said. "The flesh putrefying."

And, a little sweaty, once more he rehearsed the reasons for having left her when he had so obviously been needed.

Murdoch. The new introduction to his book. But it was no good. He knew now that he should never have returned to Spain in pursuit of . . . what? Ghosts who were to prove maddeningly elusive. The callow boy he had once been.

TWO

1

The day before, yet another reporter had tried the cottage, this one from *Maclean's*, wearing tinted aviator glasses, a safari suit, and Chelsea boots.

"Looking for somebody?" Reuben asked, stopping him on the dirt road.

"Shapiro's place?"

"Uh huh."

"I'm a personal friend of his."

"Well, yeah, right," Reuben said, looking him up and down, his grin lascivious, "but you don't have to tell me, honey. I could see that."

"Hey now, look here," the reporter said, indignant, "I didn't mean that kind of friend."

"Yeah, well. Sure. Now I only work here. But you see that old bastard up there on the porch aiming that shotgun right at your family jewels? Well, you take one step closer and he'll spray you with salt and pepper."

"Can we talk?"

"Over here," Reuben said, pulling him behind a tree.

"I'd like to ask you some questions."

"I'm not supposed to answer any," Reuben said, taking a swig from his hip flask and offering it to the reporter.

"No thanks."

"Don't you drink?" Reuben asked, affronted.

"Not this early in the day. Now you answer some questions, Granddad, and I'm going to lay twenty dollars on you."

"Shit," Reuben said, wiping his mouth with his arm, "you know what they pay me for cleaning up around here? Three-fucking-fifty an hour. I got skills, you know."

"Sure you have. And I'll bet you know plenty."

"I want thirty bucks."

The reporter counted it out and handed it over. "What sort of shape's he in?" he asked.

"Mean."

"Do the kids know about it?"

"I wouldn't waste your time asking them any questions. One's a worse liar than the other."

"Is his wife with him, or has she left?"

Reuben, his manner sly, said, "Now you didn't strike me as the jealous type."

"I'm not really a friend, I'm more like an acquaintance. And not that kind, either," he added, thrusting a photograph of Pauline at him.

"Oh her, yeah. The wife. You wanta talk to her?"

"Yes."

"Hey, there's something I always wanted to know about your crowd. Do you piss standing up like the rest of us, or do you squat?"

"Jesus Christ Almighty! I'm a married man."

"So's Shapiro."

"I'll lay more money on you after I've talked to her."

"Follow me, son."

He took the reporter into the bush, careful to lead him where it was most overgrown, and then into the swampy part, so that after brambles had nicked his safari suit, his Chelsea boots sucked up green brackish water and mud. When they came out at the brook, Reuben said, "You'll find her over there, behind that tree, reading."

As the reporter stepped gingerly beyond Reuben, balancing on a mossy rock, he suddenly felt a rod prod him in the buttocks, sending him flying into the water. He surfaced to find Reuben standing over him, rake in hand. "You're no personal friend of Josh's," he said, "and, furthermore, this is *propriété privée*. No swimming allowed. So you come out of there, sonny, right now, and get moving. Or I'll break your little fingers."

Progress. The cast had come off his pathetically atrophied right arm on Thursday, and he was now allowed to sit out on the porch for an hour every afternoon, taking the sun with his father and the senator. A caretaker had mowed the lawns and was tending to the rock garden at Trimble's Folly. Once, picking up his binoculars, Joshua was startled to see Trimble himself out there, wandering, a stricken figure, and he knew it was only a question of time before he came calling. How are you doing, old son?

Trimble had, he learned, renewed his family membership in the golf and country club, and Joshua wondered if he would come out for the opening-day sailing race and dance. Shoving it to them. Every time the phone rang, Joshua started, silently offering a year of his life if it was his wandering Pauline. It never was. All the same, he hired somebody to turn over the soil in the vegetable garden, and decided to order everything she would require from the nursery in Knowlton, sending out psychic signals.

Come home, Pauline. Pauline, my love.

One afternoon, inevitably, Reuben slipped into his room to tell him that Detective Sergeant Stuart Donald McMaster would be there at 8:30 sharp the following morning, and their long work together would have to begin, his present state of health being no excuse for further procrastination. In preparation for his arrival, Reuben set up Joshua's Sony tape recorder, no less than two dozen blank cartridges stacked alongside.

"Can you handle it?" Reuben asked.

"I wish I knew where Pauline was right now."

"So do I," Reuben said, averting his eyes.

"When I was riding all that morphine they pumped into me in the hospital, I used to dream she was there."

"Yeah. Right."

"How could she not have come to see me?"

"All she needs is a little more time alone, Josh. I'm sure of it."

"*If* she's alone. How do I know she's not with somebody else?"

"How about a Scotch?"

"Yes, please."

Reuben fetched him one.

"Hey, Josh, there's something I still gotta know about the Seligson break-in."

"What?"

"Are you absolutely sure you left a lot of those old banknotes strewn about his desk?"

"Yes. I'm sorry about that, Daddy."

"Can you remember if they were from the stack that was in sequence?"

123

"Yes, they were. Why?"

"Never mind," he said, brightening. "It's not important."

"Say, shouldn't we ask the senator to join us?"

"He's snoozing."

"How old are you now, Daddy?"

"Seventy-three, I figure."

"I'm forty-seven."

"Cheers," Reuben said, raising his glass.

"It's absurd. It's fucking ridiculous. I can't be forty-seven yet. I'm not ready."

"You'd better believe it."

"What's it like being seventy-three?"

"Well, you always seem to be getting up to piss. And it only comes in trickles."

"Anything else?"

"You get to like porno films. I have, anyway."

"Hey, remember Maw in *Trader Horny?*"

"I've managed to avoid anything she's played in," he said stiffly.

The senator wandered into the room, puffy-eyed. "Am I intruding?" he asked.

"Hell, no. But now we won't be able to talk dirty any more. I'll get you a drink."

"Thanks. How are you feeling, my boy?"

Joshua had to laugh. "I'll tell you how I feel," he said, "how I feel right now. Like the blind lottery-ticket seller."

2

In the waterfront café, where he was to become a regular, Ibiza's blind lottery-ticket seller would come wandering through the beaded door, tapping his cane, in hazard. The fishermen were fond of luring him into the rear of the café and then swiftly but surreptitiously shifting the tables and chairs around to block his passage out. As the old man lashed left and right with his cane, desperately trying to find a way out of the constantly shifting maze, the fishermen fell about laughing.

Ibiza, Ibiza.

Not him, no, no, but somebody else called Joshua Shapiro, a boy he blushed even to recall, had once been rooted there, roaring.

And yet, and yet, he thought, even as he disowned this

other Joshua, I'd give a good deal for a cup of his enthusiasm right now.

Ibiza.

There are four islands in the Balearic Archipelago: Majorca, Minorca, Ibiza, and Formentera.

Ibiza is an island of limestone hills, lush pine forests, fertile flatlands, and enticing stretches of sandy beach. There is also a salt marsh. Juniper and evergreen oak thrive there. The most gnarled of the olive, fig, and almond trees are reputed to be a thousand years old. Oranges are grown on Ibiza, but they are not nearly as sweet as those produced in the province of Valencia. The Ibizenco peasant, an obdurate man, is not highly adaptable. He survives, nothing more. Many of the island's sailors, however, mariners of prodigious skill, had traveled the world. And there was a time when Ibiza's fishing grounds were fabulously rich.

The island's capital is also called Ibiza, and is quite unforgettably approached by sea. Cubelike, sun-dappled white houses. The Upper Town and its surrounding wall, built in the sixteenth century, soaring above the natural harbor. There are passageways winding through the wall, and when the lookout signaled the appearance of a Barbary pirate ship on the horizon, the Ibizencos hastily took refuge within. Defenders assumed positions at the top of the wall, overlooking the passageway into the Upper Town, as if peering down into a well. No sooner did the *corsarios* appear at the bottom than they were bombarded with rocks. His father would have approved, Joshua thought. Real scrappers, he would have said.

Stepping down the gangplank of the *Jaime II* early one evening in 1952, an exhilarated twenty-one-year-old Joshua Shapiro was immediately hailed by a man who was to become his mentor on the island. Juanito Tur-Guerra, otherwise celebrated as Juanito Pus, owner of two battered fishing boats, a dockside *barraca*, or storage shed, and undisputed king of the waterfront.

"Venga, hombre. Aquí."

Clapping Joshua on the back, Juanito summoned fishermen to help him with his kitbag; he booked him into the small, flaking hotel on the quay and propelled him into the bar for a glass of Fundador. He was a small lithe man, his face leathery, his blue eyes flecked with mockery. Juanito had more than energy, he was a furnace. They stood at the bar for hours, joined by still more rubber-booted fishermen, laughing a good deal. Joshua established that he was a *Canadiensi*.

"Yes, but what do you do?"

"I'm a reporter. Sort of."

Juanito, like Uncle Oscar an authority on all matters, wasn't having any of it. Biting into a fresh cheroot and spitting on the floor, he revealed to the others that Joshua was obviously a rich man's son, sent to Ibiza to avoid his being drafted for military service in Korea. Joshua protested that there was no draft in Canada, but unavailingly, and the story was to stick with him for the duration of his stay.

Come midnight—groggy, staggering drunk—Joshua pleaded fatigue and inquired after his room, but Juanito insisted that they all immediately repair to Casa Rosita.

Voices subdued to whispers lest wives overhear them, they clambered over an incredibly narrow and twisting rock passageway that ran between the overhanging whitewashed houses in Sa Penya, the fishermen's quarter built on a rock promontory at the harbor mouth. Casa Rosita was the local bordello, and the arrival of Juanito and his band was greeted with whoops of delight from the girls. The girls, a frisky bunch, wore soiled housecoats unbuttoned over torn slips or bra and panties. Ascending to an upstairs bedroom with one or another of the drunken fishermen, they lugged a slopping pail of hot water, a bar of strong soap, and a freshly boiled but frayed towel.

"Is that a religious medal?" the girl asked, reaching for the long, thin key that was suspended from the silver chain round his neck.

"It's my inheritance."

The keys to the kingdom of Shapiro.

"If anything happens to me," Reuben had said, seeing him off, "everything you find in that box is yours. Do you mind if I kiss you?"

"Of course not."

"You never know. So I thought I'd ask first."

Arriving on the island, Joshua had been surprised to see the waterfront churning with strollers, but he soon came to appreciate that the weekly visit of a ship from Barcelona, Valencia, or Alicante was sufficient to bring out the crowds. An even more auspicious occasion, he discovered, was when Juanito let it out—the word flashing from bar to bar—that there would be a fresh shipment of girls for Casa Rosita on the incoming ship. The thin, pasty girls, their makeup garish, were unmistakable as they hobbled highheeled and defiant down the gangplank, straining against the weight of card-

126

board suitcases bound with rope. The fishermen, stoked with Fundador, scrutinized them from the terrace of the waterfront café, staking claims and passing judgment on their promise. Impatient as they were to introduce themselves, the fishermen understood—even as Rosita hustled her charges off, respectable people creating a disdainful passage for them—that it would be early and alone to bed for the whores tonight. In the nature of things, they would have serviced the crew in the boiler room on their passage from the peninsula.

It was at Rosita's that Joshua first met and drank with Mariano, the secret policeman. Seated at the dining-room table on a blustery afternoon in December, a basin full of glowing charcoal below to warm their feet, they chatted, baiting each other with appetite. Mariano, a wiry man, bowlegged, his skin the color of bronze, had beady gray eyes. He was from Estremadura, the province of the conquistadores, sprung from Trujillo, the same city as had Pizarro. Twenty American nations, he was fond of saying, were conceived in Trujillo.

During the Civil War, Mariano had served in the Army of the North under General Mola. After a village had been taken, in the sweep through the Tagus Valley, it was his chore to uncover and record whatever atrocities had been committed by the fleeing militiamen. He would then seek out any young men left behind, and order them stripped to the waist. Those whose shoulders bore the bruise of a rifle recoil were immediately shot. Then the churches would be reopened for mass, and there would be baptism for those born in the preceding month. Mariano, squeezing the breasts of the girl on his lap hard enough to make her cry out, said, "You have no understanding of the Spanish soul. We stopped Charlemagne. We sent Napoleon back where he came from. If necessary, we will stop Stalin in the Pyrenees."

This—deservedly, Joshua supposed—after he had mocked the troops he had just seen on maneuvers, watching their camp from a hilltop vantage point. But the soldiers had seemed very ludicrous indeed. From cosy concrete-lined trenches, they fired rifle bullets at a tank. The bullets were blanks, the tank was made of plywood. In Canada, he told Mariano, there was no compulsory military service. "Mind you, ours is not a Fascist state, in constant terror of a popular uprising."

Mariano shook with laughter. "If we didn't have military service here," he said, "the peasant boys would never learn how to brush their teeth." And then he started up the stairs, cheerfully beating the buttocks of the two squealing girls he was sending up ahead of him.

None of the whores were local girls. They came from the slums of Granada, Cadiz, and Alicante. For most of the year they traipsed from city to city, lugging pails of hot water and boiled towels, following after the fiestas where the most celebrated matadors were to perform. Litri, Aparicio, Dominguin. They prized their sojourn on tranquil Ibiza as something of a respite, certainly a time to relax.

Unfortunately, Joshua's afternoon with Mariano turned out to be the day of the mysterious mountain man, and they were asked to leave Casa Rosita. The mountain man—a sly fellow, unshaven, obese—earned his living biting the balls off sheep, the wound sealed with his healing saliva. He only came down out of the hills to the bordello once a month. The girls fawned on him, flushed with excitement. But the fishermen regarded him with disgust, spitting on the floor and trooping out, Rosita bolting the door after them. Even Juanito refused to spell out whatever service it was the mountain man performed for the girls.

Joshua began to luxuriate in the sun and in his new friends, studying maps of Spain in his hotel room before he went to bed, inking in old battle lines, planning forays onto the peninsula, trips he would finance by rewriting more *Collier's* stories with a twist in their tail for the Toronto *Star Weekly*. Then something happened.

One balmy evening, as he sat on the terrace of the waterfront café with Juanito, watching the ship from Valencia ease into the harbor, he was struck by the appearance of a tall sorrowful man leaning against the railing, biting into an ivory cigarette holder, his long angular face seared by sun and wind. He wore a white linen suit. Only after all the other passengers had disembarked did he condescend to come striding down the gangplank, followed by four sailors struggling with two steamer trunks. Then still more luggage heaped on a cart. Suitcases, a saddle, a rifle in a canvas case, and what appeared to be a furled teepee. Porters hastened to his side without being summoned, but he ignored them, as he did the two trucks that awaited his pleasure. He paced up and down until the hold doors squealed open, and then he sauntered into the bowels of the ship, and when he emerged ten minutes later he was leading a handsome brown stallion. He coaxed the stallion right onto the back of one of the trucks, secured his reins, and fed him apples out of his pockets until

128

all his luggage had been loaded onto the other truck. Then both trucks rattled off toward San Antonio.

"Now who in the hell was that?" Joshua asked.

Juanito conferred with one of the porters and returned to say, "He's a German, I think. His name is Dr. Dr. Mueller."

3

A year after the end of World War II, Prime Minister Mackenzie King said, "For the Jewish people the recent war had an especial significance. The way of life of all free peoples was threatened by Nazi and Fascist aggression. In addition, the Jewish people had the even sterner realization that for them it was not only a way of life, but life itself that was at stake."

His mood playful, Joshua once reminded his father-in-law of that typically prescient pronouncement by Wee Willie. The venerable senator was amused, but still considered the Mackenzie King Memorial Society—an organization Joshua had invented, and served as secretary—just this side of disreputable, and he adamantly refused to address it. A great loss, Joshua felt, for his father-in-law had been a member of King's wartime cabinet.

The senator was seventy-nine years old now, incredibly lean, wobbly, and arthritic. Weary of burying old colleagues, he had been, until Reuben took him in hand, increasingly inclined toward melancholy. For all his faults and the asperity of his manner, Joshua had come to adore the old man, if only because whenever Susy bounced into his stuffy Rockcliffe living room, her hair flying, he had the touching courtesy to rise out of his armchair, leaning on his malacca cane, to greet her. The senator had not enjoyed a happy life. The bride he took in his middle years, Madeleine de Gaspé Benoit, a legendary beauty in her day, was notoriously unfaithful to him and slid into drunkenness in her declining years. She died in a nursing home, in a state of delirium, even as he held her hand, and she called out another man's name. Stephen Andrew Hornby had also been disappointed in his political hopes, betrayed by Mackenzie King, whose memory he still honored. He would not allow the name of his only son, Kevin, to be mentioned in his presence. His daughter, Pauline, had also been trouble from the moment she was born. His only grandchildren, her and Joshua's lot, were half-breeds. Joshua was a prizefighter's son, a Jew. Even so, the senator invited him to lunch at the Rideau Club when he learned that Joshua was to marry his daughter.

That was in 1959, shortly before Pauline's divorce from Colin Fraser had become final, and Joshua and Pauline were already planning their eventual return to Montreal, from which he could travel in both the United States and Canada, continuing to interview survivors of the International Brigades in order to complete his long-overdue book. September it was, and flying from London to New York, on a magazine assignment, Joshua had elected to stop off in Ottawa for a hastily called Annual Day of the Mackenzie King Memorial Society and to pay his respects to the senator, whom he had never met.

Ottawa, Ottawa.

The founder of their nation's capital, appropriately enough, was an enterprising Yankee colonizer, Philemon Wright of Woburn, Massachusetts. In the winter of 1806, seven years after he had first surveyed the wilderness on the Ottawa River, he was cutting white pine and assembling the "sticks" into rafts and cribs below Chaudière Falls. The timber was bound for Britannia's fleet, temporarily deprived of its traditional supplies from the Baltic by Napoleon's blockade. The Battle of Waterloo may have been won on the playing fields of Eton, but the Battle of Trafalgar was fought on a bed of Canadian pine. Which is to say, long before Canada achieved nationhood the country was already cast in its role as hewers of wood, typically organized by an American with his eye on the main chance. For in order to deliver the timber, Wright had to undertake something that had never been done before—he was obliged to negotiate the Carillon, the Long Sault, and the Lachine, the daunting chain of rapids between him and Quebec City. Why not by-pass Lachine, he thought, taking the timber via the north shore? "The habitants who had been settled there nearly two hundred years told me it was impossible to get timber to Quebec by the route on the north side of the Isle of Montreal, but I said I would not believe it until I had tried it." Wright tried it and succeeded brilliantly in the spring of 1807.

It was the existence of a flourishing lumber-and-logging trade that inspired a certain Colonel By to found a town near Chaudière Falls in 1826. Bytown became the City of Ottawa in 1855.

And then another Yankee, this time an indigent Vermonter, Ezra Butler Eddy, came to town, opened a sawmill, and

130

with the help of his wife began making safety matches. Within two decades he was a millionaire, soon to be the leading match manufacturer in the world.

Ottawa did not become the capital of the United Provinces of Canada until Queen Victoria selected it from among a number of nondescript but ambitious colonial towns in 1857. Seven years later, the Fathers of Confederation grudgingly chose it a second time to serve as the capital of a dominion that was to sprawl from sea to sea. "The Westminster in the wilderness," scoffed an Oxford don, "a subarctic lumber-village converted by royal mandate into a political cockpit." The Americans were no kinder. Caustically observing that Ottawa had been chosen over Montreal or Toronto because it was less vulnerable to American attack, they agreed the town was safe, allowing that American troops would soon get lost looking for it. All the same, an American editor offered a formula for finding it: "Start from the North Pole; strike a bead for Lake Ontario, and the first spot where the glacier ceases and vegetation begins—that's Ottawa!"

The sulfurous stench from the E. B. Eddy plant was still stinging the streets of Ottawa when Joshua first arrived there, woozy from a transatlantic flight, to join Senator Hornby for lunch. No time was wasted on an exchange of pleasantries.

"As you know, I am opposed to this marriage," the senator said.

"Aha."

"But if it lasts any longer than the other, which I strongly doubt, I will pay for the education of any children."

"That's awfully white of you, Senator, but *I* will pay for the education of our children."

"I would like to see them go to proper schools."

"Pauline and I will be the judge of what's proper."

"The Hornbys have been educated at Bishop's for generations."

"You're forgetting something, Senator. Our children will be called Shapiro."

"Where were you educated?"

"Do you mind if I have another?"

"Please do."

"Make it a double."

"Certainly."

"I was educated at Fletcher's Field High, and from there I went on to do a stint at The Boys' Farm in Shawbridge."

"Why?"

"I got caught stealing a car."

131

"No university?" he asked without flinching.

"I'm afraid not."

"But you're a writer?"

"Of sorts."

"Where's your family from?"

"The *shtetl*."

"Ah," he said, "the Pale of Settlement."

Joshua had underestimated him.

"Your parents alive?"

"Mn hm."

"And what do they think of this marriage?"

"My mother has never given a damn what I do, and so far as my father's concerned, anything that makes me happy is fine with him."

"What does your father do?"

"If you don't mind, Senator, I think I'll have just one more."

"A double?"

"Yes, please."

He signaled for the waiter.

"My father was a prizefighter. He once went eight rounds with Sammy Angott."

"And was this Mr. Angott a pugilist of some note?"

"Indeed he was."

"And what did your father do upon his retirement?"

"Oh, many things, Senator. A good many things. A little something in the restaurant and nightclub line. Some bill-collecting. I ought to tell you that he has a prison record."

The waiter arrived with Joshua's drink.

"Oh, on second thought, Desmond, I think I'll join my guest. The same for me, please."

"But this is a double, Senator."

"I'm quite aware of that, Desmond."

"Yes, sir."

"Why was he in prison?"

"You are asking a great many questions."

"Yes. I suppose I am. And I'm looking for some straight answers."

"Why was he in prison?"

"Yes," the senator said. "Why?"

"Which time were you thinking of, Senator?"

"Good Lord, are you having me on?"

"I'm afraid not."

"Please don't take offense. But the Jews are usually such a law-abiding people."

"My father's something special."

"Well, that's something to be grateful for, isn't it?"

"Cheers," Joshua said.

"Cheers," the senator said, raising his glass unsmilingly.

"Any more questions?"

"Young man, I hardly dare."

"I should tell you that I love your daughter and I intend to make her very happy."

"I'm afraid Pauline's not much disposed to happiness. Neither was her mother."

Startled, Joshua drained his glass.

"Would you care for some wine with your lunch?"

"If you don't mind, I think I'll just have another one of these."

"Mr. Shapiro," the senator asked, calling for the waiter again, "as a matter of interest, do you usually imbibe as much before lunch?"

"Only when I'm obliged to. endure so many personal questions from somebody I've met for the first time."

"Is that how you are going to report our little meeting to Pauline?"

"Senator, as you have already made abundantly clear, you do not approve of this marriage. Even though you've never met me before. Well, that's your prerogative. But I think you are being unfair."

"That's your prerogative."

"I did not come here to ask for a damn thing. Not for a blessing or for money for our children's education. I came as a courtesy."

"But not necessarily to be courteous."

"The Shapiros have not been going to Bishop's for generations, but we are not without our own family traditions."

"Such as?"

"We do not take shit from anybody."

"I can do nothing to stop Pauline's allowance. The bequest was made by her grandmother."

"What makes you think I'm in need of her allowance?"

"Surely, as a writer of sorts, you must earn a most precarious living?"

"I stopped off here on my way to New York. I've been asked to write a piece for *Life* magazine. They will be paying me three thousand dollars and expenses."

"When Mackenzie King became our first minister of labour, his starting salary was seven thousand dollars a year; he used to take the streetcar to work."

Flushing, all Joshua could manage was, "I was never an admirer of Mr. King."

"Fortunately, he was unaware of any disapprobation on your part. Will you be expecting Pauline to convert to your faith?"

"No."

"How will your children be brought up?"

"Not to get caught stealing cars. And to jab on the move. Stick, stick, and away you go."

They repaired to another room for coffee and cognac, and there, to his future father-in-law's obvious discomfort, they were joined by Senator Pronovost. An avuncular man, his face wispy with red veins. Joshua remembered Pronovost. He had been one of Montreal's Liberal MP's.

"Gilles," Senator Hornby said, "I'd like you to meet my prospective son-in-law, Mr. Joshua Shapiro."

"Shapiro?" Pronovost asked.

"This is indeed a pleasure," Joshua said. "My father once worked for your party machine."

"Shapiro?"

"You wouldn't remember him by name. But he was one of many you hired. I think in the election of 'forty-eight he must have voted for you thirty times, maybe more."

"Shapiro, Shapiro. Wasn't there a trial?"

"Yes. You see, Senator, if you were bagman for Colucci's organization and you got nabbed, it meant three years in the slammer. But I can now see if you were bagman for the Liberal Party, you end up with a seat in the Senate. Obviously, my father collected for the wrong people."

Senator Hornby slapped his knee and laughed out loud.

"Young man," Pronovost said, "you obviously have no respect for my office."

"If you only knew," Senator Hornby said.

"I have nothing to be ashamed of," Pronovost said, glowering at Joshua.

"If that's the case," Joshua said, "then you really have a problem."

But Pronovost had already turned his back on Joshua, drifting toward another table.

"Did your father really vote for him thirty times?"

"At two dollars a crack, if memory serves."

"Oh dear, oh dear."

"Well, Senator," Joshua said, rising, "I would like to say that this has been a pleasure . . ."

His pale blue eyes watered. And suddenly he looked old, vulnerable. "Take care of Pauline. I love her."

"So do I."

They shook hands.

"I'm sure you do, but it may not be enough."

Early the next morning, too early for Joshua's taste, he was wakened by a fierce pounding on the door of his room in the Château Laurier. "Open up! Open up! We know you have a woman in there!"

The gentlemen of the William Lyon Mackenzie King Memorial Society, piling into two cars, leaving Montreal at 6:30 a.m., had arrived for their Annual Day. Portly, moon-faced Seymour Kaplan was there, Max Birenbaum, Bobby Gross, Leo Friedman, Jack Katz, Eli Seligson, and Morty Zipper, all from Montreal. Momentarily they would be joined by Lennie Fisher and Al Roth, both now living in Toronto, Mickey Stein, who was doing research in social studies at Harvard, Benny Zucker from UCLA, and Larry Cohen, who had just joined the Treasury Board in Ottawa. All of them had been pimply teenagers together at FFHS and were, for the most part, still striving. Everything possible. Joshua had already booked a private dining room, large enough to accommodate their society, at the Château, and he counted on Seymour, Keeper of the Artifacts, to decorate it appropriately.

As usual, the oak-framed photograph of Mackenzie King wearing his checkered tweed suit with cap to match, one hand caressing his Irish terrier Pat II, would be seated in the place of honor, to be toasted again and again. Another framed photograph of their cunning chipmunk would show him seated in his study, contemplating a painting of his beloved mum. Hanging on the wall would be a framed *Time* magazine cover of ice-skater Barbara Ann Scott, Canada's sweetheart of yesteryear, and a film still of Montreal actor Mark Stevens from *I Wonder Who's Kissing Her Now?* There would be an action photograph of Maurice "The Rocket" Richard, and another of Johnny Greco in the ring with David Castilloux. A Shirley Temple doll, a Betty Grable pin-up, and—a real collector's item, this—a Lili St. Cyr poster from the old Gayety Theatre. An Al Palmer gossip column from the defunct Montreal *Herald*, demanding, between gutsy paragraphs, WITH BUTTER NEARLY FIFTY CENTS A POUND, WHY NOT MARGARINE? would be in evidence. They would also have a tape of an old Foster Hewitt "Hockey

Night in Canada" broadcast. There would be records by Kay Kayser, Harry James, Tommy Dorsey, Bing Crosby, the Ink Spots, Artie Shaw, Nat King Cole, Glenn Miller, Spike Jones, Mart Kenney and His Western Gentlemen, and, of course, Deanna Durbin. Yo-yos would be available for their annual after-dinner competition. Copies of *Sunbathing*, *The Police Gazette*, and *Justice Weekly* would sit on the sideboard, as would a bottle of Kik-Cola and a sufficient number of Mae West bars for everyone. Nor would they be without stills of Bogart, Lana Turner, and John Garfield. Or their prized photograph of Igor Gouzenko, the Russian embassy clerk turned God-fearing informer, wearing a pillowslip over his head for a press conference. Also, a newspaper photograph of their favorite among extant hockey players, the aging Flopper, then still tending the nets for the perfectly dreadful Boston Bruins.

All these artifacts, and more, in everlasting memory of William Lyon Mackenzie King.

Ostensibly bland and boring, William Lyon Mackenzie King, the prime minister of their boyhood, Canada's leader for twenty-one years, was the most vile of men. Mean-spirited, cunning, somewhat demented, and a hypocrite on a grand scale. Wee Willie was born on December 17, 1874, in Berlin, Ontario. His mother, Isabel Grace Mackenzie, was the thirteenth child of William Lyon Mackenzie, the first mayor of Toronto and leader of the Upper Canada rebellion in 1837. At the age of seventeen, Willie went on to University College at the University of Toronto and from there to the University of Chicago. He had begun to keep a diary. And he was already a confirmed Gladstonian. Which is to say, a horny little fellow, bent on the salvation of prostitutes by day, he did in fact bend over them by night, forking out as much as $1.25 a trick, not counting gratuities. In 1900, at the age of twenty-five, he was called to Ottawa to organize the newly created Department of Labour. He became the department's first deputy minister. It was that same year, on Thanksgiving Day, that he espied his blessed Kingsmere, the little lake in the hills on the Quebec side of Ottawa, some eight miles from Parliament Hill. King was first elected to Parliament as a Liberal in 1908; a year later he entered Sir Wilfrid Laurier's cabinet as minister of labour. His beloved mother died in 1917, but Wee Willie was soon to commune with her spirit nightly by means of a crystal ball. In 1919, he was elected leader of the Liberal Party. Two years later he became prime minister for the first time.

Mackenzie King already owned a cottage on Kingsmere

Lake in 1920. Two years later he increased his holdings, and an estate at Kingsmere was created, King calling his house "Moorside." Another five years passed before he became "owner of house, barns, woods and another 100+ acres of land." The same year the perspicacious King also purchased an adjoining lot, in order to prevent "a sale to Jews, who have a desire to get in at Kingsmere & who would ruin the whole place," possibly by opening a kosher delicatessen.

Ah, Kingsmere, where Wee Willie was to create an artificial ruin, instantly time-honored, the "Abbey ruin," which he thought was "like the Acropolis at Athens." King diligently added to his ruins during the thirties, but he didn't make his prize catch until 1941. On the dark day following the bombing of Westminster Hall, King sent a cable to Canada House in London. Blitzed London. The cable was SECRET AND MOST IMMEDIATE. It arrived at 10 p.m. and was promptly decoded. The prime minister wanted to know if Lester B. Pearson, then with the Canadian high commissioner's office in London, could immediately prevail upon the British to round up a few stones from bombed Westminster for his ruins at Kingsmere. An embarrassed Pearson put through the request and, to his surprise, it was not met with indignant refusal. On the contrary. Historic stones were shipped safely via submarine to add a new élan to Wee Willie's ruins.

It was in 1938 that King, now a confirmed spiritualist, first met Adolf Hitler and quickly recognized something of a kindred spirit, another leader profoundly devoted to his mother's memory and the value of *Judenfrei* real estate. I believe, he wrote in his diary, the world will yet come to see a great man, a mystic, in Hitler. He "will rank some day with Joan of Arc among the deliverers of his people, & if he is only careful may yet be the deliverer of Europe."

In 1924, friends of King gave him a dog, an Irish terrier called Pat, which he soon took to be a living symbol of his mother. Kneeling in prayer before his mother's portrait in 1931, "little Pat came up from the bedroom and licked my feet—dear little soul, he is almost human. I sometimes think he is a comforter dear mother has sent me, he is filled with her spirit of patience, and tenderness & love." Pat died in his arms in 1941, even as Willie sang aloud to him "Safe in the Arms of Jesus." "I kissed the little fellow as he lay there, told him of his having been faithful and true, of his having saved my soul, and being like God." Fortunately, another Irish terrier, Pat II, soon came into his life, and before going to bed, King and his little angel dog often used to chat together

137

about the Christ child and the animals in his crib. Of Pat II's death, on August 11, 1947, the prime minister of Canada wrote, "I felt as if he had died for me, that my sins might be forgiven me." His dog's death put him in mind of Christ's crucifixion. Pat II was buried near what King called "the Bethal Stone" at Kingsmere.

King's obsession with the position of the hands of the clock seems to have begun in 1918; he regarded it as auspicious if the hands were together, as in twelve o'clock, or in a straight line, as at six o'clock. By 1932 he was attending séances and consulting mediums in Canada, the United States, and England. He also went in for table-rapping, wherein it was revealed to him in 1933 that he had been predestined to become prime minister, the fate of Canada being in his hands. Leonardo da Vinci appeared at King's little table, as did Lorenzo de' Medici and Louis Pasteur, who was good enough to prescribe for little angel dog Pat's heart condition. Another visitor to King's table, the spirit of Sir Wilfrid Laurier, assured him that President Roosevelt loved him. "He will treat you like a prince." However, when Roosevelt and Churchill came to Canada for the Quebec conference during World War II, they wouldn't let Wee Willie anywhere near the big table, and only grudgingly allowed him to have his photograph taken with them. To be fair, however, Roosevelt proved to be a lot nicer after his death. He appeared before King, begging him not to retire, if only because, said the late president, he had the wisdom that Churchill lacked, as well as "the caution and the integral honesty that holds a country together." From time to time Willie's mum would appear to "my own dearest boy, my pride and joy, best of sons." Once she went on to introduce President Roosevelt to him. "Frank, as I call him." This time out, Frank pleaded with King to take a real rest, "knock off for at least a year." He also said that it was vital that King should write his memoirs, including "the important chapter, your firm faith in a future life, that you have evidence of it."

William Lyon Mackenzie King, the longest-serving prime minister in the history of the Commonwealth, survived both his dearest loves in this world, Pat I and Pat II, and passed on to the Big Kennel in the Sky on July 22, 1950. Just as he died, thunder and lightning and torrents of rain came without any warning. The rain fell only at Kingsmere, not in Ottawa.

King, who always presented himself as a man of very modest means, earned $7,000 a year when he first became a minister in 1909. On his retirement in 1948, his pay and allowances totaled $19,000 annually. And yet—and yet—miraculously, perhaps—he died leaving a fortune of over $750,000, and this did not include the Kingsmere estate, which he left to the nation.

Their Annual Day in honor of the scheming old fraud began, quite properly, at Kingsmere, the Jews getting in to ruin the whole place at last, with a champagne breakfast on the site of the "Abbey ruins." From there they moved on to pay their respects to Pat II, at the Bethal Stone, where they sang "Safe in the Arms of Jesus," but in Yiddish, this version being the inspiration of Mickey Stein.

Then they adjourned to Laurier House.

Laurier House was left to Wee Willie by Sir Wilfrid Laurier's widow in 1922. Friends of King's clubbed together to renovate and refurbish the house for him before he moved in a year later. As usual, the gentlemen of the Mackenzie King Memorial Society began their tour of the residence from which Canada had once been governed with a visit to the dining room, the table set exactly as King had liked it. "At this table," the guide solemnly declared, "sat all past presidents of the United States, as well as Shirley Temple."

In the living room, they stood to marvel at the crystal ball that still rested on the piano, and the painting of King's mum, where he had knelt to pray nightly.

Next they assembled in their private dining room in the Château Laurier to drink more champagne. A disgruntled Seymour abruptly demanded, "How long have you known that Auden was a queer?"

"I don't know," Joshua replied, surprised. "For years, I guess. Why?"

"First Dostoevsky and then that little Eliot, whose lines I once committed to memory, turn out to be *farbrinter* anti-Semites, and now I find out that Auden, my Auden, has been a cocksucker all these years. 'Lay your sleeping head, my love,' yeah, but you know where. What can you put your trust in these days?"

Lennie Fisher, his manner urgent, strongly recommended ITT.

Seymour, just married the previous summer, was showing all the out-of-towners, including Joshua, photographs of his wife, apologizing each time. "I know it's a corny thing to do, but . . ."

At the time, Seymour was still running his bookshop on University Street, roosting in the apartment upstairs. If an

139

unsuspecting matron wandered in and asked for Taylor Caldwell's *Dear and Glorious Physician*, he would explode, "This is a bookshop, madame, not a shit-bin. You want shit, shop at Burton's. Go." But he would thrust Kafka on certain students, giving it away, saying they needed it. He was enjoying himself in the bookshop, but he couldn't earn a living there. He was married now and in three years he would be thirty. Imagine, he said, thirty. "My father pops into the shop once a week and says, 'So, enough of this foolishness. Who did I build the business for if not for you?' "

"What are you going to do?"

"Molly's great, you know. I'm really serious about this marriage. She says I can do whatever I want."

"And you?"

"I'm weak, Josh. I really hate being without money. But knitwear? With an M.A. in English lit?"

Lennie Fisher floated from group to group, urging everybody to get into Xerox now.

Max Birenbaum, whose wife was expecting again within a week, started each time the phone rang. "If it's for me, I'm right here."

Bobby Gross, prospering as a lawyer, was thinking of buying a house in Westmount.

"You go right ahead," Max said, "but I'll never step in there. Count on it."

"You make that a promise," Bobby said, "and I'll buy."

Then, arms around each other, Max and Bobby sang "Hail, Comrade Stalin," followed by "A Company Union Is a No Good Union."

A squinting, tight-lipped Eli Seligson drove Joshua into a corner to tell him that he had read his article on the Aldermaston march in *Esquire* and, so far as he was concerned, it was sentimental, left-wing horseshit. "The others may be impressed, but not me. You know what your problem is? You think you're too good for us."

"Eli, baby, I *am* too good for you."

"Boy, are you ever a *putz*. Is it true that you're coming back to live here?"

"Yes. Next year, probably."

"And you're writing a book about the Spanish Civil War, of all things?"

"Yes."

"So what?"

Al Roth, who was in real estate, advised all of them, no matter where they lived, to stop burning money on rent. He enjoined them to get out of their apartments and buy houses right now. "Borrow, if you haven't got the cash. You can't go wrong. Especially in Montreal."

Talk about money naturally led to speculation about their old classmate Izzy Singer. Izzy, wheeling and dealing before he even reached puberty, had—to everybody's chagrin, especially Seymour's—become a millionaire at last. He had, Joshua was told, first struck it rich six years earlier, peddling appliances. Izzy had taken to following the ice-truck down Clark, St. Urbain, and Waverly. Whenever the ice-truck stopped, Izzy bounded after, pounding on the door. "Why pay a dollar-eighty-five a week for ice, Missus, when I can let you have a fridge on installments for two dollars a week? Delivery this afternoon."

Seymour, warming to his pet hate, contributed a Singer anecdote of his own: "You'll never believe this, but when he was at McGill, that *grauber*, he actually took a couple of courses in architecture, not that he ever wanted to be one, that *paskudnyak*, but so that he'd know enough that they couldn't cheat him when he became a developer. Anyway, so help me God, he wrote a paper on the construction of Notre Dame, estimating from sources available the cost of the cathedral per cubic foot, and its present value as a Paris tourist attraction, arguing that it had, on balance, been a sound investment."

Nobody believed Seymour, but what was beyond dispute was that from bartering in war savings stamps in FFHS, through appliances and real estate deals, Izzy had graduated to speculation in oil and natural gas and uranium.

Morty Zipper, who worked three nights a week in a free clinic in Point St. Charles, shook his head, dismayed. "I treat kids there who are still suffering from rickets."

As they imbibed still more champagne, they turned to the serious business of the society. Joshua rose to read aloud the letter he had written to Clarence Campbell, President of the National Hockey League:

"Dear Sir, The undersigned represent a group of respectable businessmen, civil servants, professionals, and artists who convene once a year to celebrate the memory of that great political leader and statesman, William Lyon Mackenzie King—"

"Gentlemen," Seymour bellowed, raising his glass, "I give you Mackenzie King."

Everybody at the table stood up and raised his glass.

141

"—We are not a political group, but come from all parties—"

"Except the Communist Party, it goes without saying, Comrades."

"Hear! Hear!"

"—and we have only one motive: patriotism."

"Gut gezukt."

"Each year, in order better to perpetuate the late great one's memory, we try to come up with a suitable trophy or award. One year it was a dog show prize (see enclosed advertisement from *Dogs in Canada*) for the hound that best personified Pat II's godliness and bore the most striking resemblance to Mr. King's beloved mum, Isabel Grace Mackenzie. Another year, honoring yet another deeply felt interest of the late great one, it was the Mackenzie King Memorial Hooker Award, offered to two prostitutes—one English- and one French-speaking, each award worth $500—for bringing the most intense religious fervor to their work. This year," Joshua continued, "we intend to dig deeper into our collective pockets. We take great pleasure in offering the National Hockey League a trophy, sweetened, as it were, by a purse of $1,000: The William Lyon Mackenzie King Memorial Trophy."

Everybody thumped the table, and yet another toast was proposed to the late great one.

"This trophy, to be presented at the end of each season, would go to the player who, in his efforts on ice, most exemplified the undying spirit of Mackenzie King.

"Obviously, the player we have in mind would not be a high scorer, a natural star, but rather a plodder who overcomes with effort and cunning a conspicuous lack of talent, intelligence, or grace. In the nature of things, he would have to be a player who has been in the league for at least ten years, unnoticed, unheralded, but persevering. The fellow we have in mind spears when the referee has his back turned, trips an opposing player if he can get away with it, but unfailingly backs down from a fight. Preferably, he would be a man who respects his mother even more than the coach, and has a firm faith in the world-to-come. If he is on the ice when a goal is scored for his side, he argues for an assist on the play. If he is on the ice when a goal is scored by the opposition, he promptly disowns responsibility. Above all, he is a vengeful winner and a sore loser. He has no close relationships with any of his teammates. Loyalty is unknown to him. Forced into a quick decision on ice, in the heat of play, he

142

neither opts for the possibly inspired but risky choice nor stands tall and resolute on the blue line. He avoids making any decision whatsoever, heading for the safety of the bench. All the same, when many a more talented player has retired, legs gone, or has been removed from the fray in his prime through injury, our Mackenzie King Memorial Trophy winner will still be out there skating. Skating away from trouble. Persevering.

"Your Canadianism undoubted, your patriotism proven in two world wars, we hope, Mr. Campbell, that you will give this award every serious consideration. Should more information be required, or a meeting be considered advisable, we are, sir, at your service. Respectfully, Joshua Shapiro, Secretary, The Mackenzie King Memorial Society."

The letter was resoundingly applauded and approved, and Seymour Kaplan moved that it be mailed to Mr. Campbell at once.

Then a candidate was proposed for a Mackenzie King Memorial Award, one of the many statuettes of the late great one and Pat II which had been made for them by Henry Birks: Lester B. Pearson, the head of External Affairs.

Max Birenbaum made the case for Mr. Pearson. "In a recent interview," he said, "Mr. Pearson was asked if after all his years as a diplomat, and head of external affairs, he had anything to be ashamed of. His reply was at once filled with candor and quintessentially Canadian. Yes, he said, I have certainly done some things I later regretted. *I cheated in geography class when I was in grade six or seven, I think, and I've never forgotten it.*"

The award was approved without a dissenting vote.

Following dinner, chaos. Against a background of records by Artie Shaw, Tommy Dorsey, Glenn Miller, and the rest, they began to reminisce about the old days at FFHS. Strappings were reenacted, basketball games played again. Petting sessions with Bessie Orbach were savored once more. Mickey Stein won the yo-yo contest yet again, walking the dog, going round the world, and eating spaghetti without faltering, scooping up a well-deserved pot of $200. Then they split into two sides and, taking an empty bottle of Mumm's for a puck, started to replay the Stanley Cup Final of 1947, which led to an expression of displeasure by the management of the Château. The house detective paid them a visit. "Now, come on," he said, "you're all grown-up men here."

"Don't judge us too harshly," Joshua replied.

Saner voices mollified the house detective. They promised

to be good and adjourn within the hour. And then somebody, fortunately, remembered the birthday cake, thirty candles for Al Roth, the third of their number to reach such a debilitating age.

Al blew out the candles. And then, tears welling in his eyes, proclaimed, "You're the best fucking bunch of guys anybody could have ever been to school with, and if any of you come to Toronto on a visit, you're staying at my place. No hotels. I won't hear of it."

Eli Seligson cornered Joshua again. "There's something I want to tell you," he said, swaying.

"Go ahead."

"I never liked you."

Finally, inevitably, Joshua called for silence and went to the record player and put on his cherished album of songs by the men of the International Brigades, ending with "Los Quatro Generales." They raised their glasses one more time, drinking a solemn toast to the men who had died in Spain. Those who had clung like burrs to the long expresses that lurched through the unjust lands, through the night, through the alpine tunnel. They who had walked the passes, come to present their lives.

4

After weeks of carousing on Ibiza, taking in the cockfights with Juanito and his cronies, staggering out of Rosita's at dawn, Joshua certainly couldn't claim to be paddling his own canoe through the storms of temptation. There was simply no stroke, stroke, stroke. The truth was, he had to admit, he was not so much interested in writing as in being a writer. Somebody well known. But his twenty-first birthday had come and gone and he was not yet famous. He not only embraced unclean women, but gorged himself on forbidden foods: *gambas, calamares*, spider crab. Only eight years after his bar-mitzvah, whorehouse orgies.

Gehenna beckoned.

But to be fair to himself, his bar-mitzvah, he recalled, had not exactly got him off to an auspicious start if he was meant to mature into an observant Jew.

"Don't worry, kiddo," his mother had said. "You're going to have a party. Oh boy, are you ever going to have a party!"

In the morning, she had actually roused herself to make

144

him breakfast and, charged with enthusiasm, she said, "Make me a list."

"Of what?"

"The boys you want for your party."

"Forget it," he said.

"I'm going to be a good mother from now on, Josh. No more fucking with Ryan." And then, looking at him quizzically, she added, "Something tells me it upsets you."

"I don't want a party."

"Why not?"

"What would we do?"

"Well, we won't play pin-the-tail-on-the-donkey or parcheesi. It's going to be a surprise."

When he came home from school he found his mother on her knees, scrubbing the floors. The beds had been made, the dishes washed. The garbage was ready to be carted out. "You have an appointment with Mandelcorn for six o'clock. He's going to teach you all the mumbo-jumbo you need for the synagogue. If he asks if we eat kosher here, you say yes," and once more she demanded a list of boys.

A week before his bar-mitzvah she decorated the hall with crepe paper and Chinese lanterns. Streamers ran from wall to wall in the living room. Balloons hung from every light fixture.

Gifts began to arrive. Uncle Harvey sent phylacteries, a silver wine goblet, and $25 in war savings certificates. Euclid delivered Ed Ryan's peace offering—a sharkskin windbreaker, THE CHAMP embossed on the back, the pockets stuffed with silver dollars. Colucci sent books: a biography of Marconi, an illustrated history of the Jewish people, and a collection of Winston Churchill's speeches. There was also a case of V.O. in a box tied with a ribbon.

Saturday morning, in the synagogue, Joshua stumbled through the blessings he was obliged to pronounce, older members of the congregation shaking their heads, amazed that anyone, even a gangster's boy, could be so ignorant. And what about the mother? A Leventhal girl. Her eyelashes false, her cheeks rouged. Reeking of perfume.

No sooner did they get home than his mother wiggled out of her dress, buttoned on a housecoat, and, consulting her newly acquired cookbook, set to work in the kitchen. Louis Armstrong belted out "The Saints Go Marching In" as her marble cake was mixed and then slapped into the oven. She poured what looked like a half-bottle of kirsch into her fruit salad. Onions flew in all directions as, bolstered with Dewar's, she started in on the chopped liver. Meatballs, varying a good deal in size, were pitched into a pan and then stacked on a platter like cannonballs. Her sponge cake failed to rise, her cheese pie obstinately refused to set. Boiled chicken pieces, churning in fat, bounced back from her probing fork again and again. Burnt edges had to be scraped off her chocolate chip cookies.

Of the twenty boys Joshua had invited to his party the following afternoon, only twelve turned up—the others, he gathered, having been forbidden to attend. Seymour Kaplan was there, of course, so were Morty Zipper, Mickey Stein, Bernie Zucker, Bobby Gross, Max Birenbaum, Yossel Kugelman, his cousin Sheldon, and, to his surprise, Eli Seligson and Izzy Singer. They were all combed and shined, wearing their High Holiday suits, but Joshua could see at once that they were ill at ease. Most of them did not know what to expect. Neither did Joshua, decidedly apprehensive, as his mother had been into the Dewar's again since shortly after breakfast, her mood menacingly cheerful.

The boys had been gathered in the living room for only half an hour, increasingly fidgety, when it became obvious to them that there was not going to be a movie or whatever. In fact, it seemed like there was going to be absolutely nothing to do.

"Who would like to play Information, Please?" his mother called out cheerily.

Groans and moans.

"What about sardines?"

"Hey, we're not kids any more," Mickey admonished her.

"Good. That's what I thought. All right, Josh. Draw the blinds."

Oh boy, a movie after all.

But Joshua knew different, because she was already screwing in the red light bulb that throbbed on and off.

"Maw, you can't."

"That's what they said to the Wright Brothers."

"They wouldn't understand."

"Shettup and put on the record."

"Maw, please."

"Do as I ask. Come on, Josh."

So he put on "Snake Hips."

"Now don't anybody move," his mother said, running off.

The baffled boys sat on the floor, as instructed. Even as they were becoming restless, there was a rap on the door and Joshua started playing "Snake Hips" again. Then the door

146

opened enough to allow a long black-stockinged leg ending in a spike-heeled shoe to come slithering through. It was withdrawn just as swiftly, as if bitten, making the startled boys wonder if it had been an apparition. Then it came creeping through again. The leg, seemingly disembodied, was now being caressed by a feathery pink fan. Higher, higher. The spike-heeled shoe slipped off to reveal toenails painted green. The leg rubbed longingly against the doorknob. It slid away, rose again. With maddening slowness the door opened to throbbing drums, a pulsating red light, and in glided Joshua's mother, her eyes saying peekaboo behind feathery fans. Silver stars had been pasted to her legs. She wore a see-through scarlet blouse and a black skirt slit to her thighs.

"I've got to go home," Izzy Singer called out, petrified, diving for his coat and fleeing the house.

"Snake Hips" started yet again and, with a wicked wink of a loosening false eyelash, Mrs. Shapiro turned her back to the boys. Hands on her knees, she gyrated her upturned ass at them. She straightened up, unzipping her skirt, wiggling out of it. Next she peeled off her blouse, letting it float to the floor. Then she whirled around to confront the boys in mock horror. Her ruby-red lips forming an enormous outraged *O*, arms folded saucily over her breasts, legs squeezed together. Frozen there, reduced to panties, belt, and stockings, she suddenly hissed at Joshua: "Now."

"What?"

"Now, I said."

Remembering, Joshua slipped two fingers into his mouth to whistle, he stamped his feet, and the boys quickly followed suit.

Now those wanton fans, with a will of their own, began to stroke her, allowing the briefest of peeks at the perkiest breasts on any mother on the street.

Tears rolled down Eli Seligson's cheeks. Sheldon was drenched in sweat. But the others simply squatted there, stunned, some with their mouths open, as, responding to the beat of the drums, she began to bump and grind to a finale.

And, suddenly, the record was done. Mrs. Shapiro slipped into her housecoat, switched on the lights, lit a Pall Mall, retrieved her Dewar's and a splash from a table, and sat down on a stool to chat with her audience. "Did you like it?" she asked.

A flushed Seymour leaped up to applaud.

"I'm turning pro, you know. I'm going to be playing at the Roxy here."

147

Holy shit, Joshua thought.

"Now I want everybody who got a hard-on watching my act to be a good boy and put up his hand."

Seymour's hand shot up.

"Oh, come on, boys, I couldn't have been that lousy."

Three more hands were raised, then two more.

"Joshua doesn't count, because I'm his mother and it wouldn't be according to Hoyle."

5

Going to bed without Pauline curled into him made him grieve, it was something he could not get used to. But he refused to take Valium or anything like that to encourage sleep. Instead he found that at least once a week there was nothing for it like a stiff J&B taken with his favorite CBC-TV public affairs program. Oh, what a solemn and hard-hitting bunch his rivals were out there in Toronto. Our moral guardians, unfailingly vigilant, who could be counted on for an hour of weekly outrage, fitting nicely into four fifteen-minute slots. Uncompromising they were in pursuit of garage mechanics who replaced *perfectly good mufflers* in your car. Or slickers who overcharged to inject plastic hairs *that wouldn't last* into bald heads. Or language schools that made *false promises* to immigrants. If there were a deaf-mute being denied employment as a hospital nurse or a blind man, preferably Indian, being turned down for work in an airport control tower, their fearless investigators ferreted out the perpetrators of such rank social injustice, no matter how powerful, and made it really hot for them. Some nights—vintage nights—they actually got to interview real Mafia hit men or dope smugglers, the backs of their heads to the camera, who claimed there were cops who *took bribes.*

But tonight it was politics. American cultural domination of our tundra. Probing cameras caught out corner drugstores which displayed the latest Harold Robbins but *no Canadian poets* on their paperback racks; they zoomed in on schoolchildren, *our kids*, who knew who the Fonz was but had never heard of Mackenzie King. And, suddenly—hello, hello— there he was, Pauline's first husband filling the screen, the wretched Colin Fraser. Colin, a fiery nationalist, had returned from London years ago to become curator of the rare Canadiana collection at Rocky Mountain University and, not being one to hold a personal grudge, he had paid Joshua $10,000 for the manuscript of *The Volunteers*, which was rather more than Joshua had earned in royalties during the first year of the book's publication. And now Colin, fulminating on camera, revealed that innocent Canadian children were being taught geography *from a text that included a photograph of an American rather than a homebred dinosaur.* This was more than loose talk, it could be backed up by hard fact. Colin held up the picture for everybody to see. Sneaky imperialist eyes, shrewd Yankee mouth.

Joshua, heaving with laughter, was genuinely put off when the front doorbell rang, interrupting his enjoyment of Colin.

"I just happened to be passing by," McMaster said, "I saw your lights . . ."

"I haven't been able to read your manuscript yet. I'm sorry, Stu."

But he was already inside the door and Joshua found himself pouring drinks in the living room, wondering why McMaster was staring at his dressing gown. "Oh," he groaned, remembering. "Don't worry, honey. I'm wearing men's underwear tonight. After all, it's Wednesday, isn't it?"

McMaster coughed dryly. "Hey, this sofa is what I call a *real* antique. It must have set you back thousands. Where'd you find it?"

"You'd have to ask Pauline."

McMaster was now admiring an end table. "Did she find this as well?"

"At an auction."

"Good for her. Great investment. Hey, Seymour Kaplan, ah, you did say he was a buddy of yours. Right?"

Right right.

"Tell him if at his age he's still got to neck with teenage *shiksas*, not to pick The Lookout. There's lots of chemicals changing hands among the children of The Chosen there, and we're watching it."

"Stu, has it ever occurred to you that you might be an anti-Semite?"

"Sweet Jesus, no. Hell, you're looking at the friendly neighborhood police officer who has been put in charge of finding the demon housebreaker of Westmount, which makes me a protector of your people, kind of."

"Oh, really. Why?"

"Because so far he has only hit kosher houses."

"Obviously," Joshua said, nudging him, "he knows in

149

which houses gold bars are most likely to be buried between the floorboards."

"You said it, not me. But this kook marches to a different drummer. He never takes anything."

"Maybe he's some kind of psycho."

"Maybe," McMaster said, deftly changing the subject, only to start in on Quebec again. "Doesn't it strike you as odd," he said, "that when you hear all the solutions being offered, the most obvious one has yet to be mentioned?"

"And what's that?"

"Civil war."

St. Denis Street was the city's dividing line.

East of St. Denis, where most of the French Canadians were rooted, euphoria had reigned ever since the Parti Québécois had come to power on November 15, 1976. As far as that party's young activists were concerned, the reconquest had begun and now it would be the turn of the English-speaking to make bricks out of straw. But in the West End, where the English-speaking had ruled with impunity for years, each day's news was more disheartening than the last. Joshua salvaged some joy out of imagining the terrified burghers of Upper Westmount waking each morning to read in the *Gazette* that yet another company's head office had done a midnight flit, its spokesman saying, "The move of our head office to Toronto has been on the drawing board for years and has nothing to do with the present political atmosphere in Quebec."

Aglow with ill will, Joshua sought out Pinsky on Summit Circle. "Well, Irving, just in case you didn't know, the value of your house has dropped twenty percent. So far."

Pinsky's Russian wolfhound lifted a leg, but daintily, in deference to his master, to pee against a fire hydrant.

"And what about yours?" he asked heavily.

"Down there? Below the hill? What's a house worth in the best of times? Bupkas. Besides, it's mortgaged to the hilt and, if you ask me, René Lévesque's not such a bad fellow."

"Ha. I'll remind you of that a month from now when you're still scraping the shit off your face. Take it from me, French Canadians are all alike. Lazy, stupid, corrupt, self-pitying, and, oh yes, bigoted, each one an anti-Semite," and he went on to enumerate a list of old schoolmates who were packing or had already departed.

Joshua had been away, out in California, the night the PQ had swept into office. On his return to town, Max Birenbaum explained, "After the election results came in, you could see Lévesque's followers on TV, in the Paul Sauvé Arena, out of their skulls with joy, and I swear there were old Jews so scared they moved their furniture against the door. The next morning you had to wait in line to get into your safety deposit box. People were removing the goodies and driving to Cornwall or Plattsburgh with them."

Max, now that he had married again, was in no position to remove most of his goodies. His newly acquired goodies. The ineffable Tanya, his embarrassing bride, had bought them a new house and turned it into a showplace, featured in Shaar Hashomayim's annual "Open House" tour. Pauline, feigning interest, had sweet-talked a copy of the listing out of Tanya, passing it to Joshua: "On turning the corner of Upper Belmont, on to Sunnyside, you see and practically fall upon the stunning stone home with the breath-taking Tudor style façade, a reminder of a past age, and you may imagine as you enter, that beyond the large entrance, you will see the Knights of the Round Table, a large dining table near a great hearth and unique antique pieces."

At an anniversary dinner party in Max Birenbaum's mansion, a year to the night after the PQ's astonishing electoral victory, everybody was still in a turmoil. The rats, who had made contingency plans long ago, had been fully expected to desert the sinking ship; but, come 1977, even the mice had begun to scrabble after, making for Ontari-ari-ario or Florida. So there were uneasy jokes at the table about the coming referendum and the utter looniness of an independent Quebec. Tranquil Canada dismembered. Yes, yes, Barbara said, plump cheeks glowing, maybe so, certainly we have been made to feel insecure, but how exciting it must be to be young and French Canadian right now.

Thirty years earlier, on their third date, Joshua had managed to unsnap Barbara's brassiere on a bench in Outremont Park. He was the first, she had assured him. Now, after her mastectomy, she counseled others in the hospital, a volunteer worker.

O Barbara Barbara.

Seymour wakened from a cognac-inspired reverie all his own to startle the company by saying with immense feeling, "I wish I had been old enough to fight in the Spanish Civil War."

Portly, moon-faced Seymour was in knitwear, his father's business. Countering the bewildered looks around the table,

151

he said slowly, "Like my friend the so-called writer here, I wanted to fight on the Ebro."

Even as the rest of them continued to argue heatedly about Quebec, inconsolable Seymour, sodden Seymour, well into another snifter of cognac, interrupted again. "I wanted to fight on the Ebro. Come back with a wound, maybe. Nothing serious. I mean, not like Jake Barnes. But enough so that people would point me out even now. Sure he's in knitwear, but you know that limp, he got it in Spain. Do you understand?"

Joshua not only understood, he also grasped why Seymour was drinking so heavily.

Poor Seymour, who had never got to fight in Spain, was in deep trouble. Not over a KLM stewardess this time, but because of his indiscretion with Engel's wife, while Engel lay in a hospital bed, trying to pass a kidney stone.

"Engel's wife," Joshua had protested when he first heard, "I mean, how could you even be tempted by that—"

"You don't understand. You're not into sex like me. I climbed her because she was there. Like Everest."

Seymour, a compulsive philanderer, was totally unselective. His mouth full, squirting pickle juice, he ran his hand up the legs of mountainous waitresses in delicatessens, making them quake with laughter and feel good. Disembarking from the morning train to Ottawa, joining the breathless dash to the taxi stand, he had already picked out, en route, the good bet he would invite to share his ride to the Château Laurier. Seymour subscribed to a phone call club in Chicago. For fifty dollars a year, he was able to call a toll-free station and was given the numbers of ladies eager to receive obscene phone calls. He no sooner unfastened his seat belt on the Eastern flight to New York than he was at the rear of the airplane, whispering indecencies into the stewardess's ear, making her flush with pleasure. He bantered with long-distance operators and kept a poste restante box in a downtown Post Office. On steamy nights, he parked at the Westmount Lookout and necked with buyers' secretaries from Eaton's, the Bay, and even Miracle Mart. Motel desk clerks in the Laurentians, the Adirondacks, and Cape Cod, accustomed to having Seymour register with any number of "Mrs. Kaplans," shook their heads in admiration as he moseyed up to the desk with yet another moistening wife in tow. His mother's widowed friends suffered palpitations, they melted in his arms, when he deigned to visit. If his fifteen-year-old daughter brought home classmates after school to listen to acid rock records in the furnished basement, Seymour flung his copy of *Hustler* aside, scooted downstairs, and taught them how to do the boogie-woogie. He had membership cards for all the most modish discos.

From the beginning, Seymour had been incredibly adroit at avoiding discovery. A Machiavelli among adulterers, Joshua readily agreed, once Seymour had told him about his first run-in with his wife. He had only been married to Molly for two years when he had come home from the office one night, ashen-faced, grim, not saying a word all through dinner.

"What's wrong?" she asked.

"I don't want to talk about it."

"Is it something I've done?"

"Ha," he barked, thrusting the letter at her. Anonymous. Printed. YOUR WIFE HAS A LOVER.

"Oh my," Molly exclaimed, a hand held to her cheek.

"How could you do such a thing to me?"

"Do what? You crazy fool. Who sent you this?"

"How in the hell would I know?"

"But you take their word over mine?"

"How long has this been going on?"

"Oh boy, could you ever teach Senator McCarthy lessons!"

"If I'm inadequate, tell me," he raged, simulating tears.

"Oh, Seymour, my poor darling. There's not a word of truth in it."

"There have been phone calls too. At the office. They say, 'Your wife is being banged black-and-blue on Tuesday afternoons,' and they hang up. Or 'Molly sucks,' and they hang up."

"But I'd never do such a thing. Feh!"

"Not at home, you mean. Not for your husband."

"We're not going through that again. Please, Seymour. And on Tuesday afternoons, as it so happens, I go to my social psychiatry class."

"And afterwards," he said, "you blow the instructor in some cheap motel. For me, you wouldn't even wear that lingerie I bought you."

"It's filth, it's for a whore. I swear, Seymour, you are the only man who has ever touched me."

"Who is it? Somebody who laughs behind my back at parties?"

"Are you crazy?"

"Bobby Gross!"

She began to cry. "I swear on Larry's head I've never been unfaithful to you."

But, her tears notwithstanding, he slept on the living room sofa that night, and the next, although she came to visit him, appearing in her flannel nightie. "I tried to get into those undies, but they're too small, the seam split. Look, baby!"

She was wearing the garters, pinching into her plump quivering red flesh just above the knees, as high as she could force them to fit.

"Hotcha hotcha," he said.

Only then did he notice that she had brought a basin of hot water with her, as well as a bar of soap and a towel. "What are you going to do?" he asked, alarmed.

"I'll do it for you if it's so important, but I'm going to give it a good scrubbing first and you've got to promise to pull it out before you're ready to shoot."

Seymour began to giggle.

"Look, mister, I'm not swallowing any of it. I'd only be sick."

Roaring, Seymour buried his head in his pillow.

"What's so funny?"

"Are you really having an affair?"

"No. I swear," she said. And pale, resolute, she added, "Tell me when you're tumescent and I'll start."

"Listen," he said, feeling himself shrivel down there as he sat up, "I'm hungry. Why don't we have an omelet instead? With lox and onions."

And the next morning, when the registered letter came for her from Miss O'Hara, just as that bitch had threatened, he hid behind his *Gazette* as she read it, her cheeks burning red.

"Bad news?" he asked, finally.

"Maybe I'm not the only one playing around," she sang out.

"What are you talking about?" he charged, outraged.

"You ought to read this, Mr. *Playboy* subscriber. I've never read such *shmutz*."

He grabbed it. "Holy shit! Do you know her?" he asked, struggling with the signature. "Sally O'Hare?"

"O'Hara. And do *you* know her, is more important."

"I've never heard of her in my life. You've got to believe me, Molly."

"I believe you."

He stared at her, stumped.

"And I didn't jump down your throat, did I?"

"No, dear."

"I didn't insult you with accusations based on no evidence but the word of a total stranger?"

"No, dear."

"Give it here," she said, crumpling it into a ball and throwing it in the garbage. Where it belonged, she said.

"It's incredible," Seymour ventured. "Some sex nut has obviously got it in for both of us."

She seemed pensive.

"Some psychotic," he continued. "Who knows? Maybe one of those squinty-eyed types in your social psychiatry class has the hots for you, and he's trying to stir up trouble between us."

"Wasn't there a Sally O'Hara on your switchboard?"

"Oh, you are sadly mistaken. Never," he said. "And, listen darling, I've been holding back. I've been getting more obscene phone calls about you. Right here. Where the kids could pick up the phone. So I've arranged to have our number changed. Temporarily, we're going to be unlisted."

"Isn't that a bit drastic?"

"*The kids*, Molly."

But this time Seymour had been caught with his pants down. Literally. By Engel's father-in-law, who had a key to the front door and had come to surprise his daughter with a sack of oranges he had coddled all the way from Miami, only to find her naked and moaning on the living room deep-pile wall-to-wall carpet, Seymour humping away, her legs straining heavenwards. The grizzled old man had cried out and began to pelt Seymour's bare ass with the oranges, the sack tearing, fruit flying everywhere. The tale had carried. From Côte St. Luc through Ville St. Laurent to Westmount. And Molly was unforgiving.

Throughout dinner at Max Birenbaum's she glared at him, her eyes red and swollen, interrupting his stories with deprecating remarks. "Spain yet. Sure."

Seymour, not so much contrite as seething, arranged for Joshua to meet him for lunch at Moishe's the following afternoon.

"Shit," he said, joining him late, "you know what happened to me this morning?"

Joshua ordered another Bloody Mary.

"Larry came round to the office, he wanted to talk."

Larry, Seymour's eighteen-year-old son, lived in a cold-water flat on Jeanne-Mance Street. He was with an acid rock group.

" 'Dad,' he said to me, 'I've been having an affair with an older woman.' 'How old?' I asked. 'Twenty-five,' he said. Holy shit, you know what's wrong with today's young? They advertise. They ram it into your face every chance they get. We didn't taunt our elders with our marvelous young bodies."

"We were honeys."

"My grandmother," Seymour said, "used to say, 'The years fly past, but the days are long.' "

Seymour was becoming heavy, morose, awash in self-pity.

"Molly giving you a rough time?" Joshua asked.

"Aw, that's going to be O.K.," and, in his most earnest voice, he added, "I've promised to stop fucking around."

"And how are you going to manage that?"

"Don't *you* start in on me, old buddy."

"Seymour, you don't understand. I'm a fan."

"Well, that's over. *Finito.* You are looking at a man who has developed a foolproof system for fidelity."

"Oh, really?"

"You're not going to believe this," he said. "Come." And he led him right into the men's room. "Lock the door."

"What for?"

"Lock the fucking door."

As soon as Joshua locked it, a beaming Seymour dropped his trousers. He was wearing black satin panties with a delicate lace trim.

"Wow," Joshua said, whistling.

"You can look, but you mustn't touch." Seymour wiggled his bum. "What do you think?"

"Think? Who can think? I'm trying to control myself."

"Seriously now, you'd think I was a faggot," he pleaded, "wouldn't you?"

Joshua refused to commit himself.

"Sure you would," he insisted. "Anybody would. Don't you see, you prick?"

"See what?"

"No matter how horny I get, or who I pick up wherever, I'd never pull down my pants so long as I was wearing these. Why, they're ridiculous. I'd be a laughingstock. It's my chastity belt," he said. "Absolutely foolproof."

One double cognac followed another, it was 3:30, and still they sat in the restaurant, reminiscing.

"Hey," Seymour asked, grinning, "whatever happened to Monique?"

In a foolish, drunken moment, Joshua had once been sufficiently indiscreet to tell Seymour something about Monique, and how a portrait of her in the nude had once turned up in London. Pauline and Joshua had been invited to a *vernissage* and there it was, hanging on the wall. Monique nude, circa

1953. Lying on his sofa in Tourrettes-sur-Loup. Reconstructing the room beyond the painting's perimeters, Joshua recalled his library, his battered Royal portable, and that the painting had been done only months after he had been obliged to flee Spain.

"If I had been you," Seymour said, "I would have bought the painting on the spot and hung it over my living room fireplace."

"That's because you're such a pig, Seymour."

"Yeah. Right. Have you read that La Pasionaria may be allowed back into Spain?"

"Yes. Imagine. After all these years."

"Vale más morir de pies que vivir de rodillas."

"Sí, chaver."

Ibiza, Joshua thought, strolling down the Main.

Two recurring nightmares bit into his sleep in those days. In one of them, Pauline was leaving him for a Golden Goy. Captain Cleancut. "Now that I've found out what you're really like," she said. "Intellectually bankrupt. A political fraud. Peddling yourself on TV. Unable to even turn out a column any more without leaning on your thesaurus. Telling the same tired old stories at dinner parties again and again. Jewy to a fault, overtipping wherever we go. No hell in bed. An inadequate father. I'm leaving you."

"Wait. Hold it. Why did you marry me in the first place? Didn't you love me even then?"

"Prick. I didn't know at the time that you'd behaved like a coward on Ibiza. The truth is, I married you only to shock my father."

Right right.

In the other, he was twenty-one again. Confronting Dr. Dr. Mueller.

"If you think you can rob me of my manhood, you're out of your mind. I'm not running, Mueller. Neither will I allow you to screw the Freibergs. Because in the years ahead I'm going to fall in love with Pauline. We're going to have three children. I will not be ashamed. I'm a man, not a mouse. Understand?"

Ibiza, Ibiza.

6

When Joshua decided to move out of the waterfront hotel in Ibiza to the sleepy village of San Antonio Abad on the opposite shore, Juanito found him a villa there.

The most compelling man in San Antonio was Victorio, a carpenter who hunted for fish in the evening, armed only with a net, lead weights tied to its corners. Victorio, a sinewy little man, usually turned up at the waterfront at seven, and the professional fishermen seated on the terrace of the Café Joaquin would pick up their drinks and stroll down to the waterside to watch him. Indifferent to his admirers, he would roll up his trousers and slip stealthily into the sea, hardly disturbing the waters around him. Crouching, peering, as he slid deeper into the water, watching for bubbles. And then suddenly, silently, he would twirl his net overhead like a sling and cast it. Once retrieved, the water around him began to foam and the net itself held a flopping fish of considerable size. Victorio would fling it onto the bank before he continued his hunt. Only after he had netted sufficient fish to feed his large family would he acknowledge his admirers with a shy nod, and then bundle his catch into his net and start out for his house somewhere in the surrounding hills.

There were, Joshua discovered, two Germans living in San Antonio: Frau Weiss, an emaciated retired civil servant, her glittering little eyes charged with ill will, and Dr. Dr. Mueller, the man whom he had seen disembark at Ibiza attended by such ceremony. Tall, lugubrious, with grieving blue eyes, a prominent broken nose that hadn't been mended just right, and a long thin mouth pulled downward at the sides, Dr. Dr. Mueller favored a white linen suit, the jacket slung over his shoulders continental-style. He hiked through the village each afternoon, hands clasped behind his back, slit of a mouth biting angrily on that ivory cigarette holder, and wherever he drifted he commanded a deference that infuriated Joshua. If, for instance, Joshua thrust his way to the counter of the crowded, fly-ridden butcher shop, he fully expected to have to compete with the clamoring women for service, but Dr. Dr. Mueller had only to slip through the beaded door for everybody to step back from the counter, it being understood that his needs took precedence. Officers saluted him on the road and peasants stepped aside to make his passage easier. Joshua and Dr. Dr. Mueller nodded to each other at the Café Formentor and in the post office, and then one night in Don Pedro's Bodega, Dr. Dr. Mueller invited him to his table. He stood Joshua to a *poron* of white wine and a dish of almonds, and asked him when he had last seen Paris. Joshua told him. "And you?" he asked.

"Ah, well," he replied, amused, "not as recently as you, young man. I understand that you are a Canadian."

"Yes."

"Sam Steele," he mused. "Gabriel Dumont. Dumont was a very good shot."

Baffled, Joshua asked what he was doing on Ibiza.

"I am writing my souvenirs," he said.

"About the war?" Joshua asked, fishing.

"The war doesn't interest me any more."

"Where did you serve?"

"I served on the front. And you?"

"I was too young."

"Your father, then?"

"He was too old."

"Of course," he said, and then, staggering a little, his smile lapsing, he added, "I want to relate something to you. It's all over for me, a closed book. Shawnee, Sioux, Creek, chew, nigger, it's all the same to me. I respect a man for what he is."

"Why are you called Dr. Dr. Mueller?"

"Obviously because I have two doctorates. Both awarded in Vienna. It is the custom there to use both titles. And where, may I ask, were you educated?"

"Oh, me? McGill, the Sorbonne, King's College, Cambridge."

Dr. Dr. Mueller was staying in a small hotel while the villa he had bought was being refurbished. An accomplished horseman, he was sometimes seen galloping in the hills, and it was rumored that he could camp out there for three days at a time, sleeping in the open. Drunk, they said. Come nightfall, he could usually be found drinking with the army officers at Don Pedro's. When Joshua entered they nodded cordially to him and immediately turned their backs, closing their circle at the bar. Fascists, Nazis. Then one night Dr. Dr. Mueller, obviously in the mood for some sport, did not so much invite Joshua over as summon him to report. "I am told," he said, "that the real reason you are here is to avoid doing military service in Korea."

"Yes," Joshua said.

159

Dr. Dr. Mueller frowned and slicked back his thin, nicotine-colored hair. "And your father," he asked, "who was too old to serve in the war, what does he do now?"

"He's a money-lender," Joshua shot right back, glaring at the officers. "And what, may I ask, does your father do?"

"My family comes from Dresden."

"I don't understand."

"The boy doesn't understand."

"The truth is, my father was a boxer."

"America," Dr. Dr. Mueller said, "has never produced a great boxer."

"What about Joe Louis?" Joshua countered tightly.

"Ah, but Joe Louis was an African man. He was not an American."

"He was good enough to take out Max Schmeling. June twenty-second, nineteen thirty-eight. Round one, Yankee Stadium. Art Donovan, referee."

Dr. Dr. Mueller reached for the cup of lie dice on the bar and thrust it at Joshua. "Are you a man or a mouse?" he asked.

So they rolled dice for who would pay for the next *poron* of wine, Joshua losing.

"Skoal," Dr. Dr. Mueller said, preparing to drink from the *poron.*

"L'chayim," Joshua replied.

Only a couple of weeks later a newly constructed hotel, its size modest, opened on the bay outside of San Antonio, presaging a tourist boom that was but two years away. The Casa del Sol, built on a golden beach fringed with palm trees, was owned by a tiny, bright-eyed Jewish couple, the aging Freibergs, who had been sufficiently prescient to quit Hamburg following Kristallnacht, abandoning everything, borrowing to open a brasserie in Paris, fleeing before the surging Wehrmacht once more, this time to Vichy, from there to Arles, then over the wintry Pyrenees on bleeding feet to Irun, skittering on to Burgos, then Barcelona and the black market, another stake accumulated, and now wagering everything on the future of a small hotel in the tranquil Baleares.

Among those invited to the opening-day fiesta at the Casa del Sol were the mayor and his black-suited entourage, bank functionaries, and the army officers. Joshua had just started into his first drink when he was surprised to see Dr. Dr. Mueller, Frau Weiss, and Mariano of the secret police saunter onto the terrace, taking the table adjoining his. Immediately, Freiberg summoned his wife and they conferred heatedly. He's going to refuse to serve him, Joshua thought, delighted. He's going to ask the bastard to leave. Instead, Freiberg, his manner obsequious, fetched a chilled bottle of Riesling for Dr. Dr. Mueller's table and called urgently for the *tapas* tray to be wheeled over. Incensed, Joshua got up to leave.

"One moment," Dr. Dr. Mueller called after him.

"Yes?"

"My villa is ready. I'm having people in for cocktails tomorrow. All types, you know. Perhaps you would come too?"

"I'd love to, Dr. Dr., but tomorrow is *Shabus*. The Jewish day of rest."

"So it is true," Mariano said.

"What's true?"

"You are a Jew?"

"Yes. Why?"

"I used to drink with one in Cordoba."

Joshua, cashing a check from the Toronto *Star Weekly* to make a foray onto the peninsula, had been to Cordoba the previous month.

Cordoba, birthplace of the incomparable Maimonides. The Rambam. Rabbi Moses ben Maimon, on whose grave in Tiberias on the shores of the Lake of Genesareth was inscribed: "From Moses to Moses there has been no one like Moses."

Maimonides, doctor and philosopher, the soaring Jewish intellect of the Middle Ages, wrote a book Joshua had come to cherish, *The Guide for the Perplexed*.

Men frequently think that the evils in the world are more numerous than the good things; many sayings and songs of nations dwell on this idea. They say that a good thing is found only exceptionally, whilst evil things are numerous and lasting. Not only common people make this mistake, but many who believe they are wise.

Maimonides, who was forced to flee Cordoba before the Moors when he was still a young man, journeyed on through Fez, Acre, and Jerusalem to Cairo, where he settled down as personal physician to the great Saladin. Subsequently he received a flattering offer from Palestine: "The King of the Franks in Ascalon," that is to say, Richard the Lionhearted of England, having already heard that there's nothing like a Jewish doctor, wanted him for *his* personal physician; but Maimonides declined.

Al-Razi, Maimonides observed in *The Guide for the Perplexed*, once wrote a well-known book, *On Metaphysics*.

Among other mad and foolish things, it contained the idea, discovered by him, that there exists more evil than good. For if the happiness of a man and his pleasure in the times of prosperity be compared with the mishaps that befall him—such as grief, acute pain, defects, paralysis of the limbs, fears, anxieties, and troubles—it would seem as if the existence of man is a punishment and a great evil for him.

Inflamed by the vicious sermons of the Archdeacon Ferran Martinez, a mob descended on the Juderia of Cordoba shortly after Ash Wednesday 1391, and reduced the quarter where Maimonides had been born to ashes. In a great *auto da fé* held in Cordoba in 1665, something like 400,000 maravedis was spent on the entertainments of the Inquisitors and their guests. Fifty-seven "Judaizers" were "relaxed," the three who held out to the last being roasted alive.

Forget it, Joshua thought, wandering through the old quarter. Don't be a grudgy type.

The Juderia was now a truly serene maze of impossibly narrow streets, overleaning houses starkly white, overflowing flowerpots dripping from every wall. Where once the residents had been candidates for burning, windows or delicate wrought-iron gates now opened onto inner courtyards, one more exquisite than another. But this legacy of beauty is for the enjoyment of others, Joshua thought resentfully, not me.

Canadian-born, he sometimes felt as if he were condemned to lope slant-shouldered through this world that confused him. One shoulder sloping downwards, groaning under the weight of his Jewish heritage (burnings on the market square, crazed Cossacks on the rampage, gas chambers, as well as Moses, Rabbi Akiba, and Maimonides); the other thrust heavenwards, yearning for an inheritance, any inheritance, weightier than the construction of a transcontinental railway, a reputation for honest trading, good skiing conditions.

The next morning he was in Madrid, seated on the perfectly made Plaza Mayor, sipping white wine and nibbling olives as the sun went down, feeling fine, just fine, when once more his Jewishness obtruded. Descending on him unbidden. Like a press.

Some four hundred years ago, during the Inquisition, they used to burn Jews here, right here, for sport.

Auto de fe.

The vast Plaza Mayor, its cobblestones nicely worn, its Herrera towers so lovely to contemplate, the porticoes perfection itself, had actually been the scene of numerous *autos publicos generales*, an event that once vied with bullfights in popular appeal. Many of the victims were *conversos,* Jews forcibly converted but suspected of continuing to practice their faith secretly, and usually the ceremony would be held on feast days in order to attract as large a crowd as possible, spiritual benefits being promised to all those present. There were once engravings extant which showed that two elaborate stagings were erected in the Plaza, one to accommodate those convicted and the other for the Inquisitors and their attendants. Pulpits and a temporary altar draped in black were set up between them, and windows looking out on the square went for large sums. The proceedings would begin at dawn with a procession through the narrow streets of the old city in which all the clergy would take part, headed by the standard of the Inquisition. Behind followed the condemned, those who were to escape the flames by confession and those who were for burning, the latter wearing a garment with a picture of devils thrusting heretics into the fires of hell. The spectacle, with sermons being delivered and sentences read, often spun out far into the night, and to light the brand which set the pyre on fire was considered a signal honor. First of all, however, spectators were encouraged to increase the sufferings of the condemned by lighting their beards, a practice known as "shaving the New Christians."

On this square, this outsized square, where Joshua had hoped to relax, soaking in the sun; on this square, on June 30, 1680, in the presence of Carlos II and his bride, Louise Marie d'Orléans, newly arrived from France, there was an *auto de fe* which began at six o'clock in the morning and lasted for fourteen hours. Sixty-seven penitents were reconciled. "It is said that one strikingly beautiful girl of about seventeen called out, as she passed the royal viewing stand: 'Noble Queen, cannot your royal presence save me from this? I sucked in my religion with my mother's milk; must I die for it?' In spite of this, the king himself set afire the brand which kindled the *quedamero* on which she perished."

The Jews were originally expelled from Spain by Ferdinand and Isabella in 1492, shortly after the Moors had been driven out of Granada. The king gave them three months in which to convert or leave. In 1495, an Italian Jewish traveler in Spain wrote in Hebrew:

One hundred and twenty thousand of them went to Portugal, according to a compact that a prominent man, Don Vidal bar Beneviste del Cavalleria, had made with the King of Portugal, and they paid one ducat for every soul, and the fourth part of all the merchandise they had carried thither; and he allowed them to stay in his country for six months. This King acted much worse toward them than the King of Spain, and after six months had elapsed he made slaves of all those that remained in his country, and banished seven hundred children to a remote island to settle it, and all of them died.

In 1497, the King compelled all the Jews of Portugal to become "New Christians," yet many of them continued to practice their old faith surreptitiously. In 1506, two thousand of these secret Jews were literally butchered and cremated in Lisbon. An account of the massacre, by the Catholic prelate Geronymo Osorio, has survived in Latin:

This cruel massacre was begun by five hundred, who were at last joined by several others. Transported with madness and boiling with rage, they fell upon the wretched Jews, of whom they killed great numbers, and threw many half alive into the flames. By this time several fires were kindled near the place where the first offenders had been burnt, for the canaille about the streets with eagerness and alacrity had brought fuel from all parts, that nothing might be wanting to execute this horrible design. . . . The shrieks and outcries of the women, together with the piteous supplications of the men, might, one would think, have softened the most savage heart into pity; but the actors in this horrid scene were so divested of humanity that they spared neither sex nor age, but wreaked their fury on all without distinction; so that above five hundred Jews were either killed or burnt that day.

The news of this massacre having reached the country, next day above a thousand men from the villages flocked into the city and joined the murderers, and the slaughter was renewed. . . .

Juanito, on discovering that Joshua was Jewish, slapped his cheek, amazed. The revelation emerged unforced one day as they bantered together on the sun-drenched terrace of a café. "Hey, you sit right there," Juanito said. "You wait. We've got one of those on Ibiza."

And, overriding Joshua's protests, he had scampered off with two other fishermen, across the street, charging into the bank, where they literally plucked out a teller from behind his till and frog-marched him to the café table. Carlos came from a family that had ostensibly been practicing Catholics for hundreds of years, but that was beside the point. He was one of those. He was an oily little man, scrawny, his skin walnut-brown, his eyes frightened now, and Joshua's immediate reaction was, You're not my brother, I'm not your keeper. Carlos refused the offer of a drink even as Juanito and his cronies hovered over them, boyishly pleased with their catch.

"Say something to each other in Jew," Juanito said.

"Go to hell," Joshua said.

"Come on."

Still, Joshua hesitated.

"You're a fake," Juanito hollered.

"Shema Yisrael," Carlos offered, "Adonai Elohainu, Adonai echad."

Joshua, unbidden tears welling in his eyes, recognized the phrase. Mandelcorn had taught it to him for his bar-mitzvah. My God, my God, he thought, I'm just being overwhelmed by Jews these days. First the Freibergs, now Carlos. But he was waiting outside the bank at closing time, and he took Carlos to a neighborhood café for coffee.

He was a "Marrano," he said—that is to say, a "pig," or secret Jew—whose family had been practicing the faith by stealth ever since the Inquisition. His family lived in a remote town perched atop a rocky hilltop in Majorca, and there were others like them there, maybe fifty. Officially parishioners of the Holy Family, they secretly ate unleavened bread, but only on the third day of Passover, so that no Christian informer could see them baking it on the traditional day of preparation. He told Joshua, his squeaky voice reduced to a whisper, "Every spring, one morning before the other villagers are awake, the secret worshippers sneak down to the riverbank and there they beat the waters with olive branches to celebrate the parting of the Red Sea. But that must seem crazy to you, coming from Canada. You can practice the religion openly there, can't you?"

"Yes," Joshua agreed uneasily, "but the truth is, I don't come from a very observant family."

His family, the amazing Carlos told him, had originally come from Toledo. His father still had the key to the front door of their Toledo home, a token of ownership that had been passed down through the generations. Tugging at Joshua's sleeve, he added, "It was our people, you know, who gave Toledo its name, 'Toledoth,' which means 'city of generations' in Hebrew." The city, he said, had originally been

165

settled by members of the Twelve Tribes. After Nebuchadnezzar's destruction of Jerusalem. Even the names of some neighboring villages had been derived from Israel. "Take, for instance, 'Aceca,' which in Hebrew means 'strong house.' Or 'Escalona,' from 'Askelon.' I am a Zionist. If I order another coffee," he asked, pressing Joshua's arm, "will you pay?"

"Yes. Certainly."

"I'm saving every penny. I'm going to emigrate to Israel one day. Would you mind if I had a pastry as well?"

"Oh, go ahead," Joshua said, irritated. "Just order it, will you?"

"If you don't mind my saying so—after all, I'm the older one—you shouldn't frequent the brothel. Those wretched girls carry disease."

Jews, Jews, Joshua thought, everywhere I go there are other Jews to advise me. Clutching. Claiming. I probably wouldn't even be safe in Senegal. Some big buck, his face reamed with tribal scars, his voice whiny, would drop out of his banana tree to grab my hand and say "Shalom Aleichem."

Meanwhile, there was Dr. Dr. Mueller to cope with.

Mueller and Joshua, in common with the few foreigners and the artillery officers billeted in San Antonio, habitually ate breakfast at the Café Formentor overlooking the bay. Everybody had a favorite table on the terrace, a place that was his by common consent. The next morning Joshua arrived earlier than usual and, to his own astonishment, sat down to read his mail at Dr. Dr. Mueller's table. Frau Weiss at one table and two army officers at another had already finished their breakfast, but as Mueller could now be seen approaching, still a small figure in the haze at the far side of the bay, they stayed to watch. Joshua hastily ordered a plate of fried eggs, so that he would at least have a knife beside him. He ate defiantly slowly to begin with, then quickly, finally gobbling, because just as Dr. Dr. Mueller rounded the rim of the bay, he was so scared that he had all but decided to yield the table to him, pretending that he had sat there by mistake. At last Mueller loomed over him, his smile condescending. "Good morning," he said.

"Good morning."

Dr. Dr. Mueller pulled up another wicker chair and joined him at the table. Joshua couldn't tell what the officers were thinking, they wore sunglasses, but he assumed they felt he was acting in bad taste. Frau Weiss's eyes were radiant.

Still smiling, Dr. Dr. Mueller said, "Where are my hands?"

"What?"

"My hands."

"Under the table," Joshua said, baffled.

"If I held a gun there, I could shoot your balls off, but look," he said, laughing as he placed his hands on the table, "empty."

7

"Well, yeah. Right. Can you tell me what a Job's comforter is?"

Groping, he said, "A blanket, kind of?"

"You haven't been reading it," he said, exasperated.

"What?"

"The Book." And he held it up, markers sticking out here and there.

"I'm a working man now, but."

"You call that door-to-door bit a job? Shit. A Job's comforter is like if Uncle Oscar comes by unexpected on a Friday night and tells me if I'm still up shit's creek without a paddle it's because I was not much to begin with. How old are you now, Josh?"

"Sixteen. And I still haven't been laid," he protested.

"Fucking's not on today's agenda," Reuben said, opening a bottle of Labatt's, "and besides I've already taught you everything you got to know about it."

"Like hell you have."

"Have you really not been laid yet?" he asked, astonished. Joshua nodded.

"You must be doing something wrong."

"Yeah, but what?"

"God damn it, Josh, these are the Days of Awe and this time we are going to the fucking synagogue and right now we are going to concentrate on the Jewish tradition. Now, to come clean," he said jauntily, "I'm not very Jewish."

"What do you mean, 'not very'? Either you are or you aren't."

"Boy, are you ever ignorant. Take the niggers, for instance. They come in all shades from coal-black, through shit-brown, like Sugar Ray, to just a touch of the tan. Well, it's the same with the Hebes. Like, if you're very Jewish, you wear one of those crazy fur hats and sidecurls and a beard. You know the

167

type. But me, I was just born a Hebe like some guys come into this world with a clubfoot or a stammer."

"Hey, you make it sound like it was a real disadvantage."

"Well, yeah. Right. We're not very popular."

"Why not?"

"Will you stop being so difficult and maybe show a little appreciation."

"For what?"

"I never had the benefit of a religious education like I'm giving you," he said, sulking a little.

"Why aren't we popular?"

"Go know."

"That's no answer."

"Well, one thing they don't like is that since Biblical times we have a rep for driving a hard bargain. Take old Abraham, for instance. Remember I told you about him and his son? Well, once God told Abraham he wanted to destroy the cities on the plain, Sodom and Gomorrah, because they were wide-open towns, like Montreal before that little fuck Pax Plante came along, full of nightclubs and strip joints and barbotte houses and places where you could screw clean. And Abraham says to him, 'Well, yeah, right, God, but what if there are fifty righteous men there, would you still take out the cities?' 'No, not if there were fifty.' 'And if there were only forty-five?' 'A deal,' God says. And not letting go, Abraham says, 'And what if there were only forty purity-leaguers there, what then?' 'O.K.' Anyway, he finally knocks God down to ten, bargaining with him."

"We're not the only ones who bargain."

"Right. Now about Job," he said, opening his Bible at one of his markers. "You see, if you'd only read these pages you'd learn something. God, for all his faults, 'Thou shalt not this' and 'Thou shalt not that,' was a betting man. A gambler born. And he had this big believer, Job, rich as they come but nice, and one day he bets the devil that he can take everything away from Job, absolutely everything, and he's such a mark he'll still have faith. 'Oh yeah,' the devil says, 'you've got a bet.' They shake on it. And, wham, in one day God, putting in the fix, sees that Job loses his animals and his servants and his house and even all his children, except for one. High stakes, eh? But Job, he's a tough nut, and he continues to believe in God, though he does come round to contending with him, as they say. Quote, Wherefore do the wicked live, become old, yea, and mighty in power? unquote. Which is really sticking it to God, who naturally loses his temper.

168

'Hey there,' God says, 'hey you little prick, where were you when I made the world? Can you make thunder? Or rain? Or the rest of it? Like, I'm God, the *capo* of *capos*, with one hell of a track record,' and so forth and so on. And in the end, and this is not to spoil the yarn for you, Job is rewarded by getting back everything he ever had, *but double*, his cut for helping God win his bet with Satan. But the Book of Job is more than just another gambling story with a happy ending. It has a moral. These are the Days of Awe, remember, and I want you to know that if you continue to believe in God, even when you're up shit's creek, it can pay off double at the window. If I really had to explain it, I'd say faith is a lot like playing the stock market or sitting on your luck at the poker table. Your shares may fall through the floor, like in the Great Depression, or you may not be able to buy even a pair of deuces, and if you're chicken you sell or give up your chair. But if you keep the faith and hold on to, say, GM and other blue chips, well shit, look at what they're worth today. Get it?"

"Sure," Joshua said, baffled.

"Now right here, look, it says, quote, Man that is born of woman is few of days, and full of trouble, unquote. Now you tell me," he said, "which character in the Bible was not of regular-type fucking born?"

Stumped, Joshua reached for the beer.

"Jesus H. Christ, that's who. He was made through immaculate conception. And do you know what that means?"

"Tell me?"

"It's getting knocked up by God himself, which is so rare it only happens once in the whole book, and look how many pages."

"You don't believe that shit, do you?"

"According to the covenant, the Hebes are only signed up until page eleven hundred and eighty. Hey, where you going?"

"Then we're through, aren't we?"

"Sit down. Now we turn to the New Testament. Jesus."

"Why bother?"

"For polish."

"What do you mean?"

"When you get out into the world and meet Christians, you'll find like, they lean on it an awful lot. Like, if a guy is ever going to shit on you he usually leads with a quote from it. Say, he won't let you check into one of his hotels, it's restricted, but he doesn't want you breaking the furniture or slugging him. 'Blessed are the meek,' he says, 'the meek shall inherit the earth.' Bullshit. Or, say you catch one of them in bed screwing his daughter, which they go in for a lot out on the prairies, where the winters are long. You know what they say? They say, 'Judge not, that ye be not judged.' Or, for instance, you're running a book and the mayor's bagman wants you to show your appreciation that he doesn't shut you down. He says, 'Render therefore unto Caesar the things which are Caesar's.' The dirtier the sin, the sweeter the saying. The New Testament covers everything. I recommend it highly. Now, Josh, I want you to give up that asshole job and go back to school."

"I'm not going back to school," he said, digging in, "and that job is just a handle to get me into the newspaper business."

"You mean you're going to become a reporter by ringing doorbells?"

"You better believe it."

"He was a rabbi, you know," his father said, grinning, as he passed the beer.

"Who?"

"J.C."

Joshua had to laugh.

"But he didn't like the way the temple was being run and after he was counted out by Pontius Pilate, they banged him into that stick, which is what they used to do to crooks in those days, no bail, no copping a plea, no time off for good behavior, nothing, and he died. Then his bunch, they didn't fly apart like they did here after Galento was shot down. Everybody grab, grab, grab. Guys afraid to stand in front of a window or start their cars. They stuck together, like, and started a church and it was hundreds of years before they split into rival gangs. Protestant and Catholic. The Catholic church is better run, nobody can beat them at collections, and they own property all over town. Everywhere. Well, the Catholic church was built on a rock, according to Peter, but the Protestant on the love of cunt, if you ask me, though to look at those grim bastards today, it makes you wonder. It really got going with Henry the Eighth, who was king of England, and had his mind on only one thing, nookie, and was always sniffing around for a fresh wife. But the Pope, well, he frowned on divorce. 'No soap,' he said. So Henry, he quit on him and joined up with the Protestants, who are everywhere you turn now. Me, I prefer the Catholics. I mean, you know, you become a priest and you swear off fucking for life, which means you've got to be very, very dedicated. I give them full marks."

Seizing the opening, Joshua reminded his father once more that he had yet to be laid.

"We're going to the synagogue tomorrow," he reminded him sharply.

"O.K., O.K."

"I'll tell you what. You go to the place on Union Avenue. Kitty's. But, listen here, you don't pay more than five-and-two."

"I don't get it."

His father shook his head, dismayed. "Five for the girl, two for the room, and don't say I sent you, I'm your father for Chrissakes, it would be embarrassing."

Joshua got up to go.

"Not now. Geez. These are the Days of Awe."

"When, then?"

"I don't care when, but not now."

Joshua sank to the sofa in the backyard again, sulking, and there was a long and brooding silence between them. Finally, his father said, "Go early."

"What?"

"You go early, they're cleaner and not yet wet from all the others and, look, you're a gentleman, you never hit a whore. You are very polite."

"Yeah, I know. I step into her room, I take off my hat."

"Hey, that's right, Josh," he said, pleased.

"Only I never wear one."

"Oh yes you do. Tomorrow. For the synagogue."

The next morning they started out once more for the B'nai Jacob synagogue on Fairmount Street. His father looking spiffy in his straw boater and ice-cream suit; Joshua, with his trousers pressed to perfection and his black shoes gleaming. And once more the closer they got to the synagogue, the more his father dragged his feet. "They're guys who go there every night, you know, just like to the track. It's amazing."

"Yeah, only they must be very Jewish, not like us."

Men in prayer shawls spilled over the outside steps; they gathered in knots on the sidewalk. Smoking, gossiping.

"What are they all doing out on the street?" his father asked, irritated.

"It's probably jammed inside."

"You don't see that welching son-of-a-bitch of a dentist anywhere? Orbach?"

"No. But he could be inside."

"Remember, I give you the elbow once, you stand up, twice, you sit down again."

"Right. Let's go."

"We could look for another synagogue. The one in Outremont. Near Bernard. Maybe it's not so crowded."

But when they found it, there were men gathered outside there, too.

"What do you think?" his father asked.

"It's up to you, Daddy."

"Isn't this where your Uncle Harvey and Aunt Fanny go?"

"I think so."

"Let's go get a coffee and talk it over."

8

In the autumn, that most perfect of northern seasons, Kevin's face, shining with assurance, appeared to anoint the gossip columns at least once a week, which distressed Pauline.

Westmount's prodigal son, back from playing truant in Bermuda, was here, there, and everywhere. Flourishing. Outfitted by Brisson & Brisson, driving a silvery Porsche. That season it seemed no consulate dared celebrate its national day, or new disco open its doors, without Kevin there to offer a benediction. Usually with a jowly Jack Trimble, disconcertingly merry, and a glowing Jane in tow. Whatever they were up to, it was ostensibly doing the three of them nothing but good. Although the stock market continued in the doldrums—money tighter than ever in a diminishing city—the investment fund Trimble had launched, Kevin at the helm, had got off to a rousing start.

Pauline remained unconvinced. Kevin, for his part, avoided her, even their brief phone conversations abrasive.

"How," she wanted to know, "can you afford to buy a Porsche?"

"Why," he shot right back, "are you always prepared to believe the worst of me?"

Pauline went to Ottawa to have lunch with the senator.

"Kevin's back," she said.

"I do read the financial pages, you know."

"Couldn't you see him?"

"I rather suspect," he said, "that he knows where to find me," and he immediately changed the subject.

When Joshua ran into Trimble late one afternoon on Crescent Street, and they ducked into The Troika together for drinks, it was immediately clear that his black mood had passed as swiftly as the summer. "Joshua, old son, we both misjudged Kevin badly. He's a remarkable chap. A late bloomer, certainly, but all he needed was a push. Somebody willing to show confidence in him."

"Come on," Joshua said, "you're the one who's running that fund. He's only window dressing."

"The hell he is. He makes every bleeding decision on his own. I bless the day he came back here."

"Do you now?"

"Yes, and business is only the half of it. He's got me out on the golf course a couple of afternoons a week, imagine that, and Jane is looking ten years younger. I only hope the others realize how much he's doing to prove himself. It's important to him."

Joshua shrugged.

"Those Westmount wankers, if they had to do business in London and New York, like I do, they'd find out soon enough that they're strictly third-division. They haven't got what it takes. Fortunately for them, they can believe this little provincial backwater is society. But we've been around. We know different, don't we, old son?"

"Yes, we do," he said, "but that hardly explains why you continue to play the fool for them."

"I don't get the drift," he said, hardening.

Joshua paused to light a cigarette. "You're no more British than I am, Jack."

Trimble didn't blanch. He laughed. He slapped his knee. "What in God's name are you talking about?"

"You were born right here, old son."

"I was born in Putney. I didn't settle here until 'forty-nine. Everybody knows that."

"Don't worry. I'm not about to spill the beans."

"The beans. There are no beans. You bloody imbecile. You little hack. What you mean to say is, you are not about to risk spreading slanderous stories about your betters, because you know damn well you'd be hearing from my solicitors."

"Lawyers."

"Yes," he said. "And, oh, something else," he added with a thin smile. "Your brother-in-law is giving me tennis lessons." And he stomped out of The Troika.

Joshua, feeling crummy, lingered at the bar, ordering another drink. He hadn't wanted to threaten Trimble, even obliquely. He disliked himself for it. But there was Pauline to consider, and the senator, and if there was going to be any trouble, it was best Trimble knew beforehand that he had something on him. Some muscle. And yet—and yet—the more he pondered it, ordering yet another drink, the more it seemed to him that if anybody was going to play dirty, it was most likely to be Kevin. The pusillanimous brother-in-law he was now lumbered with. So he quit the bar angry with Pauline for obliging him to hammer Trimble.

The night of the dinner party on the lake, when a turbulent Trimble had first announced his surprising association with Kevin, Joshua and Pauline had sat up talking until dawn, drinking on the tilting wraparound porch.

"What you see," she said, "is a pathetic, broken-down athlete, a forty-one-year-old boy, certainly not bright by your standards. Or Murdoch's. Or even Seymour's. But he was such a beautiful boy, Josh. So naturally graceful. A faun. Every head turned when he passed. He was a favorite of the gods, or so it seemed once. If I haven't told you about him before, it's really because of my father and you. It's surprising, but you get along so well now, you really do. I don't want to spoil that for either of you. In a certain sense you have become the son he wanted, and I just couldn't bear for you to think badly of him now."

"Why should I?" he asked, interested.

"Because Kevin is the son he destroyed."

As he started to protest, she held up her hands. "I know. Don't start. I've heard you on the subject before. We can't blame everything on our parents. *We* are responsible for what we become. And God help us all if Alex doesn't turn out just right, because you're a hard man, Joshua Shapiro, oh yes you are."

"We were talking about Kevin," he said evenly.

"You didn't like that?"

"No."

All right. O.K. Kevin, she explained, had once been all but overwhelmed with love and approval. Pauline had worshipped him. Stephen Andrew Hornby, who had always yearned for a son, wept with joy on the day he was born. But, above all, it had been their mother who had doted on him, taking him everywhere with her, even when he was a tot. To sit on Mackenzie King's lap, to be introduced to the Governor-General. If she came home late from a party, her first stop was the nursery. One governess after another was found wanting. The Swiss one bullied him too much and another one, brought over from England, didn't have quite the right accent. Kevin had hardly started school when their father began to read aloud to him every night, and to prepare him for the great things to come.

"And what about you?" Joshua asked, concerned.

"I was merely a girl."

"Right right," Joshua responded warmly, beginning to stroke her inner thigh.

But she moved away from him, absorbed in her story.

Every night, before dinner, Kevin was given a list of topics that were to be discussed at the table, and an hour to prepare himself for them in the library. Social justice. The British North America Act. The Magna Carta. His every response was applauded before their father gently corrected his errors in logic, teaching him, he hoped, how to marshal his arguments for the parliamentary debates that were bound to come. Their mother bought him a pony. He had his own French tutor. And then, without warning, their family life began to come apart. Stephen Andrew Hornby, rather than getting the portfolio he was counting on, the job that Mackenzie King had promised him, was abruptly retired to the Senate. The bone-yard. Not, mind you, because he lacked the ability, but because political cunning called for a French Canadian to be put forward at the time. So he was no longer a presence, a prince. There was no longer a quickening when Stephen Andrew Hornby entered a room, or the bar in the Rideau Club. He became sour. Difficult. Younger men didn't smile at his witticisms any more. And that's when their mother, always a flirt, began to have her affairs, discreetly at first and then with a certain defiance. And now when the senator drifted into the Rideau he imagined the other men whispering, and he wondered which one, if not all of them, had been to bed with his wife. Rightly or wrongly, he began to suspect that darling Kevin had become his wife's accomplice. Kevin would pretend that he and his mother had been together all afternoon, when the truth was he had been dropped off at a movie, while his mother romped elsewhere. Then there was the trip to Europe. A grand tour. Ostensibly, to further Kevin and Pauline's education. They would listen to the debates in Westminster. Visit the Louvre. See the Vatican. But actually it was no more than an excuse for their mother to run wild. She had begun to drink a good deal by this time, and the more she drank, the less fastidious she became about her lovers. Pauline was now talking about gondoliers and croupiers and the kind of bronzed young horrors who sat at the bar of the Ruel or on the terrace of the Carlton in Cannes, waiting. She was terrified. They were often in the bedroom next to their mother's in the hotel in Ville-Franche or St.-Paul-de-Vence or Antibes. Pauline would lie in bed with a pillow over her head, trying to shut out their love-making noises. But Kevin was enthralled. He would hold an inverted glass to the wall, listening to them. "Oh boy," he'd say, "are we ever going to have treats tomorrow. We can have anything we want tomorrow." And when they got back from Europe, Pauline ran right into their father's arms when he stepped on board the ship in Quebec City. But he took one look at Kevin and he went rigid. He knew. He took one look, and he understood he was no longer a towering figure in his son's life. Instead, he was something pathetic. An old fool. A cuckold.

As before, topics were set for discussion at the dinner table. The Family Compact. Heredity. Property rights. But now Pauline was included and listened to with kindness. And once Kevin had made his case, his manner just a little too cocksure now, the senator would sit back with an ironical smile on his face and demolish it. Kevin would have appealed to their mother for help, but if she wasn't out, she was indisposed. She seldom joined them at the dinner table any more. They were living in the Westmount house again, on Upper Lansdowne, the senator going to Ottawa for only a couple of days a week. And if he turned on Kevin in their mother's presence, she would cry, but she made no protest. And one day she just packed her bags and was gone, leaving Kevin stranded. Loving postcards came for him from New Orleans, San Francisco, and even Cairo once. And if she was in town between planes and lovers, she would take them to lunch at the Ritz, spilling her drinks, tears running down her powdered cheeks, embarrassing Kevin and frightening Pauline. Now Pauline became Kevin's only support. He began to lie, he began to cheat. He wasn't awfully good at school, and so on the way home from Selwyn House he would doctor his report card. He was a natural athlete. Star of the hockey team. Unequaled in track and field. But their father simply didn't give a damn any more.

Kevin now had to reconcile school, where masters and boys doted on him, and the lake in summer, where Jane wasn't the only girl who swooned in his presence, with what had become their grim and unyielding house on Upper Lansdowne, where disapproval was all but absolute. "Oh, and he was such a beautiful boy, Josh, he didn't deserve to be-

176

come a counter in my parents' quarrel. He was hardly to blame for Mother's infidelities. He deserved better of my father, much better. And just as my father seemed to be coming around, if only a little, my mother had her stroke, and died in a room in the Royal Vic with my father holding her hand. I have no idea what passed between them in that room, what he said or what she said, but he hardened against Kevin once more."

Kevin and Pauline were now at McGill together. He was the leading man in just about everything the drama society did, and he played hockey well enough to interest professional scouts. He won the Quebec amateur golf championship and, together against the world, they took a mixed doubles tennis title. Kevin was also briefly prime minister of McGill's mock parliament. Pauline wasn't the only one who thought he would win the roses. All the prizes. She had no idea that he was already plagiarizing his English essays out of books by forgotten writers. Or that he seldom sat down to an exam without a crib sheet. Pauline thought he was wonderful, absolutely wonderful, and began to fight with their father about him. The senator would smile, but say nothing. Pauline hated him.

"Jane, Kevin, and I became inseparable. The Three Musketeers. I took it for granted they would marry—my brother, my best friend." No, there would be a coronation. Older couples sent drinks to their table in the Ritz. They raised their glasses. Here's to us, all of us, the right sort. The best this country has to offer. And, yes, there was an MG, his, bought with some money their mother had left him, and they drove everywhere in it. Their presence was sufficient to make the tackiest roadhouse modish. If they danced in a certain bar in Ste. Adèle, it immediately became the in place. Oh, there were things, little disturbances, but Pauline didn't pay attention. He seemed to owe money everywhere. Somebody—not one of their set, certainly—once accused him of cheating in a bridge tournament. Crap. Envy. Pauline laughed it off.

Then, all too swiftly, Kevin was into law school, where their father was still a legend, and Kevin, just like the others, discovered the Jews. "What did we know about Jews? You have no idea how cocooned we were. What sheltered childhoods we led. We were the best. The brightest. *The chosen.*"

"Hey, there."

"Yes," she said, her foot riding up to rest between his legs, "the chosen. With a country to inherit."

And, suddenly, there were all those fierce, driving Jews,

177

who didn't play by their rules, each one hollering "me, me, me." My God, they demanded space, lots of space, but they didn't even know where their grandfathers came from. They interrupted you in mid-sentence. They grabbed seats in the front row in lecture rooms. They wore diamond socks. They didn't give a shit about football. Clearly, no matter how dazzling their marks, they would never be accepted into the right law firms, but they could argue rings around most of the law professors and they were not going to be denied. They had already taken over the *McGill Daily*, raging at each other in the columns, arguing about beasties Kevin and Pauline had never heard of. Trotsky. Brecht. The Rosenbergs. With their stinging wit, they drove Kevin out of the mock parliament. "One of them, a good three inches shorter than I was, a young man who was doing post-graduate work in English lit, began to send me love letters suggesting intimacies I hadn't even dreamed of yet. . . .

"Oh my, all those short, dark men with heated black eyes. The appetite. Jane and I used to joke about the need to wear another layer of panties, maybe even barbed wire. We used to giggle about being called *shiksas*. It was fun for us, but not for the boys. Kevin and the others, as hopeless as British grenadiers suddenly confronted by Indians in the underbrush, had their first intimation that just possibly they were not good enough to compete. Oh dear, oh dear, they say our fraternities were restricted. It was the only place we felt unthreatened. So up your ass, Joshua ben Reuben. We were scared."

"Good. I'm glad."

"Try to understand, darling. As far as you and Seymour and Max are concerned, we had all the advantages and you didn't. Our boring world, a make-believe ballroom, was already diminishing, and it was yours that was burgeoning. I was called a Westmount snob on campus. An anti-Semite. A racist. Horrified, I had a couple of Jewish boys to the next party at our house. What I mean to say is, I *invited* a couple. Four came. They made deprecating remarks about the tasteless food. They wanted to know if I fucked and if not, who did. One of them stepped right up to my father and asked him how much he had paid for our house."

Abbott, the best of the boys even then, simply rolled up his sleeves and began to study in earnest. But Kevin, as he was bound to, tried to get by on charm. He courted the brightest of the Jewish students, flattering, cajoling, until he sweet-talked one of them, Isenberg Pauline thought his name was, into lending him his notes and then even beginning to write

178

his papers for him. Suddenly Kevin was turning in assignments sprinkled with quotes from Laski and Brandeis. He was summoned to the dean's office. The dean would probably have settled for throwing a bad scare into him, maybe making him lose his year, but then Kevin made the mistake of trying some fancy footwork on the dean, reminding him of whose son he was, laying everything off on poor Isenberg. The scholarship boy. Clearly not one of us. The dean, a decent man, was outraged. The senator was summoned to his office, and he asked that Kevin be treated just like anybody else.

"Do you know what that means, Senator?"

"Yes, I believe I do."

Before he was expelled, the senator and Kevin had the fight that had been simmering for years. Ugly beyond belief. Kevin pleaded, he wept, he begged his father to save his skin just this once. The senator told him he was a disgrace. A weakling. Totally without scruples. He had taken advantage, and probably ruined the life, of a poor Jewish boy. The senator would certainly not intervene. A raging Kevin blamed him for his mother's death. He said she never would have become so promiscuous had the senator not become impotent. The senator didn't even raise his voice. He simply asked Kevin to leave the house.

"I won't bore you with all the details, or how much the scandal was savored in the best clubs—the senator's son, a common cheat—but a shattered Kevin now found himself something of a pariah as well. The magic was gone. Old friends and supporters melted away, except for Jane and me. Darling Jane," she said, laughing harshly. "The three of us were out drinking together, mourning his fall from grace, when Kevin didn't so much propose as say, 'We can get married now.' 'Well no,' Jane replied softly, 'neither of us has any money.' I offered them mine, an inheritance from my grandmother. 'Great, we could go to Europe,' he said to Jane. 'Yes, yes,' I pitched in, approving, 'but only until you get your bearings, and then you must return, register in another law school, and show everybody that you are made of the right stuff after all.' Jane said nothing. She was pensive. And so I made some excuse, thinking it best to leave them alone to make their plans. Afterwards, I was amazed to discover that Jane had turned him down flat: Westmount would never forget. He was tainted forevermore. 'It's been fun,' she told him, 'but you can no longer take me where I want to go. Bye bye, Kevin. Good luck.' "

"And whatever happened to Isenberg-you-think-his-name-was?"

"Oh, don't. Please don't. It's reprehensible. He was expelled too. But at the time it just didn't matter to me. All I was concerned about was salvaging my brother. I threw tantrums. I made threats. I accused my father of being perverse. I told him that far from being sad about Kevin's situation, he was secretly gloating, as if his unforgivably bad treatment of Kevin over the years had been vindicated by the way things had turned out. He replied that I had rather more to learn about human nature than I had gleaned from a course in Psychology One-oh-one. I called him a hypocrite. He had been abusive to Kevin because of what he had done to a poor Jewish boy, but he belonged to the Rideau and other clubs which didn't admit Jews, and he wasn't above joking about their 'sharp practices.'"

Kevin fled Montreal and, shortly afterwards, so did Pauline. But not before she had it out with all their old friends, telling them just what she thought about their sense of loyalty. Kevin went south and Pauline took off for Europe, never to come back, she thought. To hell with them. Everybody. She married a Communist because she thought nothing would upset her father more. She was cruel to poor Colin, unnecessarily cruel, becoming her mother for a while, carrying on with all those men, more scared than anything. Wondering, until Joshua came along, if she would also die an alcoholic in a room in the Royal Vic.

Kevin tried the golf circuit for a while, and then he wrote Pauline a pathetic letter and she sent him money and he went to Hollywood for a screen test, and ended up giving tennis lessons, and providing other services, to ladies of a certain age. "My age right now. Right? Right." He tried stockcar racing. He modeled. He coached a high school hockey team. After each disaster he was drawn back to Montreal, trying the old charm, organizing reunions, and telling transparent lies about how he was on the verge of a breakthrough. Sending out signals to Ottawa, hoping the senator would call. But he never did. And if Kevin was tolerated to begin with, he soon became a subject of ridicule. He was no longer the only one who was disappointed. Everybody now had their own little failures to cope with. Marriages. Children. Careers. They began to hate him. Why not? He had once represented all their hopes, the boy who was going to take all the prizes, and what was he now? A tawdry, sleazy adventurer. "So he clings to me after all these years. I'm the only one he doesn't have to pretend with or lie to. And I'm sorry, my love, but I still remember and cherish that golden boy who once turned everybody's head. So, yes, I helped to buy him the boat. He's cost me thousands over the years. I finance his dreams. And if you really must know, I'll end up paying for his gala country club dinner, because I won't have the others snickering about his skipping without settling the bill."

"But he isn't skipping now, is he?"

She didn't answer.

"Why can't you be pleased that Trimble, whatever his motives, is giving him a chance?"

"Running an investment trust? Kevin? It's ridiculous."

"Maybe," he suggested tentatively, "Jane got him the job?"

"Oh, sure. Suddenly. After all these years. She woke up remorseful and decided, this being Junior Red Cross Day, she would do something for Kevin."

"Possibly," he said, watching her, "she's been seeing him in Bermuda."

"No. He would have told me. I just don't understand what Jack wants with him."

"Who cares?" he said impatiently. "It's a job. An opportunity."

"You think I'm being a cunt," she said, "don't you?"

He had never heard her use the word before. "No," he said, "I certainly don't think that. I don't dislike Trimble as much as you do. Maybe he's really out to help Kevin." But his voice lacked conviction.

9

Seymour, it sometimes seemed to Joshua, put the sort of single-minded energy into seduction that other men applied to digging canals that joined oceans or sending rockets to the moon. If hitherto unsavored nookie, as he always put it, was the sweetest reward this world had to offer, no subterfuge or inconvenience was too great. Napoleon could not have put more care into the taking of Austerlitz than Seymour did into the ravishing of the receptionist at Pitney, McCabe, Thornason, Lapointe & Cohen. He would find out a girl's favorite color, what perfume she fancied, and if roses pleased her more than orchids. If she read, and a few of them did, he would contrive to surface with a signed copy of a book by her most revered author. If it was called for, he came up with rinkside tickets to the hockey game when Boston was in town. He had, in order to seduce a lecturer in Political Science 101 at Concordia U., done a crash course on Kate Millett, and for the sake of the favors of a typist at the Canadian Jewish Congress, he had got dressed in striped prison garb and tramped up and down in front of the Soviet consulate to protest the treatment of his brethren in Russia.

"Seymour," Joshua had said, aghast, "what are you doing in that ridiculous outfit?"

"You are looking at a man," he replied, "who is going to have congress with a girl from Jewish Congress."

He was exceedingly generous with gifts for his girls. Rings from Lucas, necklaces from Ogilvy's, watches from Birks. The saleslady in charge of the lingerie department at Holt Renfrew suffered through his every entrapment, agonizing with him as he tried to settle on a choice, searching for what he called the real coozy creamer. The one that would make the honey run. Truly, W. H. Auden couldn't have put more thought into finding the precise adverb than Seymour did into the selection of a pair of lace panties.

And now Joshua and the boys were setting him up.

Skimming through the Personals column in the *New York Review of Books*, Joshua had stopped short, exploding with laughter, when he read:

ATTRACTIVE, COSMOPOLITAN, VIRILE MONTREAL MAN, early forties, successful, literate, adventurous, seeks slender, loving lady friend in her thirties for sensual flights. "The grave is a fine and private place/ but none I know do there embrace." Am often in NYC and Boston areas. NYR Box 142116.

Seymour, he had thought, Seymour, you shameless pig! With the creative help of Bobby and Max, riding a shared bottle of Chivas Regal, Joshua sat down to formulate a reply to the ad, coy yet enticing, hinting at, if never quite spelling out, unimaginable delights, but politely requesting a letter, more concrete information, before a meeting could be arranged. This, just in case the ad had not been placed by Seymour. They needn't have worried. Seymour's horny reply came bouncing back in the return mail and they consulted again. This time in The King's Arms, taking a fetching television actress of Joshua's acquaintance into their confidence, and framing a reply, appropriately salacious but delicate in manner, that suggested an exploratory rendezvous, neither party under any obligation, for late-afternoon drinks in the Maritime Bar of the Ritz.

Seymour arrived, shined, scrubbed, and scented, at the appointed hour. A bottle of Mumm's, nesting in a silver bucket, was already at his side, when he noticed Joshua ensconced at the bar. He waved, his smile sickly.

"Hi, Seymour. Mind if I join you?"

"As a matter of fact, yes."

"Aw, you're kidding me," Joshua said, sitting down at the table.

"Go away. Shoo," Seymour said, his manner abrupt. "I'm waiting for somebody to join me."

"Who?"

"Who who?" Seymour shot him a perplexed look. "I don't know who." Then, in a sudden burst of good humor, he laughed at himself and explained that he was meeting a blind date. "Yes, at my age. So?"

"I didn't say that. But if that's the case—"

"Wait," he said, as Joshua rose to leave. "Don't be so touchy. Sit down."

"Make up your mind."

"She will probably turn out to be awful. One of the world's crazies. Why don't you sit here with me until I . . . She doesn't know who I am either. It's too complicated a story to go into. O.K., I'll tell you. She's one of those types who advertises in the personal columns of a newspaper, never mind which. I took a flyer. I answered. O.K., O.K., I'm a terrible man."

"What have you got there?" Joshua asked, indicating a soft leather satchel beside him on the floor.

"What have I got there? A satchel. Prick."

"What's in it?"

"Fuck off, will you? I'll settle your bill."

Joshua started to get up again.

"Sit down, for Christ's sake."

"What's in the bag?"

"My equipment. Happy now?"

"*Your what?*"

"This is a complicated world we live in now. Things aren't what they used to be. So I've got to be prepared. How do I know what she fancies, a woman who advertises for it. A little S and M. Maybe not champagne, but a joint. Or a sniff of coke. Or a special kind of tickler. Who knows? Damn it, will you leave me alone."

"I'm going."

"Just sit down here with me," Seymour said, starting each time the doors swung open. "But if I ask you to leave—suddenly—you will be a gentleman. You will understand. Oh, shit, no. This is absolutely ridiculous."

Bobby Gross's wife, Barbara, who was not privy to the full extent of their intrigue, charged through the doors, big buxom Molly padding after.

"Molly, look who's here!"

"Oooh," Molly squealed.

Both ladies were laden with parcels from Holt's and Ogilvy's. Molly had a run in her stocking. A smear of cream from a chocolate éclair clung to the moustache on her upper lip. Her leather coat was missing a button. Her voice booming, she explained that they had been out shopping when Barbara had suggested they might stop for a drink together at the Ritz before going home. Why not, she had thought, this once.

Fuck fuck fuck. Seymour, fuming, began to rub his hands against his trousers, his eyes fixed on the door.

"Oh, look," Molly exclaimed, a plump hand held to her powdery cheek, "champagne!" Her smile lapsed and her flinty eyes hardened. *"Why the champagne, Seymour?"*

"Ask him. He ordered it."

Molly turned to Joshua.

"I just got a big check," Joshua said, "totally unexpected. Why don't we ask the waiters to bring some glasses. We might as well open it now."

"What a sport he is," Seymour said, summoning the waiter.

"Champagne," Molly said, giggly.

Even as they began to chat uneasily, Molly inquiring about Pauline, Seymour, his expression dead, saw their actress drift into the oak-paneled room. Joshua did not believe in levitation, but he could have sworn Seymour was lifted briefly out of his chair before he slumped back, an older man, seething.

"You know," Molly said, "I'm going to tell you something about champagne. Quite seriously. Only yesterday one of the nurses told me it's very good for your bowels."

Seymour's muttered reply was lost.

"He has such trouble, my Seymour. No matter what I say, he won't take enough roughage. So he has to force it."

"Shame on you, Seymour."

"I don't know how interested you are, Josh, but the way we defecate is unnatural. We should squat, that's natural."

184

"Why don't you hike up your skirts," Seymour said, "and give us a demonstration right here?"

"Quack quack quack," she said. "Josh isn't bored."

Their actress was in her early thirties, with long shining black hair, flashing legs. She wore a green suede coat, unbelted, a fawn silk blouse, and a matching suede skirt. Enormous shell-frame glasses rode the crown of her black head. Lowering them to her lovely green eyes, she scanned the room, shrugged, and then strode past their table to the bar, her scent lingering. Settled into the bar stool, she crossed her long legs, delicate things rustling. Inside Seymour, Joshua sensed a volcano threatening to erupt, devouring all of them. Seymour's heart was thudding. His lips were parched. Fiddling with the stem of his champagne glass, ignoring Molly's breathless prattling, he appealed to Joshua with his melancholy eyes. The joke, conceived in drunken high spirits, Bobby and Max the spur, began to pall. It could end badly, Joshua thought.

Molly was going on compulsively about her work at the hospital, but nobody was listening.

The girls Joshua had known in high school, most of whom had worked as camp counselors in the Laurentians during the summer, had finally become their mothers, but with a crucial difference. They weren't mere homemakers, their social consciences satisfied by the peddling of raffle tickets, venturing out only to organize a bazaar for the synagogue. The daughters had been educated and, consequently, were all into something. This one ran a candle boutique in the refurbished garage that was now the Galleria Shalom, and another opened a bookshop that sold only Canadiana. Izzy Singer's wife sculpted. Pearl was a spokesperson for retarded children. Max's wife worked for a nonprofit Eskimo cooperative. Hetty conducted classes on TM at the "Y." With Molly, it was the palliative care unit. Death therapy.

Mountainous Molly, scourge of the Jewish General Hospital, strode through the halls, ferreting out the terminally ill in their most secret hiding places, terrifying them with her loving smile. She was there to help them accept the imminent corruption of the flesh graciously. Selflessly come to comfort those whose revels were ending, to make them ready for the big sleep that would round out their little lives. "It's touching, you know, but what they fear most is identity-loss." Death-therapy was, as she pointed out, a thankless chore, yet an incredibly moving experience. Life-enhancing. Which, Seymour was fond of adding, laughter moving him to tears as he told the story again and again, had begun very badly indeed for Molly.

With Lazar Bercovitch, when Molly had still been a novice death-watcher.

Entering Bercovitch's private room, her smile beatific, Molly teased him, she called him *zeyda*. Seated on his bed, tilting it just a little, she held his mottled hand. She told him naughty jokes. She flirted. She tickled him. And only when the furrier's heart had melted and, spluttering with laughter, he managed furtive squeezes of those pliant breasts, yielding as unbaked dough; only as he was wondering to what good luck did he owe this jolly fat lady's visit, did she stroke his white head and tell him, "Lazar, you are not a man to lie to yourself."

Grasping her thighs now, amazed at this unexpected gift of willing flesh, he said, "Certainly not."

"It isn't what you think it is," she cooed, taking his head to her bosom, "it's cancer of the liver."

Struggling, in fear of being smothered, the old man kicked his bony legs and protested, "I'm here for the prostate. What are you saying, you dirty whore?"

Her eyes brimming with tears of empathy, his snowy head locked in her ample arms, Molly told him that no man as loved as Lazar died. The body goes, inevitably, but the spirit lives on. Lazar would endure in his family's heart. The children would tell loving tales about him at the Passover table. So would grandchildren. Their children's children.

"You crazy bitch, may only stones drop from your womb. I'm going home on Friday."

Molly beseeched him to confront the truth together with his family. Breaking free, spindly arms flailing, Lazar caught her on the forehead with a well-aimed ball of phlegm. "Help," he hollered. "Help, help!"

Nurses, ready with a rebuke, came running, followed by an irate doctor. They spilled into the room to discover the old man raging, pelting a sobbing Molly with oranges and peaches from his bedside fruit bowl.

"Mrs. Kaplan, what are you doing here?"

"Whore. Cunt. Take her away."

The doctor pulled Molly aside. "Bernstein," he said, holding his head. "Bernstein, not Bercovitch."

"Liars, you said it was the prostate."

"I swear that's all you're being treated for, Mr. Bercovitch. You're going home on Friday."

186

"Like shit, I am. I want a second opinion. I want my son. I want my lawyer."

Molly did not make the same mistake again, but as she haunted the corridors of the Jewish General, offering solace, old women barely managing to shuffle along, espying her first, found themselves propelled by a sudden burst of energy and flitted through the nearest door. Emaciated, hollow-eyed men threw salt over their shoulders. As Molly strode down the halls, chart in hand, her massive heart thundering with love, patients shivered under their bedclothes, breathing easy only after she had padded past, this unbidden angel of death.

Seymour, ashen-faced, rose from the table.

"Are you all right, darling?"

"Don't get excited. I have to go to the toilet, that's all."

Conversation continued fitfully—the children, vacation plans, Margaret Trudeau's shenanigans—as the phone rang on the wall immediately to the right of the bar. The bartender took it, nodded, and then whispered something to the television actress, who favored Joshua with a small, meaningful smile before she set her Gauloise down in an ashtray and got up to take the call.

"We're boring you," Barbara said, appealing to Joshua.

"Oh, not at all," and he pitched into the flagging conversation with simulated vigor, as he watched the girl on the phone smile, nod, burst into spontaneous giggles, frown, protest, nod again, and finally hang up. Her manner distressed, pensive, she paid for her glass of kir, left it unfinished on the bar, and drifted out of the room, failing to acknowledge Joshua as she passed. Relieved, he became more attentive to the ladies as Seymour bounded back to the table.

Barbara glanced at her watch and announced that she had to pick up Lenore at ballet.

"Did you bring the car?" Seymour asked Molly abruptly.

"Yes," she said, immediately scooping up her handbag. The clasp was broken. The bulging velvet bag was bound together with an elastic. A Roberta. Set him back $450. God Almighty.

"I have a couple of things to discuss with my friend here. Why don't you drive Barbara home? I won't be long."

Seymour, glowering, waited until the ladies had gathered their parcels together and left, and then he said, "I never would have suspected you of being so childish."

"I'm sorry, Seymour."

187

"I know that Max must be in on this, that impotent prick, and of course Bobby. But Bobby hates me."

"What are you talking about? He's been your friend for years."

"Bobby loathes me."

"Why?"

"Because I know certain things about him."

"Like what?"

Seymour wouldn't say.

"Come on."

"He goes to Eaton's basement shirt sales. He reads condensed books. Anyway, I'm not surprised at them. But I would have expected more from you."

"Oh, come on. It was a joke."

"Some joke," Seymour said evenly. "Ha ha ha. You involved my innocent wife in this mindless prank, and that's unforgivable."

"She didn't suspect a thing."

"I admit to having certain weaknesses, human weaknesses, but I never involve my wife and children in my escapades. My utterly joyless escapades. My wife and children come first with me." Leaning closer, he added, "Do you know how many times I have alienated old friends, defending you and the shit you write?"

"I have no interest in the views of your dim-witted friends."

"You are a childish, inconsiderate, condescending, snobbish son of a bitch. May you live to suffer writer's block."

With that, Seymour shoved his chair back from the table and stomped out of the bar. Stunned, Joshua ordered a double Scotch, and it was only after he called for the waiter that he realized he had been left with the bill for the bottle of Mumm's.

There were two bars in the Ritz-Carlton. The Maritime, in the basement, which Joshua favored because of its comparative privacy, and the much more modish Café de Paris on the ground floor. Embarrassed, contrite, Joshua ascended the steps to the ground floor and paused at the newsstand to pick up some magazines. As he passed the entrance to the Café de Paris, he just caught a glimpse of Seymour, an ingratiating, sweet-talking Seymour, huddled together with the television actress at a table in the corner.

Seymour, Seymour.

He would be telling her that he had once seen her perform at the Centaur Theatre, and that he had never dreamt that he

188

would be so fortunate as to meet her. He would say that he had also seen her play Masha on CBC-TV and, though he had seen *The Three Sisters* done in the West End and on Broadway, he had never known an actress to invest the role with such purity of soul. Such incandescence. Accidentally brushing against her leg under the table, he would allow that he had friends who put tax-shelter money into films and that she must meet them, and they would go to The Troika for dinner and then continue on to her apartment in the Cartier, where he would pronounce her not only gifted and intelligent, but also beautiful, astonishingly beautiful. Unzipping here, unhooking there, licking, sucking, he would say that had she not been born Canadian, had she come from New York, she would now certainly be a star of international repute. Then he would open his satchel and invite her to step into his first gift. The come-on. A pair of low-cal, peppermint-flavored candy panties. Eating them off her, he would suddenly excuse himself and rush into the toilet to spray his erection with Long John. For endurance. Then he would return, beaming, and, one hand on his satchel, ask her what she liked best. Don't be shy.

10

Damn. Making Ibiza his base, he had come to Spain to look at battlefields, talk to survivors, learn what he could about the Spanish Civil War. Instead, he was discovering that he was Jewish. Something anybody could have told him. Ruminating on these matters, as he was out hiking one afternoon, in the ochre hills rising behind San Antonio, Joshua stumbled on a campfire smoldering in a clearing. Curious, he stepped closer.

"Don't move! Keep your hands where I can see them."

Joshua froze.

"Now turn around. Nice and easy."

Whirling, Joshua found himself confronted by Dr. Dr. Mueller, red-eyed drunk, pointing a Winchester rifle at his chest. Mueller was grizzled, unshaven, wearing a fringed leather jacket, jeans, chaps, and spurs, and tooled leather boots. "You should know better than to sneak up on a stranger's campfire in these parts."

"I wasn't sneaking up on anybody."

"You could have been a hostile," he said, lowering his rifle, "a Cheyenne Dog Soldier."

A charred pot was suspended from a tripod over the fire. "Would you care for some goulash soup?" he asked.

"Why, sure. Yes. Mighty good of you."

Dr. Dr. Mueller reached for a jug, crooked it expertly in his arm, drank, and passed it to Joshua. "This will help you wash it down."

Joshua, taking advantage of Mueller's drunken state, asked, "What did you do in the war, exactly?"

"I fought."

"Where?"

"In the high country and on the plains. Wherever we found them. And you?"

"I was too young, remember?"

Rocking, Dr. Dr. Mueller said, "I feel for your people."

"Oh, sure, and you helped as many as you could to escape."

Grieving, Dr. Dr. Mueller remembered Tohopeka, Sharp Knife's soldiers carving long strips of skin from the bodies to be dried and used for belts. "I remember when your people were many," he said, "and they owned the land from the sunrise to the sunset."

"Like hell they did."

"I knew this country when their campfires twinkled at night like the stars of the fallen sky."

"What's that?"

But suddenly Dr. Dr. Mueller's mood changed. His eyes swimming in truculence, he leaned against a flat rock and propped his arm in a wrestling position. "Come. Try me."

"I'm not interested."

"Of course."

The following evening, clean-shaven, wearing his white linen suit, and biting on his ivory cigarette holder, Dr. Dr. Mueller stood at the bar in Don Pedro's. "Are you a man or a mouse?" he called out to Joshua as he entered, and they played lie dice again.

Once more, Joshua asked, "What did you do in the war, exactly?"

"I fought."

"Where?"

"Wherever they sent me."

"But you don't care for Jews?"

"I don't care for anybody who has a yellow streak down his back," he said, and then he went on to complain loudly

190

about Spanish cuisine, saying it could not compare to the French. His French was fluent.

"I don't understand," Joshua said. "Why didn't you buy a villa on the Côte d'Azur rather than here?"

"Because I am a wanted man in France."

"Why?" Joshua demanded, his heart thumping.

"You know, Hitler was not impressed by the intelligence reports he got on the Canadian assault troops captured at Dieppe. One of your soldiers had never heard of Roosevelt, another, asked if he knew of any Germans, said, 'Sure, General Rommel and Lili Marlene.'"

Parrying Joshua's arguments about Nazi iniquity, he was fond of thrusting the siege of the Alazar at him. The cruel murder of Colonel Moscardó's son by the republicans. To which Joshua would counter, "At least he had a name, not a number."

The most direct approach to Dr. Dr. Mueller's villa, which was nestled in an enviably lovely and secluded cove two miles beyond San Antonio, was to turn off the main road about a mile out, cut across a wasp-infested olive grove, and start up a craggy mountainside that finally flattened into a rump of bleached, guano-covered rock which overlooked his place. Again and again Joshua made the trip, skirting a crest with a commanding view of the barracks and training ground. Then, sheltering behind a rock, he could see a boldly painted teepee anchored in the sand, a handsome brown stallion secured to a stake nearby. He would watch Dr. Dr. Mueller at lunch or swimming or working on his manuscript under the shade of a lemon tree, consumed with loathing for him, but unable to act.

Then one day Joshua saw him emerge from his villa in chaps and spurs, wearing six-guns. Dr. Dr. Mueller strode slowly toward the sea—froze—whirled—drew—and fired at empties of Johnny Walker lined up on a table. Thrusting his six-guns back into their holsters, he snickered, yanked a pouch out of his breast pocket, and rolled himself a cigarette. He shouted something in German, a protest, and drawing both guns again, retreated into his villa. Joshua waited. Maybe a half-hour later, Dr. Dr. Mueller sashayed through the French doors again, the very image of Marlene Dietrich in *Destry Rides Again*. He wore a blond wig, rouge, lipstick, false breasts under a black corset pinched at the waist, sheer black stockings, pink garters and slippers. Slapping imaginary groping hands away from his bosom, pouting, he drifted over to his typewriter and began to bang away at it, pausing only to dab his eyes occasionally with a black lace handkerchief.

The next evening he was holding forth at Don Pedro's again, thrusting the lie dice at Joshua. "Are you a man or a mouse?"

It was Juanito who enabled Joshua to piece together the rough outlines of Ibiza's Civil War history.

The island fell to the nationalists in 1936, following a successful uprising by the Guardia Civil. But in August 1937 a Valencian expeditionary force, led by air force captain Alberto Bayo, arrived at Ibiza in four transport ships, as well as two destroyers, a submarine, and six airplanes. The Communist poet Rafael Alberti was released from prison. The fishermen rose against the fifty men in the garrison and the island was under republican control once more—but not for long. Bayo, continuing to Majorca with twenty-five hundred men, ran into resistance from the Italian Black Shirts and, in September, a nationalist counteroffensive, supported by Italian aircraft, succeeded in routing Bayo's expeditionary force. Ibiza and Formentera were both abandoned. The nationalists killed 55 Ibizencos in an air raid. In reprisal, the anarchists shot 239 prisoners before retreating to the peninsula. And so, when the rebels finally returned, they shot another 400 Ibizencos in reprisal for the reprisal, among them Juanito's uncle.

There was more bloodshed in 1938.

One evening in May, as the German battleship *Deutschland* lay at anchor off Ibiza, two republican aircraft flew out of the sun and dropped two bombs on the ship. One hit the side of the deck, the damage it caused negligible. But the other penetrated the seamen's mess, killing 23 and wounding 75. Germany was, of course, "neutral" at the time; the *Deutschland* was on a non-intervention patrol. The republican ministry of defense hastily claimed that the battleship had fired at the airplanes, but it was a lie. To further exacerbate matters, the republican planes were flown by Russians. Hitler, according to reports, was so outraged that it took Foreign Minister Von Neurath all of six hours to calm him down. Within a week, the Reich took its revenge. Five ships, among them the pocket battleship *Admiral Scheer*, fired two hundred shots into Almeria at dawn, destroying thirty-five buildings and killing nineteen people.

Before the year was out, a group of Spanish priests in exile in Liège composed a prayer to the Virgin of the Pillar:

To you, O Mary, Queen of Peace, we always turn, we the faithful sons of Your best-loved Spain, now vilified, outraged, befouled by criminal bolshevism, depraved by Jewish Marxism, and scorned by savage communism. We pray You, tears in our eyes, to come to our help, to accord final triumph to the glorious armies of the liberator and reconqueror of Spain, the new Lelayo, the Caudillo! *Viva* Christ the King!

Strolling on the waterfront, Juanito pointed out pockmarks in the buildings made, he said, on the evening the *Deutschland* was bombed. From the heights of the old town, looking out to sea, he indicated where, during World War II, tankers flying the Spanish flag had refueled German U-boats.

One day Joshua took a knife with him and buried it close to the rock overlooking Mueller's villa. Then, alarmed at his own behavior, hardly daring to wonder at its implications, he resolved to quit Ibiza. Taking his breakfast on the terrace of the Casa del Sol one morning, he decided to leave on the *Jaime II*, bound for Valencia the next Wednesday.

The new hotel, helped by Mueller's patronage, had caught on quickly, displacing the Café Formentor as a rendezvous. Among the first guests who came to stay at the Casa del Sol there was a charabanc full of Americans. Joshua watched as they began to drift onto the terrace for breakfast. Dr. Dr. Mueller, taking his seat, waved. Joshua didn't acknowledge his greeting, which made Frau Weiss smile.

Looking out into the bay, Joshua could see three destroyers, obdurate in the morning mist, rising and falling grayly at anchor. The American Sixth Fleet. Toward Formentera, an aircraft carrier, also at anchor, rocked half-concealed in the mist. An American tourist came out, sat down at a vacant table between Joshua, Mueller, and Frau Weiss, and asked the waitress, in English, for two fried eggs, toast, marmalade, and coffee. "And just this once," he said, "forget the olive oil, will you, honey?" Then he settled back easily in his chair. An owner. Indicating the ships at sea, he winked at Mueller. "Ours," he said.

Freiberg's brother-in-law Max, a smuggler and money-changer of sorts who had arrived only a day earlier, emerged through the beaded door from the hotel and waddled over to the tourist's table, cameras and binoculars slung over his shoulder. "Good morning," he said.

"I'm not buying anything."

"On these cameras," Max said, warming to his pitch, "you do not pay tax. Like in America."

Both men were wearing beach shorts and sandals. The tourist was tall and tanned, brawny, broken-faced, his smile engaging. Max was small, pasty, and potbellied.

"Hey you," the tourist said. "Take a good look at me. Do I look like I pay tax?"

"Certainly, no."

"Then why don't you do me a big favor and fuck off?"

Max turned to Dr. Dr. Mueller, taking him for another member of the tourist party. "Would you like to look at a camera, Joe? They are German."

"If they are German," Dr. Dr. Mueller said, grinning at Joshua as he simulated an American accent, "they must be the best. How much?"

"One hundred and fifty bucks."

Dr. Dr. Mueller laughed and passed his big brown hand among the cameras and binoculars slung from Max's shoulder, much as if he were insinuating it inside a woman's blouse, and then he shook them about roughly. "Where did you steal them from?" he asked Max.

"Yeah," the tourist said, grinning, as he wiped egg yolk from his mouth with the back of his hand.

Max laughed, he slapped his thigh, his stomach shook; then, abruptly, he was solemn again. He whacked his mutilated hand against the table, like a butcher flinging a fish on the counter. He propped his left leg on a chair and ran his bad hand along a scar there. "Gestapo," he said.

Frau Weiss whistled, feigning astonishment.

"I'll give you fifty dollars cash," Dr. Dr. Mueller said playfully. "Real American dollars."

Max clacked his tongue reproachfully. He wiped the lenses of a camera and set it down tenderly on Dr. Dr. Mueller's table. Stepping back, he admired it from different angles. "You must pay two hundred dollars in New York. Don't forget taxes."

"Hey," Dr. Dr. Mueller said, smiling, "you're a very smart fellow. You're not Spanish."

Boiling with rage, Joshua watched Frau Weiss reach over and nudge Dr. Dr. Mueller.

"I'll let you have it for one hundred dollars without the case, O.K.?"

"How much for the binoculars?"

Swiftly Max polished a pair of binoculars. "They are German," he said. "The best."

Frau Weiss covered her mouth with her hand. She tittered.

"Seventy dollars," Max said.

Dr. Dr. Mueller picked up the binoculars and studied the destroyers in the bay, frowning.

"For you," Max said, "only sixty dollars."

"You are not Spanish," Mueller said.

"I am Spanish."

"You are a Jew," Mueller said, "is that not so?"

"For Christ's sake," Joshua howled, fishing into his pocket, "I'll take the fucking binoculars. Give them to me. Come on."

Max, Frau Weiss, the tourist, Dr. Dr. Mueller, all turned to look, startled, as Joshua hastily signed a traveler's check for fifty dollars, added some pesetas, and thrust the money at Max.

"The camera as well?" Max asked, beaming.

Frau Weiss clapped her hands together and laughed. The sun caught a gold filling.

"The hell." Joshua seized Max by the arm and pulled him over to Frau Weiss. He pointed at the scar on Max's leg. "Now laugh at this, you German cunt. Go ahead."

Dr. Dr. Mueller rose languidly and stepped between Joshua and Frau Weiss. "You," he said to Max.

"Yes, sir."

"Tell this rude boy when you left Germany. The truth now."

Max shrugged.

"Speak up!"

"Nineteen thirty-three."

"Gestapo. You see how they lie, Shapiro. How they exaggerate. It's all propaganda."

"Unlike Dresden," Frau Weiss said. "Everybody should be made to see Dresden."

Joshua grabbed the binoculars and flung them from the terrace. They did not, as he had intended, shatter against the rocks, but landed short, falling softly into the sand. He seized Max by his narrow shoulders, shaking him fiercely. "You don't have to be afraid of him any more. He's shit. *How did you get the scar?*"

"Let me go, you're crazy."

Joshua pushed Max from him. He stumbled backwards against Mueller's table. Dr. Dr. Mueller, shaking his head, helped him into a chair, and then grinning at Joshua, he called, "Waitress, the baby's having a tantrum. Bring me his bottle quickly."

195

Joshua quit the terrace, pursued by Dr. Dr. Mueller's laughter, but he did not leave Ibiza as planned, sailing on the *Jaime II* the following Wednesday. Because on Monday, Monique and her mother arrived.

THREE

1

> On that arid square, that fragment nipped off from hot
> Africa, soldered so crudely to inventive Europe,
>   On that tableland scored by rivers,
> Our fever's menacing shapes are precise and alive.

For many members of Joshua's generation, Spain was above all a territory of the heart. A country of the imagination. Too young to have fought there, but necessarily convinced that they would have gone, proving to themselves and the essential Mr. Hemingway that they did not lack for *cojones*, it was the first political kiss. Not so much a received political idea as a moral inheritance.

When John Osborne's Jimmy Porter, in *Look Back in Anger*, mourned that there were no more good, clean causes left, Joshua glowed in his Royal Court seat, nodding yes, yes, but once there was Spain. The Ebro. Guadalajara. The men of the International Brigades defending Madrid with no better map than a plan of the town torn from a Baedeker. André Malraux's flying squadron. Dr. Norman Bethune's blood plasma group. Arthur Koestler awaiting execution by a firing squad. Christopher Caudwell presenting his life. George Orwell, in the trenches, refusing to fire on a Fascist because he was squatting with his trousers rolled to his ankles, preparing to defecate, and it seemed wrong to kill another man in that posture.

Sometimes life improves on art. Or, looked at another way, when Joshua last caught sight of Osborne, somebody he had once taken for a spokesman, he was reposing in a photograph for the benefit of the women's page of the London *Sunday Times*, acting out exactly the sort of item that Jimmy Porter used to read aloud, outraged, to his wife at the ironingboard.

LOOK!
His Clothes and Hers
Jill Bennett and John Osborne

The playwright, spade-bearded, reclined languorously on a chic, ultramodern chair. Radiating content.

> JOHN OSBORNE is wearing a cashmere sweater from a selection costing £12 at Doug Hayward, and tartan trousers, £26 at Doug Hayward.

In the text, running underneath, John and Jill chat.

> *Jill (Mrs. Osborne)*: I change my scent all the time. Today I'm wearing Calandre by Paco Rabanne. But I'm mad about Guerlain's No. 90 and Calèche and Joy. And John always wears whatever I have on. He never bothers with after-shave.
> *John:* After-shave is for pooves.

Ah, but once there was Spain. Once, writers had been committed to revolutionary change, not their own absurdity. Instead of *Catch-22*, there was *La Condition Humaine;* rather than Portnoy, Robert Jordan.

In London, in 1953, shortly after Joshua had been obliged to flee from Ibiza, the notion of attempting a book on the men who had fought in the International Brigades grew into an obsession. He began to sift Charing Cross Road bookshelves for anything about the Civil War. Memoirs, old Gollancz Left Book Club editions, pamphlets. He started a file on the names of volunteers as they appeared in the books he devoured or in old copies of the *New Statesman* and the *Daily Worker*. He had no literary connections, he was working in a vacuum, squeezing out a living of sorts by filling in three nights a week on the Canadian Press desk and doing the occasional broadcast for the CBC. Then, slowly, things began to fall into place. A piece he had written about traveling through Spain, visiting the old battle sites, was accepted by *Encounter*. He earned a stint doing a novel-review column for the *Spectator*.

In those days you were expected to churn out copy on a batch of four books, but, in recognition of the pittance paid, you were allowed to actually carry off twelve, each one worth half the retail price at a bookshop on Fleet Street. One day Joshua entered the literary editor's poky little Gower Street office to discover a wiry figure already plundering the novel shelves, obviously a veteran man-of-letters, for he was hastily snatching up books not on the basis of such trifles as the author's name or the publisher's imprint, but on the only important consideration: the retail price. "Ah," he'd say, appropriating a 21-shilling novel. "Lovely." Next he seized another fat one, a 25-shilling beauty. "This looks fascinating."

"Murdoch, you bastard. Leave something for me."

Together they hopped a bus to Fleet Street, flogging those books they had no intention of reading, let alone reviewing, and then they made off for the nearest pub. "The art books, my dear," Murdoch said, quoting an earlier reviewer, Evelyn Waugh. "That's the stuff we want to get our grubby hands on. Some of them fetch as much as three guineas each."

Then Murdoch asked him about Ibiza. Hesitantly, his bruises still raw, Joshua told him something about his adventures with Juanito. But he did not mention Monique. He was still too ashamed. And then, floating on too many large gins, he found himself saying how he had outwitted and finally humiliated Dr. Dr. Mueller. Murdoch begged for more and more details. Improvising, Joshua obliged him with lies even larger.

He didn't tell him—he couldn't possibly tell him—that he had written to the Freibergs, a long and convoluted letter of apology, explaining himself as best he could and asking if they were all right. Please be all right. His letter had gone unanswered, which, all things considered, did not surprise him.

With Murdoch, he became a regular at the Mandrake Club. And on wintry Friday afternoons they waited impatiently there for Murdoch's wife, a secretary in a publishing house, to drift in with her pay envelope, enabling them to settle the week's account. As soon as Murdoch had become sodden and truculent, and they had taken him back to their flat to tuck him in, Margaret and Joshua used to sit together in the kitchen, drinking. One night he reached out to feel her breasts. "Yoicks," she said.

At the time, Murdoch and Margaret lived in Kentish Town and Joshua had a small flat in Chelsea.

In the seedy early fifties, long before London had been

pronounced swinging, Chelsea's most celebrated tomcat was Eliot, a resident of Cheyne Walk, and the only boutiques worth seeking out on the King's Road were dark, smelly little places stacked with second-hand books. Joshua's modest flat on the then tatty end of the King's Road lent him the use of place-names that matched his mood perfectly. His bus stop was Lot's Road; his local, the World's End. Stepping out in his baggy utility tweeds, he could, if he chose to, stroll toward squalid Fulham, lingering at smog-encrusted windows of row upon row of decrepit junk and second-hand furniture shops, munching fish and chips wrapped in a greasy *News of the World*. Or if he wandered the other way, toward Sloane Square, there were an abundance of foul Anglo-Indian and Chinese restaurants, second-hand bookshops, tobacconists, and barbershops with big flashing Durex signs in the window, and chemists, their dusty, faded window displays proffering rupture belts and salves that promised relief from itchy hemorrhoids.

Murdoch, whose first novel had been published to hosannas, was already famous as well as feared, though not yet in the money. He was still supplementing his income from royalties by reviewing here, pounding out a telly column there, and reading for a publisher somewhere else. Moved by his condition, even more parlous than his own, Joshua advised him to order all his food, even whatever clothes he required, from Harrod's. "Open an account. Get your bloody publisher to sign for you, if necessary. And then, so far as gullible tradesmen are concerned, you are no longer a yabbo but a proper gentleman. The Harrod's accounts are sent out quarterly. When it comes, ignore it. A month will pass before you are sent a polite reminder. Then you run through the itemized account and query a jar of mustard here, a tin of sardines there. This creates unimaginable confusion. Wretched little clerks, who cycle to work from darkest Clapham, scurry from desk to desk in the basement. Files are pried open. Sales slips consulted. Ledgers double-checked. Months will pass before somebody comes up with the actual signed sales slip, including the mustard or sardines. The next step calls for a little guile. You write an indignant letter querying the authenticity of the signature on the sales slip. More confusion. Consternation in the very bowels of the emporium. Further delays. Six months will pass before you have to settle the account and by that time, I hope, you will have the necessary money. If not, keep the correspondence going."

A publisher Joshua met at a *New Statesman* party invited

him to lunch, asked to see some pages from his manuscript about Spain, and ten days later mailed him a contract, with the promise of a much needed £150 advance. That night, in a mood to celebrate, Joshua crashed a party at the home of an Australian actress who lived in a rambling old house in Earl's Court. Celia was an ardent left-winger. And in those days, before the Khrushchev speech had confirmed Stalin's obloquy to even the most obdurate, before the uprising in Hungary, many of her friends were still active in the Party. These friends, Joshua would discover later, after he had become a regular at Celia's gatherings, included one Colin Fraser and his dazzling, reputedly promiscuous wife, Pauline.

Meanwhile, there were problems.

Murdoch's second novel was (deservedly, Joshua thought) even more highly praised than his first, but it didn't even earn enough to clear his overdraft. Margaret already had one child and eighteen months later gave birth to another, obliging her to leave her job. Something, Joshua thought, had to be done.

Yes, yes, but what?

On a letterhead pinched from the office of *Encounter,* Joshua wrote to the curator of the rare manuscript collection at the University of Texas, saying that he had been commissioned to write an essay on the novels of Sidney Murdoch. He would be in Texas in the spring, he added, and would be grateful if he could be allowed access to the Murdoch papers. There were, a librarian replied, no Murdoch papers in Texas. Joshua wrote back immediately to say that he was astounded and, for good measure, he enclosed a batch of Murdoch's most flattering reviews. The librarian wrote again to say that the curator was then traveling in Italy, but Professor Shapiro's letter would be brought to his attention on his return. Joshua took the University of Texas letter to a printer on the Old Kent Road and asked him to reproduce twenty copies of the letterhead. He then wrote to all the dealers he could find listed, asking them if they had any Murdoch papers available. Finally, an unsavory American dealer was snared on his hook. He approached Murdoch with a view to purchasing his papers. Murdoch promptly unloaded everything he had on him, earning about five hundred pounds, and when the dealer came back for more, he was not about to admit the cupboard was bare. Instead, he went Joshua one better. He improvised.

Visiting Murdoch's flat in Kentish Town one night, Joshua came upon his two-year-old daughter, Jessica, howling on the floor, yanking at a soggy nappy, while Murdoch, determined to shut her up, was rubbing her lips with cognac. Ralph, squatting in another corner of the freezing living room, his nose running, was totally absorbed in a box of Ritz crackers. Joshua's immediate problem was that he didn't know where to stand. The floor was covered end to end with typewritten pages.

"Where's Margaret?" he asked at once.

"Clever. Oh, very clever indeed."

"What's that supposed to mean?"

"Little greaser."

Rattled, Joshua inadvertently stepped on a manuscript page. He withdrew his foot immediately.

"Oh, no. That's just the thing. Step on some more of them, please."

"I'm sorry. It was an accident."

"But I happen to be serious. Tread on the bloody pages before your shoes dry."

Joshua did as he was asked.

"Margaret finally found out about me and Lucinda and stormed out of here late last night. If she is leaving me for good this time, she had better come back for this lot." Murdoch poured him a cognac, his smile fierce. "Do you really fancy her that much, Joshua?"

"Don't be ridiculous."

Murdoch wasn't convinced.

"I rather suspected you were into her knickers once she began to insist how you were the most pathetically unattractive of all my friends."

"Not bloody likely."

"Too bad. Ah well, somebody will marry her, don't you think? Now that I've had her teeth capped. Scheming little mouse. Her behavior was perfectly proper until I settled the dentist's bill. No NHS for her. It had to be Wimpole Street. Seriously, don't you think somebody will marry her?"

"With two kids?"

"Aha," he exclaimed.

"I'm not having an affair with Margaret."

"Then why has she suddenly taken to bathing before going out shopping in the afternoon?"

"She could be having an affair with somebody else."

"Then why would your phone be off the hook those same afternoons? Don't deny it. I checked with the operator."

"I could be having an affair with somebody else, too."

"Oh, really," he asked, interested, "who with?"

Joshua didn't answer.

"I smell a dirty rat."

"What about Lucinda?"

"I'm afraid she's preggers."

"Is she expecting you to marry her, then?"

"Margaret's simply aching to find out the answer to that one, isn't she?"

"How would I know?"

"Judas!"

"Are you in love with Lucinda?"

"Oh, don't be such a bore, Joshua."

He helped Murdoch stow the drugged children into a bed that reeked of urine and then drank more cognac with him as he continued about his work. Pages, dripping with beer, were hung out to dry before the faltering fire. He scribbled corrections on other pages, while Joshua crumpled and uncrumpled further sheets for him. More pages were burned here and there with a cigarette, others were stained with tea. The manuscript, he explained, had come to him unsolicited from a young writer in search of advice. Once it had been properly aged, Murdoch planned to sell it to the dealer as an early effort of his that he had, on reflection, decided not to publish. He refilled their glasses and they drank to that, regarding each other warily. "The irony is," he said, "that I don't really enjoy the actual fucking that much. I find women terrifying. And they're all much the same in bed, aren't they?"

"Then why must you change partners so often?"

Murdoch contemplated that one. "Well," he said at last, "it is becoming disconcertingly easier for me to start an affair rather than a new novel. And what I do enjoy are the deceits. The stratagems. The dangers. All the lovely little lies. Mind you, I'd never stoop to cuckolding a good friend. I'm not a total shit. I know, I know, 'I'm not having an affair with Margaret.' Balls, you aren't."

Murdoch began to strut.

"I shouldn't tell you this, but no matter how flattering she is to you now, the truth is she could never finish your boring little article in *Encounter*."

"Sidney, you are pathetically insecure."

"Of course I am. Aren't you?"

"What are you going to do about Lucinda?"

"The proper thing, it goes without saying. But the poor child," he added, unable to repress a grin, "is under age and can't possibly marry without her parents' consent."

"Which just might be forthcoming, given the compromising circs."

"Shit. Shit. Shit. What a pain in the ass you are. Can you lend me a hundred quid?"

"Wait. Hold it. I think I've got a better idea," Joshua said, beaming at Murdoch with drunken benevolence. "You and I, Sidney, might just be able to earn a tidy sum in the great state of Texas," and he went on to improvise his scheme.

"Of course, of course."

"We could backdate the stuff to Cambridge."

Murdoch splashed more cognac into their glasses. "Ah, Murdoch," he sang out, "mad, bad, and dangerous to know. Yes. Good. Excellent. It could bring a small fortune. Of course you realize that I am famous while you are merely well known, and only in Staggers and Naggers circles at that. So you would have to agree to a sixty-forty split in my favor. What do you say?"

Joshua agreed at once, and in the weeks that followed, they both avoided real work, laboring to outdo each other in their joint project. All unavailingly, alas. For before they could market the stuff, Murdoch ran afoul of the Texans. His instantly aged manuscript, sold to the university, turned up in print, the real and inconsiderate author earning a good deal of attention. The Texans took umbrage, so did the real author, and Murdoch found himself threatened with a lawsuit, until he explained away his swindle as an absent-minded mistake. Letters gone into the wrong envelopes. Happens all the time, don't you know?

On the other hand, their work could not be written off as a total loss. At least to Murdoch, the custodian. A malevolent stranger (Margaret, Murdoch hinted darkly) stumbled on the stuff, photostated some of the more outrageous chunks, and mailed them to Lucinda's parents in South Ken. They absolutely forbade the marriage. Lucinda was dispatched to Switzerland, and Margaret—sweet, ostensibly dependent Margaret —emerging after an understandable period of despair, was astonished to discover how capable she really was. "People used to think I was mute, an idiot," she told Joshua, "because whenever we went to dinner parties I could never get a word in edgeways, everybody was so intent on Sidney's bon mots. And you know how he loves to perform. Holding forth at anybody's table. Polishing his anecdotes. Now when I'm invited out, people actually listen to what I have to say. There are men who find me both attractive and witty."

Joshua had now become a regular at Celia's delightful bottle parties, which abounded in left-wing journalists, contributors to the *New Statesman* and *Tribune,* and American refugees from McCarthyism. Hollywood people. There were also impecunious Africans, an engaging, hard-drinking bunch, seemingly indolent, who were to disappear only to return a decade later, Joshua was to discover on a visit to London, borne to the same parties in chauffeured limousines, unraveling turtleneck sweaters now eschewed for three-piece gray suits, this one the foreign minister of Malawi, that one the freshly appointed Zambian ambassador to the Court of St. James's. Each one bearing a willing, flushed Belgravia rose on his arm, the black man's burden. And then, yet another decade later, settling into the *New York Times* in The King's Arms, jesting with The Flopper, he would read of these genial men he had known in their prime, one executed by the latest supreme liberator of Kinshasa, the severed head of another found floating in the Upper Volta River.

It was as a result of a chance encounter at one of Celia's parties that Joshua actually made direct contact with the dreaded Party and, incidentally, Pauline.

The dazzling, baffling Pauline, whom he would sometimes espy being not so surreptitiously fondled by a black man, headed for another part of the room at even a hint of his approach. And if he pursued, doggedly, she would move away yet again, her long legs rustling.

Then one night at Celia's somebody cornered Joshua, saying, "I'll bet you'd be afraid to speak at the Communist Party Writer's Group?"

Pauline, for a change, was sufficiently close to overhear, and he could tell by her face that she expected a craven response from him.

"Certainly not," he said.

"Jolly good. We'll expect you a week Wednesday. You can speak on modern American writing."

Early that Wednesday evening, in The Bale of Hay, Joshua pleaded with a drunken Murdoch to come along with him.

"Oh, but it's no good, my dear. If I go, the room's bound to tilt in my direction. You'll be totally ignored."

"I'll take that chance."

"The women who attend those lectures are perfectly dreadful. The pong. They have moustaches. They wear elastic stockings. And they always want you to sign some bloody petition. Let them get Amis. He's willing to sign anything, if only because his name comes even before 'Auden.' But nobody reads as far as the M's."

"If you don't come with me, Sidney, I'm going to sign your

name to every petition going, and you will never get to be a visiting lecturer at Iowa or Stanford."

"They'll only serve punch or some vile Georgian wine, and they'll expect us to sing songs with them."

"They've promised a bottle of Scotch," Joshua lied.

The house was in Highgate. At least thirty comrades had been prepared for, but only sixteen had turned up.

"The Bulgarian folk dancers opened in the West End tonight," the host, a *Daily Worker* editor, explained consolingly.

They waited another half-hour in the dowdy living room, sipping plonk, until three more people drifted in. Everybody in the group was supposed to be a writer, but most of the audience was composed of plump, good-natured matrons who had brought their knitting. Joshua was given a fulsome introduction and dug right in to pontificate—knowledgeably, he hoped—about younger American writers. Mailer, Styron, Salinger, Capote. Nobody was interested. Nobody, that is, except for a febrile Colin Fraser, who scribbled notes throughout his lecture. Unlike Pauline, who appeared to be reading the *New Statesman,* rattling the pages as noisily as possible. Infuriated, Joshua decided to get a rise out of them. Although he admired the political stance of progressive writers such as Howard Fast, he said, he much preferred reading reactionaries like Faulkner or Evelyn Waugh.

"Why," a woman immediately demanded, "won't they let Howard Fast out of jail?"

"Because he's done such violence to the English language," Murdoch called out.

Everybody turned to glare.

"I'm Sidney Murdoch," he said, grinning.

"Oh, is that who you are," Pauline said. "I thought for a moment that you were Mary McCarthy."

Murdoch shrank back into his folding chair, seething.

"Is it true," another woman demanded, "that a progressive writer can't find a publisher in the United States today?"

"Would you say that all American writers are corrupted by success?"

Joshua managed to excuse himself early, but he was stopped at the door by Colin Fraser, notebook in hand, a disapproving Pauline trailing after.

"I've seen you at Celia's," Colin gushed. "We're Canadians too," and, introducing Pauline, he suggested they move on to the nearest coffee bar.

"Coffee keeps me awake," Murdoch protested.

"Well then, let's go to our place. Digs. We can knock back a few jars there."

Emerging from the Haverstock Hill tube station, strolling back to their place, Joshua managed a quick word alone with Murdoch. "I want you to wait until I've gone to the toilet, and then you are to tell her how absolutely wonderful I am."

"But I'd like to fuck her myself," Murdoch pointed out, grieving.

"God damn it, Sidney. This is important to me."

"Do you think he's a poof?"

"I hope so."

Colin Fraser, scrawny, pallid, angular, constantly jerking his oblong head to clear stringy brown hair from troubled blue eyes, sprang from Ottawa, an ambassador's son. He was a literary scholar, doing research in the British Museum on the novels of Jack Lindsay and others, and working on a progressive novel of his own, its theme the Winnipeg general strike. He and Pauline lived in a dank little basement bed-sitter in England's Lane, where, fortunately, there was a half-bottle of gin available, as well as beer, but only old mustard or jam jars to serve as glasses. They lived in penury (self-inflicted). Colin had his scholarship and Pauline was working as a supply teacher, mostly in terrifying secondary moderns in Brixton or North Kensington. Neither of them, as a matter of principle, was dipping into family money. Colin, in fact, had renounced his sizable inheritance. "I had a look at the trust fund portfolio once," he said indignantly. "It holds shares in South Africa and in companies that produce arms that were used in the Korean war of aggression."

"Oh, shocking," Murdoch said.

Colin read *Peace News*, he subscribed to *Tribune*. He would, Joshua was to discover, journey to any church hall or school basement, no matter how difficult to get to, if only there was a minister appearing on the platform there, who would rebuke him for having been born white, an exploiter of Africa's soul, or failing that, if there was some frizzy-haired matron in sensible shoes who had just returned from liberated China to show a jumpy, out-of-focus documentary about the joys of life in a Cantonese bicycle factory. Having discovered that Joshua was from Montreal, he droned on and on about French Canadians and how badly exploited they were. Joshua was inclined to scoff, but nodded instead, agreeing to anything, his eyes fastened longingly on Pauline. Maddeningly beautiful, perversely hostile. She was drinking heavily, seemingly embarrassed by Colin's progressive bromides, but fiercely protective, not yielding an inch. She was clearly more intelligent than he was; he couldn't figure out what they were doing together.

Murdoch, having performed his commission during Joshua's calculated absence, laying it on Pauline about his incomparable merits, had begun to doze. He was bored. And so was Joshua. But he was determined not to leave without a moment alone with Pauline. Finally, the insufferable Colin rose to go to the toilet. Joshua quickly sat down beside Pauline. "Would you have lunch with me tomorrow?" he asked.

"Only," she said, her smile sweet, "if you promise me that we can go back to your place afterwards and fuck like crazy."

Joshua turned pale. Murdoch wakened, gaping.

"No. We can't go to lunch. I'm a married woman."

"Yes. Certainly. I appreciate that. But I thought maybe——"

"Besides, I don't like you."

"Neither do I," a revived Murdoch said. "He's poking my wife on Wednesday afternoons. She comes home late. I have to make do with a cold plate and maybe yesterday's trifle reheated."

"Don't pay any attention to him," Joshua said, and once more he asked, "Please come to lunch with me."

She was hesitating, possibly about to acquiesce, when Colin bounded back into the room, beaming. "This is fun," he said. "This is damn good fun. I so enjoy the company of creative comrades."

Pauline, betrayed, grabbed her coat and stomped out of the bed-sitter.

"I'll get her," Joshua offered.

"No. She does it from time to time," Colin said, not the least distressed. And all at once he seemed to relax, as if to say, Now they could really talk. Saying how highly he valued Joshua's opinion, he asked if he would read his manuscript. Oh, with pleasure, Joshua said icily. And then next Wednesday, Colin said, he could come to dinner, and they would discuss it.

"He's busy on Wednesdays," Murdoch said.

In the morning, Joshua wakened to find a letter from Peabody, who was working for *Esquire*, along with an issue of the magazine including a piece of Joshua's on London. Janet had given birth to their first child only a month earlier. "I'm writing this by the seaside, on the beach where I used to build sandcastles as a boy. We're staying in East Hampton

208

for the summer, at my father's place, and the day of Jeremy's birth my father and I solemnly planted an apple tree to mark the event. The tree my father planted the day I was born still bears sweet fruit, even as Janet has, but I fear my father will not live to see this tree mature. He's seventy-one and suffered his second stroke last winter. I read Dickens aloud to him at night, even as he once did for me, and I assure my mother on the hour that I do not smell gas in the kitchen and that I will wear a hat in the sun. I waken each morning at dawn, a voyeur, concealed in the grass that grows on top of a dune, come to watch Janet nurse Jeremy in the sand by the sea. It is an exquisite sight, beyond my powers of description, and my only fear, embarrassingly coarse, is that such is my reverence for mother and son joined in such poignant embrace that I will never lust for her again. I have decided to lay down a library rather than a wine cellar for Jeremy, all our favorite books, and I would appreciate suggestions. Yes, I know, Isaac Babel.

"Janet, who was working at *Time* until swollen with seed, is a splendid girl. After she has nursed Jeremy, she sets him down tenderly in a wicker basket in the shade, unpins her black hair, shakes it out, and plunges into the sea. My God, Joshua, old Feodor be damned, and crabby old Eliot as well, there's a lot to be said for this life. In the evening we soak our freshly cut corn in a bucket of sea water and then roast them over a charcoal fire. This we follow with bluefish, caught that very morning, and fruits de pays, as we used to say. Come home, troubled spirit. Janet longs to know you and even I have come to miss your surly presence. I'll be taking a leave of absence this autumn to work for Adlai, assuming that he will run again, but I doubt that he has the fire to take Ike. Even so, I'm glad to be back. Come home, Joshua."

Having suffered through Colin's unspeakably bad and sentimental attempt at a novel, Murdoch howling at passages Joshua read aloud to him, he made his way to the basement bed-sitter on Wednesday night, armed with a dozen red roses. But Pauline had outwitted him. She wasn't there, but at the local Odeon, he was told.

"She felt we could talk more freely on our own," Colin said. "Well, I'm all pins and needles. What do you think?"

"I think your novel's absolutely marvelous," Joshua said, "and that you should send it to a publisher immediately. Don't change a word."

They sat down to eat bangers and mash Colin had thoughtfully prepared. The bangers, squirting hot fat like pus, were pink through the middle and the potatoes abounded in rock-hard lumps. "Shall I be mum and pour?" he asked.

"Sure."

Joshua indicated the set of golf clubs leaning against the wall. "Don't tell me," he began.

"Oh, no. I don't play. They belong to her darling brother, who's visiting London at the moment." And then Colin went on to say how they must all return to Canada soon and work together to expel the American exploiters. "If you only knew," he said, "how much I envy you your working-class experience."

"Well, Colin, old fuck," Joshua said, beginning to play with him, "I wouldn't mind having your inheritance. I wouldn't turn my back on it."

"Oh yes, you most certainly would," Colin said, all twinkly.

Midnight came and went and there was no Pauline. "Well," Joshua said, getting up to go, "I do hope to see you both at Celia's on Saturday night."

"You've got your eye on Pauline," Colin said.

"Oh no I haven't."

"Take care. She may not be the stuff your dreams are made of."

There was a couple locked in a heated argument in a parked Hillman across the street, but as Joshua emerged onto the pavement the man who was with Pauline quickly doused the inside light. Joshua hurried away, bent into the slashing rain. Local Odeon my ass, he thought.

They did show up at Celia's on Saturday night, but Pauline infuriatingly defeated his every approach, sliding away from him each time he started in her direction. She was drinking heavily again and laughing too much. Bitch. He hated her. But she was also beautiful, wearing a tight black silk dress that buttoned down the front. Joshua kept his hands in his pockets, drifting to another part of the living room, looking for an argument. But he couldn't stay away and neither, if he'd only realized it then, could she, constantly fluttering around him, tantalizingly just out of reach. When he next caught sight of Pauline, she was hanging on the arm of a big handsome black, a talented West Indian writer Joshua knew. Bitch bitch. He also began to drink too much, seeking out strangers to insult, and when he next did a compulsive circuit of the rooms, he couldn't find Colin or Pauline anywhere. Heading for the toilet, he concluded that they both had left, and good riddance too. His mistake. He opened the toilet door to find Pauline and the West Indian writer in a fierce embrace. Pauline was bent over almost backwards, his basketball-player-size hands with their pink palms driving her silken buttocks to him. Elbowing past them, Joshua whacked back the toilet seat.

"Oh, come on, man," the West Indian moaned, "please."

Joshua contrived to piss in a pleasingly high arc, singing in his froggiest voice, "Tote dat barge, lift dat bale, git a little drink and you land in jay-il, but ole man rivah, dat ole man rivah . . ."

The West Indian began to heave with laughter.

"I thought you were a married woman," Joshua called over his shoulder.

"I don't want you coming round to our place any more and patronizing him. He's a much better man than you are."

"Or woman," Joshua shot back, slamming the door on them.

A fresh drink in trembling hand, maybe a half-glass of straight Scotch, he drove an unsuspecting blacklisted screenwriter against the wall, excoriating him and his kind.

In those days, when the blacklist was most rigorously applied, many of them had to write or direct episodes of the Robin Hood series under pseudonyms for producer Hannah Weinstein. With a stroke, $10,000-a-week masters reduced to £500-an-episode navvies. Oh God, Joshua thought, film-makers of the left actually driven to living off capital. But, mindful of their heritage (the Paris Commune, the storming of the Winter Palace, Lillian Hellman saying no to the resounding sound of her own applause), they sneaked progressive thoughts into the Robin Hood series. So a soulful Jewish tailor might be discovered in Sherwood Forest, doing piecework for the dastardly sheriff of the *shtetl* of Nottingham, who maintained a non-union shop. The tailor, scratching his snowy head, ruminating under an oak tree, anticipating Proudhon, might tell Friar Tuck that all property was theft. In Nottingham itself, miraculously, a black might be found, maybe a runaway slave, and Robin and the *chevra* would do battle for his equal rights. Put plainly, though the work was demeaning, no opportunity was lost to educate the masses. *De haut en bas.*

And now Joshua, cheeks scorching, found himself actually shouting at one of them. "And what about Isaac Babel," he wanted to know, "Mandelstam, and the rest? Aren't you, with all your whining, marginally—yeah, *marginally*—better off

211

than they were, and when did any of you ever speak up for them?"

"Hey, I thought you were the kid who was the Spanish Civil War buff?"

"I am," he replied, embarrassed.

"Which side are you on?"

"Well now, I've got a problem," Joshua said, his anger dissolving into laughter, "I can tolerate everything about the left but its advocates. And now," he added, "I think I'd better get the hell out of here."

Joshua managed to acquire the West Indian writer's new novel and wrote a most vitriolic review of it for the *Spectator*, suggesting that it was the kind of self-pitying cry that could only appeal to vacuous but rich white women liberals who, in their quest for sexual punishment, were excited by inchoate black anger; and he mailed a copy to Pauline.

"Oh, are you ever a shit," she said, on the phone immediately.

"Come to lunch with me."

"Certainly not."

"Why?"

"You are utterly without scruples," she said, hanging up.

Yes. Right. And I am also going mad, he thought. Absolutely mad.

Night after night he would sit in his flat drinking prodigiously, and in his mind's eye, unbutton that black silk dress, undo the filigreed bra, allowing her glorious breasts to spring free, pausing to kiss them reverently before he stopped to remove her black pumps, roll down her stockings and yes, oh yes, relieve her of her silken panties (modestly white, he decided) and then, imagining unspeakable yet tender acts of love, he would rush into the toilet to masturbate, emerging humiliated, a pimply teenager again, pumping away. He hated her. He wanted to hurt her. He swore he would never take her to lunch even if she came to him on bended knees. *Bended knees*, he thought, *trying to unzip him with her teeth.* No, no. Stop that. Sure, he'd take her to lunch. To Lyon's Corner House. Or the ABC on Bayswater Road. Heh heh heh. And the next afternoon he would find himself in Hampstead, searching in one pub after another, hoping to run into her. Consuming large gins here and there, grinning foolishly, as in his mind's eye he bathed her, he powdered her, he perfumed her. And then he combed through all the neighboring Odeons and Granadas. And what if he found her necking with some pink-tongued, big black ape? Murder, that's what.

Then one demented morning he even set his breakfast table for two, chatting with an imaginary Pauline over a cuppa.

"I'm sorry," she said demurely, "now you must think I'm wanton."

After last night, she meant.

"On the contrary," he said, "it is I who hope you don't think me a beast now."

"A beast?" she asked, shining with gratitude. "Oh, no. At last I know what it's like to have a real man make love to me."

"Come here, my sweet."

"Oh, yes, please. But wherever do you get the strength?"

Margaret came round on Wednesday afternoon to discover that his bruised member wouldn't rise; he had been stricken with impotence.

"Poor Mr. McThing won't stand to attention," she simpered.

"God damn it," he said, leaping off the bed, "this is my cock. It's not called Mr. McThing or Captain Hook. Don't any of you nutty people on this ridiculous offshore island ever get beyond the nursery?"

Weeping softly, Margaret began to dress, tying the straps of her somewhat faded bra together with a safety pin.

"And, furthermore," Joshua said, "Sidney's known about our Wednesday afternoons for ages."

"That hardly matters any more, does it?"

"He's my friend."

"And wasn't he your friend when you invited me to come here in the first place?"

"Oh, shit, Maggie. I'm sorry. I'm going crazy. I'm a wreck. I'm in love with a nigger-loving whore."

He actually began to shop for her. At Woolland's. Harrod's. A Bali "Self-Expression" Seamless Front Closure Contour Bra. From Yves St. Laurent, a tempting two-part party-goer for Yves-tide, just a whisper of silk ruffles. From Givenchy, a smock that smacked of Paris, complete with maddening slit leg show and tiny tucks. He bought her a scooped draw-stringer by Renata, with an all-encompassing whirl of softness in a sizzling sateen print. Softie, slim lingerie after Dior and more, much more of the sort of thing that he only intended to allow her to wear in their bedroom.

He sent her the copy of *Esquire* with his piece on London. And he phoned again and again. If Colin answered, he hung up. If she answered, she hung up.

Letters bounced back unopened.

She was not to be seen at Celia's any more, probably because there were too many white men there.

Bitch. Whore. Cunt.

He punished her, no longer taking his purchases from Woolland's and Harrod's to bed with him, but shoving them into a dresser drawer. Undressing her in his mind's eye, vengefully now, he was pleased to discover that she had droopy tits and swampy pubic hair, where only crabs nested. Smelly down there. Yes. He was better off uninvolved.

He began to write for the *New Statesman* as often as possible, because he knew she read it, maybe even in bed when Colin was out giving of his thin blood to Korean orphans or demonstrating against the Bomb. Yes, in bed, his cunning prose fondling her warm high bosom as she leaned over to put out a cigarette. Or in her sweetly scented bathroom, his words nestling in her lap as she applied lotions to her leg hairs, those long bare legs outstretched. Or maybe she even sat on his paragraphs in the kitchen, taking a solitary cup of tea, the heat of his adjectives penetrating those sensuous buttocks. Oh my God, he thought, lying alone on his lumpy sofa, erect and dripping.

Oh yes, oh yes, ostensibly pronouncing on the contemporary American novel or Teddy Boys or Canadian politics, he was really writing for an audience of one, spinning love letters in the sober pages of the *Statesman* with hidden salacious messages, just for her. For her to ponder in bed or to sit on or touch with those long cool fingers. He also began to attend every left-wing occasion, however dreary, advertised in the back pages of the *Statesman*, because he hoped she might be there. So he dozed through China Friendship lectures, readings by Bulgarian poets, and celebrations of the new Russian technology. And he did find her, more than once, only to be cruelly rebuffed and end up encouraging the solemn Colin to try yet another publisher, maybe one less reactionary, with his appalling novel. Prick.

Pauline gradually came to count on his intruding presence and was disappointed, she had to acknowledge, when he didn't turn up for an opening night at Joan Littlewood's theatre in East Stratford. Didn't he know they would be there?

On their return to their bed-sitter, Colin was the first to notice something amiss. Probing for the remembered heel of gin on a shelf, he was surprised to find a full bottle and beside it a little stranger. "How many times," he asked, "have I told you not to buy South African sherry?"

"But I haven't."

"Who did, then?" he asked, even as he dipped into the larder for a jam jar, drawing back, bitten. There sat a dozen new bourgeois tumblers. "Did you buy glasses?" he asked.

"Yes," she said, her manner as nonchalant as she could manage, for she had already reached into the wardrobe for her dressing gown, only to be startled by its unsuspected weight. There was a bar of Givenchy soap in one pocket and a small bottle of Lanvin cologne in the other.

"Anything wrong?" he asked.

"No."

But when she pulled back the bedspread, she was hard-put to suppress a gasp at what she found lying there.

Softie, slim lingerie after Dior.

Joshua waited anxiously by the phone the next morning, he didn't dare leave his flat, but there was no call.

O.K., that's it. He'd had enough. He was through with her. Absolutely. And so, on impulse, the following Saturday afternoon Joshua lugged the boxes from Woolland's, Harrod's, and Dior to a Hampstead garden party that had been organized to raise money for the latest bunch of Africans triumphant in Kenya or Nigeria. She had to be there with the other nigger-lovers. He caught her alone and thrust the lot at her.

"What's this?"

"They don't fit me, you bitch," he said, his manner ferocious, "so you might as well have them," and he fled before she could shove them back at him, even as the congregation was singing a CND marching song, to the tune of *Clementine:*

> In the heart of ancient London
> Lived a man and daughter fair
> With the pep that marks the hep-cat,
> But her daddy was a square.

Then suddenly, it was November 4, 1956, and Joshua stood in Trafalgar Square, along with thousands of others, come to hear Nye Bevan speak, and, in his case, possibly, just possibly, catch a glimpse of Pauline.

Any way you looked at it, it was a black Sunday. At breakfast Joshua read in the *Observer* that a high American government official had said, "There are people inside the National Security Council who have already urged that we use tactical atomic weapons . . . to help Hungary. . . . If the Hungarians are still fighting on Wednesday, we will be closer to war than we have been since August 1939."

Three-thirty in the afternoon, as Joshua stood in front of Canada House, in Trafalgar Square, Russian tanks had already encircled Budapest, an Anglo-French invasion fleet had set sail from Cyprus, pipelines in Iraq and Syria were aflame, and Israeli troops had routed the Egyptian army in Sinai.

Thousands had been drawn to the meeting organized by the Labour Party and the Trades Union Congress. Pauline simply had to be amongst them, but where, and how to find her?

People filled the square, they filled the streets bordering the square, and they spilled over the steps of the National Gallery and St. Martins-in-the-Field. It was the largest demonstration since the war and many who had come to protest were astonishingly young. They had, it's true, a special interest. Many had already been called up. Others were expecting to be called up soon.

The audacious Nye Bevan was at his corrosive best. While the pigeons of Trafalgar Square, temporarily homeless, swooped and complained above, he said, "If Eden is sincere in what he is saying—and he may be—then he is too stupid to be prime minister. He is either a knave or a fool. In both capacities, we don't want him."

"Eden must go!" the crowd roared back. "Eden must go!"

A perplexed Tory to Joshua's right countered with, "Yes, but who's going to replace him?"

Once Bevan had finished, the aroused crowd churned about hopelessly for a moment or two, private arguments flaring up here and there, and then, suddenly, spontaneously, it knit into a marching group. A toothy girl in a green cashmere twin set turned to her escort. "I say," she said, "they're actually going to march on Downing Street."

March on Downing Street they did, thousands upon thousands of them, bringing traffic to a dead stop, waving banners and shouting, "Eden must go! Eden must go!"

And there she was. Unmistakably. Pauline, Pauline. And, oh my God, she was wearing her tempting two-part party-goer for Yves-tide, with its whisper of silk ruffles.

To hell with Hungary! Fuck Suez! Oh my darling, my love, but beside her bobbed the ineffable Colin, beet-faced, hollering, "Eden must go!"

And you too, you little prick!

Bobbies, many of them young, apple-cheeked boys, stood about ten feet apart all the way down Whitehall, even as

Joshua, possessed of an insane will, bulled his way through the crowd, hopping up and down for a glimpse of honey-colored hair, listening for the whisper of silk ruffles above the din.

Pauline, Pauline.

At first the bobbies didn't interfere, but when the demonstrators reached Downing Street, out charged the mounted police. "Shame," the crowd chanted. "Shame!"

A long, pallid, black-bowlered man banged his furled umbrella on the pavement again and again. "Well done, the police," he shouted. "Well done, the police."

Joshua came up behind her and she turned, just for an instant, and smiled before she turned away again, driving her back shamelessly into him.

Heaven.

And he knew, he could swear, she was also wearing her Bali "Self-Expression" Seamless Front Closure Contour Bra, and time and patience would reveal what more.

"Eden must go!" cried a crazed, unknowing Colin.

His arms slid around her waist, her honey-colored hair was driven into his face, and he began to tug her back and away.

The crowd surged forward, trying to breach Downing Street, the mounted police pushed them back again, then the crowd heaved again; and Joshua was dizzy with Pauline's perfume.

"Stop pulling. Patience," she said. "We've got to wait for Colin."

"He's just been arrested," Joshua said.

"Where?"

"I saw."

"You didn't."

"It's the pokey for him tonight. He'll be absolutely thrilled."

"You're lying," she said gaily, not taking her hand from his, falling against him again, laughing.

Joshua kissed Pauline on the mouth for the very first time. "Marry me," he said.

"You're crazy."

"Marry me, marry me."

"But I've already got a husband."

"Of sorts."

"Joshua!"

"I'll take care of him. I come from a family of gangsters."

"Oh, I'll bet," she said.

When they finally quit Whitehall around six o'clock, the

traffic had started to move once more and the pigeons were in possession of Trafalgar Square again. The next morning in bed they read in the *Daily Mail* that even while they had been heaving and chanting, Sir Anthony Eden had been sitting in session at Number 10 with leading cabinet ministers. The *Mail* observed that the demonstrators' ranks had included "large numbers of coloured men, some accompanied by white women. There were also Greeks, Cypriots, Indians, Pakistanis—many of them waving communist publications. . . ."

Once more, a spiffy Canadian contingent had been overlooked.

But the definitive pronouncement on Suez was not made until 1967, when Paul Johnson, then the editor of the *New Statesman*, wrote:

For many people of my generation, Suez was the most exciting time of our lives—the equivalent of the Spanish Civil War for our elders. The issues seemed absolutely clear-cut: right on one side, wrong on the other. We lobbied MPs, stuck up posters, broke up cocktail parties with our angry arguments. It was my first experience of public speaking—standing on a rickety chair outside factory gates and haranguing a sea of sullen faces. On Suez Sunday we all thronged to a monster rally in Trafalgar Square, where Nye Bevan made one of the most sparkling speeches of his life. Then the cry: "To Downing Street"—and the huge, uncontrollable surge into Whitehall. From being comfortably ensconced in the middle of the mob, I suddenly found myself mysteriously in the front rank, with mounted police advancing purposefully towards us. I remember thinking: "I'm glad they're not French cops." Then a few minutes of complete confusion, in which I lost my umbrella and a button from my coat. Some of us reassembled at the Ritz for tea, where a kind waiter took my coat away to have a button sewn on.

Such, such were the terrifying barricades of the London fifties.

2

"You married a very classy tootsie, my boy. I'll bet with her background, she goes to the toilet she doesn't even look in the bowl."

"Oh, thanks, Maw. Thanks a lot."

"And I want to thank you," his mother said, "for inviting us to your wedding. I never realized you were that ashamed of us."

"There was nobody from her family there either," he said, and for the umpteenth time he explained that they had married the day after Pauline's divorce had come through. "Maw, she was eight months pregnant with Alex. We couldn't wait."

"Like father," she said, "like son."

"But I wasn't born," he protested, "until two years after your marriage."

"You saw the certificate?"

No.

"Pour me another drink, *yingele mein*."

He did, but he was infuriated; he was also sorely disappointed, because he had been looking forward to his return to Montreal after so long an absence abroad. 1963 it was and, apart from a couple of flying visits home, he had been away for twelve years. He was returning with a pregnant wife, a child, a growing reputation as a journalist, and an unfinished book. He had, since he had first started on *The Volunteers*, interviewed survivors of the International Brigades in England and France, and now he felt that, making Montreal his base, he would be able to seek out the many American and Canadian veterans he had corresponded with. Fortunately, money was not an immediate problem. He had already signed to write a monthly column on sports for a Toronto magazine. His New York connections were good. A documentary series he had written on the history of boxing for BBC-TV had been sold in Canada, Australia, and New Zealand; a shortened version was scheduled to appear on CBS. All this had earned him a chunk of money sufficient to put down a deposit on a modest house on a terraced street in Lower Westmount. He had been looking forward to his return home because the move had been sweetened for him by the incredible news about his parents. Imagine, after all these years, Reuben and Esther reconciled. Actually living together again. His mother had, she was to tell Joshua, made the reconciliation possible by sacrificing her career as an exotic dancer. For his father's sake.

"For my sake? Shit. She's got fifty-five years and maybe three hundred fifty thousand miles on her."

"So what? Sally Rand's still stripping and she's a lot older than I am. And Margie Hart's still out there. 'If I Shake, It's for Mother's Sake.' Did you hear the one about Lois DeFee?"

Six-foot-six Lois DeFee, the "Eiffel Eyeful," had married a midget.

Q. How did the midget make love to Lois?

A. Somebody put him up to it.

His mother, who had yet to discover that her future would be in skin flicks, had already turned the first of her many emotional flipflops. She had discovered God, the messenger coming in the mousy shape of a little rebbe from the Chabad Lubavitch. Together they had scoured her kitchen stove, thrown out all the dishes, and replaced them with kosher ones. A mezuzah was hammered into the front door. "By rights," Esther informed his stunned father, "I should have my head shaven and wear a wig."

"How come?"

"So I shouldn't be sexy for other men."

"And you think if you walk around here looking like a peeled hardboiled egg, *I'm* going to find you sexy?"

His father was still toiling for Colucci, organizing construction workers, sort of. A week before Joshua and his family were to sail home, Reuben phoned to warn him about Esther. "She's, like, very Jewish these days."

Their first visitor on Wood Avenue was Jane Trimble, and even before his father made it to the house, Uncle Oscar phoned.

"Hey, Dimwit, Denny Dimwit, you're back?"

"Yes."

"So what?"

"How are you, Uncle Oscar?"

"Jiffy-sunglasses, what do you think?"

"I don't understand."

"Prick, what's to understand? It's sunny out, blinding, see, so you dip into your pocket for your tube of Jiffy and just spray it on your regular eyeglasses. Instant sunglasses."

"Hey, that sounds terrific."

"There's a problem."

"What?"

"The formula, prick. What do I put in the spray?"

Reuben arrived early the following morning with a case of chilled Labatt's, a dozen red roses, a battery-powered fire engine, and a doll that squeaked when spanked. He immediately charmed Alex, but he was shy with Pauline. Stealing approving glances at her when her back was turned, giving Joshua the thumbs-up sign, but shy with her until she said, "I'm so sorry, Mr. Shapiro—"

"Reuben."

"—there's not even a chair for you to sit on yet."

"Aw, don't worry, kid. The furniture's going to be here in an hour."

"What furniture?"

"Well, yeah, right. The furniture. Didn't you tell her, Josh?"

"You tell her, Daddy."

"You like antiques. Joshua said so. Well, they're on the way."

"Is that right, Josh?"

Joshua nodded and abruptly turned his back to jimmy open another packing case. Reuben began to stack dishes.

"Now hold it, everybody. Stop. I don't mean to appear ungrateful, but did it ever occur to either of you that *I* might want to select the furnishings for my house?"

"Why, sure. That's how come I got it on approval. Isn't that so, Josh?"

"Damn right."

"Anything you don't want, it goes right back and fuck it. Excuse me."

"And where will this furniture be coming from?"

"Yeah, where," Reuben said, scratching his head. "Why, from the antique shop."

"Which one?"

"Ask Josh."

"Huchette's."

"You said it. It's in St. Jerome. You turn left at the Esso station."

"I never heard of it," Pauline said, anticipating a shipment of garish furnishings she wouldn't be able to return without hurting her father-in-law's feelings. Damn it, Josh.

"Well, this Huchette runs this kinda warehouse for my old friend Colucci, and I had the pick of everything."

An enormous moving van pulled up in front of the house, and the men began to unload. A long oak refectory table. Eight high-backed chairs. A beautiful grandfather clock. Winged leather armchairs. A quilted sofa. A brass bedstead. Bureaus. An antique mirror. Pauline stood there speechless, amazed, and then she suddenly cried, "Stop!"

The men set down the heavy oak breakfront, panting.

"I thought this was the kinda stuff she liked," Reuben said, shooting Joshua a dark look.

"Of course I like it. It's beautiful. But have you any idea what these things cost today?"

Reuben rocked on his heels, beaming. "It's, like, my wedding gift."

"But we can't accept all this from you, Reuben. It's far too much."

Reuben broke open a bottle of Labatt's.

"Why don't we just let the men put everything down," Joshua said, "and we'll discuss it after they've gone."

Pauline wavered.

"O.K., boys," Reuben said. "Bring in the rest."

A rolltop desk. A marble-topped table with a wrought-iron base. Beds. A color-TV set. Lamps. Another sofa. And still the men were returning to the van for more. Pauline, distressed, summoned Joshua into the kitchen. "He's not a rich man. We can't take all these things from him. It's indecent."

"Yeah, but he's very touchy. We don't want to hurt his feelings."

Finally, the movers left and Joshua and Reuben watched anxiously as an awed and obviously perplexed Pauline moved among her new possessions, peering into a drawer here, running her hand along a surface there, standing back the better to ponder a wing-chair. And then she stooped behind the color-TV set, lingering there, before she shot bolt upright, her expression severe. "Now sit down, please," she said.

Reuben sat down.

"Both of you."

Joshua took the other wing-chair.

"Have all these things been stolen from somewhere?" she asked in a quivering voice.

Joshua sighed and contemplated the ceiling.

"How could you think such a thing?" Reuben asked.

"Because," she said, "if you will look closely at the back of the color-TV set, you cannot fail to observe that somebody has gone to a good deal of trouble to file off the serial number."

"Holy shit," Reuben said, "but those dealers are just not to be trusted. One's more crooked than the next." He examined the set himself. "Fortunately, this doesn't come from Huchette. I picked it up on Craig Street and it's going right back there."

"Why don't we just call the cops?" Joshua asked.

"Well, yeah, right. Good thinking. We could report it. What do you say, Pauline?"

She hesitated. Somewhat—if far from totally—reassured,

222

she backed off a little. "You do whatever you think best. I'd better make some lunch for Alex."

The following night Reuben and Esther took them out to dinner in a kosher restaurant. Pauline had already warmed to Reuben and felt easy with him, but Esther scared her. A born-again, dark, brooding Esther.

"In which faith," Esther wanted to know, "will my grand-children be raised?"

"Cut the crap," Reuben said.

Nervous, and more than somewhat high, Pauline told Reuben what a gentleman his son had become. She said he never entered her boudoir without folding his trousers neat and washing up good, even if he no longer kept his wallet under his pillow. She also allowed that he had yet to hit her.

"He never should of told you any of that," Reuben said, his manner solemn yet pleased.

But Esther, Joshua could see, was fulminating, obviously feeling left out.

And now, two nights later, seated with her in his parents' N.D.G. apartment, Reuben out at Blue Bonnets, she said, "Pour me another drink, *yingele mein*," and he fixed her a Dewar's and a splash.

"Poor Ruby," she said.

"I didn't say that."

"But right now you feel sorry for him, you feel he never would have had to marry me if not for you."

Once, Joshua had summoned up the courage to ask his father why he had married Esther in the first place.

"You think it was my idea? She was a boxing freak. She used to come to my fights shrieking, shouting curses at the referee, sobbing any time I was hit. Hanging around outside the dressing room. A Leventhal girl. I don't know how many times she proposed before I said yes, on condition she promised to stay away from my fights. I looked like a fool."

"Didn't you ever love her?" Joshua demanded angrily.

"I forget."

"That's a hell of a thing to say."

"Those Leventhals gave me a lot of trouble. They treated me like dirt."

Joshua fetched another glass and poured himself a drink.

"I know why you hate me," Esther said.

"What are you talking about?"

"Ed Ryan. Remember?"

"I remember."

"You came back from Belmont Park that day and you

knew, just seeing me standing there, and you gave me that look, his look, and then he came back from Michigan, the second time I mean, and it didn't matter how many whores he had while he was hiding out, or what I went through worrying about him, he found out, maybe that gangster Colucci told him, and Ed Ryan ended up a cripple and me a drunk, my son."

"I didn't know anything about his whores, not then, but I do remember that you used to lock me out of the house so that you and Ryan wouldn't be disturbed."

"Let me tell you something about your precious father. He's incapable of a relationship with any woman who expects more than five-and-two from him, and don't tell me you don't know what that means. You used to go to Kitty's too. Like father, like son."

"I would come home from school and your bedroom would stink of Ed Ryan's cigar smoke."

"My, my. Mr. Ryan used to bring me flowers. Your father gave me a dose."

"Oh God, Maw, there are some things I don't need to know."

"Do you know how long Mr. Ryan was after me, and all the others, with your father in prison if he wasn't in hiding?"

"I don't give a damn."

"You don't give a damn about me. All right. I deserve it. I never wanted you," she said, reaching for the bottle. "Remember, I used to have to shoot a roll of film of you every week. His precious boy. You know why? He was afraid of what I might do to you. When you were a baby with the croup, I couldn't get any sleep, I was going crazy, I once hit you so hard he had to send for the doctor. I hated changing your shitty diapers. If you hadn't been born, I would have been with him in Michigan and we might have started a new life there. There was still hope for us then."

"But I thought you only married him because I was coming."

"I was beautiful enough to be in the movies. They wanted me to do a test."

"Who?"

"Who? Where? Why? When? I don't have to answer questions for the cops any more. People, that's who. You adore him, don't you?"

"Yes."

"And if I told you that he killed at least one man I know of, what would you think of that, Mr. Writer?"

"In the ring?" Joshua put in nervously.

"He was fast. Oh, on his good days there were none faster. Stick, stick, and away you go. But he didn't knock out too many people." She paused. "No. Not in the ring. He took out a man on a back road on our side of the Vermont border. When he was running booze for the Gurskys. A gun fight."

"I see."

"Tell me," she asked, smiling, "does the senator's daughter know what kind of family she's married into?"

"I suppose not."

Esther laughed. So did Joshua.

"Neither did I. Him. The crazy Oscar. Your Uncle Harvey begged me not to throw everything away for your father. He wanted to send me to McGill. But I was highly sexed and Reuben was like nobody I had ever known before, and he told me he was going to be a champion and I believed him and look at him now. An ex-con in a Panama hat. A hoodlum's bum-boy. Did you know he used to break people's hands for Colucci?"

"Yes, I knew."

"Tell the senator's daughter."

"What have you got against Pauline?"

"Her age. And the way you follow her everywhere with your eyes. I'm leaving your beloved father as soon as I can find work. Getting together again was a mistake."

"But I thought it was your idea?"

"Think again. Anyway, it isn't working. I want more than five-and-two out of this lousy life."

"What will you do?"

"I have plans."

"Can I do anything to help?"

"I don't need your money. I have family of my own."

Joshua winced.

"That hurt. Good. You've hurt me plenty. Hey," she asked, relenting, "what happened when the Alabama Assassin met the Brockton Blockbuster?"

"Rocky Marciano dumped him in the eighth round."

His mother began to sob. "And who did Floyd Patterson beat for the crown?"

"Archie Moore. Fifth round. Chicago. November thirtieth, fifty-six."

"Maybe I'll just find myself a younger man," she said, pouring herself another drink, "who can fuck me like Mr. Royal once did."

"God damn it, Maw."

225

"Don't you ever cry?"

"No."

"I'm not that old, you know. I can still handle it. She'd understand, your classy-assy tootsie. Because she's been around, my son. If you don't know, I do."

"Pauline and I will be just fine."

"This is the six o'clock news. Brought to you by ungrateful children, highly recommended by doctors everywhere. Good evening, Mr. and Mrs. America, and all the ships at sea. Hear this. Joshua Shapiro married above himself."

"Like father," he said, taunting her, "like son."

"I was one of the Leventhal girls."

"Wowee," he said. But she didn't react. She didn't remember.

"You never cared for them, any of them, but when you were in trouble with the cops, who always came through for you? Your beloved father or Uncle Harvey?"

"Daddy once told me that they treated him like dirt."

"O.K. So? We were much more cultivated people. I could play the piano. We wore white gloves on the High Holidays, the Leventhal girls. I didn't jump out of my pants at the sight of a policeman. My father used to take me to lectures. John Mason Brown. Pierre van Paassen. We attended symphony concerts. You know, I once asked your father if he would take me to *Macbeth*, Donald Wolfit was in town, at His Majesty's, and do you know what he said? 'Shakespeare,' he said. 'Take away the fancy costumes and the swordplay and what are you left with? Poetry, for Christ's sake!' "

Joshua could not hold back his laughter.

"I knew you'd find that funny," and now she was laughing and weeping at the same time. *"Tell him not to leave me again. Speak to him."*

"But I thought you said—"

"You thought. I said. He did. I didn't. Fuck you," she shouted, knocking his glass to the floor.

Joshua took his shaking mother in his arms. He stroked her thick black hair. My God, she's small. I never realized.

"Let me go," she said, breaking free.

"Do you want me to speak to him?"

"Certainly not."

"What do you want?"

"Who knows?"

He stooped to pick up the broken glass.

"Do you at least earn enough to support your family, Mr. Writer, or are you living off her stocks and bonds?"

"I haven't taken a penny from her."

"You will. Wait. Then her background will come out. Westmount will be heard from. Watch out for your balls, kiddo."

3

Money, money.

Once, no thought for tomorrow, he could con Barclay's into an overdraft and, his pockets stuffed with crinkly, white, handkerchief-sized fivers, splurge on Front Closure Bras, draw-stringers from Renata, and softie, slim lingerie from Dior. His *finca* in San Antonio, with a cook thrown in, had set him back no more than $50 a month. A £150 publisher's advance had been sufficient to put him merrily to work on a book. His first book. But now the $25,000 in advances he had squeezed out of Toronto and New York publishers to write the definitive book on hockey seemed a pittance, an insulting reward, for the work he knew would be involved in researching and writing the book. Now he had a wife born to champagne as well as Kool-Aid in her fridge and three kids who expected the *right* ski boots. Now he was earning more money than he had ever dreamed of, and yet there never seemed to be enough.

Where it sprang from, as well as how it went, continued to confound him.

There was the fat check for the sports column he still cranked out monthly; a thin trickle of royalties on paperback reissues of books he'd otherwise rather not be reminded of; magazine assignments out of New York; and, above all, the money he earned doing television work for CBC Interviews. And documentaries that he narrated himself.

Each year he solemnly entered these projected earnings into a ledger with reassuringly lined pages, estimated his outgoings, conscientiously adding ten percent, and tottered out of his office to tell Pauline this was the year, the biggie, when he was bound to come out a big five thousand ahead minimum. How about that? Hug hug. Kiss kiss. But when the year was out, he unfailingly emerged $7,500 short and found himself, a Grub Street Mr. Micawber, counting on something turning up.

Once it had been the sale of his manuscripts to that twit Colin Fraser in Calgary. Fraser, who had come out of the

227

closet, as it were, and was living with a young actor. Another time it was a whacking royalty check out of East Germany for the people's edition of *The Volunteers*. But what now, Joshua?

"So, yes," Pauline had said, "I helped to buy him the boat. He's cost me thousands over the years. I finance his dreams."

Never mind his dreams, darling, what about my nightmares?

But the truth was, Pauline couldn't help. What with inflation, the money that still dribbled in from her trust fund was negligible. So Joshua had, he calculated, two options. He could negotiate a larger mortgage on their house, creaming off the cash, or he could finally fall back on his inheritance, the long thin key that still hung from a silvery chain round his neck. But he was superstitious about that key, he really didn't want to know how many stocks and bonds or whatever were fattening in Reuben's safety deposit box. It was only to be used, he felt, in the event of a real catastrophe. If, for instance, anything happened to him, and Pauline was left to cope with the children. And neither did he want Pauline to know he was troubled about money. She was far too edgy these days, even short-fused, the continuing presence in the city of that late bloomer, Kevin Hornby, seemingly casting a pall on her days.

Jolly Jack Trimble was also becoming a nuisance.

Only a week after Joshua had confronted him in The Troika, he had phoned to invite him to meet there yet again.

"I want to apologize for being such a nit. Of course," he implored, "you were only trying to take the mickey out of me when you went on about my not being born British."

"Yeah. Right," Joshua said uneasily.

"And certainly," Trimble said, those hard little eyes glittering, "the joke stopped right there."

"Yes. Certainly."

"I asked you to meet me here," he said, "because I'm on to something hot. I can't even whisper the name of the stock, it's that confidential, but if you can let me have ten thousand, I can double it for you in three weeks."

"Jack, I don't play the market."

"This isn't playing, it's a dead cert. Do you understand me?"

"I'm afraid I do," Joshua said, stiffening, "and I don't care for it. And anyway, I wouldn't know where to lay my hands on ten thousand."

"Borrow it from your bank."

"I'm already into my bank for all they will tolerate."

"I'll sign for the loan. Or I can even lend you the money."

"Jack, this really isn't necessary. You don't owe me a thing."

"Of course I don't owe you a thing," he said, his cheeks flaring red. "What an absurd thing to say. I'm just trying to be a friend. I thought you would appreciate that."

As autumn yielded to winter, the trees bare, fur coats being redeemed from storage, Christmas decorations going up everywhere, the investment trust that was Kevin's special domain in Trimble's office began to attract attention. In this country, a sour Joshua noted, where prophets were without honor, but profitmakers venerated, he was becoming a figure. He was acclaimed in the *Financial Post;* there was a short, snappy profile in the business pages of *Maclean's.* "Westmount's Whizz Kid." In all his interviews, Kevin paid fulsome tribute to Trimble, the acknowledged financial wizard who had given him his chance, and his slippery benefactor unfailingly responded in kind. "Kevin Hornby," he told one reporter after another, "is the Guy Lafleur of this office. He's a natural. If Coral is this year's success story, well, he deserves all the credit. I consider myself lucky to be able to share in the profits."

The profits, on the evidence, were prodigious, not only shareholders but also Kevin quivering with delight as Coral fattened on points day after day.

WESTMOUNT WHIZZ KID FLIES OWN PLANE ran a headline in the *Gazette.* Kevin was no longer dependent on the vagaries of commercial airline schedules, but could now pilot his own Beechcraft to New York or Toronto or Calgary or wherever it was crucial for him to strike next. He was, the reporter noted, the only son of Senator Stephen Andrew Hornby, and a portrait of that grand old man held pride of place in his office. "I'm just crazy about having the old s.o.b. hanging up there," he was quoted as saying. "Keeping me honest. Watching over me and my work."

Joshua ran into Kevin, inevitably, on Sherbrooke Street, immediately in front of the Cartier, where he had taken an apartment. Kevin insisted he come right upstairs with him for a drink.

"You have no idea how inadequate I feel in the presence of people with real talent. People like you. All I make is money," he said, dimpling.

"On the evidence, a good deal of it, too," Joshua ventured, scanning the apartment.

229

Trophies trooped across the mantelpiece. Golf, bridge, fishing. And there were photographs of Kevin everywhere. Standing alongside an enormous marlin hanging from a dockside scale. Golden-haired, younger, assuming a linebackers' stance, a McGill Redman. Cuddling with two starlets from *Thunderball*. There was also a framed photograph of Kevin and Pauline, embracing on a tennis court. The Mixed Doubles Champions. But that had been in 1952, and the man who sat before him now carefully combed his hair to conceal a burgeoning bald spot. His eyes were pouchy, rimmed with red. He was putting on a paunch. His hands were far from steady.

"Coral's been my salvation," he said.

"I read somewhere that Jack thinks you're the Guy Lafleur of brokers."

"Well, that was typically generous of him. But I wouldn't go that far. I prefer to think I've been lucky. How's Trout?"

"Pauline's just fine, but she's worried about you."

"Worried? I'm doing fabulously well. She ought to be pleased."

"Oh, but of course, she's pleased. So am I."

"Don't get pompous with me, please."

"As long," Joshua continued, "as you don't do anything to hurt her or the senator."

"Do you speak for my dear father as well now?"

"No," Joshua said, retreating, "not really."

"But I understand that the two of you get on famously."

"Does that surprise you?"

"How is the old boy these days?"

"Thriving, considering his age."

"Interesting, don't you think, that I should have to ask a stranger about my father?"

"Why don't you drive out to Ottawa and surprise him with a visit? He might respond to that."

"Or show me the door again."

"Give him the option."

"No way."

A week later, Kevin was adjudged one of Montreal's Most Desirable Bachelors in a feature that appeared in *Chatelaine*. The magazine came out on the day of Trimble's annual Guy Fawkes party and a twinkly-eyed Kevin, arriving late, a fashion model on each arm, took the inevitable ribbing good-naturedly. It was, by common consent, the most opulent of Trimble's parties and, sometime later, cursed with hindsight,

230

Joshua would come to wonder whether he already knew there would never be another.

The theme, naturally, was resoundingly British. Union Jack lampshades and wastepaper baskets and ashtrays everywhere. Smoked salmon had been flown in from Harrod's, and the kippers that would be offered to those who stayed on for breakfast, from Fortnum's. Waitresses offered a Queen Elizabeth rose to each lady as she drifted into the living room. Waiters, dressed like buskers, held forth over a counter offering cockles and winkles; they brought round trays laden with sizzling brown bangers or Scotch ale, as well as champagne. There was a pearly king and queen and disco music from a group called The Lambeth Walk. An actor with a cockney accent had been hired to fry the fish and chips. Dover sole. The real stuff. "And only the bona fide Québécois here," a bouncy, rosy-cheeked Trimble announced to cheers, "will be allowed to sprinkle vinegar on their *pommes frites.*"

Wet snow had begun to fall before the fireworks display in the garden, but it did not detract from its splendor. Everybody oohed, everybody aahed. Catherine wheels. Exploding stars. Whooshing rockets. Sprinklers. Cracklers. Chasers. Raining comets. And, finally, the *pièce de résistance:* A rubber-booted Charlie moved out to light a long fuse attached to an elaborate frame, retreated, and a moment later everybody applauded; there were even some defiant cheers, as the unmistakable images of Her Majesty Queen Elizabeth II and Prince Philip leaped and spluttered before they illuminated the troubled skies of loyal Westmount, a colony besieged.

In the opinion of some, this last display was needlessly provocative, considering the times. Izzy Singer sought out the *Star*'s society columnist and drove her into a corner.

"I've already got your name," she said impatiently, "*and* Mrs. Singer's dress. A sheath of cerulean blue printed silk."

No, no, Izzy pointed out, this time he emphatically didn't want his name listed among the guests.

A bad business, somebody else suggested. After all, Trimble's neighbors did include a Parti Québécois cabinet minister.

"Oh, let him get stuffed," Trimble said.

And then Trimble, who had seemed to be everywhere at once, was suddenly nowhere to be found. The lights dimmed and knowing guests began to giggle, explaining to newcomers that it was time for his number. One year, memorably, it had been "Maybe It's Because I'm a Londoner That I Love London So."

Wait. He's really something else. Hilarious. Wicked. A card. And now, incredibly, he was sashaying out there, even as The Lambeth Walk played a fanfare. Garishly rouged, his cupid's mouth smeared with lipstick. Wearing a wig. Trimble in drag. My, my. His gay nineties gown uplifted by enormous balloon breasts. Strutting in high button boots. The jowly, hard-eyed Trimble, leering at his squealing guests and singing in a cockney accent:

"My word, I've had a party,
My word, I've had a spree!
Believe me or believe me not,
It's all the same to me!
I'm wild with exaltation,
I'm dizzy with success,
For I've danced with a man who—
Well, you'll never guess!

I've danced with a man who's danced with a girl
Who's danced with the Prince of Wales!
I'm crazy with excitement,
Completely off the rails!
And when he said to me what she said to him
The Prince remark'd to her,
It was simply grand!
He said, 'Topping band!'
And she said, 'Delightful, sir!'
Glory, glory hallelujah,
I'm the luckiest of females,
For I've danced with a man who's danced with a girl
Who's danced with the Prince of Wales!"

As the lights had dimmed, Joshua caught a glimpse of Jane burying her head in Kevin's chest, in mock or possibly even real horror. But now, as the lights brightened again to appreciative laughter and applause, she was standing alone. Kevin had gone. And Pauline was not to be seen anywhere. Jane waved a hand at Joshua and drifted to a corner of the room, waiting for him to join her. "They're in the library," she said. "Having it out. About time too. You haven't told me how lovely I look tonight."

"I was saving it for a more intimate moment."

"She can't stand not being his games mistress any more. 'Kevin take a giant step, Kevin don't.' If I were unkind—"

"If you were what?"

"—I might even venture that she's somewhat chagrined to find him standing on his own two feet at last."

232

"Don't ever underestimate my wife."

"Everybody's getting into Coral. Abbott, Hickey, McTeer, the Friars . . . They were holding off, frankly dubious, but now they're falling all over themselves to invest."

"Possibly," Joshua said, "nothing breeds forgiveness or makes Westmount's heart palpitate quite so much as the smell of quick money."

"Oh, but here comes Pauline," she said, brightening, leaning over to kiss him tenderly on the cheek as she approached.

Pauline had been crying and wanted to leave immediately.

Once they were in the car, she said, "He's buying a condominium downtown. A hundred thousand dollars. He's looking at properties on the lake. Oh, and he and Jack are considering going into film production. Something to do with tax shelters. He wanted to know if you had any script ideas?"

"Gee," Joshua said. "Golly."

"And lookee here," she said, handing him a folded envelope, as they pulled up in front of the house. "Repayment in part."

There was a check for $5,000, and a certificate declaring her the owner of another $5,000 worth of Coral shares.

"He says the shares are already worth better than eight thousand and that I should hold on to them. I think I'll do just that, but you can have the check if you make me forget that I'm a mother of three tonight."

4

Good news.

The next morning's mail brought a letter from his American publisher, suggesting the time could be ripe for another edition of *The Volunteers*, if only Joshua was willing to return to Spain to gather material for a new introduction.

The Volunteers, eight years in the making, had finally been published in 1966. The Canadian edition had sold some six hundred copies; the American, nearly five thousand; and the British, more than three. But there had been a gratifying number of translations. Reviews had been surprisingly widespread and, for the most part, flattering. And, best of all, two weeks before the book was to appear in England, Pauline and the kids had presented him with an airplane ticket to London, so that he could be there for publication.

London, demented London, already pronounced swinging in 1966, the party in full flow.

Jean Shrimpton yielded to Twiggy; the Beatles to the Rolling Stones. Germaine Greer, reviewing a cookery book in the *Spectator—Consuming Passions, A History of English Food and Appetite*—rebuked the author, Philippa Pullar, for saying "not a word about the charming practice of marinading fish between the vulvae to make a delicacy for a lover." Which was a long way from the schmaltz herring Morty Zipper's grandmother used to make for them.

Strolling down to The World's End, once his local pub, the very morning of his arrival, Joshua was struck by the transformation of this once flaking street into the most saucy of boulevards. Tarted-up junk shops were now offering "antiques" at insanely inflated prices. The surly King's Road chemist of blessed memory, the greengrocer and sweets shop proprietor who had struggled for years, realizing a small annual profit, had finally struck an unexpected bonanza, letting their leaseholds go for a ransom to Le Drugstore, boutiques called Skin, Just Men, or Take 6, and to frightfully in restaurants and clubs such as Alvaro's and Dell'Aretusa.

Joshua learned that Alvaro Maccioni, the former waiter who ran both places, had appointed a committee of fifteen social savants to pronounce on applications to join Dell'Aretusa. Only the rich, only the famous, need apply.

"It's not," Alvaro told a reporter, "that I choose these people because I think they are better, but because they have things to talk about. The man who gets up in the morning and goes to the factory every day to produce some tool or something—what does he have to tell me of life? I have nothing against the poor devil, but you can't make conversation with him unless it's about football or women."

Joshua had come to the King's Road, at Margaret's request, to take his godson to lunch. Murdoch's boy Ralph. Ralph was in trouble at St. Paul's. He had been caught smoking pot. Murdoch hadn't helped matters any by telling the headmaster that he was a bloody hypocrite and that in any event pot would soon be legalized. Waiting for Ralph in The Eight Bells, Joshua leafed through one of the new magazines, *Climax,* that he had picked up in a neighboring newsagent's shop.

GET YOUR OWN VICKY MOSS COCK CANDLE

This is it, gang, your chance to have your very own Vicky Moss Cock Candle, a beautiful multi-coloured realistic candle of a rigid cock, unavailable anywhere else. A guaranteed conversation piece, these candles are so realistic they could even be used as the real thing, but we offer them as a novelty only. Comes in two sizes, regular and the Vicky Moss Cannonball Special.

For the sake of Ralph's generation, Joshua, Murdoch, and the others had once won a famous victory. After Ypres, following the Battle of Britain, never had so many adolescents owed so much to so few libertarians. When our St. Crispin's Day came, Joshua thought, we certainly held that thin red line. Writing intrepid letters to the *Times* and taking the stand as indignant witnesses, they had seen to it that the ban on one of the most tedious novels ever written, *Lady Chatterley's Lover*, was lifted. And lucky Ralph's inheritance was now *Climax, Forum,* and the porn flicks.

Ralph and his kind had not been raised on crippling Jewish, Calvinist, or Catholic lies. Self-serving lies. Unlike their fathers, they had not been shackled by the manifest hypocrisies of either church or synagogue. Ralph had been brought up to masturbate not in fear of being struck blind, but with pride in his stroke. There were no forbidden foods in his heritage. Or original sins. Liberated from a stultifying class system, he was attracted by a society built on caste. Which is to say, his was a free and questing spirit, impressed more than anything with the wisdom of the East, the inner peace he sensed among the swollen-bellied, starving masses of India. Ralph was also fascinated by pagan rituals. Although Joshua hadn't seen him in years, he immediately recognized him as he came swaggering into the pub. Ralph had grown into a tall, gangling young man, with Margaret's crooked teeth and Murdoch's weak, squinting eyes and lank, unruly hair. He wore a velvet blouse, unlaced to the navel, bell-bottom trousers, and sandals. He twitched, he bit his nails.

"Are you taking me to Alvaro's, Joshua?"

"I'm not a member," he said, telling him about Alvaro's interview with the *Standard*. "Besides, most of the writers I know only talk about women or sports. And if it's not that, it's royalties. We'd never do."

Joshua took him to a decent but unfashionable Italian basement restaurant instead, and there Ralph told him that he wished to become a writer. "But my father says I shouldn't call myself Murdoch. He says critics would only compare my work to his, to my disadvantage."

235

"Your father has many endearing qualities, but he can also be an oaf. Call yourself anything you like."

"I don't dig his stuff, anyway. You both write about how groovy it was to be born poor. But that's superficial. All that kitchen-sink stuff has become a bore."

"How were we to know?"

"And he's writing very badly now. Margaret can't get him the advances he once got. The Americans are no longer interested in him."

"I understand that you're in some kind of trouble at school."

"Oh, shit, it was only pot. And they're taking me back. They only throw you out if you're caught pushing. Besides, Margaret smokes with her boyfriends. Or my uncles, as they once were," he said, smirking. "I want to go to America."

"Sure. Why not? But finish school first."

"Can you help me get into films?"

"I thought you wanted to be a writer?"

"I want to direct my own scripts."

"One of the few directors I know," Joshua said stiffly, "began as a clapper boy. Are you willing to do that?"

Ralph's smile was pitying. "Man," he said, "but you and my father make a pair. You no longer work your way up from the bottom floor. Those days are past."

"How do you get to direct your own scripts then?"

"You make yourself a reputation."

"And how do you do that?" Joshua asked, paying the bill.

"I'm going to be in next week's *Private Eye*. They found out about St. Paul's and they're giving me a mention."

"And that's a start?"

"Yes," he said, grinning.

Before they parted, Ralph borrowed £10. Margaret had warned Joshua that he tried to borrow £10 here, a fiver there, from all her friends, and not to give him anything. But such was Joshua's distaste for Ralph that he could not deny him.

"Thanks, Uncle," Ralph said with a meaningful smile, and then he was gone.

At a dinner party the same evening, Joshua discovered that the lady seated next to him had just returned from Ibiza. Such a darling place.

Had she been to San Antonio, Joshua demanded, excited.

Yes.

Had she run into a German there? Tall, sorrowful. A Dr. Dr. Mueller.

No.

236

What about the Casa del Sol?

Good heavens, but there were so many hotels there now, it was difficult to remember the names.

In the morning, Joshua stopped at a travel agency on Sloane Square. "Is it possible for you to book me a hotel on Ibiza?" he asked.

Certainly, sir.

"The Casa del Sol," he said.

But she could find no listing for it.

"It's in San Antonio," he said.

"I'm sorry, sir. I simply can't find it."

"But I've stayed there."

"When?"

"Nineteen fifty-two."

"Well now, that was fourteen years ago, wasn't it? There have been a good many changes on Ibiza since then."

Seething, Joshua turned into the King's Road and promptly split his trousers down the backside. He tried to buy another pair, but in all the fabled boutiques of Chelsea he could not find a pair without bellbottoms. All at once, he was filled with a fierce resentment against style-making London, the new modish foolery. And his indignation was compounded by an especially mindless week, which had seen a new pronouncement in the *Evening Standard* by Mary Quant. Think pink, Miss Quant cooed, and suggested that next year's clothes could do more to highlight the inherent loveliness of pubic hair. Furthermore, Miss Quant revealed that her mate diverted himself after a hard day at the office by trimming her own pubic hair into a heart shape, making her vagina a living valentine, so to speak.

Joshua retreated into the nearest pub, drank a large gin, and another, and another, and then phoned Pauline. "I'm coming home," he said.

Where a pleasant surprise awaited him.

The paperback rights to *The Volunteers* had been sold in the United States for a modest advance, even by the standards of those years, and he took his father out to lunch to celebrate. "Twenty-five hundred bucks," Reuben said. "Well, that's great. Really great. Hey, Josh, aren't those paperback books handled by magazine distributors, like?"

In New York, a year later, Joshua's paperback editor took him out to an expensive dinner and told him how pleased everybody was with his surprisingly good sales. "The book is ordering astonishingly well in places like Phoenix, Chicago, Detroit, New Orleans, and Florida. And, oh yes, Louisville,

Kentucky, where I always thought they never read about anything but horse-racing. Frankly, we never expected there would be such interest in a book, however talented," he put in quickly, "about the Spanish Civil War."

"Obviously," Joshua said, reaching for his drink, "there's been strong word-of-mouth in some areas."

5

A week after Trimble's Guy Fawkes party, Joshua sat in his study unable to work, fingering the long thin key to the Kingdom of Shapiro, wondering if, after all, the time had come to crack the safety deposit box in Cornwall. Or cash the check Kevin had given to Pauline. Then, miraculously, the phone rang and something did turn up. Peabody at *Playboy*. As they couldn't afford Harold Robbins, he said, and Jacqueline Susann wasn't available, would he consider doing a piece for them on the new Hollywood? Only three days later, Joshua flew out to L.A.

Joshua loved Hollywood and its confident hustlers. On a previous visit he had delighted in spinning through the canyons in somebody else's Mercedes, gearing down to consider the more outlandish mansions, each garden perfect. He liked to wander through the unbelievably opulent men's shops on Rodeo, startling the prissy clerks by bargaining. He enjoyed the tanned, trim, middle-aged producers on health diets, toting scripts to market in Gucci attaché cases, even as their East Side grandfathers had once carried sewing machines on their shoulders. They strutted into the Polo Lounge or La Scala or Dominic's, bound in safari suits, blissfully playing the room, death just another sour-grapes rumor out of the East, bad word of mouth, something that used to figure in grainy European-made films, which everybody knew were bum grossers.

Strolling down Wilshire Boulevard, the morning after his arrival, he ran into Murdoch, a Sidney Murdoch so bloated he hardly recognized him. The two friends, who hadn't seen each other in half-a-dozen years, fell tearfully into each other's arms and immediately repaired to La Scala for lunch.

"Who would have dreamed," Murdoch said, recalling their first meeting, "that we ever would have lived to run into each other here?"

"Those unforgiving literary lads we once were."

"Are you appalled, dear boy?"

"Absolutely not."

"I'm thrilled. And I want you to know I'm doing splendidly here."

Murdoch had been raised on the Hollywood of Bette Davis, Joan Crawford, Gary Cooper, Cary Grant, Bogart, and Rita Hayworth. The scandalous life of the stars. The depravity that was the rule on board Errol Flynn's yacht and in Charlie Chaplin's mansion. He had flown out to Hollywood on an assignment grudgingly dredged up by a fearful Margaret, who had long been his literary agent as well as Joshua's. Margaret was understandably concerned about his venture and lectured him severely about his drinking and his lechery. "You don't understand what you're getting into. Hollywood's quieter than Leatherhead on a Saturday night and considerably more boring."

"Oh yes, I'm sure," Murdoch said, filled with glee.

Murdoch, innocent Murdoch, his once magical powers failing, had been hired by Bill Markham to write a treatment based on his magnificent second novel, set in the Midlands. Determined not to be mistaken for just another British ninny on arrival, he had put a good deal of uncharacteristic thought into his transatlantic attire. Gone were the hush puppies, the shirts from Marks & Spencer, the baggy tweed suit from Cecil Gee's. Murdoch had floated off the plane wearing a floppy widebrimmed felt hat, dark glasses, a foulard from Sulka, a shirt from Mr. Fish with more stripes than an old-fashioned barber pole, flared trousers, and soft Chelsea boots. The studio flunkey who had been dispatched to drive him to The Beverly Hills Hotel chatted knowledgeably, he thought, about the delights of Covent Garden and the Royal Shakespeare Company.

"Oh, who gives a damn about all those prancing pooves," Murdoch said.

The flunkey said he would be sending a limo round to pick up Murdoch at seven for a dinner party at the Markhams'. Murdoch, anticipating a poolside quivering with *Playboy* centerfolds, juicy as they were wanton, hurried into the shower and soaped his hairy belly. He shook talcum powder over his genitals. But when he arrived at the Markhams' mansion, he discovered that he was the only guest; he was dining alone with Bill and his cultivated wife, Ellen. Svelte, bony Ellen, who wore black hair straight back, gathered with a jade clip. She wore a silk shirt and narrow black slacks. Her antique

239

man's pocket watch, settled between small tight breasts, was suspended from her long neck by a gold chain.

"How good of you to have me here," a deflated Murdoch said.

The dinner party wasn't at poolside, either, but at a table set in a room that had been cleverly redone with fittings transported from a seedy Camden Town pub, complete with jars of Scotch eggs floating in filthy brine and a mottled mirror advertising Watney's.

"I can't imagine what awful things you've heard about film people," Ellen said, "but I want you to know that Bill brought you out here because he has the highest regard for your integrity."

When she leaned forward to flick her cigarette at the ashtray, her pocket watch dipped, dangling free, and when she leaned back again, it swung with her, landing between her breasts with a most disconcerting thud. "You have written a seminal novel," she crooned.

"It's a minor masterpiece," Markham pitched in, suppressing a yawn.

"But I'm willing to make any changes you require," Murdoch offered affably.

"Oh, dear. No. You mustn't think for a moment," Ellen said, affronted, "that *everybody* in Hollywood is only interested in money. That would be selling us short."

Ignoring her, Murdoch appealed to Markham. "Do you think we could get Ava Gardner to play Mavis?"

"We could get Ava Gardner to play anything," Markham said, aghast. "She must be fifty now."

"Oh yes. How stupid of me. What about Raquel Welch?"

"*Tell him,*" Ellen said.

"Sidney, this is going to be our Tiffany project."

Murdoch began to fizz with pleasure and anticipation.

"We're not going after prurience in this film. We're going to shoot this back in Leeds with *real* actresses."

"There," Ellen said, "aren't you relieved?," and she asked him if he knew Doris Lessing.

Seated with Joshua at La Scala three days later, Murdoch had to admit that he had phoned Markham three times since that first meeting and he had yet to call back. "But I'm not the least bit worried," he said. "I've written a splendid treatment. Awfully sexy. I've put in all the filth I could only hint at in the novel. Joshua, they are justifiably put off by literary types here because of their pretensions. They find me refresh-

240

ing, because I'm prepared to adjust. I'm willing to write for the market."

They were well into the Remy Martin before Murdoch announced how proud he was of Margaret. "When I took her on," he said, "she was no more than a mouse, incredibly shy, with those perfectly dreadful teeth, and look at her now. Thriving. Running my life, the bitch. Mind you, she never remarried, but," he shrugged, "after me . . ."

They contemplated their drinks, two middle-aged cronies in a strange land.

"There's something I always wanted to ask you, Joshua. It's about Cambridge."

"Yes."

"I don't know quite how to put this . . ."

Joshua waited, bemused, his manner unhelpful.

"Remember, ah, Joanna?"

"Indeed I do."

"I feel we've known each other so long we can ask each other anything."

"Would you come to the point, please."

"Did you realize we were young then?"

"No."

"Neither did I. But we were, you know."

"I know now."

"Bloody hell, isn't it?"

"Yes."

"Was it you who nicked her pearl necklace that time?"

"Certainly it was."

"You did?" he asked, startled.

"Yes."

"But how could you do such a thing?"

"I had no money to eat with, and she looked just as splendid without the necklace."

"Easy as that?"

"Yes."

"I don't believe you, my dear. You're lying."

"Of course I am."

Murdoch grinned, relieved.

"But then," Joshua said, "we're both liars, aren't we? Professionals, at that."

"Artificers," he said, "not liars."

"Liars," Joshua insisted. "Both of us."

Joshua was wakened by an early phone call in his room at the Beverly Wilshire the next morning. Good news. There was a film producer in town foolish enough to want his services—Benny Leopold of Mandrake Productions. "I need you," he said urgently.

Benny Leopold was a Toronto real estate developer, a millionaire several times over, with an obsession: the movies. He wanted to produce. He was a chunky little man, a natty dresser, no more than five feet two, with mournful wobbly eyes and hair everywhere, winding out of his ears, curling out of his nostrils, even on the backs of his fingers. He had to sit on a cushion to see out of the windshield of his Rolls Royce. He took Joshua to Ma Maison and there he laid everything on the table. "On her deathbed," he said, contemplating his cutlery, "my mother, may she rest in peace, made me promise that one day I would make a movie about the Jewish immigration to Canada in 1902, the struggles, the hardships our people went through, not glossing over our sexual hang-ups. Something, you know, adult—"

"You're not suggesting nude scenes, are you?" Joshua asked, appalled.

"Only if they are artistically necessary." He had a script, he said, written by an American with more than one first-class screen credit, but it needed more work. "He hasn't got the background right. Now I've read *The Volunteers* and some of your other stuff, and I'm convinced you could at least get the documentary details right. Have you ever written a screenplay?"

"Certainly."

Leopold looked pensive. "I'm afraid I don't recall ever seeing your name . . ."

"Of course not," Joshua said. "I've always used a pseudonym for my film work."

"Well," Leopold said, "this is a wonderful opportunity I'm offering you. I'm talking about a go-project, all the money there, and I'm prepared to guarantee you a co-credit." Of course, he added, since Joshua was hardly a name writer, and would require a good deal of artistic guidance from Leopold, he mustn't expect an enormous fee; and then straightening out imaginary creases in the tablecloth, he whispered an offer.

"So your mother, may she rest in peace, not only specified that you make a movie with lots of tit shots," Joshua said, ordering another cognac, "but also that you hire a writer cheap."

Outraged, Leopold all but shot out of his chair. "That's not fair. You don't know anything about me, my *modus operandi*."

"Right."

242

"Well," he continued, eyes pleading, "aren't you going to ask me anything about myself?"

"I wouldn't know where to begin."

"Please ask me what I'm like."

"What are you like?"

"Frank."

"That's refreshing."

"Aren't you going to ask me anything else?"

"Give me a hint."

"Come on, fella. You constipated? Don't hold back. Between us, everything has got to be in the open. Ask me more."

"O.K., what more can you tell me about yourself?"

"I'm a former Communist. My god failed," he said, making it sound like a death in the family.

"I'm sorry to hear that."

"It happens. Now I hope you can see that I'm a straight-dealer."

"Good."

"Good? Don't you know anything about this town? This den of thieves? *Rare, you mean*. And what about my credits? Don't you even want to know about my track record?"

"What about your credits, then?"

Leopold seemed to take on height, dimension. "I've made two movies," he declared, telling Joshua their titles.

"I'm afraid I haven't seen either of them."

"You haven't seen them. Prick. What about me?"

"I don't understand."

"The first picture I made," Leopold said, head rocking, hands clasped between his knees, "failed to win distribution."

"Was it that bad?"

"I don't know. I can't show it. Not even to friends." How was he to know, he explained, that the film unit he hired in Toronto, such obliging fellas, were non-union. The print had been declared black and no lab would process it for him.

"What happened to your other film?"

"It was a co-production with Eastern Europe. In fact, if I may say so, *the first Eugene O'Neill ever made in Hungarian*."

"What happened?"

"What happened? Distribution was in the hands of the reactionaries. They wouldn't touch it. But what the shit, you're new to the game, you win a few, you lose a few. But now I'm ready to fly, baby, you and me together."

Murdoch, inevitably, began to run into trouble. He vomited over a jade collection at a party in Bel Air and he was thrown out of yet another mansion for pawing the hostess, a privilege she only allowed to names that went over the titles. Then Markham had to move him out of The Beverly Hills Hotel after he had made a nuisance of himself once too often at the pool. Murdoch phoned to protest. He was told Markham was in conference, but a room had been booked for him at the Century Plaza. Not a suite, but a room.

Murdoch had nowhere to go that night, but Joshua had been invited to a left-wing producer's mansion right out there in Malibu, and he was foolish enough to spring the sodden Murdoch on the company. An old friend who just happens to be in town, Joshua said. Distinguished British novelist. *New Statesman* contributor. Certainly, bring him along.

There were more than twenty rooms in the producer's mansion, which had been built in the Spanish style, smack on the ocean, a high electrified fence enclosing its ten choice acres. Approaching the estate, Joshua braked and hopped out of his rented Cougar to press a buzzer posted on the gate. A disembodied voice established who they were before the gates slid open and they started into the winding driveway, both of them gaping at cascading fountains and towering iron sculptures that reminded Joshua of his Uncle Oscar's scrap yard. An eager red-jacketed young man, carrying a huge umbrella, came on the trot out of nowhere to shelter them from the light drizzle as they stepped out of their car. Taking the keys, he smiled winningly and handed each of them a postcard. On one side, there was a glossy of him, pumping iron, with his vital statistics as well as the name of his agent listed below. On the other side, there was a list of his television credits.

The walls of the long tiled wall that led into the enormous living room were lined with paintings. A Warhol, a Lichtenstein, a Miró, a Leger. A reverently lit bust of Bobby Kennedy rested on a pedestal in an alcove. In the opposite alcove there was a matching bust of Ché.

The other guests were already there. Two bona fide stars, one male, one female. A once justifiably famous director, who now did Gallo wine commercials; his wife or daughter, it was difficult to be sure. Their host, his wife. Their host, beaming, told Joshua how much he admired his book on the men of the International Brigades, paying him the ultimate compliment. "There's a picture buried in there somewhere."

As soon as Murdoch and Joshua were introduced, a solemn waiter wheeled a tray over toward them. The tray's

244

surface was embossed with the Stars and Stripes. It was laden with coke, various uppers and downers, and an inlaid box overflowing with Colombia Gold, cigarette papers, and a rolling machine. "Mn," Joshua said, contemplating the tray, "you wouldn't have any chopped liver, would you?"

"Or a bag of all-sorts?" Murdoch asked.

No.

"In that case, we'll both have Scotch."

To Murdoch's chagrin, Joshua was the one who was seated next to the female star. Who wouldn't eat California grapes. Who was for abortion-on-demand and ERA, but against Zionist duplicity and colored toilet paper. She was awfully good to look at, and Murdoch, glassy-eyed, couldn't stop staring. With fetching concern, those celebrated eyes dazzling, she asked him about the National Front and Paki-bashing, even as Murdoch was trying to peek down her cleavage.

"I fancy you, my dear," Murdoch allowed.

Ignoring him, the star cut into another conversation, this one about cancer-giving food additives. "Do you realize," she said, her voice charged with moral outrage, "that the potato chips we buy in supermarkets are only twenty percent potato and the other eighty percent chemicals?"

Murdoch rocked with laughter. "Obviously, my dear, you are sadly obtuse, but you do have quite the most famous pair of titties I have ever seen. I hope you won't misunderstand," he said, reaching out for her, "if I just—"

Which was when he earned his well-deserved slap across the face.

"Fuck," Murdoch said, knocking back his chair and bringing up his lunch over the floor of imported tiles.

"O.K., everybody. Easy," Joshua said, rising. "I'll take him home."

But outside, Murdoch announced that he wasn't going home yet. "Let's go and drink in that bar where those writers who use electric typewriters can be found."

"The Polo Lounge?"

"Yes."

"No."

"You're ashamed of me," Murdoch said, "because I'm not Jewish. After all these years, you have finally acquired a social advantage."

They drifted into the Polo Lounge and did indeed find a table occupied by a screenwriter Joshua knew, a girl who could only have been a starlet on his arm. The screenwriter, bronzed and denimed, his copper bracelet proof against cancer, recognized Murdoch's name. "Hey, you were once one of the Angry Young Men, weren't you?"

Murdoch turned pale. His forehead sweaty. "Get me to the gent's. Quickly, Joshua."

He held Murdoch's head, as he retched again and again, bringing up bile. Then he propped him up against the bathroom wall, washed his face with paper towels that he had soaked in cold water, lighted a cigarette, and thrust it between lips that had gone purply. "Sidney, we've been drinking together for more years than I care to count. Why all this vomiting, suddenly?"

"It's the chemicals."

"What chemicals?"

"Would you get me back to my hotel?"

He got Murdoch into his room, out of his smelly clothes and into bed, and then he had to help him into the toilet again, where he rested on wobbly knees, chalky head lolling over the bowl, heaving miserably, without anything to bring up. Finally, Joshua managed to lead him back to his bed again. "Shall I call a doctor?" he asked.

"No, please. I'm fine now. You know, I adore it here. Everybody's so wonderfully silly. They haven't even heard that they're going to die."

Joshua drew a blanket over him.

"Groucho, if you remember, once said he wouldn't belong to any club that would have him. Well, what ruined me, Joshua, was publication. I used to be consumed with such a respect for literature. The great tradition. But if even I could make some, and win praise for it, there couldn't be that much in it. I now think they were all as vain and calculating and fraudulent as I am. Will. Dr. Johnson. Miss Austen. The lot. Prancing fools. Would you think it a bore to stay?"

Joshua hesitated.

"I'm afraid of being alone."

Joshua plucked a pillow from the bed and curled up on the floor.

"I forgive you for fucking Margaret."

Twenty years ago. More.

"I don't care for anything I've written. Not a word of it. I'm going to become a package like that screenwriter, and make lots and lots of money."

In their drunken stupor, they had forgotten to put the latch on the door or the DO NOT DISTURB sign on the handle outside. Joshua was jolted awake shortly after seven, a black maid staring down at him. "Oh, sorry," she said, retreating.

Murdoch was sleeping soundly, but Joshua's immediate concern, beyond a hammering head, was that Pauline had probably been trying to reach him at the Beverly Wilshire, discovered he hadn't spent the night there, and assumed that he was at an orgy. Joshua left a hasty note for Murdoch, paused to retrieve a man's pocket watch from the bedside table, and took a taxi back to his hotel. Pauline had called four times, Leopold twice, and Markham three times. Joshua called Pauline first, a frantic Pauline, and then he called Leopold.

"We can start work tomorrow," Leopold said.

"Benny, I'm considering more than one offer here. I haven't made up my mind yet."

"You've got to say yes," Leopold said, his manner grave. "I need you. You are absolutely the only writer I know who can save this project."

Joshua met a perplexed, jumpy Markham for lunch, Ma Maison again, Markham not looking at him as they took their table, but soaking in the room. "Always good to see you, Josh. You look great. Here comes Sue Mengers. You want to meet her? It could be useful."

"No thanks."

"What are you doing here?"

He didn't mention *Playboy*, but told him about Leopold, looking for information.

"There's Natalie Wood. I wouldn't put her into anything any more. . . . Ordinarily, I wouldn't take a call from anybody like Leopold. But when he phoned, and I heard you were in town, I figured it was to check you out. I told him you were a great talent. Take the job."

"You're holding something back."

"You have no idea," Markham said, "how much I miss the old days in St.-Germain-des-Prés. Look, it's Betty Bacall. With David fucking Susskind. I guess she's willing to do TV now."

"How's Ellen?"

"I'll get to that. First, tell me who ever would have believed that James Edward Peabody, one of Camelot's most promising, would end up toiling for *Playboy?*"

"They print articles by some damn good writers, you know."

"Between the pubic hairs. He's a drunk. His hands shake. He called me once when I was passing through Chicago, as supercilious as ever, and I squeezed him into a lunch, if only for old times' sake. Sure enough, he had a young girlfriend who acts. He also had a script idea for me, who hasn't? Well, he was in such pitiful shape, I tried to shove something his way, a retainer as a talent-spotter. But he wanted more money than I could reasonably justify. Hey, there's Mary Tyler Moore with a little prick from the William Morris office. Josh, is it true that you and Sidney Murdoch are old friends?"

"Yes."

"Good. I'm counting on you to help me get rid of that loopy Englishman."

"You brought him out here," Joshua said coldly.

"It was only because of Ellen."

Ellen, Joshua remembered, took slightly out-of-focus mood photographs for *Vogue*.

"She must have read everything he ever wrote for the *New Statesman*," Markham said, "all his novels, everything, she's some reader, and he writes a treatment of his novel, it's a minor classic, that is just this side of hard-core. It's been a shock to her. She's hurting, Josh."

Ellen, Markham explained, had been an admirer of Murdoch since her Bryn Mawr days, and for years she had pleaded with him to get the studio to make a movie out of Murdoch's second novel. So Markham had bought him for their tenth wedding anniversary, a gift, a surprise, and now she wanted him returned, like an unsatisfactory package from Neiman-Marcus. But Markham was determined to handle the matter delicately. Ellen, he said, was very sensitive. "He's got to go, Josh. I've got him coming round to the house for drinks at six, and I want you to be there when I tell him. He makes me nervous with all his 'dear boys' and all that other British bullshit."

"O.K. I'll come. On condition that you pay up his contract, no tricks, and fly him home first-class."

"I was going to do that anyway. What do you take me for?"

So Murdoch, shaky but sodden again, finally got his Beverly Hills poolside party. No *Playboy* centerfolds, just a tight-lipped Markham, Ellen, and Joshua. Sipping champagne, but eschewing the smoked salmon, he took the bad news unemotionally, it seemed, even as Ellen, kneeling in the grass here, perching on a canvas chair there, snapped photographs of the rejected but renowned British novelist, ostensibly at ease in her garden, a first-class BOAC ticket to London tucked into his napkin. This time out, Joshua thought, I'm going to be the one to heave up the contents of my stomach.

Then, as Murdoch's dismissal seemed to be passing without incident, he suddenly called for the Remy Martin bottle, poured an enormous quantity of cognac into his champagne glass, stirred the mixture with his finger and turned to Joshua. "I was lecturing at some grotty little university in New England once," he said, not looking at Ellen, still clicking away, lying prone on the grass, "one of those finishing schools for the intellectually inadequate daughters of the new rich, when one of them leaps up to ask, 'What makes you think your work will last, Mr. Murdoch?' To which I replied, 'I would rather that the novels were interred, all of them, and that I danced on the grave myself.' I was determined to outlive everybody, Josh, even my grasping children. Especially Ralph, who is growing into a very nasty piece of work indeed." Murdoch paused to fart resoundingly. "I do beg your pardon," he said, "but, not to worry, my dears, I believe the wind is blowing toward the flats. Where was I, Josh?"

"Outliving everybody," Joshua said, reaching for the cognac bottle himself.

"But it's not to be. I'm dying, you know. Leukemia. The ailment of the royals."

Joshua choked, tears welling in his eyes. Murdoch, ever-conscious of his audience, leaned drunkenly toward him, offering him his big wet lips, and said, "Kiss me, Hardy."

Joshua kissed him full on the mouth, the unspeakable Ellen clicking away, enthralled.

"And now," Murdoch said, rising shakily, clutching Joshua's hand, his face the color of wasting snow, "I've simply got to lie down."

Ellen led them to a guest room, hastily spreading beach towels over the quilted cover before Joshua lowered him tenderly onto the bed. "Do you need anything?" he asked.

"Just let me close my eyes. Five minutes is all I need."

Joshua waited until he had begun to snore before he joined the Markhams on the terrace again.

Ellen had been crying. "To look at him now," she said, "and to remember what a talent he once was."

"You promised me that you would pay off his contract," Joshua said to Markham, "but you didn't even mention it."

"I don't own the studio, Joshua. I have people to answer to there."

"God damn you. God damn both of you. You're not fit to shine his shoes."

"Do you know he had a boy in his hotel room yesterday?" Markham charged. "He was with him all night."

"I knew," Ellen said, "for all his braggadocio, he couldn't cope with women."

"That wasn't a boy, Bill, it was me."

"Like fuck it was," Markham said, just a hint of a wobble in his voice.

"Don't worry. You're not my type. You never were." And, with a sweep of his arm, Joshua sent the champagne tray flying, glasses shattering against the flagstones.

"Those were my Baccarat glasses," Ellen shrieked, fleeing for the house.

"Why didn't you tell me you were in town for *Playboy*? Ashamed?" Markham asked.

"You're rotten, Bill, always were."

"Oh, I forgot to tell you why that prick Leopold needs you, Joshua. It had nothing whatsoever to do with your legendary skills. He's financed by Canadian tax shelter money. In order to qualify, he has to have so much native content in his wretched films. It's your Canadian name he wants on the script, that's all. Mind you, any Canadian name will do. I think it's worth a point-and-a-half under their quaint system. But in your particular case," he said, rising from his chair, "that strikes me as about a point too high."

Joshua surprised him with a not-very-satisfying right to the jaw, but it did knock Markham off balance, enabling Joshua to drive his shoulder into him, sending him sprawling backwards into the pool. Markham surfaced to see a crazed Joshua swinging a wrought-iron chair overhead. He immediately ducked again, avoiding it. Another chair went flying into the pool and then the table itself rolled over the edge, before Markham made it out of the water on the far side. He watched, heaving, as Joshua rolled a potted palm to the edge, kicking it over into the deep end, and then he ran for the house. Joshua kicked open the French doors, swept the jar of pickled eggs off the polished brass counter and smashed it against a wall. He was reaching for the Watney's mirror when he saw Ellen standing there, hands on her hips. "Having fun?" she asked.

"You bet."

Then he heard the police siren in the distance.

"Where's Bill?" he asked.

"He's coming. Don't worry."

"Ellen, my sweet," Joshua said, slipping behind the bar to pour himself a cognac, "if you have me arrested, I'm going to tell Bill that you were in Sidney's hotel room."

"You're out of your mind," she said.

250

Joshua reached into his pocket, pulled out an antique man's pocket watch on a long gold chain and dangled it before her. "He can handle women," he said, "but he happens to be very fastidious."

"You give me that!"

"I don't want to be arrested," Joshua said. "I also want Sidney's contract paid out. Every fucking cent."

The police car rocked to a stop outside.

"Bill," she hollered, running toward the front door, "Bill!"

Leopold was camped in the lobby of the Beverly Wilshire. Bouncing to his feet the instant Joshua came through the door. "When do we start work?" he burbled.

"Benny, only one thing worries me. You said I was the only writer who could save this project—"

"Am I frank? I'm frank," he said.

"—that wouldn't be because you need a Canadian or you lose your tax shelter money?"

"Certainly not."

"Good. We'll start work tomorrow. Book a table for lunch at Ma Maison. I'll meet you there at one."

"Done," he said.

And the next morning, at 10 a.m., Joshua was on a plane to Montreal.

6

"Oh my God, Daddy. Some fucking inheritance. How could you do this to me?"

"Well, yeah. Right. What do you think, Pauline?"

"I think you're both crazy."

"The money's still good," Reuben insisted, "just a little old, that's all."

Joshua sent a wad of fifties flying toward the ceiling. "I need another drink, darling."

"Let him fetch his own, he's got no respect."

"You heard your father."

"O.K., O.K., but count it out again, will you, please."

Flying home from L.A., Joshua was returning as broke as when he had left. Thirty-five thousand feet over Utah he began to finger that long thin key, saying to himself, what the hell, it's mine, salvation time has come. And so, early in the morning the day after his return, he drove out to the Royal

Bank of Canada, which was on the main street of Cornwall just across the border in Ontario, where they had kind of boxes. Smiling too much, his throat dry, he presented a letter to the manager, showing him his passport, and, with trembling hands, shoveled the contents of the box into a suitcase that he had brought with him. Easy as that. The quantity of the banknotes, some of them $100-bill bundles, overwhelmed him. *My God, I'm rich. Loaded.* He sang all the way home, careful not to exceed the speed limit, and only after he had led Pauline into the bedroom and emptied the suitcase on the carpet did he grasp the nature of his problem. There was a lot of money there, more than he had ever seen before, but it was vintage money. The banknotes were dated 1925, 1935, or '37, and there was even a bundle of brand-new 1923 $2 bills, with a portrait of H.R.H. Edward, Prince of Wales, in the uniform of the Welsh Guards. For the rest, there were some $500 bills, issued in 1925, with a portrait of King George V; a pack of Silver Jubilee $25 bills, showing Their Majesties King George V and Queen Mary in their coronation robes; a stack of hundreds, issued the same year, with a portrait of Prince Henry, Duke of Gloucester; and a goodly number of 1937 King George VI bills in fives, tens, twenties, and fifties.

Reuben was summoned, but couldn't get to the house until late the following evening. "Well," he said, "you've finally been to Cornwall."

"Right."

"I thought you'd cleaned out that box years ago."

"How could I? What if you needed it?"

Pauline counted out the money again. "There's thirty-two-thousand eight hundred and twenty-two dollars here, if you want to include the shinplasters."

Shinplasters, twenty-five-cent Dominion of Canada banknotes, first appeared in 1870, but were still being issued as late as 1929.

"Those are real collectors' items," Reuben said.

"Everything here is a collector's item. What am I going to do with it?"

"Well, yeah, right. You dress up good, see. A three-piece suit, no flash in the tie or pointy shoes, and you step into a bank and ask to see the manager. Gee, you say, golly, I'm Senator Hornby's son-in-law (you don't have to say you're Jewish, and these days they don't ask outright any more, it's not the style), there I was digging away in my garden out there on Lake Memphremagog one Saturday aft and clunk,

252

clunk, I hit this old chest. Talk about pulling a lunch pail out of the toilet bowl. Gee whiz, look what I found."

"I already thought of that."

"Good."

"Bad. A bank manager has to inform the mint when this sort of stuff comes in, especially in large quantities, the money goes back there, and then some smart-ass discovers my father has a prison record and back you go."

"You're not to redeem this money anywhere," Pauline said, alarmed.

"I know, I know."

"What a couple of banana-heads you are. You don't take it into one bank, you move it around."

"Sure, I get into my car and drive across Canada, cashing a hundred in every bank I pass, and five years later I'm home again, and they still send the bills back to the mint."

"What I don't understand," Pauline said, "is why you didn't invest the money, even in government bonds. It could have been worth four times as much now."

"Well, yeah," Reuben said, scratching his head, "right. But like Josh here once told me, I've led an unexamined life."

"Tell her where the money comes from, Daddy."

"Places."

"Look," Joshua said, brandishing a bundle of King George VI fifties, "these are all in sequence. They've never even been in circulation."

"Oh, those," he said, grinning in fond remembrance, "they come from the Bank of Nova Scotia in Ste. Agathe."

"Did you also rob banks?" Pauline asked.

"How could you even think such a thing?"

"But it comes from a bank robbery," Joshua put in.

"Well, yeah, possibly."

"And it can be traced back to you?"

"Listen, they bust three banks a day here, maybe four if it isn't too cold, and what we're talking about is the thirties. How long do you think they hold a grudge?"

"This is impossible."

"Most of the money's clean, Josh."

"How did you earn it?" Pauline asked.

"He was in insurance, sort of."

"Yeah. Right."

"Then why did you have to hide it in a box?"

"Well," Reuben said, groping, "it was the income tax. I never cared for it."

253

"Don't you pay tax?" she asked.

"Not yet."

"And look at this," Joshua said, waving a stack of Silver Jubilee twenty-fives at him, "also unused and in sequence."

"Shit, you think the money in your pocket hasn't got a past? I mean, do you demand the family background of every banknote you're handed? Let Pauline deposit some of it. Or the senator."

"It's not them I'm worried about, it's you."

Reuben retrieved a Prince Henry one-hundred from the pile. "We could run the money down to New York to a coin dealer. These must be very rare now."

Joshua looked interested.

"A lot of these notes, you know, have to be worth much more than the face value now. And those dealers don't ask questions."

The two men began to study the different banknotes.

"What we need is a catalogue," Joshua said, "with a price list."

"Yeah, right."

"No," Pauline said, "absolutely no."

They looked at her, startled to find she was still there.

"And why do we need the money, anyway?" she demanded.

Joshua poured himself another drink.

"You short, Josh?" Reuben asked.

"Some."

"Well, how much money do we need?" Pauline asked.

Joshua frowned, embarrassed for her. Reuben looked disgusted.

"What's wrong?"

"Shapiros don't take money from women," Reuben said, appalled.

"I'm not a woman, I'm his wife. How much do we need?"

"You heard my father."

"You mean it's O.K. to rob banks and collect insurance, as you both put it, and break hands and not pay taxes," she said, her voice rising, "but it's immoral to take money from your wife?"

"I brought him up good."

"O.K.," Pauline said, "take the money down to New York, you can both go to jail as far as I'm concerned," and she left the bedroom, slamming the door behind her.

"I hate to criticize," Reuben said, "but you'd think, what

with all the privileges they had, the fancy schools, Westmount and all that shit, that they would at least have been brought up to know right from wrong."

7

Monique and her mother arrived in Ibiza on a balmy Monday evening on the ship from Barcelona.

Monique's mother was fierce, stout, her round face flushed and her hair dyed red. Clutching a glossy black purse, she wobbled on spike-like high heels. But slender, olive-skinned Monique, bracelets jangling, black hair flying in her face, was something else again; flouncing down the gangplank, the first three buttons of her black blouse undone to reveal a swelling bosom, a maddening hint of white filigree. My, my. She also wore narrow black slacks and leather sandals. Her pouting lips were painted red, just like her toenails. Her eyes were hidden behind dark sunglasses. Only eight years after he had given up *Terry and the Pirates*, the Dragon Lady's kid sister floats ashore.

Juanito, who was seated with Joshua on the terrace of the waterfront café, bit into his cheroot, spat, and summoned a blue-smocked dockhand to his side. Then he informed Joshua that mother and daughter had come down from Paris. The father, deceased, had been Spanish. A doctor, a Socialist. On the crossing, if a man approached Monique on deck, the mother had been right there, snarling.

Joshua shrugged, feigning indifference, as he watched the determined Carlos, his day at the bank done, weaving among passengers on the dock, peddling bottles of *gaseosa*. Carlos also dealt in contraband American cigarettes now, buying them from the sailors, selling them in the cafés. With the proceeds, he had already bought a Hebrew dictionary. A grammar. He subscribed to an Israeli newspaper, *Maariv*. "When the time comes to emigrate," he said, "I'll be ready. Nobody will take me for a fool."

Passengers milled about impatiently, their luggage already assembled at their sides, clapping hands or hollering for porters, all unavailingly, as four men in blue smocks came sniffing around Monique and her mother, circling. The pair were obviously waiting for a missing piece of luggage. It arrived, a splendid wicker case gently deposited on top of four suitcases by a sailor. Monique's mother dug into her purse, surfacing

255

with some coins, but the sailor nodded no, smiling shyly at Monique as he retreated. The porters, ramming their carts ahead of them, closed in, almost colliding. Monique's mother settled on the ugliest of the four and indicated the oldest and most grizzled of Ibiza's three taxi drivers: Rafael. And in a moment mother and daughter were gone.

Strolling down to the *barraca*, Joshua hung back while Juanito, pad in hand, inspected dripping overflowing boxes of inkfish, lobster, and sea bass, all of which would be loaded onto the ship in the evening. His spunky ten-year-old son, also called Juanito, came skipping along after them, sipping a *gaseosa* he had bought from Carlos.

"What shall we do tonight?" Juanito asked.

"I don't know," a dispirited Joshua replied, "but I'm not going to Rosita's again."

Juanito, concerned, said, "We could go to Santa Eulalia."

But Joshua wasn't listening. Would he even know how to talk to a proper girl any more? After all that crazed whoring.

"A friend is killing a pig. He's going to roast it. There will be a party. What do you say?"

More seamed, unknowable faces. Two weeks earlier, he had turned twenty-one. "Come home," his father wrote. "I miss you."

"Maybe I'll just take the bus back to San Antonio. I don't want to end up drunk again tonight."

Juanito cuffed him playfully on the shoulder. "I am your friend. Tonight you should be with friends."

Rafael pulled up in his quaking old Ford and Juanito sauntered over to chat with him. Leaning against the car window, he nodded again and again. Finally, he called Joshua over to join them. "The girl's name is Monique and they are staying at the Casa del Sol. Her mother brought her here to get her away from a boyfriend. There was some trouble."

"How does Rafael know all this?" Joshua asked.

"She never stopped talking, the mother. Rafael is dumb as they come," Juanito said, yanking the taxi driver's ear, "and ugly, but he was in Marseilles for three years and understands French. They quarreled all the way to San Antonio. The mother did up the top buttons of her blouse before she let her out of the taxi. Aii-aii. She can swear, the young one. She made Rafael's ears burn."

They didn't go to the party in Santa Eulalia after all. Joshua wasn't up to it and Juanito refused to go without him. Instead Juanito took him to a small restaurant run by a crony of his, a former ship's cook. Juanito told him how much he had enjoyed the stories of Jack London and that he would like to see snow before he died. Maybe Joshua would invite him to Canada one day, he suggested, and they would fish through the ice with the Eskimos. He also insisted that he had only been joking the night he had said Blasco Ibañez was a real writer and Joshua was merely a kid. He was willing to bet Joshua was a very talented young man.

Monique, whom Joshua had found so bedazzling on first glance, wasn't the first foreign young lady to have come to Ibiza while he was rooted there. One evening a British girl and her aunt, touring the Mediterranean islands, disembarked from the *Jaime II*. The aunt, a pulpy lady, seemingly rigid, carried a flowery parasol. The girl, engagingly freckled, was holding an easel and a painting box as she came tripping down the gangplank. She was a big girl, buxom and broad-hipped, a schoolteacher from Kingston-on-Thames. The first night she wandered late and alone, her manner tentative, into the noisy waterfront bar, immediately rendering it quiet. Juanito took it that having ventured into such a squalid bar alone, the girl, however demurely dressed, was a whore. Red hot. Crazy for it. Joshua cautioned him that she seemed a most well-bred young lady and this was certainly not the case. But Juanito, hastily cleaning his fingernails with a matchstick as he cursed Joshua for a fool, demanded that he introduce him. So Joshua invited the girl to their table. Her name was Peggy. She graciously allowed that her Spanish was bloody awful, actually, and that she would be happy for some English-speaking company. Peggy, who mucked about with paints, inquired about the most super vistas the island had to offer.

Juanito, his manner abrupt, said, "Tell her in English that I think she is beautiful."

"Juanito recommends the area around Santa Eulalia."

"How would one get there?"

Joshua told her where the bus stopped.

"Does she like me?" Juanito asked.

"She says you could do with a bath and a shave."

Juanito spat on the floor.

"I take it your friend is one of the local peasants. They don't speak proper Spanish, don't you know. It's a dialect."

"Juanito's a fine fellow."

"Ask her, nicely, if she has ever been on board a fishing boat."

"Man, it stinks below decks on your boats. You want her to be ill?"

Juanito, fixing her with his most enchanting smile, looked as if he might leap out of his trousers and mount her right there.

"Is he tiddly?" Peggy asked.

"Ask her, you bastard, if she would like to see the secret passage through the wall of the old town."

"Juanito suggests that there are some fine views to be seen from the old town."

"I would love to paint him."

"She paints. She would like to know if you would pose for her."

"I'm not a homosexual. Tell her I am in love with her."

"Go to hell, Juanito."

Peggy, lapsing into Spanish, smiled sweetly and said, *"Mi alegro de esta aquí."*

"Oh," Juanito responded, hugely encouraged, and he promptly ordered another round of drinks and shifted his chair tighter to Peggy.

"Oh, dear," she said, appealing to Joshua with her big blue eyes.

"You go now," Juanito said. "Good night."

"You're frightening her."

"You know nothing. Go now."

"Are we in for a sticky time?" Peggy asked.

Joshua eased his chair back a little from the table.

"You're not thinking of leaving me alone with him, are you?"

"No," he said, changing his mind, and appealing to Juanito once more to contain himself.

"You are not my friend. You are a son of a whore."

"What was that he said?"

"He finds you pleasing to look at."

"Cheek."

"Tell her I know a beach where we can swim now."

"She's scared of you."

"Say I will bring her freshly caught inkfish for breakfast."

"Tell her yourself," Joshua replied hotly.

Now it was a somewhat flustered Peggy who pushed back her chair, rising. "Would it be too much to ask you to take me back to my hotel?"

"Of course not."

As Joshua got up, Juanito cursed him. "Don't come round to my bar any more. You have no friends on Ibiza."

Taking Peggy's plump freckled arm, Joshua escorted her back to her hotel. He was eager to return to Juanito, to explain himself, but she suggested a nightcap. The bar was closed. However, as she still seemed distressed, he agreed to join her for a smoke on the dark and seemingly abandoned terrace. "It's going to be as bad as Italy here," she said, "all those perfectly frightful little men trying to pinch your bottom wherever you go."

There was a stirring in the darkest corner of the bar. Somebody broke wind. Peering, Joshua made out Peggy's aunt, her mouth agape, a nearly empty bottle of Fundador on the table before her. Peggy snatched his hand impatiently. "Take me for a walk," she said.

Damn it, Juanito would be seething, convinced they were now romping in bed together. He led Peggy to a secluded spot on the hotel grounds and they sat together on a rock looking out to sea. Peggy rested her chin, doubling just a little, on her apple-pie knees and gathered her white cashmere sweater around her.

"Chilly?" Joshua asked.

"Mmmn."

"Maybe you ought to go to bed?"

"Me, and my cuddly Mr. Pooh Bear," she said all twinkly. "What fun."

Joshua smiled.

"You can't imagine how difficult it is for two respectable women to travel alone on the Continent. They all want to get their filthy hands into your knickers. On the beach at San Remo, the Italian men stroll about in the briefest of shorts. When they sit down," she said, pressing his arm, "you can actually see their extraordinaries."

"You can?"

"They have filthy, waxy ears," she said with immense feeling. "Not like mine," she added, tilting her face for his benefit, "all soft and nibbly."

There was a long pause and then Peggy bounded to her feet. "Well then," she said.

"Will your aunt be all right?" Joshua asked, as they passed her again.

"Oh, let her be. I don't share with her, you know. We have separate rooms."

They were now standing in the dark at the foot of the staircase inside the hotel.

"I suppose," Peggy said, "I had better move a chair against the door before getting ready for bed. Or, God knows, somebody might barge in and find me standing there. Starkers," she added, giggly.

"That will hardly be necessary," Joshua replied in his most reassuring voice.

"Mmmn. Quite." Extending her hand, her manner unaccountably sharp once more, she said, "I would like to thank you for being so wonderfully gallant and rescuing me from God knows what."

"I will expect you and your aunt for tea tomorrow."

"Now that's *something* to look forward to," she said, and she started up the stairs at last, enabling him to hurry back to the bar and explain himself to Juanito.

Drunk and belligerent, Juanito was astonished to see him. "You mean that after all that you didn't even fuck her?"

Joshua told him yet again that Peggy was a well-bred young lady, utterly respectable, and furthermore, he pointed out, in civilized countries it was possible to escort a frightened young lady home without taking it as license to leap into bed with her. There were other rules of social conduct, he added, than those that applied at Casa Rosita.

"You know nothing," Juanito said. "You're still a kid."

Peggy and her aunt failed to turn up for tea the next afternoon, which baffled Joshua, but she greeted him warmly when he discovered her at work two days later in the bay of San Antonio. Seated on a canvas stool, her easel set out before her, a broad-brimmed straw hat shading her oval face, but her reddening freckled shoulders bare, she was seemingly indifferent to the onlookers she had attracted: some of the local children, the village carpenter, and two army officers. One of the officers, the tall, bronzed Jose González, was familiar to Joshua. An accomplished horseman, he was a native of Cadiz. Occasionally they drank together, González practicing his English.

"I'm sorry about the other afternoon," Peggy said gaily, "but my aunt wasn't up to scratch, as you can well imagine, and I had no way of getting in touch with you."

"Would you like to have a drink when you're done here?"

"I'd love to, but fools walk in. I've already accepted Captain González's invitation." Peggy crinkled her peeling nose. "Do you think I'm in for another spot of trouble?"

"Why, Jose is a gentleman of the old school."

González and Peggy became inseparable. They were seen together strolling hand in hand on the beaches after dark, cuddling in Don Pedro's Bodega, Peggy chewing on his ear, or embracing ardently on the waterfront. They were seen everywhere, in fact, except in the bar of Peggy's hotel, a sanctuary her bilious aunt never quit, disgusted busboys heaving her onto her bed each night. More than once, González, understandably unfamiliar with English slang, sought Joshua's advice privately. "Is not 'to come' a regular verb, as if you invite, I come to your house?"

"Yes, that's right."

"Then what does it mean, please, 'Come, baby. Come now.' If you are already there?"

Another time it was, "Are 'extraordinaries' a measure of the unusual or the street word for the male organs?"

Infuriated with himself, deeply embarrassed by his innocence, Joshua avoided Juanito for a couple of weeks rather than risk his ridicule. When they got together again, however, Juanito did not tease him. He did not taunt him with Peggy and González; instead he gratuitously told him a story about some foolishness he had committed when *he* had only been twenty-one years old.

Juanito, my friend.

If I ever have a son, Joshua vowed, I will try to be just as understanding. Then he laughed aloud, it seemed such an outrageous notion. Imagine, he thought. Me, a son.

8

False spring. After a benign evening of melting snows, the temperature suddenly took a dive, the streets freezing again, but Joshua wasn't the only one out there. Pinsky and his Russian wolfhound blocked his path. "Did you catch the National?" he asked. "Your friend Lévesque was shitting on us again. He said the Jews were edgy. They're bums, every one of them. A bunch of know-nothing pricks. A Jew in their mind is a stereotype."

"Why don't you leave, Pinsky?"

"Where would I go? Tahiti?"

"That's the stuff."

"*With Gilda?* What would she do without a phone?"

"Why not Toronto?"

The worst thing Joshua could have said, as it turned out.

"Don't quote me on this, you bastard, but I was in Toronto last Tuesday with a bunch of the boys." By "the boys" Pinsky meant pillars of the community. UJA heavies, synagogue presidents, Jewish Congress apparatchiks. "We flew in for a secret meeting with our counterparts there. The Toronto *chevra*. We had come to spell it out. The day was dawning

261

when we might all have to leave Quebec. In our innocence we expected our brothers, remembering the Holocaust, to greet us with open arms. A little love. Fat chance. 'Don't be hasty,' they said. 'We'd love to have you here, you're family, but it wouldn't look good for the Jews to run, and to tell you the truth, things aren't so hot here.' Sons of bitches. Forest Hill *dreck*. What they meant to say is, they don't want to cut up the pie. Except for the bunch that was into real estate. They wanted us to move right now, the more the better. They practically came in their pants at the thought of the action. How's your wife?"

"Improving."

"You never should have taken Jonathan Cole off the case."

"Oh, really, and would that be your considered opinion?"

"Not mine. His."

"He discussed Pauline with you?"

"We jog together."

The next morning, a Monday, a fine, powdery snow began to fall on streets already encrusted with a scalp of ice. It was still snowing on Thursday, the morning Alex, who had just acquired his driving license, borrowed the car to return some records to a friend in N.D.G. An hour later the phone rang. It was Alex; he had been in an accident. "Are you hurt?" Joshua asked.

"No."

"Was anybody hurt?"

"No."

"O.K. Relax. And tell me what happened."

Descending Clarke, a steep hill at the best of times but uncommonly treacherous in winter, he had geared down for a red light at Sherbrooke Street and then obviously braked too hard, only to find himself sliding helplessly past the light and into the oncoming traffic. He bounced off not one, not two, but three cars. He was now parked round the corner, being questioned by the cops, one of whom wanted to speak to him. "Don't worry about a thing," Joshua said. "I'll grab a taxi and be right over, but put him on."

"Clickety-click, clickety-click. I told the kid not to disturb the master at work, but he insisted on calling you."

"He did the right thing. He told me nobody was hurt."

"Right. But one of the cars he barely dented belongs to a real meatball. One of your more excitable co-religionists. A Mr. Henigman. I think he's going to claim psychological damage. I figure he'll also claim the collision rendered him impotent, but if you're lucky he'll only sue for five million.

This has been a bad year for men's suits, and most of those bastards are in trouble with the tax inspectors. Or don't you read the *Gazette?*"

"He's in men's suits?"

"He gave me his card already, yet. Oy vey. He says, I drop into his factory I'll walk out dressed like a prince. So if the meatball sues, we'll get him on attempted bribery of a police officer."

"I'll be right over, Stu. Hold on."

Alex, his cheeks burnt red by the wind, was waiting in the snow. So was McMaster.

"Some day," Joshua said.

"Cold as a witch's tit," McMaster said.

Taking Alex by the arm, Joshua pulled him aside. "You O.K.?"

"Yeah. The brakes grabbed. There's something wrong with your brakes."

"There's nothing wrong with the brakes, the car just came out of the garage."

"Well you just better have them checked out again, Daddy."

Joshua shook his head impatiently.

"O.K. What do I know?"

"I didn't say that. Were they rough on you?"

"Oh, no. But whenever I tried to say anything they just said, 'Now you shettup, kid.' Then the usual happened," he added hotly.

"What do you mean?"

"They looked at my name, established I was your son, and suddenly I smelled roses."

The morning Alex was born, Joshua had wept in the hospital men's room. A son, a son.

"McMaster is crazy. Hey," Joshua said, grinning, "don't look so long in the face. It doesn't matter. One day get me to tell you about *my* first accident."

"Yeah, you probably hit four cars, and this was nothing."

Joshua embraced him, took the car keys, said he would handle things now, and sent him off to classes. He was late, surely, but there was no determination in his gait. Probably he was headed elsewhere.

"You shouldn't kiss your kid in the street like that," McMaster said. "It must be embarrassing for him."

"He never protested," Joshua said, startled.

"How could he?"

Joshua allowed McMaster to lead him across the street to the drugstore and they sipped coffee together at the counter.

"Have you read my manuscript yet?"

"Yes, I have. Stu, what you really ought to do is write your autobiography. Memoirs of an honest cop."

"Geez. Yeah. I've got tons of material. If only you could give me hand with the writing of it."

"I'm afraid not."

"Isn't there anything I could say," he asked, "that might change your mind?"

"Sorry, no."

"I figured," he said, his eyes hot, and he asked Joshua if he had read about the incident in Dr. Jonathan Cole's house.

Yes. The item in the *Gazette* had caught his eye at breakfast. According to the report, the author of *Your Kind, My Kind, Mankind* had only discovered there was something screwy the morning after his return from Banff. Dr. Cole had been in Banff with his wife, the noted local composer, presenting a paper at an international medical conference. His mansion, a graystone, was high on Edgehill Road, its parquet floors protected by wall-to-wall carpets. The grand piano on which Bessie had composed *The Golan Heights Sonata* was a Steinway. Bessie's stirring sonata had first been performed in honor of Moshe Dayan, in town for an Emergency Bond Drive dinner. It was available, Bessie pointed out to the reporter, on records or sheets from Masada Music Inc., a nonprofit division of Catmore Holdings Company, an outfit whose name was derived from those of the two Cole children, Catherine and Mortimer.

McMaster filled in the juicy details that had not appeared in the *Gazette* story. The Coles, he said, had not discovered that anything was out of joint in their house until the morning after their return from the west. Jonathan and Bessie had come home late and gone upstairs to bed immediately. Bessie without flushing herself out with herbal tea, Jonathan eschewing his Water-Pic toothbrush for once. Standing on her medically balanced bathroom scale the next morning, Bessie was startled to discover that she had ostensibly gained five pounds, although she had certainly not overeaten in Banff. A considerably revived Jonathan emerged from the shower and then absently started to slip into the suit he usually wore to the office. The trousers didn't fit. They were incredibly tight; he couldn't button them. Baffled, Jonathan studied the suit carefully. Yes, it certainly was his office suit. He tried the jacket. It wouldn't button properly. Jonathan stripped down

264

again and then stepped on the bathroom scale. Amazingly, he seemed to have gained five pounds. Yet he had jogged every morning in Banff and his stomach was rock-hard as usual. Distressed, uneasy, he slipped into his dressing gown and wandered downstairs for breakfast. Bessie wasn't in the kitchen. He found her sitting on the living room sofa, weeping.

"What's ailing you?"

"Can't you see, lummox?"

He couldn't.

"The furniture."

"Holy shit!"

Somebody had cunningly rearranged the living room furniture. Nothing was in its accustomed place. And yet—and yet—as they flew from place to place, they could find nothing missing. That the sterling silver, however valuable, had not been taken was readily understandable: each piece of cutlery was boldly initialed "JC," and therefore its ownership could have been easily established. But the interloper had not made off with Bessie's furs, neither had he attempted to crack the wall safe. The hi-fi, the color-TV sets, the Nikons, the Bell-Howell film camera, the Cuisinart, anything else easily pawnable, were all in place. Not one piece of Eskimo whale-bone sculpture had been disturbed. But, on closer inspection, the real act of vandalism, mindless vandalism, committed by the housebreaker became apparent. The A. Y. Jackson landscape, the pride of Dr. Cole's collection, a picture he was fond of describing as serene, enjoyable beyond all his other possessions, had been defaced. Somebody had carefully removed the artist's signature, probably with turpentine, and signed it with his own hand, "this copy by Hershl Sugarman." Jonathan let out a terrifying cry. "Look at that," he howled at his wife, "will you fucking look at that," and he reminded her that he had been absolutely against Brenda visiting her family in Barbados while they were away.

"Fortunately," Bessie said, trying to comfort him, "whoever it was didn't actually damage the picture."

The insurance claim adjuster who had been summoned to the house, McMaster continued, was sympathetic but in a quandary. Yes, he had to agree, there was possibly, just possibly, a decrease in value, but the case was so odd he would have to take it under advisement. After all, the Jackson had been authenticated and the painting itself had not been damaged.

"I suppose," Joshua said, "this qualifies as one of your unusual break-ins."

"Uh huh."

"Do you think it was the same bunch that got into Pinsky's wine cellar?"

"I figure they're a bunch of kids, stoned out of their skulls, and when we catch 'em, they'll turn out to come from good families, connected people, and they'll get off with suspended sentences. So what else is new?"

Shrugging, Joshua lighted a cigarette.

"Once, I don't know how many years ago, maybe twenty, a couple of meatballs broke into old Judge Gilbert's place on Argyle. You remember Gilbert—Mr. Community Pillar. Reform Club, Mount Royal, etc. etc. Only he had a weakness. A sweet tooth. He liked being blown by under-age hookers in his chambers, him sporting his wig and robes all the while. His missus, on the other hand, liked nothing but CC, a secret drinker—she could go through a bottle a day, maybe more. Never saw her she wasn't pissola. Anyhoo, these meatballs broke in, made off with the family silver and hey, hey, lots of unexplained cash from the wall safe. We took them in the lane behind Wood Avenue. A couple of Pepsis, real mon-sewers out of St. Henri, shit-scared. One of them has a gun and gets me in the thigh—just this much higher and to the right, and you're now looking at the first soprano in the choir at Saint James' United. Anyhoo, there was better than twenty thousand, unexplained, in those long brown envelopes, which is to say every time we risk our necks, bringing in a couple of meatballs, the judge does a little business with Brother Colucci or whoever, and they are back on the street even before we are out of the hospital. So he comes to see me in the hospital, your Judge Gilbert, says he's recommending me for a St. George's Medal, and slips me two hundred bucks. Wow. Hot damn. Two months later I had me a little NB. My nervous breakdown. You had yours yet?"

"Not yet."

"I wake up, I'm sweating. I go to sleep, I'm sweating. For ten days I don't shit. I think I'm being followed everywhere. One day I'm supposed to be getting into my patrol car, I start to turn the door handle and I freeze right there. It takes my partner and another guy to uncurl my fist from the handle. And I can't stop shaking. Aw, cops. Uneducated. On the take. Who cares what they go through? You been following Watergate? Sure you have. Well, lookit, now each and every one of those fuckers comes out with his book. Best sellers.

Movie rights. The works. But what happened to the honest cop who was responsible for them being caught in the first place? You never hear about him. Just a little nigger, lucky if he was taking home two-fifty a week, and he spots the tape on the door and blows the whistle. Now you and I know niggers and how lackadaisical they are about their work. Look at Willie Davis when we had him in the outfield here. If a ball was hit right at him, O.K., but he wasn't going to chase it under a hot sun. Like it was pussy or chitlins. No suh. But this little nigger, he blows the whistle, and maybe John Dean, now that he's made his fortune, slips him two hundred bucks." McMaster shrugged. "Hey, have you caught the new picture at the Pussycat yet?"

The Pussycat was a downtown porn cinema.

"No. Why?"

"Just asking," McMaster said, smirking.

So he discovered *Office Party* was playing at the Pussycat. Among its featured players, Esty Blossom.

Shit shit shit. At an age when other Jewish mothers, sprouting moustaches, were past vice-presidents of ORT or delivering meals-on-wheels or convening fashion shows for the Hospital of Hope, his mother was up there on the big screen blowing men half her age.

Office Party must have been made at least a year earlier, because now Esther was out of skin flicks, having graduated to women's lib. The Movement. To begin with, Joshua heard that the harridans on the extreme edge of the movement had greeted his mother's conversion with glee. Esther, the exploited one. The reformed sex-object. Obliged by coarse producers to cavort nude on screen for their profit until, betrayed by her body, she was cast aside. The girls were overjoyed. Salt of the earth, his mommy. Badly used for years by a punch-drunk husband, a hoodlum usually on the lam. Neglected by what they described in their magazine as her famous and affluent son, that vastly overrated sexist journalist and TV commentator, Joshua Shapiro. Oh yes, they were congratulating themselves on their prize catch, this living metaphor for male chauvinist abuse, until the afternoon they took themselves to Ottawa to demonstrate for abortion-on-demand. Out there on Parliament Hill, all those truculent ladies without makeup or bras, their armpits defiantly hairy, placards held high, scorn in their eyes, Esther to the fore. Fighting Esther, charged with love for the cause and her new-found sisters. Alas, little did the sisters grasp that Esther was an experienced scene-stealer. A real pro. Only when the

267

television cameras began to pan toward her did she whip out her placard from under her fringed poncho. The cameraman froze. Timorous but socially conscious MP's who had grudgingly ventured out of the House to reason with the ladies stared, aghast. An alert RCMP constable started toward her, on the double. Esther, glorying in the attention, leaped up and down, brandishing her placard:

> SMELLY IT MAY BE
> BUT MY CUNT BELONGS TO ME

9

Now that they had converted to Celsius, waking on wintry mornings in Montreal, roused to the strident morning newscast by his digital clock radio, Joshua could no longer figure out how cold it was outside. The bouncy announcer, charged with cheer, cried out that it was two above, or nine below, but even though Teddy, the family mathematician, had explained the conversion formula to him again and again, he simply couldn't be bothered. He preferred to stand by the open window and guess how insufferably cold it really was out there. The kids were finding him increasingly grumpy. What they didn't grasp was that he was also becoming paranoid. Imagining that he was being followed on his nightly walks. Last night he even thought that he had seen McMaster.

Once, when he could readily have agreed that thirty was old, it had been his life's ambition to write something that would last. A page. A paragraph. A sentence, even. Now aged forty-seven and counting, as sportswriters were fond of saying, he stood tall for his morning piss and noticed, much to his chagrin, that looking down he couldn't quite see his very own penis. It was hidden below his obtruding belly. He resolved to diet. His new ambition, as serious as the earlier one, was to be so flat of stomach come his forty-eighth birthday that he would be able to look down in the morning and see it. Good morning, big boy.

It was just after 7 a.m. Joshua heard doors slam, feet pounding up and down the stairs, as Teddy searched for his gym shoes and Susy rattled the bathroom door, pleading with Alex to come out of the shower. Alex would have already brought in the *Gazette* and had his first phone call of the day. He will prepare his lunch, exactly to his taste, and forget it on the kitchen counter. Getting out of bed, Joshua reflected that, all things considered, he was glad to be a family man. Everything would be perfect, he thought, if only Pauline were here.

". . . among those awarded the Order of Canada today," the radio newscaster announced in a booming voice, "was Montreal tycoon Isaac Singer. . . ."

Izzy Singer, O.C. Imagine; Izzy had at last squeezed a booby prize out of all that frenetic effort. Joshua laughed aloud, remembering.

1967. The Grey Cup game. A game Joshua had covered for *Sports Illustrated*, cleverly combining the assignment with an Annual Day of the Mackenzie King Memorial Society, a reunion he all but ruined for everybody, having impetuously invited Izzy Singer to join them.

In those days, of course, Izzy no longer drove his battered Ford V-8 down St. Urbain, chasing after the ice-truck, peddling refrigerators. A millionaire since 1960, Izzy was by that time a veritable merchant prince. He rode herd over shopping centers he owned in Montreal, Calgary, and Vancouver. Condominiums in Florida. A fast-food chain that ran from sea to sea. Office towers in Toronto, Atlanta, and Los Angeles. Oil leases in the Northwest Territories. Forests in the Maritimes. Mineral rights in northern British Columbia. The option on seas of prairie grain. And more, much more, a sprawling empire he bestrode not as a proud colossus but like a worried ant.

Izzy, Izzy.

Joshua had nothing in common with him but Room 42, FFHS, and a memory that would not allow him to despise Izzy as did Seymour and the others. At Izzy's twelfth birthday party his mother had insisted that he play the violin for the boys, who sat there smirking, waiting to see what fumble-fingers, who couldn't even make the class softball team, could do. Izzy stood there—pale, thin, trembling—playing some gypsy air scratchily. His mother beaming, his aunts bubbling, until their pride was betrayed by a stream of hot piss darkening Izzy's trousers, spreading in a tell-tale puddle round his shiny new pair of shoes.

And then in 1967, out of nowhere it seemed, Izzy invited him to lunch at Ruby Foo's, a roadhouse that served sickly sweet liberal Jewish Chinese Food, his notion of heaven. "Even with all my accountants dreaming up things, those shmocks," he said, "I'm paying five thousand dollars a week tax. That's two hundred and sixty thousand dollars a year.

I've had drinks with your father-in-law at the Rideau Club. Nice guy."

A compact, bristling little man, an arctic owl, with large shell-rimmed glasses and blank brown eyes, Izzy knew enough to wear a Savile Row suit, shirts that had been tailored for him on Jermyn Street, and shoes made especially to fit his tiny feet. Ostensibly, the perfect prosperity package. But his onyx cufflinks were just a mite too large, and the initials woven into the breast pocket of his shirt too prominent. Izzy, of St. Urbain born, was still pissing in his pants as he played. He now also suffered from a most disconcerting facial twitch, his right cheek doing an all-but-perpetual dance. "I haven't got any friends here any more," he said. "I can't afford it. I'm invited to a party, the minute I come through the door, somebody has come round offering me a deal. They phone me at home too, before I've even brushed my teeth. You need a good dentist? Hershorn. The best. Tell him I sent you, you won't have to wait three weeks for an appointment. Really, Joshua, you ought to have them capped, all those spaces between look bad. Especially on TV. Hey, we really made something of ourselves, you and me. You and I. Which?"

"Me," Joshua said.

"You're wearing a nice jacket. British. Cashmere. The best. I have four."

"If you're so disgustingly rich, Izzy, why don't you retire?"

"Because money's like a soufflé, you've got it, you've got to keep a constant eye on the oven, either it keeps rising or it flattens. Inflation. I hear you don't fuck around, you're faithful to your wife. That's a plus. Me too, I'm faithful. I mean, you're going to be screwing other women all the time like that crazy Seymour, you can bring home the syph. How many times a week do you still fuck? Average?"

"Fifteen."

"Ha ha. We fuck on the average three times. More on vacation. Becky bought a copy of *The Joy of Sex*, we're still making sensual discoveries. Joshua, come back to my office with me, there's something I want to talk to you about."

Izzy's office occupied a floor in one of the city's new office towers.

"I believe in coming right to the point," he said. "No shmoozing. I'd like to get into the Senate. If you whispered that in your father-in-law's ear, I wouldn't complain. I'm a big contributor to the Liberals. He must know that. So?"

"Ask him yourself," Joshua said angrily and, eager to

270

change the subject, he muttered that he was leaving in the morning for the Grey Cup weekend in Ottawa, to be followed by the Annual Day of the Mackenzie King Memorial Society.

"Gee, I never see any of the old bunch," Izzy said wistfully.

"Would you like to come?" Joshua asked, trapped.

"O.K. Done. How many tickets do you need for the game? I'll pay."

"Izzy, we've already got our tickets."

"Yeah, but where? With my muscle, it would be the owner's box."

In Ottawa, Joshua felt he could not really avoid lunch with his father-in-law at his home in Rockcliffe. Their relationship was still rather stiff in those days, so he was startled to hear the senator say, after the briefest exchange of pleasantries, "It's time I told you how very pleased I am that you married Pauline. I want to apologize for my churlish behavior on your first visit here. It was inexcusable."

"I could have been more polite myself."

They both laughed, recalling the things they had said to each other, and Joshua felt himself suffused with the beginning of a warm regard for his father-in-law. What promised to be a kinship, two men bound together by their love for Pauline.

"There's something I want you to know. I'm transferring the family cottage on Lake Memphremagog to your name and Pauline's. Why should you be troubled by death duties when the time comes?"

"I'd rather," Joshua said, intent on earning points, "that you just put it in Pauline's name."

"As you like," the senator said, obviously relieved.

In his mind's eye, Joshua saw the cot in the maid's room. With the rubber sheet.

"I'd be most grateful," the senator said, "if you could all manage to come out and visit me next summer. I'd like to see my grandchildren out there."

They talked about Jane Austen, Dr. Johnson, and Mrs. Thrale, and then the senator revealed a taste, surprising to Joshua, for the novels of Hammett, Chandler, and Macdonald. They discovered they shared an enthusiasm for Bath. The senator told him that he had once met Isadora at a party in Haut-de-Cagnes, but she had cut him. "I suppose," he said, "she realized what a boring old stick I was."

271

Emboldened, Joshua asked him about his meeting with Izzy Singer.

"Yes, I remember," he said, amused, "he phoned me out of the blue to say he was an old friend of yours."

Joshua blanched.

"Don't worry, I've had a long experience of the type. I got the idea quickly enough. But I was curious, and I asked him to join me for drinks at the Rideau, knowing how much that would please him. He's an amazing fellow. Commendably forthright. He wants to be appointed to the Senate."

"Did he offer you money?" Joshua asked, ashamed.

"Some directorships," he said, averting his eyes. "You know, I can't imagine why a man of his flair and accomplishment would want to get into the Senate."

"There's some chance, then?"

"None whatsoever. He wants it too badly. That will never do in Ottawa."

"Did you tell him that?"

"I think he should be allowed to try. He shouldn't be denied that."

"Noblesse oblige."

"Oh, come now, that's a bit rich. I'm merely tolerated these days. An aging ornament. You'd be surprised how little influence I have."

Joshua got out of his taxi outside the National Press Club, badly in need of a drink, troubled by his meeting with the senator. The streets of Ottawa were icy, bitterly cold, but, for all that, a parade was in progress. Desperately high-spirited westerners come to town to see their American imports, NFL rejects to the man, do battle with the East's imports for Canada's national football trophy, the Grey Cup. The Saskatchewan Rough Riders vs. the Hamilton Ti-Cats. Paunchy men on horseback, their faces seared red by the wind, yodeled at passing secretaries huddled into their fur collars. Yahoo.

Back at the Château Laurier, the grizzled, middle-aged bellhops had broken out in rakish Grey Cup boaters. More westerners in high heels and Stetsons milled about, many of them reeling. All the unanchored lobby furniture had been removed. Joshua showed his room key to the man guarding the elevator, entitling him to ascend, and he was soon joined by his colleagues in the Mackenzie King Memorial Society. Seymour, Max Birenbaum, Bobby Gross, Leo Friedman, Jack Katz, Eli Seligson, and Morty Zipper of the Montreal contingent. Joshua told them, somewhat defiantly, that they were to be joined by Izzy Singer, but not until early Saturday morning.

"Shit," Seymour said, "now you've gone and done it. While George Reed is making his run, he'll be counting the gate and figuring out how many hot dogs are being sold."

"Cool it," Joshua pleaded.

"You don't know the half of it. I ran into him in Florida once. Izzy Singer relaxing. Poolside. You know what he was doing? He was sitting there, with a notebook in his hand, marking his three kids for diving, on a scale of one to ten, with a prize for the winner."

The out-of-towners began to trickle in. Mickey Stein, now a professor of social studies at Harvard; Benjy Zucker, a dean at UCLA; and Larry Cohen, a deputy minister at Consumer Affairs. Lennie Fisher and Al Roth had flown in from Toronto.

Izzy arrived in time for breakfast the following morning, catching up with the boys at their table in the Château dining room. His cheek dancing, he threw a clutch of game tickets on the tablecloth. "You know what scalpers are asking for those seats?"

Nobody knew where to look. They buttered toast or stared glumly at their newspapers. Except for Lennie Fisher, who leaped up to find a chair for Izzy.

"Oh, will you sit down and shettup," Joshua said to Izzy. "We've all had a late night."

"I've had champagne sent to your room for tomorrow night. A case. Dom Perignon. I also brought a side of smoked salmon with me."

"Sit down," Joshua said.

"I thought we were going to have us a ball here. What's the matter with everybody?"

Izzy's deerstalker hat matched his brown cashmere coat. His binoculars had been made in Germany, the best. A Nikon in a soft leather case was suspended from his shoulder. He also carried a Hudson's Bay blanket and a pillow in a celluloid case.

"I'm going to get you laid," Seymour said, his smile menacing. "After dinner tomorrow night."

"I thought," Izzy said, his voice wobbly, "there were no girls at these dinners."

"There are no girls," Joshua assured him.

"I swear," Seymour said, "that when she's finished with you, your tongue will be hanging out. Your cock will be raw

273

and bruised. We'll have to carry you all the way back to Montreal."

Izzy's seats were better than theirs, but the boys accepted them grudgingly, only Lennie Fisher acknowledging his largesse. "I was at Becky's last show," he said. "I think her work is marvelous."

Izzy's wife, Becky, sculpted. She made pieces out of fish bones. In an interview with the *Gazette,* arranged by Izzy (a major advertiser), she had said, "My children, bless their hearts, couldn't be more understanding. If my atelier door is closed, they walk about on tiptoe. I don't think Leonard Woolf himself could have been more patient than my husband."

A bitterly cold wind cut across the frozen playing field, the Ti-Cats jumping up and down on the sidelines. One-two-three-four. Between exercises they blew on their reddening fingers and stamped their feet together.

Then the Rough Riders trotted onto the field, their partisans in the stadium roaring. Izzy tugged at Joshua's sleeve. "I've got to pee."

"Turn right at the top of the stairs."

"But it won't come if there are other people there."

"Then wait."

"I can't."

"Izzy, I'm running out of ideas."

"Come on," Lennie Fisher said. "I'll take you back to the hotel. We'll keep the taxi waiting and we'll be back before they even kick off."

On the field, they watched a milling group of scrawny girls in green-and-white tights, their teeth chattering, their noses running. The Riderettes. Pimply sex kittens of the prairie. Fortunately, a thoughtful bandmaster had provided them with woolies, sadly loose-fitting, to wear over their stockings. The girls bobbed up and down, running in place, to keep warm. Suddenly, a TV camera came into play, the drums went boom, and the intrepid girls, after one last wipe of the nose with chapped hands, flashed radiant smiles and began to strut across the frozen field.

"Get 'em, get 'em," the Riderettes chanted. But the Riders were down 17–0 at half-time.

"I'm freezing," Joshua said to Seymour. "Let's watch the rest of the game on TV back in my room."

As they moved past Izzy, only his owlish shell-framed glasses showing over his Hudson's Bay blanket, he asked, "Do you have to pee?"

274

"No," Seymour barked. "We're going to get you that girl now. A real wild one. Wow."

Rather than risk the hallelujah streets of Ottawa again that night, the boys decided to order food from Nate's Delicatessen and to play poker in Seymour's room, turning in early with tomorrow's Memorial Day festivities in mind. Izzy pulled Joshua aside to say he couldn't play. Relieved, Joshua still felt obliged to ask him why.

"If I win, everybody will be angry with me, and if I lose, they'll say so what, he can afford it."

"Don't believe him," Seymour said, overhearing. "He's going back to his suite because he knows I'm sending the girl in there. She's going to screw his head off."

Their Annual Day couldn't begin with a champagne breakfast on the site of the "Abbey ruins." Snowy Kingsmere was shut down for the winter. So they drank their champagne at the gates, Mickey Stein leading them in his Yiddish rendition of "Safe in the Arms of Jesus."

"What if somebody comes?" Izzy asked, embarrassed.

Plump, good-natured Mickey Stein, to whom they had used to hurry with their jokes even back in FFHS days, just for the joy of seeing him heave with laughter, was a milkman's son. He had been able to afford McGill only because he had won a scholarship. And now, a full professor at Harvard, he pronounced to the sons of the American rich on the nuclear family, male bonding, and cultural patterns among the Assyro-Babylonians in Persia during the Sassanian Dynasty. "Joshua," he said, "you don't understand what publication means. I don't write for the masses. I compose a three-thousand-word argument for publication in a journal with a circulation of, say, fifteen hundred. The editorial committee broods for six months before they accept my piece, and then we write to and fro for another six months, quarreling over commas. A year later my reflections on the eschatology of the heretical dharmas is published, I Xerox two thousand copies for other professors, the Ford Foundation gives me a grant, and I'm able to take Sylvia to conferences in Tokyo, Stockholm, and Grenoble. Where we meet with other bores. And you want to know what? I'm beginning to suspect the delivery of milk is a more socially beneficial activity. Here's to us, *chaverim*."

Their other academic, sweet Benny Zucker, a dean at UCLA, was not to be outdone. "Scratch Stein here and what will you find? A thwarted Socialist. A loser. Who has he backed in recent elections? Gene McCarthy. He'll never learn

275

to be a proper goniff. He's mired in the wrong discipline. But me, I now own a wall of honorary degrees. My legendary services as an industrial consultant are fought over. I have an agent. And once a year he sends me down from the mountain with my tablets. To conventions for overachievers in Hawaii. Or orientation courses for top-level executives on an Arizona ranch. I am even known among the oilmen of Dallas. And wherever I go, standing at the podium, removing my reading glasses to emphasize a point, I tell the movers and shakers that our researchers at UCLA, computer-programmed, tested in the field, indicate that there is more stress among executives than bartenders and, furthermore, that there is a definite correlation between energy loss and age. And they shake their heads, flabbergasted, delighted with me, thinking, boy those Jews are clever. You've really got to hand it to them."

"How much," Izzy demanded, "do you get paid for such a lecture?"

"Well," Zucker said, elated, "not to brag, two grand, minimum."

"We had Elie Wiesel speak at our Bond Drive Dinner last summer, we paid him five thousand dollars."

"Oh, well," Zucker allowed, retreating, "it was just a story to amuse the boys. I never suggested others weren't being paid more."

Seymour looked ready to erupt. "Izzy," he said, "I've decided you're not getting fucked after all. Instead, I'm going to kill you."

"I don't like you either," Izzy protested, his cheek doing a jig, "but at least I know how to behave."

At Laurier House they marveled once more at the crystal ball on the piano and the painting of Wee Willie's mum. "He wasn't prime minister for nothing," Izzy said, pointing out that Joshua's father-in-law had been a member of King's wartime cabinet. "I've had drinks with the senator. At the Rideau," he said. "What a gentleman!"

Finally, they assembled in their private dining room in the Château Laurier, all the society's artifacts already in place.

"Geez," Izzy said, astonished, "aren't you guys ever going to grow up?"

Lennie Fisher enjoined them to get out of stocks and into commodity futures or gold. "I'll bet even Izzy would agree with me."

"I no longer discuss the portfolios I control in public," Izzy said, "because I always end up being quoted in the financial pages. Things move up or down, I'm blamed."

Everybody congratulated Larry Cohen on his appointment as a deputy minister.

"What are you being paid?" Izzy asked.

Reluctantly, Larry told him.

"You could do a lot better in the private sector. You know how much tax I pay? Five thousand dollars a week."

Eli Seligson, whom Joshua had been avoiding, finally caught up with him and pulled out a scathing article about his work from the *Detroit Jewish Press*. "This is what the authorities on such matters think about the shit you write."

Sliding away from him, Joshua proposed the first toast. "Gentlemen," he said, raising his glass, "I give you William Lyon Mackenzie King."

Then Seymour stood on his chair to propose the next toast. "Here's to the kisses we snatched and vice versa."

"Feh," Izzy said.

Mickey Stein won the yo-yo contest once more, but then the hockey game turned nasty. "This year," Seymour said, his smile innocent, "we're going to allow checking," and the next thing they knew, Izzy Singer was sprawled on the floor, whimpering, groping for his glasses.

"God damn it, Seymour, that was hardly necessary."

Lennie Fisher began to circle around Seymour, bobbing and weaving.

"Oh, go away," Joshua said, "you little suck-hole."

"I'll take him too," Seymour said, struggling with his jacket.

"I've got a disc problem," Eli Seligson announced, retreating.

Mickey Stein began to shake with laughter.

"Get off the floor, you twitchy little snake," Seymour yelled.

"For all your big talk," Izzy said, "what are you? A sweater manufacturer."

"I'm going to wipe him out," Seymour said.

Joshua drove Seymour into the bathroom, shutting the door behind them.

"Go back to your friend," Seymour said.

"Oh, cool off, you prick."

They both began to laugh. Seymour lifted the seat, moving back further and further, pissing in a high arc, singing, " 'I'll be with you in apple blossom time, I'll be with you, to change your name to mine.' . . . I'm afraid of dying," he said. "You?"

"Yeah."

277

"Who needs it?"

"Right."

"Did you have a good look at Al Roth?"

"What's wrong with him?"

"His wife's having an affair."

"How do you know?"

Zipping up, Seymour winked. "How are the kids?"

"Fine."

"I don't even know that I like mine. I mean, really like them." Seymour sighed. "Pauline doesn't care for me."

"That's not true."

"You're lucky, Josh. Terrific wife. Great kids. Talent. I hate you. I hope you die first."

"Not if I can help it."

"The most fun was the bookshop. All those nervy kids coming in, stealing, thinking I didn't know. Izzy Singer's a rat. He hurt Benny Zucker. That really burns me. Why did you bring him here?"

Joshua told him about Izzy Singer being forced to play the violin by his mother, a stream of hot piss running down his leg.

"Oh, yeah, I remember now. I was there. I don't know, Josh. I don't know. We're going to be forty soon. We've got to start being more selective about our friends."

When they got back into the suite, Izzy was already into his topcoat. "I don't feel well," he said. And, looking imploringly at Joshua, he added, "There's a plane leaving in forty-five minutes. I'm going to catch it."

"O.K.," Joshua said. "I'll come too."

"But we haven't even played your Civil War album yet," Seymour complained.

"I invited him, I'll see him home."

It was an uncharacteristically subdued, somewhat diminished Izzy who sat with Joshua on the airplane, twitching, as they skittered over wads of moonlit cloud. "What can you see in that animal?" he asked.

"Seymour?"

"Seymour."

"Appetite."

Even though it was late, Izzy insisted that Joshua join him at his mansion for a nightcap. Becky, fortunately, was in bed. So was the butler. Izzy had to fetch the cognac himself. "It's forty years old," he said. Surrounded by his possessions, high in Westmount, he seemed reassured. Everything opulent, everything in conflict. A Riopelle. A Chagall. A high modern marble fireplace, its inner frame bronze, surrounded by eighteenth-century English antiques. Round tables dressed in full skirts. Silk embroidered sofas. Velvet cushions. A collection of jade lying on glass shelves. An Aubusson rug. Picture window looking out on the pool. It seemed, at first glance, not so much a home as Izzy's notion of the ultimate hotel suite. Automatically, you looked around for a check-in desk. Izzy felt it was a pity that Joshua couldn't see the bathroom off the master bedroom, with its large circular bath and sauna, where the Empress Becky could powder and oil herself before retiring to her atelier. But he did take Joshua into the kitchen. Farmhouse beams. Copper pots of all sizes suspended from the ceiling. Butcher's block. Commodious counter. Gourmet gas stove. "I had everything ripped out when we moved in," he said. "Sixty grand, just for the kitchen."

"Does Becky know how to cook?"

"She doesn't have to."

Wearily, Joshua agreed to one more cognac before leaving. Izzy sipped camomile tea.

"You want to see my library? Two thousand eight hundred books. First editions. The complete Oxford Dictionary. Lots of Judaica. I belong to the Book-of-the-Month. The Literary Guild. The Fortune Book Club. The History Book Club. You name it."

Joshua didn't find out how badly the night had ended for Izzy until some years later, after he had got to know McMaster.

Before turning in, Izzy had freed his Alsatians from the basement, and then set up his photoelectric cell detector and vibration detector and ultrasonic alarm system. But he couldn't sleep. He was consumed with hunger. There was smoked meat in the massive fridge. Bagels. Potato salad. Lox. Chopped liver. He knew that, and just thinking about it fed his hunger pangs. But Izzy also had a problem. His alarms were all locked into a time-set, they couldn't be switched off manually and would not run down until 6:30 a.m., when staff rose. In order to get at the succulence that awaited in the kitchen, Izzy would have to pass below the photoelectric cell signal, careful not to break its hidden light pattern, which would activate the alarm. He would have to move softly, lest he trip the sensitive vibration detector. It would also be necessary to evade the sound-wave pattern of the ultrasonic system. This called for guile. Cunning Izzy, advancing along the floor of the upstairs hall like an infantry veteran, propelling himself on his elbows, passed below the first light beams.

Then he slithered successfully down the stairs. Here, happily, the beams and detectors were all hip-high, allowing for free movement of the dogs. Izzy was able to crawl as far as the kitchen on his hands and knees, one Alsatian sniffing at his asshole, probing with his wet snout, the other lapping at his ear. Carrying God knows how many diseases on that slobbery tongue. Shit. Fuck.

In the kitchen, still on his knees, Izzy skillfully managed to pry open the fridge and reach up slowly for the smoked meat platter. The chopped liver. Rye bread. Potato salad. Lacking a plate (dishes too high, damn it) or a knife (out of reach too), he spread the stuff on the terracotta floor and triumphantly began to fix himself a sandwich. Then the dogs, agreeably surprised, began to move in on him, tearing the best slices of meat from the platter and lapping up gobs of chopped liver. Shit. Fuck. Cunt. Fending one dog off with his arm, Izzy was just in time to notice the other attacking his sandwich. Enraged, crying, "Bad. Bad," Izzy began to flail away at the dogs. This they interpreted as play and one of them leaped to his hind legs, breaking a light beam. Which set off the photoelectric cell detector.

"You putz," Izzy shouted, leaping up to defend himself.

Which set off the vibration detector and ultrasonic alarm system.

Bells rang. Alarms whirred. Spotlights were ignited in the garden. Lights lit up a monitor board in Westmount Police Station. Staff came on the trot. Becky, screaming, locked herself in the bedroom.

Izzy, struggling with the dogs on the kitchen floor, began to sob.

Sirens wailed.

And, within minutes, two policemen were charging into the house, guns drawn.

"Please, please. It's only me. Izzy Singer. There's been a horrible mistake. A false alarm."

10

Although Joshua espied Monique and her mother at breakfast the morning after their arrival, seated only two tables away from him on the terrace of the Casa del Sol, he made no attempt to introduce himself. Pretending to read, he fed on surreptitious glances at her mouth, her bosom, her legs. He also contrived to stroll in the vicinity as she lay languorously on the sands in her maddening black bikini, but he pretended to be self-absorbed as he passed. He would never have approached her directly, risking rejection, if not for Dr. Dr. Mueller.

One evening, just before he parted the beaded door to Don Pedro's Bodega, he heard the sound of Monique's laughter coming from inside. A dark, throaty call. *She would be standing at the bar, and when one of the officers insulted her, questioning her virtue, he would send him flying across the room with a smartly delivered uppercut. Monique would melt, moaning, into his arms and he would carry her off to his place.*

> *But did thee feel the earth move?*
> *Yes. As I died. Put thy arms around me, please.*

Monique was seated at a corner table, sipping wine with Dr. Dr. Mueller, the first three buttons of her blouse undone. They were speaking English together, Mueller carrying on in his most worldly manner. The usual bunch of officers were lounging about, chatting in groups, mindful of Mueller's seductive intent and respecting his need for privacy. Gentlemen, the lot.

Provoked by Dr. Dr. Mueller's presence, Joshua picked up the lie dice from the bar, turned to their table, and asked, "Are you a man or a mouse?"

The officers appeared to be distressed, if hardly surprised, by his boorish intrusion, but Dr. Dr. Mueller seemed amused. He beckoned to Joshua with a smile tolerant of awkward boys. So he and Monique were finally introduced. They shook hands, French-style. Then he and Dr. Dr. Mueller began to throw dice, ostensibly for drinks. Dr. Dr. Mueller won and, according to the rules of the game, Joshua paid for the *poron* but they had to drink it at Mueller's table.

"I have seen you so often," Monique said, "but I thought you would never say hello."

"Hello."

"He calls himself a writer," Dr. Dr. Mueller said.

"I could tell you were an artist."

"I'm a reporter."

"I suspect," Dr. Dr. Mueller said with a wink, "that our young friend is writing a report about whores. Or why would he be at Casa Rosita so often?"

281

But Monique, far from being offended, seemed enthralled. "You frequent a brothel here?"

Trapped between the need to drink quickly and the realization that once he finished his share of the *poron* he would be obliged to quit the table, Joshua sat there, briefly paralyzed, a stupid grin on his face.

"The lovely lady is waiting for an answer," Dr. Dr. Mueller said.

"I've been there with the fishermen on occasion."

"Would you take me there once? I have never been to a brothel."

"I do not think your mother would approve," Dr. Dr. Mueller said. "I believe you would be better off going horseback-riding with me tomorrow. My friend Captain González will make the arrangements."

"I love horses."

"Why don't you speak French, Dr. Dr. Mueller, as a courtesy to a visitor from Paris?"

"Do you speak French?" she asked.

"He picked it up during the war, with the army of occupation."

"I see," she said, her voice gratifyingly icy.

"Anybody who was not a mouse or, forgive me, a child at the time, fought in the war. I fought for my country. The French fought for theirs. But it's all over for me now, a closed book. I respect a man for what he is," he said, thrusting the lie dice at Joshua.

"You wish to roll again?" Joshua asked, astonished.

"I think one of the officers would like to have a turn with you. We will excuse you."

"Wait," Monique said. "Do you write in the manner of the avant-garde?"

Venturing a guess, Joshua said, "Yes."

"Have you read *Ubu Roi?*"

"Oh, yes, and I enjoyed it enormously."

To the indignation of Dr. Dr. Mueller, Monique leaped up, with a perceptible bounce of her marvelous bosom, and took him by the hand. "This has been very pleasant, Gunther. I thank you for inviting me to a drink."

"You are going?"

"My mother is waiting for me."

Dr. Dr. Mueller grabbed Joshua by the arm, holding him down in his chair. "Then we will have another game of lie dice after all."

But Monique wasn't finished. Smiling at Joshua, she said, "I was hoping you would take me back to my hotel."

So Joshua sailed right out of there arm-in-arm with Monique, leaving Dr. Dr. Mueller behind. He was not only amazed but exhilarated, and fearful as well. For he grasped that he had done the unspeakable. He had humiliated Dr. Dr. Mueller before the officers.

Monique kicked off her sandals and without actually discussing it they avoided the dirt road, starting back to the Casa del Sol across the sandy shore on the rim of the bay.

"Why did you never greet me on the terrace?"

Joshua confessed to being shy.

"I asked Gunther about you one morning and he said there was once an English girl here and she told Captain González that you were a homosexual. I thought maybe that's why—"

"No. Honestly."

They sat down together near the shore. Joshua lighted a cigarette. Monique closed her eyes and inhaled with great ceremony. "I love the tang of the sea air," she said.

"Yeah, sure," he agreed, swallowing hard.

"Oh, to be at one with nature. Savage nature."

Oh, why don't you shettup, he thought in spite of himself.

Still breathing deep, Monique recited some lines about the sea, by Rimbaud, with enormous feeling, her bosom rising and falling. My, my. Scratching around for some saltwater poetry of his own, the best Joshua could come up with, under the circumstances, was, "Break, break, break/ At the foot of thy crags, O, sea/ I would that my tongue could utter/ the thoughts that arise in me," lines he had once had to copy out fifty times after he had been caught winging a blackboard brush at Seymour Kaplan.

"Breathe deeply," Monique said, "and you will smell eternity. This is the air the Phoenicians smelled when they came here so long ago."

"Um, is it true your mother is waiting for you?"

"She will wait. It makes her angry, but she knows I cannot live without the fucking."

Could he have heard her right? Joshua fondled her, greedy but inept. She began to moan. He pulled back, burnt. "Anything wrong?" he asked.

"Oh, you have a way of doing that," she replied hoarsely.

Hey, hey, she had been moaning with pleasure.

". . . of touching me there . . ."

Kitty's and Casa Rosita notwithstanding, Joshua was still a sexual innocent. Only two years earlier, visiting a summer

283

camp in the Laurentians where Bobby Gross was working as arts and crafts director, his ignorance had been certified in the company of his peers. Bobby had boasted that Aviva, dramatics, had invited him to masturbate her the night before. Right out there on the baseball diamond. The outfield.

"Ah, who are you trying to kid," Joshua had said, nobody's fool even then, "how can a girl masturbate?"

Whoops of laughter greeted his remark and he had been sick with embarrassment for days. And now, looking down, he could see Monique's eyes rolling. Soon only the whites were visible. Sweet Jesus, what next?

A twig cracked in the darkness beyond the trees. An animal, he thought.

"I cannot bear the idea of growing old," Monique said. "I will kill myself before I am thirty."

"You mustn't even think that," he implored her.

Monique was already undoing the rest of the buttons of her black blouse, tossing it on the sand and unhooking her bra. Looking back, Joshua still couldn't say whether he was more alarmed than aroused, but, within an instant, they were locked together, Monique's skillful tongue flicking in and out of his mouth. Strolling back to his place they stopped to embrace again and again, his hands kneading her breasts. Monique was inclined to moan, disconcertingly, and he, already spent, was suffering from a painful and persistent drip. Back at his place, he made a mess of it. He was no longer of much use and it was a subdued and forgiving Monique he led back to the Casa del Sol in the early hours of the morning. Her mother, she said, was bound to be waiting on the terrace. So they parted on the beach, having arranged to meet for a swim after breakfast. Starting home again, he was pursued by the clamor of their raised voices, the echo of racing high-heeled footsteps against the marble tiles, a slamming door. Joshua cursed himself for his ineptitude and wondered if Monique would now be convinced that he was a homosexual after all and would consequently become agonizingly unobtainable again. Joking about him with Dr. Dr. Mueller. He's not a man, Gunther, he's a mouse. *Mueller*. Before going to sleep, Joshua locked his door and moved a chair against it, propped under the knob. He secured the windows and took a hammer to bed with him. *You are not only a plagiarist but you are also impotent. A coward. I hate you.*

After breakfast, even as her mother glared at them from the hotel terrace, they swam together in the bay. Monique thrusting her breasts against him under water, jiggling them against his chest. Monique fishing into his trunks, making him leap, astonished, but finding him happily erect. They swam to a lick of sand, obscured by palm trees, and there they indulged in some rather more gladdening a,b,c,d. Then they returned hand-in-hand to the hotel so that Monique could change her clothes. A waitress, mopping tables on the terrace, told him that he was wanted in the kitchen, and there he found a flushed Freiberg waiting for him with his wife and Max.

Mrs. Freiberg, her black eyes smoldering, hissed, "You mustn't come to fuck with that girl on our beach. I would also prefer it if you ate your breakfast elsewhere from now on."

"Don't you serve Jews here?" Joshua asked.

Freiberg spat on the floor.

"What's the worst thing that ever happened to you?" Max asked. "Wait. I'll guess. Your pet dog was run over by a car. No, you were naughty and your mummy made you go to bed without your supper. Have you ever eaten the flesh of sewer rats?"

"Where'd you get your scar?" Joshua demanded, his cheeks on fire.

"They beat the shit out of me, what do you think?"

"Why wouldn't you say as much to him?"

"Do you speak Yiddish?" Max asked.

"Only a little. Why?"

"Because you are a *putz!*"

"Maybe," Joshua said, turning to leave, "but I wouldn't serve that bastard Riesling at my hotel."

Mariano was seated on the terrace, sipping coffee. "Come here," he said to Joshua.

"What is it?"

Grinning, he slipped Joshua a coffin small enough to lie in the palm of his hand. "Open it," he said.

As Joshua slid it open, an enormous erection popped up from between the legs of the carved corpse inside.

Monique emerged from the hotel, he took her back to his place, and this time he did not fail her. They made love through the afternoon, the night, and, with considerably diminished ardor on his part, through the early hours of the morning. Finally, he delivered her back to the hotel and tottered home to fall into a deep sleep. It was the same the next day, the day after, and the day after that. Between Monique's visits, Joshua wandered from room to room in a stupor, aching everywhere, wondering when he would hear from Dr. Dr. Mueller.

Seemingly, Dr. Dr. Mueller had been rendered inert by his humiliation before the army officers. Joshua ran into him twice on the terrace of the Casa del Sol. Once, actually buying a camera with an elaborate lens from Freiberg's brother-in-law, Max; another time, eating ice cream with Monique's mother. Joshua was too discreet ever to take Monique to Don Pedro's Bodega after that first night, but he still frequented the place himself. Dr. Dr. Mueller, if he was there, greeted him with a cordial smile, but they did not talk and there were no more games of lie dice. A gratifying change had come over the officers. Where once, with the exception of González, they had been no more than correct in his company, now they actually drank and joked with him. Jiménez, the jolliest of the captains, took to teasing him. "Man, she must keep you very busy. We no longer see you strolling on the hill overlooking the barracks."

"He's too tired to climb hills these days," another officer pitched in.

"Oh, well," Joshua said, savoring his role, "there may be some truth in that."

"Say," Jiménez asked, "what were you doing up there, anyway? Hunting butterflies?"

He didn't dare acknowledge that he had been on his way to Dr. Dr. Mueller's villa. "Oh, just walking. Looking around."

"Juan says you were spying on us."

"He's absolutely right," Joshua agreed, relieved.

Although he still drank with the fishermen and shared their scorn for the military, the truth was he was flattered by his hard-won approval from the officers. He savored their knowing smiles when he passed them on the road with Monique, the sex-crazed morsel he had plucked from Dr. Dr. Mueller's grasp.

His triumph, it seemed to him, had connotations larger than mere sexual appetite fulfilled. He had demonstrated that, given the choice, a young lady of taste preferred the attentions of a skinny working-class Jew to that of an arguably aristocratic, yet moldering, German. He had taken on a Nazi *mano a mano* and demonstrated to Mr. Hemingway and himself that he did not lack for *cojones*. After months of despairing about his inadequacies, he had, to his delight, turned out to be one hell of a fellow, manly beyond his wildest dreams.

One night, feeding on such conceits, he asked Monique

what had led her to choose him over Dr. Dr. Mueller. Then he lay back, waiting for the compliments to fall like rain.

"Oh, that was easy. Have you ever looked at him closely?" That Jew-hating monster. Nazi scum. "Sure I have."

"He has tiny ears. Very small fingers. His big toes hardly exist."

"What's that got to do with anything?" he demanded.

Monique, redeeming herself somewhat, went on to say that she had noticed Joshua on the terrace on her first day at the Casa del Sol and had immediately resolved to make him her lover.

"Why?" he asked, shameless.

"You had such big ears. And your nose! My God! And your big toes, just look at them!"

"I don't understand."

"In my experience, men with such extremities usually have a very big one."

"You mean, that's all there was to it?"

"Oh, yes. Why?"

"No reason," he said, crushed, "just wondering."

With a familiar urgency Monique now announced, "I promised to be back at the hotel by two tonight."

Which meant there was no more time for idle talk. He was being called on once more to compensate with energy for what he lacked in dimension. An exception to her rule, alas. Happily, he hopped to it. Such, indeed, was his twenty-one-year-old abandon that he still had no idea that he was being set up by Dr. Dr. Mueller.

11

"Well, yeah. Right. What's tomorrow?"

"The Habs against the Leafs. If The Rocket puts it in the nets, that makes it ten games in a row."

"Try again."

"It's Purim."

"Hey," his father said, astonished, "how did you know that?"

"Morty Zipper told me."

"O.K. Not bad. Now tell me what it means," and here he dragged out his Bible, searching for the right passage, "to have a Mordecai at your gates."

Mordecai "Three-Fingers" Brown was the only one he

knew of by that name, but he had been a pitcher long ago. "You're going to tell me anyway. Why do we always have to turn these lessons into a kind of quiz?"

His father broke open a bottle of Labatt's.

"I want you to stay away from Kitty's. Every time she opens the door to bring in the milk, she says you're standing there with your tongue hanging out."

"You're the one who told me to go early."

"Yeah, but not every day. Shit."

"My pimples are drying out. Look."

"Yeah, and they've left your cheeks looking like a sieve." Joshua bristled.

"I'm sorry, I didn't mean that. Now about Purim. I'm no rabbi, you know, but I'm trying to teach you to the best of my ability so you should be aware of our tradition. I only hope I'm doing it proper."

"What's wrong, Daddy?"

"Well I've read this Book of Esther three times now and, like, Mordecai is a guy we're supposed to honor on Purim. But the way I see it, reading between the lines, he was a real conniver, a suck-hole, a very bloodthirsty fella. . . ."

"Oh yeah?"

"And—not that I want you repeating this to your Uncle Harvey—and certainly the first Jewish pimp."

"Can I say something?"

"I don't want to hear anything about what you're doing at Kitty's. I'm your father, for Christsake!"

"About the Bible, I mean."

"Oh, yeah, sure, that's why we're sitting here."

"You don't seem to care for just about anybody in it, except for the hairy guy who was always cooking up stews for his father."

"Esau."

"Yeah."

"Yeah."

"Why don't we just drop it?"

"Because you've quit school and it's left to me, of all people, to knock an education into you. Now Mordecai was Kish's kid, a Benjamite. That means from one of the two tribes that were left about the time the Jews had been muscled out of Palestine and were mostly hacking it in old Persia. There were twelve tribes who signed up with Jehovah, the covenant, but ten were lost since," he said, his voice trailing.

"How lost?" Joshua pounced.

"Shit, Josh. Lost. Disappeared. Like the Montreal Maroons or the Ottawa Senators or the Brooklyn Americans; I mean, they just aren't here any more."

"They *disbanded*, they weren't lost. How can ten whole fucking tribes just disappear?"

"The same way you build the world in six days, is how. This is the Bible we're studying, it's been translated into every language you ever heard of and has sold more copies than any book in the world. So pay attention. We are now talking about Persia during the days of King Ahasuerus, see. The king's wife, a real bitch, was called Vashti, and one day the king calls for her, he was at this banquet with all his followers and maybe he feels like a piece of ass, and she wouldn't come, which really burned him. He dumped her and got this idea to run a beauty contest, but only for broads who still had their cherry, and you could enter from any one of his hundred and twenty-seven provinces. Which brings me to old Mordecai. He was taking care of his dead uncle's girl Esther, who was also known as Hadassah, like the group your Aunt Fanny belongs to, always trying to hit you with raffle tickets. Only she wasn't a *yenta* like them, this Esther, but stacked, a looker, and Mordecai put her in the contest. Now we have lots of beauty contests, you know, like they had one to find a Scarlett O'Hara to play in *Gone With the Wind*. Or like Miss America. But if you won this one, you didn't just get to travel with the Bob Hope Show, you got to be Queen of Persia and all its provinces."

"Where does our family come from?"

"Oh, some shitty little village in Poland. Chickens used to run around right in the house. Do you remember your grandfather?"

"Not very well. Did you like him?"

"Well, he used to knock me around, you know, and he was bad news," his father said, laughing fondly. "You know what he used to do? Greenhorns, you know, new arrivals from the old country, would get off the train with their bundles, scared shitless, and my father would come up to them with this pad in his hand and bark, 'What's your name, Jew?' 'Bishinsky,' they'd say, teeth chattering, or 'Pfeffershnit.' And he'd holler, 'You crazy Jews, this is the British fucking Empire and you can't call yourself by such horseshit names here. You there, you are now called "Bishop," ' and he'd hand him the name on a sheet of paper torn from his pad, 'and you, your name is now "Pepper," and that will be five dollars each.' Trouble is, the old bastard couldn't spell good and to this day there are

289

families in Montreal called Bishop who spell their names B-e-a-s-c-h-i-p. Do you really not remember him that well?"

"Do you remember *your* grandfather?"

"Oh, yeah, sure. He was a crippler back in Russia, where he originally came from. If you didn't want to serve in the Czar's army, he would put one of your balls on an anvil and smash it. Or shoot a toe off for you. Or maybe just puncture an ear drum. It was good work, but seasonal."

"We're some bunch, the Shapiros."

"Have another beer, kid."

"Sure."

"Now Mordecai, he entered Esther in the contest and in those days, before Kotex, they all must have smelled real bad down there, because it took twelve months to clean them up for the king. Quote, six months with oil and myrrh, and six months with sweet odors, and with other things for the purifying of the women, unquote. Anyway, she won. Esther took the crown. But Mordecai he had duped the king, he had no idea Esther was Jewish. And now that he had planted her in the king's bed, he began sitting at the king's gate. And there he once heard two guys plotting to rub out Ahasuerus and he put the finger on them and they were both hanged. Now the king's minister, Haman, he used to see this old kvetchy Hebe sitting at the king's gate and Mordecai would never bow his head to him, which made him wonder about his muscle. With all his blessings, Haman used to see him there and wonder, quote, Yet all this availeth me nothing, so long as I see Mordecai sitting at the king's gate, unquote. It burned him, it really burned him. So he went out and got the king's permission not only to hang Mordecai, but to kill every Hebe in Persia and all its provinces. O.K. Sure. What he didn't know was that Mordecai had his uncle's looker of a daughter planted inside, screwing the royal head off every night, and he got Esther to work on the king and one, two, three, the tables are reversed. Not only is Haman hanging on the gallows he set up for Mordecai, but the king now turns around and grants the right to the Jews, quote, to destroy, to slay, and to cause to perish, all the power of the people and province that would assault them, both little ones and women, and to take the spoil of them for prey, unquote. And listen to this, the people of Persia are now so shit-scared that many of them become Jews. Even so, Mordecai and his followers they kill some seventy-five thousand enemies, men, women, and children, which is why we celebrate Purim, quote, a day of feasting and gladness, unquote. And old Mordecai, really

290

leaning on his connections now, ends up prime minister in Haman's place.

"Now I've told you I read this story three times, and the way I see it there are two morals buried in it. One, Mordecai's rise out of nowhere proves something I've always tried to knock into your head. It doesn't matter what you know, but who you know. Two, according to the law and what the rabbis say even now, it is an offense to marry out of our religion—we are not supposed to tie the knot with a *goy* or a *shiksa*. But nowhere in the Book of Esther do you find God hollering because she married a *goy*, and I never heard any rabbi complain either. So, if I interpret the law correctly, you are not allowed to marry out of the faith unless it's into a royal family. Interesting, eh?"

12

How was Joshua to know they would fly to the moon? Gun down another Kennedy? Get Nixon? Trade Bobby Orr? Or that the honest crook and the worldly senator would become such devoted friends?

His father, his father-in-law.

Given to drinking together in the Rideau Club, the senator beckoning cabinet members to their table to be introduced. "I would like you to meet my son-in-law's father. Reuben Shapiro. He is the most perspicacious Bible scholar I've ever met and a former lightweight boxing champion of Canada. He went eight rounds against Mr. Samuel Angott, and I'm proud to say I once had the signal honor of being his wheelman. Isn't that so, Reuben?"

"Damn right."

Then, leaning back in his chair, the senator might add, "We're looking for a little action tonight. Maybe a poker game."

Ever since his initial meeting with the senator Joshua, brooding on him, had magnified the man as a much-needed figure of rectitude come into his life. Unwinding the spool of that first encounter again and again, he had grown increasingly ashamed of his brash behavior. The truth was, he had reflected more than once, that had he been Pauline's father, he would not have wanted her to marry the likes of Joshua Shapiro. With hindsight, Joshua had come to respect, even cherish, the senator, and to measure his own moral lapses against what he took to be the senator's uncompromising standards. The old virtues of the men who had forged colony into country, refining a frontier society. So he had been considerably more sorrowful than triumphant to discover that the senator was considering accepting a couple of directorships in companies controlled by Izzy Singer. He was indignant that Izzy, who knew the price of everything, had turned out to be a better judge of character than he was. He hadn't grasped, as Pauline had always known and accepted, that her revered father was the sum of old alliances, with political connections he could redeem at his convenience. His senatorial endowment policy. Obviously, his father-in-law was a man of sensibility and tact. His fingernails clean. His library beyond reproach. Without a police sheet. But there was a little of Colucci in his soul.

Which certainly explained why his father was so amused by him, if not why the senator had come to hold his father in such surprisingly high regard.

It was Joshua, his mood defiant, who had arranged the senator's meeting with his father.

He and Pauline, as requested by the senator, drove out to inspect her inheritance on Lake Memphremagog in the spring of 1968, with Alex, Susy, and the infant Teddy, whom Pauline was still nursing at the time. They had only been installed in the sinking old house with the wraparound porch for a few days when Joshua invited his father out for the weekend. His step jaunty, Reuben disembarked from the bus in Magog, wearing his straw boater, an ice-cream suit, and one of his vintage hand-painted ties. Autumn, a veritable riot of color, comes to the Laurentian Shield. He arrived on a Friday night, laden with toys for the kids, and the senator, as Joshua should have expected, was far too experienced a man to betray even a flicker of surprise at his father's appearance. But he did seem a bit chuffed that the children, who were unfailingly reserved in his presence, flew right into Reuben's arms, competing for kisses. And Joshua feared that it was not generosity, but a spirit of grandfatherly competition that prompted him to invite his father to join him and Alex on a fishing expedition early the next morning. It was June, the lake still running cold, hungering bass, perch, and even landlocked salmon swimming in shallow waters. Joshua never did find out all that passed between them on that outing, but if the senator, an experienced angler, thought that Reuben would prove comically inept on the lake, he was in for a surprise. Hunkered down in Michigan more than once, Reuben had learned to handle rod and reel with élan.

"Oh, you just help yourself to any lure you want," the senator had said, opening the tackle box. "They're all much the same."

"Yeah. Right," Reuben said, anticipating the senator's hand, snatching just the right lure out of a tray before the senator could grab it.

"Now I'm going to throw this line the best I can, Alex, and then, you and me, we're going to reel it in together, but slowly."

Reuben, who could cast as expertly as he could jab, immediately struck for the dark shady waters just short of where the lily pads were beginning to send up shoots. When they finally came in, late in the afternoon, Alex was waving eight fish on a dancing line, shouting that he and Reuben had landed six of them together. Joshua was concerned—needlessly, as it turned out. For whatever had passed between his father and the senator on the lake, the amazing thing was that the senator didn't seem to mind about the fish. He was flushed and exuberant. "I don't mind telling you," he said, "that we have some damn good fun out there."

And, on the evidence, a good deal of rye as well. Reuben and the senator drained the last of the V.O. before the fire, and the senator asked him how he had become so familiar with the Bible.

"Well," Reuben said, "in the days when I was no more than a club fighter really, and I would have to stay in all those crummy hotels on the road, there was no TV in the rooms. We didn't even have beds with Magic Fingers yet. I could never get to sleep the night before a fight, so I found myself reading the Good Book, in which I have instructed my worthless son here."

Pauline, going on very little sleep, nursing Teddy on demand, suddenly let out a sharp cry. She had invited twelve people over on Sunday afternoon and had just discovered there was very little to drink in the house and, of course, the liquor commission in Magog was already closed for the weekend.

"Couldn't we borrow some bottles from the Hickeys?" the senator asked.

"They're not invited."

"What about the McTeers?"

"And they'll be reminding me about it for the next twenty years. Shit."

"I know you're tired," Joshua said, "but would you please stop overreacting to the most trivial—"

Teddy let out a yelp from his crib. Anticipating, Joshua grabbed Pauline. "Sit, for Christ's sake. He'll wait a minute."

"Oh, a hell of a lot you know about these things," she said, dashing up the stairs.

The senator frowned and began to poke the fire.

"Yeah, well," Reuben asked, "are we anywhere near a village called Vale Perkins here?"

"Indeed we are."

"Then we can't be far from Owl's Head?"

"I had no idea you were familiar with this region," the senator said.

"Well, like, I was in the liquor business once. Deliveries, sort of. And in those days I got to know some of the back roads that lead into Vermont from here."

"Holy cow," the senator said, "you were a bootlegger!"

"Now what I'm going to need," Reuben said, "is a flashlight, maybe a couple of shovels, two empty boxes, and have you got a crowbar?"

"Yes, in the basement."

"Josh, I'm going to need you."

"Can I come?" Alex asked.

"Geez, can you come? I'm counting on you, kid. You're going to be my lookout man."

"And what about me?" the senator demanded, aggrieved.

"Well now, you're a very respectable fella. I really don't know."

"It's my car," he said, petulant.

"Yeah. Right."

"Let me be your wheelman."

"Well . . ."

"I'll bring my piece."

"*Your what?*"

"My cannon."

When the senator reappeared, he was carrying a pail of water and an old 12-gauge shotgun that had last been used to scare raccoons out of the cornfield.

"Holy shit," Reuben said, "what do we want with that thing?"

"In case we run into the heat."

"Oh, yeah. Right. Good thinking. But just be careful where you point it."

Pauline drifted down the stairs, Teddy suckling happily at

her breast, to find them standing there with flashlights, shovels, crowbar, and shotgun. "What's going on?" she asked.

"We're going to find you some booze," Reuben said. "At least, that's the general idea."

"Reuben, you are not to break into anybody's house here."

"Oh, no. Hell. Nothing like that."

"Are you going with them, Daddy?"

"Yes," the senator cried out defiantly.

"At your age?"

"Damn it, Pauline, I'm the wheelman," he said, hurrying on ahead to avoid further recriminations.

"Joshua, what's happening?"

"I don't know."

"Come on, fellas."

They found the senator squatting at the rear of his station wagon, rubbing mud on the license plate.

"Hey," Reuben said, nudging Joshua, "I can see you've been around."

The senator grinned, immensely pleased.

"Now just let me have a look at that shotgun," Reuben asked. And, borrowing it for a moment, he slid round to the other side of the car.

They drove to Vale Perkins and then on to Owl's Head. Beyond it, Reuben pointed out another dirt road that led into Vermont. "We want to go as far as the border," he said, "turn around and then track back exactly one mile."

The senator took it slowly.

"O.K. Stop right here."

Flashlight in hand, Reuben got out to scrutinize the trees by the roadside, and then he started tentatively into the woods. He was back in five minutes. "This may turn out to be a wild goose chase," he said.

"What do you mean?" the senator asked.

"Well, it's been a long time since I last passed through here. You and me, senator, we've begun to shrink, but these goddamn trees here they just keep putting on new growth."

They stopped another hundred yards down the road and Reuben got out to examine an old cedar tree, running his hands along the bark. "O.K., just pull up here, boys."

"Do you want us to stash our wheels anywhere, Reuben?"

"Shit, no. Just come on out of there."

Following Reuben, they climbed over a fence with a NO TRESPASSING sign nailed to it, the senator carrying his cannon. Reuben began to study the trees again, running his hand along the bark here and there. Finally he seemed to find

295

whatever it was he wanted, and he set out through the grass, stopped abruptly, and called for Alex and Joshua. "O.K., Josh, you start digging here and you here, Alex," and then he moved off to sit down on a rock with the senator. "Maybe," he said, "you should be sitting back on the road? Lookout."

But the senator wasn't budging. "If anybody comes," he said, "we're fishermen digging for nightcrawlers."

"Hey, Senator, I sure coulda used a fella of your skills back in the old days."

"This is such grand fun, Reuben."

Alex called out to say that he had hit wood.

"Well, well, why don't you get your father to help you uncover it, then?"

Within twenty minutes the unmistakable outlines of a coffin began to emerge.

"Put down that shovel immediately," Joshua said to Alex, and he charged over to his father, pulling him aside. "Are you crazy, Daddy, bringing Alex out here. Is this your idea of a joke? There's a coffin in there."

"Oh, really," Reuben said, reaching for his crowbar.

"Let's get out of here right now."

"I'm staying," Alex said.

The senator joined them. "Is there really a stiff in there?" he asked in a faltering voice.

"What a bunch," Reuben said, exasperated. "Alex, we should of come out alone."

"Yeah."

"Now you boys just dig out that coffin. I know what I'm doing."

When they had finally cleared the cheap, rotting pine coffin, Reuben moved around it, jimmying the lid here and there. Joshua's heart thudded. The senator, for all his bold talk, looked old and weary. But Alex was elated. "O.K.," Reuben said, "anybody here believe in ghosts?"

Nobody answered.

"If it's a vampire, I think what you're supposed to do is drive a stake through its heart."

Nobody laughed.

"O.K. Stand back. Ready. Steady. Go," Reuben said, and with one twist of the crowbar he swung back the splintering lid to reveal a cornucopia of booze. Top Hat Whisky, Scotland's Pride, Edinburgh Castle, Hi-Life.

"Holy cow," the senator exclaimed.

As Alex reached down to retrieve a bottle of Top Hat,

296

Reuben cautioned him. "Hold it, kid. You don't want to drink that shit."

"What?"

"Too much sulfuric acid. The Gurskys didn't know too much about distilling in those days. There was so much rust in this brew they had to run it through a loaf of bread, not that it really helped. You sip that and your fingers will go numb. Now there," he said, pointing at two strapped boxes, "there's the stuff we want."

They retrieved the boxes and unstrapped them to uncover a dozen bottles of Johnny Walker Black and a dozen of Gordon's Gin. Reuben opened a bottle of Johnny Walker, took a swig, and passed it to the senator, who drank and passed it to Joshua.

"I'm so excited," the senator said, "I've just got to piss right here and now. Anybody mind?"

"Certainly not."

And then, his cheeks flushed, the senator added, "Anybody care to join me?"

Alex and Joshua transferred the good liquor to their own cartons and, on Reuben's instructions, resealed the coffin and shoveled earth over it again.

"How did it get there in the first place, Reuben?"

"I really wouldn't know about that, Senator, but if I had to guess I'd say in a hearse, most likely."

They started back for the road, the senator leading. "Damn it," he suddenly exclaimed, trotting back toward them, "it's the heat."

They all turned to Reuben, but he offered no guidance.

"I knew we should have hidden the car," the senator said.

Parked right behind their station wagon, headlights blazing, was the village taxi. And leaning against it, wizened, mottled old Orville Moon. Lizardy eyes, yellowed teeth. "Why, Senator Hornby," he said, astonished, "what are you doing here?"

"Looking for nightcrawlers."

"You came all this way for worms?"

"That's right."

Moon indicated the senator's shotgun. "And were you going to shoot the meaner ones between the eyes?"

Alex sat down on his carton. So did Joshua.

"For worms," Moon said, "they sure do rattle a lot."

"Look here, Orville, if not for me you'd still be singing for your pension. I also got your cousin that beer license."

"True enough."

"Out of our way, then."

"There's some deer that's been shot out of season around here."

"Now you just scat, Orville."

Pauline was waiting for them in the living room.

"I pissed outside," the senator told her, excited, "out in a field there."

Alex and Joshua carted in the liquor.

"Boy, did we ever have fun!" the senator said.

"Stop waving that cannon around like that," Reuben said. "Here. Give it to me."

Reuben gestured for Joshua to follow him out onto the porch, where he showed him the empty breech. He held the bullets in his hand. "I wasn't taking any chances. I emptied it before we got into the car."

The senator was just a bit of a problem the following afternoon.

"You'll never guess where this hootch comes from," he said, pouring a Scotch for Dickie Abbott.

"Hey now," Reuben said, "I never took you for a canary."

"Damn right. Mum's the word. But it was aged in the casket, wasn't it, old pal?"

"If you say so, Senator."

Later Joshua found Pauline soaking in the bath. Pauline, Pauline. Joshua let out a yelp, stripped down, and lowered himself into the tub behind her.

"What if Alex comes in?" she asked.

"Well now," he said, beginning to lather her breasts, "don't you think it's time he learned about alternative life-styles?"

"I'm not protesting. I just think maybe we should lock the door."

"Maybe I've made a mistake about avoiding it out here. Possibly we should try a summer on the lake."

"You have no idea of the kind of people who come out here in summer. You'd only be miserable, Josh."

"What about you?"

"I was brought up with them."

"I could build a fence around the property. Electrified. This is where the Shapiros live. Bless them. Jane Trimble and cancer keep out."

"If only it were that simple."

"Hey, you're becoming awfully serious."

"Darling, if you're going to do that—"

"Do you want me to stop?"

298

"Certainly not. But lock the door, please."

"I love you. But I can't understand why you ever married me. I never would have."

"You didn't make it easy to say no."

"Did you love me then?"

"I wasn't sure."

"And now?"

"Please lock the door."

"You haven't answered my question."

"I love you. I'm also afraid."

"Of what?"

"The others."

FOUR

1

". . . And then I said," McMaster droned on, as the Sony whirled, " 'Look, Colucci, you dumb dago, you North End asshole, I don't know what you've got going with anybody else in Number Four, but you can stuff that envelope where the monkey put his fingers.' Cut. Stop. Correction. And then I said, 'Look, Colucci, you are dissimulating, you are not a credit to your people, like Dante or Mayor La Guardia, I don't know what arrangement you have with other officers in this station, but I do not accept emoluments, and therefore please put that envelope back in your pocket.' Is that better?"

"Terrific," Joshua said.

"You'll clean up all the other dirty parts as we go along."

"Sure."

Reuben appeared in the doorway. "The Flopper's on the phone. What do you think?"

"I'll take it."

Shooting McMaster a sour look in passing, Reuben passed him the phone.

"Lookit," The Flopper hollered over the din of The King's Arms, "tell ya why I called. There's a sale on Wonder Bras at the Bay, and we thought we'd pick up some, only we don't know what size cup ya take."

"Very funny. Ha, ha."

"You sound lousy. Now you take care of yourself, you son of a bitch," The Flopper pleaded in a throbbing voice. "Here's Rog."

Roger's voice was thick. More of the correspondence had

been leaked, he said, and it was going to run in *Maclean's* under the photograph of the two of them kissing. "Issue a statement," he said, "and I'll see that it goes out on the wires immediately."

"You think that would change anything?"

"His kid was on the National last night. They interviewed him in London. What a shifty little bastard."

"Well, he has his grievances."

"Issue a statement. One minute. Robbie wants to say something."

Robbie was also drunk. "I don't give a shit about you, darling. What I want to know is, how is Pauline?"

Joshua choked.

"Joshua?"

"I don't know where she is," Joshua said, signaling his father to take the phone from him.

"That's it," Reuben said, "he's tired now," and he hung up and turned to McMaster. "I think he's had enough of your memoirs for one day."

"He's not tired. Besides, we've got a best seller in the making here."

"Josh?"

"I'm all right."

"Anything I can get for you while I'm here, then?" Reuben asked McMaster.

McMaster rocked in a wicker chair, sucking on a soggy White Owl, his colorful shirt unbuttoned, his hairy belly bursting out of his double-knit tartan trousers, his dainty feet encased in white golf shoes. "Yeah, another Laurentide. But just bring me the can. I'll open it myself, if you don't mind?"

"Don't you trust me?"

"You bring it to me in a glass and your boy here has the first sip."

"Why can't we be friends, Stu? Here," he said, extending his hand, "shake."

"Daddy," Joshua called out, terrified, "don't."

"Don't worry," McMaster said, "I know better than to shake that hand."

"Yeah, well," Reuben said, leaving, "I'll give you another hour with him and that's it for today."

After McMaster had finally gone, Joshua was able to make it upstairs to his study and, looking across the bay, he saw Trimble out on his dock. He'll be coming here, Joshua thought. If not today, tomorrow.

Joshua wished he were on morphine again.

Ensconced in the hospital, his body throbbing, he had, under the influence of morphine shots, dreamed again and again that Pauline was there, adrift over his bed, and then he would call out her name, only to have one of the nurses loom into sharp focus.

"What is it, Mr. Shapiro?"

Apprehensive, unable to work, Joshua began to sift through cardboard boxes that had not been unpacked since they had left London, sorting out old papers. Somehow a photograph of Monique and him in San Antonio had survived the years. She was snuggled into that black bikini and he was grinning beneath a broad-brimmed straw hat. Look at him, the prick. He also found a handbill saying that Litri, Aparacio, and Luis Miguel Dominguin would be in Valencia for the Fallas, and a yellowing flyer from the Florida, *Boite de Nuit*, Calvo Sotelo 17, Valencia, which proclaimed "El más extraordinario programa de Grandes Atraccionies, Presentación de Sugestivas Estrellas, con Lolita Madrid y Bella Nelly." Something else he had unwittingly dragged across continents was three stapled sheets from the Office Espagnol de Tourisme, announcing "Voyage aux Îles Baleares, séjour très agréable en toutes saisons."

My, my.

2

Monique's stout, fleshy mother continued to fulminate on the terrace of the Casa del Sol, resolutely refusing to acknowledge Joshua whenever he passed her table, but she seemed to have become reconciled to her daughter passing most of her nights at Joshua's place. Certainly she never intruded on them. Then, one morning, he was awakened by a visitor. Wiry, beady-eyed Mariano. It was, Mariano said, his duty to put a number of questions to him. "You must remember," he began, "that in Spain we expect foreigners to behave with a certain decorum."

Joshua suppressed a smile.

"You have committed certain indecent acts on public beaches."

"What are you talking about?"

"Your conduct has come to the attention of the bishop, and he is outraged."

303

"Are you going to have a little *auto de fe* just because Monique and I have kissed on a beach?"

"You have been seen nude together on Las Salinas and twice on the beach of the Casa del Sol."

"Seen by whom?"

"You deny it?"

"Of course I do."

Hugely embarrassed, Mariano sighed and said, "There are photographs of the two of you."

"Are you serious?"

"They are the kind of photographs they sell in Pigalle."

"What happens now?"

"It's not good. I'm trying to help, but not everybody is your friend here."

"Have you come here to arrest me?"

"Oh, no," he said, offended, "but I must urge you to go carefully."

"May I see the photographs, please?"

"I haven't brought them with me, but they exist."

That afternoon, emerging drunk from Don Pedro's, squinting against the sun, Joshua started down the hot dusty road winding out of San Antonio until he was about a mile out, and then he cut across the olive grove and sank to the grass under a gnarled tree. He awoke an hour later, no longer dizzy. He climbed the mountainside and once he reached the hump of guano-covered rock overlooking Dr. Dr. Mueller's villa he had, it seemed to him, sweated out his drunkenness. He dug his knife out and clambered down the rock face into Dr. Dr. Mueller's garden, skinning his knee against a jutting rock.

"Mueller," he called.

No answer.

"It's me, Mr. Mr. Shapiro."

Nobody home. Lucky you, he thought, and now if you know what's good for you, beat it. But instead he used his knife to pry open the terrace doors. Inside, it was soothingly cool. He had no idea where he might have hidden the photographs. Neither did he know exactly what he was going to do. There were, of course, no lampshades made of human skin or unmarked bars of soap lying about. There was a sentimental photograph of what appeared to be an Indian camp caught at dusk, only one of the braves was drinking Steffens Pils out of a bottle, and underneath was the inscription "Gemeinschaft Nord-deutscher Indianerfreunde." A buffalo robe hung on one wall, and there were crossed tomahawks over

304

the mantelpiece. There was also a framed photograph of a severe-looking man with a handlebar moustache in the uniform of the Kaiser's army. His father? Another photograph, this one of an elegant lady with coiled blonde hair seated on a sofa with two plump boys. The lady wore a high, frilly-collared black dress, the boys school uniforms, and all three stared solemnly into the camera. Underneath, somebody had inscribed in ink "Dresden, 1943." Joshua studied Mueller's foreign-language bookshelves, infuriated because the books were, he had to admit, mostly in good taste or, at worst, innocuous. Hemingway, Maugham, Michael Arlen, Charles Morgan, and what appeared to be the complete works of Zane Grey. There was a shelf of German books on natural life. Everything from horse-breeding to a history of leopards. And then, in a glass case, three rows of paperback westerns in German by Gus McCabe.

Turning to the records strewn on the table, Joshua was disgruntled not to find anything Wagnerian. Some Gene Autry, a *Carmen* album, *The Best of Maurice Chevalier*, Beethoven's Second Symphony. Frustrated, he scooped up a lamp with a porcelain base in the shape of a waltzing eighteenth-century couple, flung it toward the ceiling, and watched it splatter on the floor, slivers everywhere. He found the camera with the long-range lens and smashed that too.

Bureau drawers in the master bedroom revealed no photographs of Monique and himself, but film stills had been tacked to the walls everywhere. William S. Hart, Hopalong Cassidy, Randolph Scott, Joel McCrea as Buffalo Bill, Gary Cooper, Wallace Beery, Andy Devine. Another photograph, stuck in the mirror, showed Mueller wearing chaps and spurs, six-guns drawn. There was a hairnet lying on the bureau and a crash diet torn from the pages of *Look*. Tailor's dummies lined one wall. One wore a gunfighter's outfit, another a saloon girl's costume, a third was dressed as a plains Indian. Six-guns in a holster were slung from a bedpost.

The bathroom medicine cabinet yielded vitamin tablets, a powder for the cleansing of dentures, a salve to relieve rectal itch, and a tube of hand lotion.

In the living room, Joshua picked up a batch of records and smashed them against the corner of a table, immediately regretting it. This is childish, he thought, and he stooped to retrieve pieces of the broken lamp base from the floor. Suddenly, he was disturbed by a noise coming from the front of the villa. Voices? A dog? Springing dizzily to his feet, he bolted out of the house, continuing across the garden in a

305

half-crouch, and starting to climb the rocks. He ran—stumbling—rising—running again. He ran and ran. Down the mountainside, across the olive grove. He didn't stop until he emerged on the road. The bus to Ibiza was approaching. He waved it down and clambered inside. Only then did he realize that his arms were badly scratched and that he was drenched in sweat.

Sometime past midnight, in Ibiza, Juanito caught up with him in the waterfront café. "Come on," he said.

"Where?"

"Rosita's."

"I don't want to go to Rosita's. I've had enough of that."

"Come on."

"I said no. Leave me alone."

He was careful to be back in San Antonio in time for breakfast at the Casa del Sol, the Freibergs be damned. Otherwise he felt Mueller would certainly be suspicious. But when Mueller finally moseyed onto the terrace in his white linen suit, he didn't even acknowledge him. He heard no more from Mariano. A week passed before Mueller sat down at his table in Don Pedro's. "My place was broken into the other day," he said thickly.

"Oh?"

"Vandals."

"Did they do much damage?"

"Sufficient. They took things too. My diamond stickpin is gone. So is my camera. They found my traveler's checks," and, biting into his ivory cigarette holder, he added, "Eighteen hundred dollars is missing."

"Why, my dear Dr. Dr.," Joshua said, "how I've underestimated you."

"Drunken fishermen must have taken it. Fortunately, I'm insured. I have already phoned the American Express in Madrid and warned them that somebody would be passing forged checks."

"What did they say?"

"Oh, they were very kind. They are sending new checks. Mariano is sending them a copy of his report."

"Well, well."

"Have *you* had any trouble?"

"Yes. With hostiles."

"What?"

"Cheyenne Dog Soldiers. But I managed to run them off my property. Me and my six-guns."

"Take my advice," Dr. Dr. Mueller said, rising, "don't leave any money sitting around."

Joshua found Freiberg's brother-in-law, Max, sunning himself on the beach. Prodding him with his foot, he demanded, "Did you change any money for that Nazi in the last few days?"

"What Nazi?"

"Dr. Dr. Mueller."

"He's no Nazi," Max roared, shaking with laughter.

"He's a wanted man in France," Joshua charged hotly, "isn't he?"

"Do you know what that drunkard did in the war?"

Joshua didn't know.

"He was with a government office in Berlin. He sat on his ass and wrote propaganda. He never got to the front, but eventually it came to him."

"He was with the army of occupation in France."

"Writing articles."

"Why is he wanted in France?"

"Not because of the war," Max said, disgusted, "but because of something he did in nineteen-fifty. He assaulted a girl in Nice. A whore. I hear he tried to scalp her. You know how he is when he's drunk. He could have thought he was Chief Crazy Horse."

"Why are you frightened of him?"

"Frightened? We are not frightened. But he is not without influence here."

"Did you change any money for him in the last few days?"

Max wasn't saying.

"Maybe you're the *putz*, not me. He's reporting the checks as stolen. He says his villa has been broken into."

Max laughed. His belly shook.

"What's so funny?"

"Who would have suspected Mueller of having a *yiddishe kop*?"

"I'll kill you," Joshua said, grabbing him. "Honest to God, I'll kill you one of these days."

Max broke free of him. "I'm O.K. If I changed any money for Mueller at the unofficial rate, the check would be in Geneva by now. But what about you? Are you O.K.?"

Mariano was waiting for him at his place.

"Where do you get your money?" he asked abruptly.

"I earn it."

"Perhaps by writing reports for your government." Incredibly enough, Mariano was suggesting he might be a spy. "We have a big military station here. You have been seen observing the soldiers from the hilltop more than once."

"With their pathetic wooden tank and rifles firing blanks."

"You have made a statement in the presence of three army officers that you were spying on them."

"We were drinking together. I was joking."

"That's not what they say."

"They're lying."

"They are officers."

"Fuck you, Mariano."

"You are the one who is lying, just as you lied about the fornications on the beach until I told you that I had proof."

"That was different."

"Mueller has been robbed of eighteen hundred dollars in traveler's checks."

"He's lying."

"Everybody is lying but you."

"Oh, what's the use? Come to the point, Mariano."

"You are nobody, but Dr. Dr. Mueller is a celebrated author in his own country. Gus McCabe, the western writer. He also has admirers in high places in Madrid. He says you are an anarchist with your own concubine here, and that you robbed his villa. The officers have also signed a statement. Because you are so young, I would like to help. If you leave Spain of your own accord within forty-eight hours, the complaint will stop with me and you will be able to enter this country freely again."

"Hold it, Mariano. Stop right there. I want to know if it was the fucking Freibergs who told you that Monique and I could be found nude on their beach?"

"A complaint has also been filed against the Freibergs. It seems their wiring has not been installed according to strict government regulations. It may be necessary to shut down the Casa del Sol."

"God damn him, what does he want from the Freibergs? They had nothing to do with me. I can testify to that."

"I did not say he filed the complaint. But if their wiring is faulty, there is nothing you can do."

"You're a snake, Mariano. You really are."

"You do not seem to understand that if you don't leave here within forty-eight hours, you will have to face certain charges. You will go to prison, most likely."

Run, Joshua, run.

But he had no money. Certainly not enough to get him to Paris. With Juanito's help, he sold his portable typewriter.

Whatever clothes he wasn't wearing. He met with Monique, they agreed to get together in Nice in two weeks' time, and then he hurried to the Casa del Sol, running all the way. "I must see the Freibergs immediately," he told the desk clerk.

But they weren't there. They were in Palma, consulting a lawyer.

"How long will they be gone?"

"Three days, maybe four."

"What about Max?"

"He's with them."

Joshua scribbled a note, left it for them, and then he booked passage on the *Jaime II*, sailing for Valencia the same evening. Juanito carried two cases of fresh fish on board for the captain, assuring Joshua of a cabin for the crossing.

Standing on the deck, waiting for the ship to pull out, he could see Dr. Dr. Mueller with a party of giggly American ladies at the café on the waterfront. It was a Wednesday. Mueller, he imagined, had taken them to the cockfights. The ladies would have been outraged, aroused, and they would have taken many photographs. Dr. Dr. Mueller would have made his set pronouncement. "The Spaniards," he would have said, "are not as sophisticated as we are. They are born to cruelty."

Dr. Dr. Mueller pointed him out to one of the ladies and whispered something in her ear. She laughed. Joshua turned away from the railing and walked slowly, he hoped, to starboard.

Run, Joshua, run. You're not a man, but a mouse.

3

The whispers and informed warnings had been circulating for weeks. Coral stopped fattening on points. It stalled one morning, tottered the next, and on the opening of business at the Montreal Stock Exchange on a dry, sub-zero Wednesday it began to plunge, frenetic investors bailing out. There was no *Gazette* the next Monday, because of a printer's walkout; they seldom watched the local TV news, so the scandal didn't catch up with them until Tuesday. In the morning, Kevin's picture was not only on the front page (a stricken but far-from-surprised Pauline absorbing every detail), but also in the business section and, ironically, on the society page again. The headline on the society page ran:

" 'Among those enjoying the music of Perry Carman and his Orchestra on Saturday night,' " Joshua read aloud, savoring each idiocy, " 'were Richard Abbott, Q.C., and Mrs. Abbott, whose gown of pink georgette was worn with a stole of matching ostrich fronds; Mr. Gavin McTeer, and Mrs. McTeer, wearing a halter of black, sequined crepe; Isaac Singer, O.C., and Mrs. Singer, who had a rope of fragrant-smelling freesia around her neck and wore a sheath gown of off-white silk jersey; Mr. Eli Seligson, and Mrs. Seligson, wearing écru silk; Mr. Jeremy Gursky, and Mrs. Gursky, in a pajama ensemble of fuchsia and green patterned chiffon; Mr. Jack Trimble, and Mrs. Trimble, whose gown of—' "

"Oh, stop it. Please, darling."

"Wait. Here comes the good part. 'The evening's highlight was a slick, short performance given by selected members of the ballet company and a group of good-natured men-about-town, ready to draw chuckles at their dancing technique. "Le ballet aquatique égyptien" saw the boys, among them Kevin Hornby, as towel-clad water-bearers, attempting to portray figures on an Egyptian frieze.' "

The story in the business section was succinct. An immediate halt had been called to trading in the shares of Coral Trust, this year's high-flier on the MSE, pending an investigation by the Quebec Securities Commission. The story on the front page offered hardly any more details, but was, nevertheless, charged with ominous undertones. The RCMP had raided the Stock Exchange Tower offices of Westmount Whizz Kid Kevin Hornby, seizing documents and correspondence. Hornby, outraged, claimed to be totally surprised by the move and pleaded with investors to remain calm. There had been no irregularities at Coral, he maintained, and he welcomed any investigation, which could only vindicate him. Jack Trimble, also on the Coral board, stated that he had complete confidence in his associate, the man in charge of the enterprise, but, on the advice of his lawyers, could not comment at this point in time.

Joshua, who was bound for London on the evening flight and from there to Spain, had already packed. They had taken the children out to dinner the night before and now, as was their habit when he had to make a trip, they went to a small French restaurant they favored for lunch, ordering champagne.

"I wish you were coming with me," he said.

"And I wish you weren't going."

"I have to."

"I know."

"I've left the envelope in my top right-hand desk drawer."

A ritual comparatively new with him. *In the event of an airplane crash, I leave everything I own to my wife Pauline.* (Signed) *Joshua Shapiro.* Her eyes filled with angry tears, she said, "I hate your fucking envelope. I don't want to know about it."

"But you have to."

"What will you say to that wretched Mueller after all these years?"

"I wish I knew."

"I wonder what would have happened if we'd met much earlier. Right here. When I was at McGill."

The mixed doubles champion. "We would have loathed each other on sight. Nothing would have been possible."

"Do you ever think that you've had enough and wish you were single again?"

"No."

"Liar."

"And you?"

"I sometimes wonder how the kids have survived this long. All those protruding table corners. The wall plugs. Whooping cough. Measles. But Alex is already growing away from me. Susy will be next. Ten years from now they'll phone each other to say 'It's Sunday, *you* visit Mother this week.' Have you ever been unfaithful to me?"

"No."

"But don't you ever want another woman? Jane, for instance."

"Certainly not Jane."

"Who, then?"

"Strangers sometimes. A woman I might pass on the street."

"And what do you do about it?"

"Nothing."

"It wouldn't be very flattering if you were faithful to me only because an affair would be something you couldn't handle. I once told Jane that you were wonderful in bed."

"Wouldn't you say that was somewhat perverse?"

"There are times when I feel that if only you betrayed me, I could draw back a little. I might feel safer."

"I see," he said sharply.

"You simply don't understand how much I've got at risk. I can't imagine my life without you any more."

"But I'd be equally lost if anything happened to you."

"It would take time, but you'd adjust."

"I don't like the turn this conversation is taking."

"But we seldom talk about anything any more. We meet in the hall to split duties. You go to Steinberg's, I'll take the shirts to Troy. Possibly our life together has come to lack a certain intensity. Oh, now you're really getting angry."

"I'm not getting angry."

"You're already in Spain."

"Damn it."

"There are other couples, you know, who wonder about us even now. They can't understand what we have in common."

"And you?" he asked.

"The truth?"

"Please."

"When you fly off like this, I wish I were less dependent. I wish there was more of me," and tears began to slide down her cheeks.

Pauline's cheeks.

It was four o'clock, snowing again, and they were drinking coffee and cognacs together in the living room, reminiscing about halcyon days in London, when Kevin arrived, ashen-faced in spite of the cold, coming to the house directly from Dickie Abbott's law office.

"Trout, I've got to talk to you. Would you mind, Joshua?"

Possibly, had he not already had so much to drink, Joshua would have left them alone. As it was, he didn't budge.

"I'd only tell him everything later," Pauline said.

Joshua fetched another snifter and poured Kevin a cognac. He fiddled uneasily with his glass, staring at the carpet. "I've got two tickets to the Boston game on Saturday night, if you want them?"

"Thanks, but I won't be here."

"He's flying to London tonight."

"What fun," Kevin said, brightening.

"Yeah," Joshua said morosely.

"He's going to a funeral."

"Oh, I'm sorry. I was hoping to go over for Wimbledon this summer. Did you ever go when you were living there?"

"Trout did, not me."

Pauline shot him a reproving look.

"Well, I suppose you've seen the *Gazette?*"

"Yes," Pauline said in a barely audible voice, imagining her father opening the paper in Ottawa. Kevin again.

"Trout, whatever happens, I want you to know I didn't steal. It's all lies. Everything. From the first day to the last, I never really grasped what was going on at Coral."

"You were quoted in *Maclean's*," Joshua said, "as saying that not a dime of Coral's money was invested without your approval."

"They made that up. They were lying."

"Jack Trimble assured me you made all the decisions."

"He made a point of telling everybody that. He knew what was coming. He was lying."

"Everybody's a liar but you," Joshua said, suddenly turning pale. Echoes, echoes.

"Yes," he said. "I should have gone right on to Georgian Bay. I never should have stopped here. The truth is, Jack has loathed my guts since the day I flew in."

"Why did he offer you the job, then?" Pauline asked.

"It was Jane's idea. She told him everybody in the old bunch would think he was a fine fellow if only he could manage the redemption of poor old Kevin. And he took me on because he was already in deep trouble with his investments and I fit right into his plans. He set me up, Trout. I'm his patsy."

"Look here," Joshua said, "you're not going to lay everything off on Jack just because he wasn't at L.C.C. or Selwyn House with you."

"I'm not laying anything off on him. I'm telling you the truth."

"How come you were so thick all winter, seen everywhere together, like the Three Musketeers?"

"He's a very devious man."

"And so are you."

"Would it be too much to ask if I could speak to my sister alone?"

"How long have you been having an affair with Jane?"

"That's none of your goddamn business."

"He's right, Josh."

"It wasn't my doing, Trout. I wanted no part of it. Remember the evening you both came to dinner on the lake? Well, they had a fearful row in their bedroom that morning. I think it was over me. He wanted me to clear out. He drove into Montreal without even saying goodbye to me; it was awfully early, and he wasn't supposed to come back until six. I thought Jane and I would be O.K. together, because Charlie

313

would be there and little Alice, but they were sent off to the sailing club and she was everywhere I went in the house. Taunting me one minute, thrusting herself at me the next, drinking all the while. Saying I was a total failure, a fraud, a disappointment to everybody, a gigolo, and then making sexy suggestions. Could I still get it up, or was I thirty seconds of action and an hour of apology, like all the other so-called studs on the lake? I retreated to the boathouse, saying I was going to pack my scuba-diving equipment, and the next thing I knew she's there, peeling off her bikini top, down on her knees, taking me."

"You mean to say," Joshua asked, simulating horror, "she took advantage of you?"

"I'm just telling you what happened."

"Jane's not nearly so desperate or lacking in subtlety that she's got to fling herself at somebody like that."

"Women have always found me very attractive."

"You're full of shit," Joshua said.

"Will you please let him finish," Pauline said.

"She was like a crazed woman, Trout, I couldn't stop her. When we finally came out of the boathouse, it was maybe four-thirty and Jack's Jaguar was parked at the top of the hill. We hadn't even heard him arrive. We slipped back into the boathouse and decided to return to the house separately. She continued up the hill and I went for a swim. When I got back to the house, determined to announce I would be off in the morning, Jack, to my amazement, was a totally different man. All sweetness and light. Jane was fondling his neck and he couldn't stop grinning. 'Sit down,' he said. 'I've got an offer to make you, old son.' "

"And, in return, you've been screwing his wife ever since."

"I don't have to take that from you, Shapiro."

Still, Pauline was silent, pensive.

"She used to sneak down to see you in Bermuda, and that's where you worked on her to cajole Jack into getting you the job."

"You're out of your tree."

Joshua lit one cigarette off another.

"Why," Pauline asked in a quiet voice, "do you dislike Kevin so much?"

His stomach churned.

"Why, darling?"

"Let me ask him a question instead. Why would Jack run Coral into the ground?"

"He was dangerously overextended last summer, heading

for real trouble. Speculations in oil leases. A wrong guess on how far the dollar would sink. Too many millions bet on property in Montreal. A combination of factors, all squeezing his cash flow. He was short in Zurich. He had overdue notes out in New York. I have good reason to believe he was only one step ahead of the securities commission when I came along and he launched Coral, using me as bait. We made money at first, good money, and then he began unloading worthless holdings from other funds into Coral at book-value prices. Oil leases. Real estate. The whole ball of wax."

"Why didn't you protest?" Pauline asked.

"I didn't understand what was going on. I was euphoric. I thought we were doing great. I was foolish enough to think Daddy would read about me and be proud. I was earning bonuses. Fifty thousand one time, twenty-five thousand another. I had no idea anything was improper until the rumors started, and then I Xeroxed some papers and took them to Dickie Abbott's office. He was horrified to see what I'd signed."

"Did you really not understand what was going on?" Pauline asked imploringly.

"Whenever I'd query something he'd say, 'You don't worry your head about that, old son, let's take the afternoon off and golf.' Or 'It's nothing, just more government bumpf, sign the damn stuff and we'll go and take in the boat show at Place Bonaventure.' He was a desperate man. Foxy as a—" He stopped short.

"As a what?"

"As hell. He arranged everything so that he comes out clean. Clean? My innocent benefactor betrayed. And I'm the swindler. Trout, they've sealed my bank account. Government inspectors are going through it right now, and they're going to find things I'll never be able to explain. He used to put checks through my account, big ones, saying not to worry, it's a tax thing. Do you realize who was in Coral, and I mean up to the neck? The McTeers, Abbott, the Friars, the Harpers, everybody we were at McGill with. The entire country club. Some of them may come out of it ruined, and I was the one who talked them into it. They're going to think I was in on it all along. They'll say I've got at least a million stashed away in Switzerland," he said, his voice quavering.

Joshua poured him another cognac and Kevin accepted it with a trembling hand. "I need your help, Trout."

"I don't understand. What could I do?"

Kevin hesitated.

"Well?"

"You could testify," he said, his eyes welling with tears, "that you saw me sign Coral papers without reading them."

"Is that true, Pauline?" Joshua asked.

"The day she came to look at my apartment," he continued, staring at her, "Jack just happened to send somebody round from the office with some papers. I asked for time to read them. He said his instructions were, I was to sign them without delay—Jack needed them. I signed. You must remember, Trout."

"Do you?" Joshua asked.

But Pauline didn't answer immediately, watching Kevin, who had begun to weep into his handkerchief.

"If you could bring yourself to testify," he said, after he had paused to blow his nose, "it would be a considerable help. Jack thinks the world of you. It would rattle him if he thought you were going to take the stand against him."

"Can my children be of any help?" Joshua asked.

"I don't understand."

"Let's do everything possible to save your skin."

"Look here, you don't seem to grasp what's at stake. I could go to prison. They could sentence me to as much as ten years."

"Your sort doesn't do time," Joshua said. "You'd be out on bail and the trial would drag on and on and, what with appeals and all, you'd be fifty before anything happened and by that time you'll be living it up in Panama."

"I did not steal from my friends and I'm not running away again. I would like Trout to testify."

"How do I know that all that stuff with the papers to sign wasn't a charade, staged for her benefit?"

"Obviously, you don't think very much of me."

"If Pauline wants to testify, she will. That's up to her. And now, if you don't mind, I'd like to speak to her. I've got a plane to catch in an hour."

"Have a safe trip," Kevin said and, hurrying into his coat, he was gone.

"You didn't behave well," Pauline protested, distressed.

Joshua poured himself another cognac.

"I've never seen you so demented."

"He doctored his report cards. He cheated in bridge tournaments. He got somebody else to write his law school assignments for him. He used to come back here again and again telling everybody lies. He's weak. He's rotten."

"Yes, he's weak, and yes, he may even be rotten. But he

316

also happens to be my only brother. What am I supposed to do, Josh? Pack him off to prison with a kiss on the cheek?"

"Jack put out for him and in return he's been screwing his wife and skimming money out of Coral, and now that he's been caught with his hand in the till he's trying to dump on Jack just like he once did on what's-his-name Isenberg."

"All the same, I don't think he'd steal from Abbott and the others. He hasn't got the brains or the courage."

"Well, you ought to know. He's your brother."

"Yes, he is. And what, my darling, if he is also innocent?"

"Or the world's flat, after all?"

"Can you hate him that much?"

"We'd better call the kids in," he said, taking her in his arms. "I've got to leave for the airport in half an hour."

"Yes," she said, her head resting on his shoulder.

"Do you want me to call your father?"

"No thanks. I'll handle it. Will you phone me from the airport?"

"Certainly."

She waited for his call and then hurried into a taxi, getting out at the Ritz. She found Kevin seated at a corner table in the Maritime Bar.

"I knew you'd come," he said, reaching for her hand.

She withdrew it immediately.

"I'm not going to prison, Trout."

"Will you order me a drink, please."

He ordered her a glass of white wine.

"That was unforgivable, Kevin, cornering me like that. You know damn well I never saw you sign any papers without reading them."

"But you could have, honestly, if only you'd stayed on for another fifteen minutes."

"Kevin, are you lying again?"

"No."

"You've lied so often," she said wearily.

"I'm not lying about this. You've just got to help me, Trout."

"And what if I can't?"

"But you've never let me down before."

"I'm not going to let him down. Don't you understand?"

"No," he said, baffled. "I don't."

"Well then, let me explain something to you. We've been married for eighteen years now. He has his bad days and I have mine. We don't wake up every morning bursting into

317

song. But we're perverse. No matter what, he doesn't lie to me, I don't lie to him. And now you've already involved me in a lie, if only by my omission."

"Come on now. Stretching the truth a little on my behalf can hardly do him any harm."

"I can't seem to make you understand."

"If I'm put away, it could kill Daddy."

"Oh, that's cheap. Really unforgivable. You don't give a shit about him."

"Unlike your husband. They get on famously, I understand."

"Why couldn't you think about Daddy before you started your fiddling?"

"I have not been fiddling."

"If you only knew how much I wished I knew if you were telling the truth."

"I know Joshua's never had our advantages," he said, "but that's no reason for him to be so prejudiced against me."

"Oh, what do you know about Joshua? When you were practicing your tennis stroke, he was sitting up in some squalid room on Dorchester Boulevard, teaching himself to become a journalist."

"I'm told his father is an errand boy for the Mafia."

"Reuben?" she asked, startled.

"Yes."

"Go fuck yourself."

"Well, you've certainly picked up their idiom, haven't you?"

"You're such a fool, Kevin."

"You seem to get on well enough now, but you know and I know that you married Joshua hoping to shock everybody."

"Did Jane tell you that?"

"I do some of my own thinking."

"Well, that would be a change. Now let me tell you something. He's not only my husband, but I love him. We have three children. A life. I'm not putting it at risk to save your skin when I don't even know if you're lying again."

"I'm not lying. I am also counting on your testimony."

"On my lying for you, you mean?"

"I'm not going to prison, Trout, no matter what."

"I certainly hope not."

"You don't understand."

4

Sidney Alexander Murdoch, who would have been forty-nine years old in May, was cremated in Golders Green in the presence of his two wives, several mistresses, and six children. There was also a surprising number of literary people at the crematorium. A few were really old friends and had come to mourn. But still more were either clients of Margaret's or had obviously turned up because they grasped that certain important publishers and critics were bound to be there, and maybe even a *Daily Express* photographer. The obituary in the *Times* had been flattering, setting out how Murdoch, the son of a Bradford newsagent, a council school boy, had won a double first at King's College, Cambridge, and gone on from there to a certain literary eminence.

Following the cremation, some of them adjourned to Margaret's house in NW3, where Joshua got drunk as quickly as possible. Margaret was gray-haired now, lumpy, her figure considerably thickened. Once, Joshua recalled, four-year-old Ralph had stumbled on them pawing each other in the Kentish Town kitchen. Good grief, he had thought, chilled, I'm his Ed Ryan. He told Margaret that he was bound for Spain, on a commission from his American publishers, to write an introduction for a new edition of *The Volunteers*, and she assured him that she could easily arrange for another British edition as well. He had caught up with Margaret in her enormous kitchen, complete with red Aga cooker, butcher's block, and intimidating row of Sabatier knives, and he reminded her of the Mandrake Club and how he and Murdoch had used to wait for her to turn up on Friday afternoons with her weekly paycheck, less than eight pounds after taxes. This set them to listing other regulars at the Mandrake, older than they were, who had preceded Murdoch to the grave. Dylan, John Davenport, and the difficult, unappreciated Julian Maclaren-Ross.

Overhearing them, a snowy-haired man asked, "And whatever became of Tambimutto?"

"Or Ruthven Todd," somebody else recalled.

"Who was he?" a writer, much younger than they were, asked.

Joshua retreated to a corner of the kitchen, wondering if a future generation of Cambridge snots, riffling David's bookstall, would stumble on an early edition of one of Murdoch's novels, the reviewers' quotes on the faded jacket dazzling. "Not to be missed." "Brilliant." "A minor masterpiece."

It's a mug's game.

Yes, he thought, and then, grinning foolishly, he recalled the evening he had barged in on Murdoch trying to instantly age that young writer's manuscript, hoping to pass it off as his own and sell it to the University of Texas.

"Wait. Hold it. I think I've got a better idea," Joshua had said, beaming at Murdoch with drunken benevolence. "You and I, Sidney, might just be able to earn a tidy sum in the great state of Texas if you were willing to engage in a vile, salacious homosexual correspondence with me. Sickeningly explicit."

"Of course, of course."

"We could backdate the stuff to Cambridge."

Murdoch had splashed more cognac into both their glasses. "Sidney Murdoch's period of poovery, hitherto unsuspected. . . . Ah, Murdoch," he sang out, "mad, bad, and dangerous to know. Yes. Good. Excellent. It could bring in a small fortune. Of course, you realize that I am famous while you are merely well known, and only in Staggers and Naggers circles at that. So you would have to agree to a sixty-forty split in my favor. What do you say?"

Joshua had agreed at once and, in the weeks that followed, they had both avoided real work, exchanging letters that outdid each other in slander and depravity, not only involving themselves, a love that dared not speak its name, but also literary enemies, old friends they took for prigs, and family pets. Recalling some of the more outrageous passages in a correspondence long since—Joshua assumed—destroyed, he laughed out loud.

My, my.

Ralph, who was lecturing at Cambridge, had come down for the service, his long hair gathered in a pigtail, wearing a Superman T-shirt, the badge riding his breast proclaiming "TRY INCEST/ The Game the Entire Family Can Play." "I want to speak to you about his papers," he said.

"What about them?"

"Didn't you sell yours to some provincial Canadian university for a lot of bread?"

"Yes. Rocky Mountain U. But I'm afraid they're so provincial they're mostly interested in Canadian papers."

"But he was really famous in his time."

"Look," Joshua said angrily, "the man to try there is a Dr. Colin Fraser. Oh, and Ralph . . ."

"Yes?"

"I think you're full of shit."

The next day Joshua wandered through Soho, visiting the pubs he and Pauline used to frequent while they were waiting for her divorce from Colin to come through. "What I can't understand," she had said, "is why he is being so cooperative."

"He thinks I'm a comrade," Joshua had replied, his mood light, "and he'd never do one of us in."

"I wonder."

He phoned Pauline at eleven, six o'clock their time, so that he could speak to the children as well.

"They've taken away Kevin's passport," she said. "Jack's telling everyone he's sure there's been no deliberate wrongdoing, just some bad luck with certain investments that would have righted themselves in time, and he is absolutely confident that Kevin will be able to explain everything. He believes in him, he says."

"It's not necessary to like Jack," he reminded her, "to believe that he's telling the truth." Like that sewer rat Nixon, he added to himself, remembering, rather than the gentlemanly Hiss.

"He's lying."

"Have you spoken to your father?"

"He's no more help than you are. He always said Kevin was no good."

No sooner did he hang up than Joshua began to feel melancholy. Lonely. And then, looking up the number of an old Fleet Street chum, he suddenly grasped that he couldn't make out the dancing names in the telephone book unless he held the page a good distance away from his eyes. Now I'm going to need reading glasses, he thought.

Wandering down Carlisle Street, he was reminded of those long afternoons that had used to unwind in the Partisan Coffee Bar and of the silly left-wing attitudes they had cherished at the time. Jesus, when he looked back on himself at any age, Joshua then rather than now, it seemed he had always been such a horse's ass. O.K., he was willing to accept that, given his present unquestioned wisdom. But didn't it mean that if he ever reached sixty, he would take himself to have been just as much of an oaf in his late forties? Yes? No? He had no answers.

The next morning he was in Madrid, back after rather more

than a quarter of a century. In 1952, cars had been rare in Madrid, but the mountain air bracingly pure. Now the industrial smog didn't burn off until 10 a.m., and the streets stank of diesel fuel at all hours. In Madrid, in 1952, children of Teddy's age had fought each other to shine Joshua's shoes for a nickel. They had begged for pennies or cigarettes, their facial skin broken with running sores. Sipping cognac on the Gran Via, more than twenty-five years later, he was no longer badgered by shoeshine boys, but he couldn't help noticing the preponderance of amputees out working the street. Soldiers of the Ebro, defenders of the University City. Now aged men, leathery-skinned, hands hard as bark, missing an arm or a leg. Corner cigarette vendors, lottery ticket sellers. *"Para hoy! Para hoy!"*

Seated on the terrace of a stylish café, Joshua remembered the stacks of *Life* his father had kept in the den. Going through them one by one, razoring out anything that had to do with the Spanish Civil War. Once Madrid had come to mean no less than *la tomba del fascismo* to him, *¡No Pasaran!*, and the cry of La Pasionaria, "Vale mas morir de pies que vivir de rodillas," but that night he was to dine at the expensive Casa Botin, a few steps down from the Plaza Mayor, on Calle Cuchilleros. In 1924, the restaurant had been much favored by the young Ernest Hemingway; now the multinational corporation men had come. At the table next to Joshua's a slender American in a charcoal-gray suit made notes even as he drank. His gold-plated ballpoint, a Cross; his leather-bound diary, a Gucci. "I'm a team player," he said feelingly. "I don't know if they appreciate that at home."

His companion, unattentive, frowned at his menu. "How do you say 'without garlic'?"

Joshua's companion, Paco, was a member of the central committee of the no-longer-illegal Spanish Communist Party. Paco had been to prison, once for two-and-a-half years, another time for a six-month stay. He had been beaten up in a number of police stations and had the scars to prove it. "In the old days," he said, "when you signed a statement, the important thing was to leave absolutely no room for additions between the final sentence and your signature, but now . . ." He shrugged.

Now, Joshua thought, hardly anything means what it used to.

In 1936, the Archbishop of Toledo had been able to hail Franco as a modern crusader and bless the nationalist rebels who would crush "the modern monster, Marxism, or Communism, the seven-headed hydra, symbol of all heresies." To be fair, in those days the Reds they had celebrated on St. Urbain Street had indeed been hell-raisers, potential church-burners, dedicated to establishing the dictatorship of the proletariat by whatever means available. These enlightened days, however, there were Catholic priests petitioning for the right to marry and commissars who didn't purge the ideologically impure on Sundays. Rabbis, who once gave you a clap on the ear if you sat down to eat without pronouncing the prescribed blessing, now wrote books telling you everything you wanted to know about cunnilingus, assuring the faithful that having consulted Rabbi Akiba, taking Maimonides into consideration, they found it no violation of the dietary laws to eat your wife even though she didn't have cloven hooves. I'm O.K., you're O.K. Abortion, once a disgrace, would now appear to be every embryo's birthright. Furthermore, as Germaine Greer had ordained, any sister unwilling to drink her own menstrual blood, though not necessarily with the fish course, had yet to be truly liberated. Our consciousness, Joshua thought, continues to be raised.

Comrade Paco took *Playboy*. He drove a Seat, the Spanish-assembled Fiat. He was thirty-eight, already bald, with horn-rimmed glasses, a smile calculated to please, a conservative suit. A reasonable man, Paco hankered not so much for a dictatorship of the proletariat as just a little more democracy at home. A *soupçon*. "Did you know," he asked, "that two members of our central committee are priests?" Last year, he added, he had been invited to the United States to address a reunion of survivors of the Abraham Lincoln Brigade. "When I told them about the priests, they were astonished. We owe these men a good deal, but they are sadly out of touch. I met Teddy Kennedy. Do you know him?"

"Yes. Certainly. As a matter of fact, when I told him I was coming to Spain, he asked me to give you his regards."

"Are you teasing me?" Paco asked, palpitating.

"And why would I do a thing like that, Comrade?"

Still working on his research, Joshua went to lunch the next day with the elegant Antonio, a former Foreign Office official in the government of cautious old men that had ruled through Franco's last illness and the immediate post-Franco period. They ate in the opulent Club 31, hard by the Alcala Arch and surrounded by *haute couture* salons. The sweetly perfumed, bejeweled lady at the table next to theirs wore a silver lamé dress. A Piaget wristwatch. Her handbag was made of baby crocodile.

"Is it correct to say," Joshua asked, "that there are now all of two hundred and forty political parties in Spain?"

"That," he said, his smile rueful, "is only counting coalitions."

He wouldn't be able to write the new introduction, he no longer gave a damn. Not only Spain had changed in twenty-five years, but so have I.

Ah, but possibly not Ibiza, he thought, ensconced in his rented car, starting south.

Tooling down the Nationale IV, heading uneasily toward Ibiza, Ibiza at last, Joshua imagined Juanito and himself taking off on a drunk of heroic proportions. Unless, he thought, his mood darkening, Juanito did not remember him. Or, still worse, remembering, might not cherish the relationship as he had come to over the years. No, that was impossible. There would be a memorable reunion. Yes, yes, Shapiro, gather ye epiphanies while ye may. He would find the Freibergs, who would absolve him of all wrongdoing. He would confront Mueller. Mueller, who must be sixty-five years old now, maybe a couple of years more, and me—O Jesus—older than he was then.

Joshua made his first overnight stop at a *parador* in Arruzafa, a hilltop commanding the heights over Cordoba and a sweeping view of the Guadalquivir Valley. A Spanish paradox: although his balcony overlooked an orange grove, the trees laden with plump ripe fruit, Joshua was served tinned orange juice for breakfast, freshly squeezed being unavailable. On second thought, however, it did not seem so utterly Spanish to him, or even a paradox, but just a conceit of the poor who had belatedly come into funds.

Like Uncle Oscar.

Poor Oscar, who had once intruded on his contemplation of Franco's picture in *Life*, had now lived long enough to see all his dreams of riches collapse. He was reduced to driving a taxi these days; and Joshua never hailed one on the streets of Montreal without fearing that he might have unwittingly hired his uncle as a chauffeur. And yet Oscar, sagacious Oscar, had been the first Shapiro to quit St. Urbain for the pleasures of tree-lined Outremont. From cold-water flat to apartment—a real apartment, with a shower! A shower Joshua was invited to gawk at, if not allowed to use. Furthermore, such had been Uncle Oscar's brief postwar affluence that he could actually afford to serve his children tinned fruit in summer. But it took more than that to impress Esty Blossom. "He's only showing off," she said.

Joshua had last heard from Uncle Oscar only a couple of days before he had flown to London. He had phoned, typically, at 1 a.m.

"Motorized suitcases!"

"What's that?"

"Look here, Dimwit, you've seen the toy cars kids run by remote control. Teddy must have one. Well, why not suitcases? It would eliminate schlepping at airports and train stations."

"And what if there's a power failure?"

"Prick. You carry your own battery pack."

"Or what if you run down another suitcase or maybe even a cripple in the terminal?"

"You'd carry motorized suitcase insurance."

"I don't know, Uncle Oscar, I just don't know."

"If I had phoned you a year ago and said 'Pet rocks,' you would've called me crazy. You know what that guy is worth now? MILLIONS!"

From Cordoba, Joshua continued on to Seville. From there to Granada. His sense of unease growing, a palpable presence, the closer he got to Ibiza. What in the hell's wrong with you, he thought. Once you enjoyed travel beyond almost anything. Shapiro on the road alone, out there adventuring. Or Shapiro and Peabody bouncing through the Alpes-Maritimes in the old *deux-chevaux*. But now—and how it infuriated him—the road filled him with fear and apprehension. He could have a heart attack in his hotel room. Or his car might crash. And what—oh my God, no—if he were never to see Pauline or the children or his father again, so many things left unsaid? Two a.m. in his hotel room, 9 p.m. at home. He put through a call to Montreal, but he was told there would be a two-hour delay. O.K., calm down. But in the morning the first thing he did was check out his tires and then his brakes before hitting the road again, his hands clammy.

Coming out of the Sierras at Motril, he joined the main road to Malaga, and for the second time in his life followed the route of the retreating republican army. The road to Almeria, as Joshua now traversed it some forty years after the republicans' retreat, had been subject to violence of a different order, this time out the land rather than the people being brutalized. The road was crammed with new hotels and condominiums, hammered into every available clifftop and cove.

Haphazardly built, without a thought for tomorrow. SPRECHEN DEUTSCH HIER. WE SERVE FISH AND CHIPS.

He turned in his rented car in Almeria and spent the night there, bound for Ibiza in the morning. Such, however, were the vicissitudes of Spanish air schedules that he could not fly directly to Valencia, continuing from there to Ibiza, but was obliged to fly all the way back to Madrid, and from there to Valencia, catching yet another flight for the twenty-minute hop to the island.

If his mood had been one of gathering apprehension before, now it was downright filthy. There was no such nicety as women or children first or even seat selection on an internal Air Iberia flight. Instead, you hovered near the gate, prepared to scrimmage, elbows at a ready angle, flight bags a weapon, once your flight was called. Then you were shoveled into a bus, rammed in tight, until it was all but impossible to shut the doors. Next the driver lighted a cigarette and the bus waited on the apron while, your face pressed against the window, you watched the inevitable second bus pull up, only to take on the remaining two or three passengers and the flight crew. Then the buses toured the tarmac, giving the driver an opportunity to pick up speed before he finally braked to an abrupt stop before your plane, sending the passengers flying against each other and the windows. The doors opened, achingly slow, and the passengers scrambled, trotting toward the rear entry door of the airplane, elbowing, shoving, never giving an inch. When Joshua finally clambered on board himself, bruised and cursing, it was to discover that the quick and the brave had already claimed most of the vacant seats, laying out coats and satchels, a measure of ownership, and standing guard, glowering.

Finally he made it as far as Valencia, only to find out that something was amiss there. Too many belligerent Guardia Civil were milling about, rifles slung from their shoulders. Men and women passengers for Ibiza were brusquely separated. Passports or identity cards were demanded. Bags were searched. Then they entered separate waiting rooms to be frisked in the presence of plainclothesmen. Joshua's tight-lipped request for an explanation was countered with shrugs. Then, suddenly, the crisis had seemingly passed and passengers were hurried off through the blustery night and onto their airplane. For the first time in years, Joshua was wretchedly ill in flight, heaving up the contents of his churning stomach again and again. After more than twenty-five years he was returning to Ibiza, his cherished Ibiza, ashen-faced and drenched in sweat.

Ashen-faced and drenched in sweat, come to think of it, was just how he had left the island in 1952.

5

Seymour's coronary struck him, not as he had always feared, in an out-of-town motel, making love to a stranger, but in the security of his own home. He had been unwinding in his living room, after a grueling day, munching chopped liver and crackers, sipping a restorative Scotch, watching Walter Cronkite, when he felt something like a barrel stave tighten round his chest. Sweat broke from his every pore. And the stave, impossibly, tightened further. "Molly," he managed to call out, "take me to the hospital. I'm having a heart attack."

"Oh, come on. None of your jokes now. The table's set and everything."

"Call Morty Zipper."

"I'm waiting for an important phone call," Larry warned, irritated.

"Help. I'm dying."

"Everything happens to me," Molly said.

"Molly," he groaned.

"All right. I'm coming, I'm coming."

"Hear O Israel, the Lord is our God, the Lord is One."

One glance at him in his chair and Molly's heart began to palpitate. "Oh, my," she said.

"I love you and the children. I always have," he said. "Now please call Morty Zipper. Or an ambulance. Both."

Molly hurried to the phone. Quaking, tears running down her cheeks, she held his hand while they waited for the ambulance.

"Remember, I have twelve shirts at Troy. The muffler has to be changed on the Buick. Izzy Singer is not to come to my funeral. No rabbis. I want Josh to speak over me."

"Don't talk like that. Stop. You're going to be all right."

"I'm dying."

"Death isn't the end. The body goes, inevitably, but the spirit lives on. Our children will tell loving tales about you at the Passover table."

"Larry?"

"So will your children's children."

"How did I ever marry such a cunt?"

"Don't you dare talk to her like that," Larry said, shifting in and out of focus.

"Sh, darling."

"Josh left a black bag in my bedroom cupboard just before he took off for Spain. It's very personal stuff. His. You're not to open it. Just return it to him."

"You're not supposed to talk."

"Don't say in the *Star* obit 'the beloved husband of,' 'the beloved father of.' I hate all that Hallmark cards shit. Just the facts."

"It could be only heartburn. Or indigestion."

But the men had already come with the stretcher and the oxygen tanks. One of the paramedics immediately recognized Molly. "Hey, how'd you get here so quickly, love?" he asked, grinning, pausing to rub her bottom in passing.

Molly leaped free of him. "You don't understand," she said stiffly, her cheeks crimson. *"He's my husband."*

"Oh, geez. Sorry."

"Don't you dare touch me," Seymour moaned, horrified.

"Easy, old fellow. Easy now."

6

There had been no airport on Ibiza in 1952, no paved roads winding out of town, and only a few cars and a handful of small hotels. In those days, even the bus ride to San Antonio, some twelve kilometers distant, was an adventure. The bus was a hybrid. The chassis was of World War I vintage, a former U.S. Army vehicle, and the body, reconstituted many times, was made of wood, slapped together with a hammer and nails. Now, returning, Joshua discovered that all the roads had been paved. Private cars were abundant, there were modern taxis everywhere, and a fleet of spanking new buses of the Côte d'Azur type ran between Ibiza and San Antonio on the half hour, punctually.

Joshua arrived at midnight and took a taxi directly to one of the smart new hotels. Standing on the balcony, looking out to sea, he could not get his bearings. The old town, the watchtower, the familiar harbor were all obscured from view. All he could see were hotels—hotels everywhere—and new condominiums, their balconies confronting the sea like enormous bureaus with all the drawers left open; and then, his eyes moist, he recalled Peabody, charged with concern, Peabody, his smile tender, saying "Try Ibiza."

"Ibiza?"

"Ibiza."

Peabody, who had used to stride down the Boulevard St. Germain, the world itself his inheritance, was on the Ganges now, searching for his firstborn son, Jeremy. Janet's sweet fruit. Jeremy had last been heard from in Goa, eight months earlier, headed for Varanasi. Peabody was advertising in English-language newspapers all through Asia, sticking Jeremy's photograph up on café walls and leaving copies with the police and the most likely hotels.

The last time they had talked on the phone, Peabody had said, "Damn it, Joshua, but weren't we a grand bunch once?"

"Damn right we were."

"Except for Bill Markham."

"Yes."

The harbor was obscured from Joshua's view, but in his mind's eye he was twenty-one again, seated at the dockside café with Juanito, watching a tall sorrowful man leaning against the deck railing, biting into an ivory cigarette holder. Mueller, sauntering into the bowels of the ship, emerging with his handsome brown stallion.

Are you a man or a mouse?

One a.m. on Ibiza, eight o'clock in Montreal. Eight p.m. home time. Family time. Susy would be chattering away at Pauline, Pauline attentive, as they did the dishes together in the kitchen. Alex would be out, of course, but Teddy would be chewing on a pencil at the dining room table, pretending to concentrate on his homework. Joshua tried to put through a phone call, but was told there would be a two-hour delay.

Hell.

"I don't want to be left alone," she had said. "I hear every creak in the house. I dream I'm in my coffin."

After breakfast the following morning, Joshua rented a car and drove to the old town through streets that had simply not existed in his time, streets of boutiques, pizzerias, pubs, and restaurants. Even the harbor, vastly extended, was not as he had remembered it. There was no longer a *barraca* at the edge of Sa Penya. Affronted, Joshua stopped a policeman and asked him if he knew where he could find Juanito Pus.

The policeman scratched his head, baffled. "What does he do?"

"Why, he's a fisherman, of course. He was always on the waterfront. Everybody knows him."

"You've been here before, then?"

"I used to live here, maybe twenty-five years ago."

"Twenty-five years?" He whistled. "Well, the fishermen use another harbor now." And he pointed out a cove, beyond the new yacht basin, where impressively expensive-looking boats rocked at anchor. Joshua drove there at once and was relieved to find fishermen mending their nets on the quay. "I'm looking for Juanito Pus," he said.

"The old one?"

"Yes," Joshua allowed, "the old one."

Juanito hadn't fished for years, they told him, but the family ran a stall in the fish market and Joshua should be able to find him there. So he started back to the old town, parked, and wandered among the stalls of the fish market, searching for a familiar face. Somebody found him first. A man who looked exactly like the Juanito he remembered, with the same endearing smile. The man grabbed Joshua by the shoulders and exclaimed, "The Canadian!"

Grinning back, his heart hammering, all Joshua could manage was a nod.

It was Juanito's son, somebody he had known as a twelve-year-old puppy, a waterfront urchin, now a grown man of thirty-seven. Young Juanito explained that his son had been in an accident and his father was at the hospital sitting with the boy right now. They gossiped for a bit—Joshua's Spanish rusty, infuriatingly inadequate—and then Juanito gave him directions. But at the clinic, the receptionist told him that Juanito had left and the boy was asleep. Disappointed, Joshua returned to his hotel and again tried to put through a call to Pauline. This time he was told there would be a four-hour delay. Joshua poured himself a stiff Scotch and sat out on his balcony, looking out to sea.

"I wish you were coming with me," he had said.

"And I wish you weren't going."

"I have to."

"You're already in Spain."

Damn it.

In Montreal, he was here; in Ibiza, he brooded on home. Inadequate in both places. What a prick you are, Joshua.

After dinner, he drove out to the Mar y Sol, parked his rented car, and set out on foot for Sa Penya. Its main street, actually an alley, where only fishermen and whores and donkeys had trod before, had been turned into a mall, and there was not a donkey hutch anywhere that hadn't been converted into a restaurant or bar or boutique selling leather or jewelry. Tall, black-haired Argentinian boys sprawled on the pavement, joints being passed from hand to hand, their wares laid out on carpets before them. Rings, bracelets, pendants. A plump, curly-haired girl, wearing a T-shirt embossed with the slogan SO THAT WHALES CAN LIVE, GROW JOJOBA, sat with them, plucking away at a guitar. Middle-aged homosexual couples fluttered past. Joshua avoided the posh basement bars, throbbing with acid rock rather than flamenco, and inquired after Juanito in the sleazy ones, where the locals obviously found refuge. Finally, he came up with his address and found the narrow house, only four doors beyond the winding passageway that had once led to Casa Rosita. But then his nerve failed him. Oddly enough, he had never been to Juanito's place. He did not even know his wife. And it was eleven o'clock—maybe they had already gone to bed. He decided not to intrude. Instead, he drifted down to one of the new cafés on the main street and sat down to have a drink on the terrace.

The days are long, Seymour's grandmother had said, but the years fly past.

The Mackenzie King Memorial Society seldom convened for their Annual Day any more, their last reunion a disaster.

Plump, good-natured Mickey Stein, recuperating from a heart by-pass operation in Houston, had been unable to attend. Jack Katz and Al Roth were suing each other over a real estate deal in Toronto. Max Birenbaum had come, but stomped out in a huff, unable to endure the ribbing he was getting about his hair transplant. Larry Cohen, with the Department of Revenue now, had spent the evening avoiding a fulminating Bobby Gross, who was being taken to court on a tax-evasion charge.

"You know what your hero, E. M. Forster, once said?" Bobby charged, finally cornering Larry. "If I had to choose between betraying my friend or my government, I wish I'd have the courage to choose my friend."

"That's a loose paraphrase and he wasn't talking about chiseling. Besides, I have nothing to do with the case. I can't help."

Lennie Fisher, who had been accepted as a member by the Royal Yacht Club of Ontario, invited everybody to join him for drinks on his sloop if and when they were in Toronto. "And I want you to know," he said again and again, "if I'm moored in the outer basin, it's only because everybody has to wait their turn for a berth in the inner basin. It has absolutely nothing to do with my being Jewish."

"Even in the old days," Seymour Kaplan said, "you were always the class *tuchus-lecker*."

"What you mean to say is, I don't look back on FFHS as the good old days, the glory days, because my life hasn't been a downhill slope."

The reunion was haunted by sweet Benny Zucker, gaunt now, his skull protruding through flesh drawn taut, telling everybody, "Boy, was I ever lucky. It was really a close shave. It weighed five pounds and six ounces, but it turned out to be nonmalignant."

"You're looking great," Joshua said.

"If it was terminal, they'd have me on chemotherapy now, wouldn't they, Morty?"

"Damn right," Morty Zipper said, slipping out into the hall to bite back his tears.

"How long has he got?" Joshua asked, bringing him a cognac.

"I wish it were Eli. Is that a terrible thing to say?"

In the morning, Joshua drove right to the clinic. It was sweltering in there. The boy, who had been struck by a taxi, lay in bed with both his broken legs suspended by pulleys from the ceiling. He was thin, pale, his eyes dull. Joshua guessed that he was eight years old, but small for his age. He was twelve. "My father was going to drop by your hotel last night," young Juanito said, "but he did not wish to disturb you." Juanito, he added, had just left and could be found at home.

So Joshua returned to Sa Penya once more and started out for Juanito's house. Suddenly, he was hailed from behind and turning, he saw a shrunken old man with a seamed face, wet eyes, and a sunken mouth. To his intense embarrassment, he did not immediately grasp that this was Juanito. Yesterday's furnace. Well, *he* was no longer a skinny, callow punk in jeans, encouraging a beard. He touched Juanito's cheek and the old man grinned, revealing long yellowing teeth with many a gap between. They strolled arm-in-arm, not speaking, but exchanging wry glances, to the waterfront café where they had taken their first drink together. "Juanito, my friend," Joshua said, coughing to clear his throat, "this certainly calls for a cognac."

"But I don't drink any more," he protested. "Not for the last eight years. The doctors, you know." With a trembling hand he put on his glasses for Joshua, smiling shyly, explaining that his failing eyesight had improved with abstinence.

"What happened to the *barraca?*"

Gone, gone, just like his fishing tubs, which had been lost in bad times. Ibiza's fabled fishing grounds were no more, he explained, and smiling ruefully he added, "There are very many foreigners here today."

Once fish had been so abundant as to be all but worthless on the island, the bulk of the overnight catch being sent to market in Valencia, the rest sold for pennies outside the *barraca* as a courtesy to the local women. Now, although some of the old men still stubbornly fished the once-fertile bank, there was hardly enough to feed the locals. The new hotels, the condominiums, in Ibiza and San Antonio, the entirely new seaside villages squeezed into every available cove by German developers, everybody dumping raw sewage into the sea, had driven the fish away. Juanito shrugged. He bit off the tip of a cigar and spat on the pavement. "Ibiza is prosperous now." He told Joshua of shrewd old cronies who had sold their worthless *fincas* to crazed foreigners for fortunes. "You should have bought when you were here." Then he burst out laughing. "We had to sell your clothes and your typewriter, remember?"

When the fishing had failed, Juanito, like his father and his grandfather before him, had gone to sea, sailing to the French ports, North Africa, and the Canaries. Fourteen years at sea, he said, signing on as a cook, but now he managed on his small pension and the help he got from his son.

"He has grown into a fine fellow," Joshua said, "and he looks just like you."

"He is a good man, but he is too wild. He drinks too much."

"Hey, Juanito. Come on, man."

Something of the old fire flared in his rheumy eyes. He grinned broadly. "Remember, we were going to fish together with the Eskimos one day. Through the ice."

They passed the next morning together, reminiscing and driving about the island, Juanito shaking his head in wonder, amused that Joshua could actually afford a rented car.

"You are no longer poor, then?"

"No."

"Are you rich?"

"Not really."

"But you own a car?"

"Yes," he allowed.

333

"And a house in the country?"

"It belongs to my wife."

If Ibiza had changed and grown incredibly, the San Antonio he had known simply didn't exist any more. It was gone. In place of the sweet, somnolent village there was a thrusting resort town, not unlike Juan-les-Pins, with a paved esplanade, elegant shops, a huge yacht basin, and an endless run of large hotels. Nobody could possibly walk into the sea and hunt fish from this waterfront any more—it was a four-foot drop from the new concrete pilings. Don Pedro's Bodega had been supplanted by a discotheque: Snoopy's Place. The only army officers about were retired British majors, reading the *Daily Telegraph* on the terraces of cafés that offered tea and muffins. The barracks, Juanito said, had been shut down years ago. There was now no military presence on the island. González, Jiménez, the others, all gone. "And whatever happened to the Freibergs?" Joshua asked.

Juanito looked baffled.

"You know, the Casa del Sol. The original owners." And he told Juanito how he had once tried to reach them by phone from London.

"Oh, the Jewish couple. I remember. But why would you phone them?" he asked, affronted. "You never even wrote to me."

"What became of them?"

"He got sick. His heart. They sold their hotel for a huge profit at the beginning of the boom here and moved to Malaga, I think."

"Did Mariano close down their hotel after I left?"

"No. Why?"

"He told me that a complaint had been filed. Their wiring was faulty. He might have to close them down."

Juanito laughed. "He lived off that one for years, the bastard. He never closed anybody down, but he used to collect on it again and again." Juanito grinned and shook his head. "I am a family man," he suddenly declared with feeling. "We are both family men. One life, one wife."

"And what," Joshua asked playfully, "about Casa Rosita?"

"It is no longer here. Not for years. All the casas have been closed down by the government."

"And where could I find Mariano?"

"He retired years ago. But he knew how to take care of himself, he owns property all over the island. If you are really

334

interested in seeing the bastard, you can usually find him in Los Molinos."

Bolstered by still more cognac, Joshua asked, "And Dr. Dr. Mueller?"

"Why in the hell would you want to see him again?" Juanito asked, spitting.

"Revenge," Joshua said, feeling foolish.

"What are you," Juanito asked, amused, "a Spaniard now?"

"I am no longer a kid now. I have kids of my own."

"Will you kill him?"

"No," Joshua said, startled.

"What, then?"

"Just tell me where I can find the bastard."

"In the cemetery," Juanito said. "He's dead."

"God damn it," Joshua cried out. "God damn it to hell." All this way for nothing.

"I thought you came here to see your old friend Juanito, not some crazy German."

"Yes. Certainly. Of course I did."

"Well, I'm no longer a young man," he said, querulous. "I'm tired now. Take me home, please."

"When did he die?"

"Five years ago. Maybe six."

"How?"

"Cancer."

Joshua drove Juanito home and continued on to Los Molinos, one of the new hotels, where he found Mariano seated at a table in the bar, reading a newspaper. Bronzed and wiry as ever, but the beady eyes clouded with cataracts now. Mariano had obviously suffered a stroke. His thin mouth was slightly askew and his left arm hung limply from his side. He did not recognize Joshua at first. But after a belligerent Joshua reminded him of who he was, he seemed delighted to see him, which was disconcerting.

"You were such a skinny kid. So hot-tempered. But those were the great years here. Afterwards, the real trouble started. Hippies. Hashish. Lesbians. Homosexuals. The dregs of Europe and America. I can't tell you the problems we had here. The dike was breached, and now look what's happening to Spain. Poor Spain. Once we were the owners of the world. Nobody can forgive us that we discovered America. But now we are a poor people and everybody is ready to shit on us. Soon England will be the same. Sure Franco was a dictator, but we had a good life under him. There was law and order.

Now they are going to legalize the Communist Party again. La Pasionaria is back. We will go the way of Italy. There will be guns in the street. Like Lisbon. Hey, look at you! Obviously, you are a respectable man now. It's odd, you know, how things turn out. Do you remember Don Pedro's? Well, after you left, things changed there for Mueller. The officers felt that he had played dirty."

"The officers turned in a sworn statement against me."

"Oh sure, that was Jiménez, Juan. But González and some of the others, the younger ones, they felt ashamed. You were only a kid, you know, and they felt Mueller had done you in only because you were a Jew. Horseshit. Here in Spain we are all Jews. Well, not everybody. But at least one in ten has Jewish blood, if you go back far enough. I have nothing against the Jews."

"Why, you even used to know one in Cordoba."

"One? Many. Majorca is thick with Jews. They are very clever and it is better not to mess with them. But, man, you certainly come from a difficult people."

"Stiff-necked."

"Remember Carlos? You know, the mousy little bank teller. He saved his salary for ten years, I don't think he ever ate in a restaurant or went to a movie, never marrying, saving to emigrate to his promised land, and in the end they wouldn't have him. His family hadn't been Jewish for hundreds of years as far as they were concerned. Your rabbis said his mother was officially a Catholic. What they called their law of return didn't apply to him or hundreds of others in Majorca who wanted to go. How about that?"

"Is he still here, then?"

"He left years ago, for South America somewhere. Let me order more drinks. It is really very good to see you again. Hey, remember those afternoons at Rosita's?"

"What I remember is that you were going to shut down the Casa del Sol."

"Oh, really. Why?"

"Their wiring was faulty."

Mariano laughed. He slapped his knee with his good hand. "I'd forgotten all about that." He paused, pondering. "Now it is obviously *my* wiring that is faulty. I don't recall. Did I close them down?"

"No."

"Good."

"You came to my house and you said you had photographs

336

of me and Monique. The kind they sell in Pigalle. I can remember your exact words. 'In Spain,' you said, 'we expect foreigners to behave with a certain decorum.' "

"Hey, she must have been some fuck, that girl. Whatever happened to her?"

"I have no idea."

"Probably fat now. Like the mother. Always look at the mother. But those photographs—now I remember—they may have been shocking in those days. But now." He made a deprecating gesture. "Do you read *Hustler* magazine?"

"No."

"Sometimes they are left behind by tourists." He leaned closer to Joshua, his eyes heated. "Girls masturbating. Licking each other. Amazing stuff."

"Mariano," Joshua cut in, exasperated, "I did not steal Mueller's traveler's checks."

"You did. You didn't. Ancient history. Who cares now?"

How could you hit an old man with a crippled left arm, however vile? "But you gave me forty-eight hours to get out of here because of those charges."

"I enforced the law. It was my job. But I never promised anybody justice. Do you have a good life in Canada?"

"Yes."

"Then forget it. I have survived two strokes. But almost everybody I know is dead now. Would you do me a favor?"

"For you, Mariano, anything."

"I will leave you my address. When you get home, mail me copies of *Hustler*. It is difficult to find here. And, say, we must have dinner together. How long will you stay in Ibiza?"

"I'm leaving tomorrow."

But he had one more trip to make.

Without even the benefit of a kitchen knife this time, Joshua drove back toward San Antonio, parked about a mile out on the hot asphalt highway winding out into the new suburbs, cut through the parking lot behind a pizza parlor, past a Hamburger Heaven, and crossed a miniature golf course that had used to be an olive grove. He climbed the mountainside—stopping more than once, winded—before he finally reached the hump of rock that had once overlooked Dr. Dr. Mueller's villa. There was no teepee. No brown stallion. Certainly no villa. Instead, a six-story condominium, the concrete already cracked, the paint flaking here and there. The Don Quixote Estate. Joshua sat down on the rock and laughed until he almost cried.

Starting back to his car—walking, not running—he was

337

overcome with both relief and disappointment. *You did. You didn't. Ancient history.* But *my* ancient history, damn it. He paused to set his wristwatch to Montreal time. Home time. Family time.

Mueller has been robbed of eighteen hundred dollars in traveler's checks.

He's lying.

Everybody's lying but you, Mariano said.

Jack Trimble assured me you made all the decisions.

He made a point of telling everybody that. He knew what was coming. He was lying.

Everybody's a liar but you, Joshua said.

And what, he thought, if Kevin was telling the truth? Absolutely impossible. All the same, he was Pauline's brother. The senator's only son. He would have to be helped. *I will be Victorio,* Joshua thought. *I will be the honest fisherman. I will cast my net into the water and bring out sufficient fish to feed my family. My loved ones.*

Back in his hotel room, exhilarated, he poured himself a stiff Scotch. He decided that he would not write a new introduction to *The Volunteers.* That was from another time, another place. Let it rest. He put through a call to Pauline and was able to reach her after only an hour's delay. "Pauline, my love, I've been trying to reach you for three days. How are you?"

No answer.

"Darling?"

"Kevin's dead," she said in a wobbly voice. "His plane crashed."

"What?"

"He's killed himself."

"Pauline, I'll come as fast as I can. I'll grab the first plane out of here."

"Oh, Joshua, why couldn't we have helped him?"

7

Reuben met him at the airport and drove him right out to the Royal Victoria Hospital, where Pauline lay in bed, heavily sedated.

"Don't worry," Reuben said. "She'll be home in a few days."

The newspaper accounts of the crash did not suggest

338

suicide, but an accident. A mechanical failure. Kevin had not filed a flight plan, but apparently had just taken his Beechcraft up for a spin to relax his nerves. It had been cold, but clear. Later there was some light snow. He had crashed into Owl's Head mountain on Lake Memphremagog. Dying on impact. Neck broken. Back smashed. He was forty-two years old. The newspaper accounts described him as the only son of Senator Stephen Andrew Hornby, and observed that Kevin had once been a sportsman of note. A one-time McGill Redman. An outstanding hockey player. Tennis player of considerable accomplishment. A former Quebec Amateur Golf Champion. Latterly a prominent broker and man-about-town, who was under investigation by the securities commission at the time of his death. Foul play was not suspected.

"Did he leave a note?" Joshua asked.

"No, but Pauline's convinced he committed suicide."

"God damn it, she didn't need this. Neither did the senator."

"Or Kevin," Reuben said sharply.

"O.K., O.K."

"What do you think?"

"He didn't want to go to prison. They don't dress for dinner there."

Reuben looked at him, surprised. "What have you got against him?"

The days stretched into weeks and then one morning Joshua wakened, hung over again, to the chilling realization that Pauline had now been in the hospital for almost a month, wasting. Although his debts were mounting and his hockey book, hardly begun, was already long overdue, he couldn't work. He was spending far too much of his time at The King's Arms. And one afternoon, surprisingly, his cousin Sheldon sought him out there. Before he could even join Sheldon at his table, The Flopper looked down from his customary stool at the bar and called Joshua to his side. "Who's the fancy fella?" he asked.

"He's no fancy fella. He's my cousin."

"Lookit, peckerhead, whoever he is, I betcha he never pissed in a hotel sink."

Poor Sheldon had once been the most promising of his generation of Leventhals. An unrecognized Quiz Kid. One day president of the Junior Red Cross; the next, a star on the McGill campus. Stroke, stroke, stroke. Graduating *cum laude*, the family pride. And now, twenty-five years later, his face fleshy but his beard trim, his fingernails manicured, reeking of a leathery cologne, Sheldon was big in storm windows, his father-in-law's business.

"Are you enjoying it?" Joshua asked.

"Storm windows?"

"Well then, why don't you try plumbing?" Joshua suggested, shooting him a fierce look.

But Sheldon didn't catch the reference. "I don't care for the direction this country is taking," he said. "I've published eight letters to the editor of the *Star* in the past two years. Have you read them?"

"I'm afraid not."

"They are widely admired. Lots of people have complimented me on them. Complete strangers. Gentiles among them." Sheldon leaned forward to press Joshua's arm, his eyes imploring. "I'd like to get into punditry. I want to be a pundit. Help me, Josh." And he unclicked his attaché case and thrust two columns at him. One was about Israel, the other dealt with Quebec. The first column began: " 'What is truth?' asked Pontius Pilate." Joshua giggled.

"What's so funny?"

"Sheldon, you once made a big mistake in your life. You should have let me play with your Lionel train set. We could have taken turns operating it."

"What are you talking about?"

"Go away," he said. "Please go away," and he quit the table, watching poor Sheldon flee, embarrassed.

Shapiro, you are indeed an abomination, Joshua thought, as he drifted back to join the regulars at the bar: Roger, Robbie, The Flopper. The Flopper was expounding on the injustice of the prodigious sums now being paid to untried juniors, venturing that even Guy Lafleur would never have been such a star in the old six-team league. "Lookit," he said, "half of his goals are scored against the Minnesota No-Stars or the California Seal Pups." He was willing to acknowledge, however, that even he had benefited from expansion. A few years back, fifty years old but owning up only to forty-two, he had been briefly reactivated, earning big money for the first time in his career with the Miami Screaming Eagles. "The trouble with the Eagles," he readily admitted, "was we only played positional when we lined up outside room four-oh-eight in the Ramada Inn, in Edmonton, to be blown by Miss Rita Kowalchuk, a great hockey fan."

Drinking himself to bed each night, Joshua became obsessed with the notion that he was waking each morning with fewer gray cells than he had gone to sleep with. Cherished little cerebral circuits shorting or expiring every night, flooded by alcohol. Then one night, as he lay half asleep on his sofa, the phone rang, jolting him. It was Jane Trimble, unable to find him at The King's Arms, standing on his doorstep a half-hour later. "Well," she said, "Sir Galahad at home." Sweeping past him into the study, relieving him of his Scotch in passing. "I thought you'd be undressed. How disappointing!"

"Damn it, Jane, what do you want here at this hour?"

"Not that," she said, surprising him with a cool hand between his legs. "But, oh my. You're not as indifferent as you pretend."

Joshua broke free to pick up the phone.

"Who are you calling, darling?"

"Jack, to come and get you."

"Joshua and Jack. Jack and Joshua. How different you are. He was absolutely thrilled to be accepted by the old crowd, and you think you're doing us a favor just by tolerating us from time to time. St.-Urbain-boy *oblige*. You're also far more attracted to me than you admit, but you wouldn't want to hurt Pauline. On a scale of one to ten, how am I doing?"

"Lousy," he replied with too much anger, starting to dial their number on the phone again.

"Jack can't come to get me. He's in Toronto."

"I'll call a taxi, then."

"You call a taxi and I'm going to get out of my clothes," she said, flicking her tongue at him as she unbuttoned her blouse and slithered out of it.

Joshua ducked into the kitchen to pour himself a drink. She followed, which infuriated him, because he was stirred by the sight of her creamy breasts all but popping out of her slip of a bra. "Put on your blouse. One of the kids might come down."

"And discover us necking? *Ça, alors.*"

"I'll drive you home, if you like."

"I don't like. And neither," she shouted, "do I wish to be humiliated, you fuck. You arrogant prick. Just who do you think you are?"

"Now you lower your goddamn voice, or I'll pick you up and shove you out in the snow just as you are."

"Why, I'll bet you would," she said, sinking to the sofa, her skirt riding up. Tears rolled down her cheeks, smearing her eye shadow. "We used to walk home from ECS together, smoking Sweet Caps, Pauline and I. Oh God."

"How's Jack?"

"How's Jack? Everybody's treating him like shit. All he ever did was make money for them, those fools, and now they blame him for Kevin's suicide. We're ruined, both of us. I want more," she said, thrusting her glass at him.

He poured her another drink.

"Remember the night of our champagne dinner on the lake? Jack oozing good feeling. 'Kevin is joining my firm,' " she said, mocking his accent. "Weren't you surprised, old son?"

"Let's just say it was not exactly my idea of a fun evening."

"Jack drove into town that morning and wasn't supposed to return until five. *Malheureusement*, he was back at four and saw us together."

"You and Kevin."

"Me and Kevin. We were going to get married once, but I backed off, frightened. I'm sure I'm not telling you anything you don't know," she said, leaning over for him to light her cigarette, "but I was concerned about the closeness of his relationship with Pauline. Does that trouble you?"

"Immensely. But I try to be brave."

"Really, I was very pleased when she married you, because for a time there I thought she'd never find a man who could displace Kevin in her affections."

"Ah, but aren't you sweet? I think Pauline is blessed in having you for a friend. Now, just between us, when did you first start slipping down to Bermuda to see Kevin?"

"It was only once, and I was with somebody else at the time. Dickie Abbott, does that surprise you? We ran into Kevin by accident."

"And you immediately said, 'Hey there, Kevin baby, why don't you fly up to the lake and visit your sister? She seems happy. Let's see what we can do about that.' "

"I most certainly did not suggest that he come up here."

"Neither did you sweet-talk poor Jack into taking him on."

"As a matter of fact, no, I didn't. It was Jack's idea."

"And he also suggested that the two of you ought to have an affair, if only for old times' sake."

"I thought that might bother Pauline," she said, her smile provocative, "but I didn't dare to hope that it would make you jealous."

"I was thinking of Jack."

"Jack worshipped Kevin. He's everything he ever wanted to be."

"I'd like to know what really happened that afternoon."

"Jack and I quarreled at breakfast. Over Charlie again. And then he drove into town, leaving me alone with Kevin. Well, not alone. There were the kids. But Kevin sent them off to the sailing club, and when I still didn't emerge from my bedroom, he brought me lunch on a tray. We talked about the old days and how difficult it used to be to shake Pauline, if only to find time to be alone. He told me how I was even more beautiful now, if possible, than I had been then. And naturally he tried to climb into bed with me, but I wasn't having any of it. Shit, I had to lock the bathroom door in order to get dressed. He followed me everywhere I went in the house like a puppy, flattering, pawing, trying to steal kisses. Doesn't that have a nice Victorian sound? He told me that in all our years apart he had never found another woman who was my equal. It was embarrassing, very embarrassing, and so I made an excuse about having to check out something in the boathouse, and I suggested that he join me for a swim afterwards. Anything to cool him off. And the next thing I knew, he sneaked up behind me in the boathouse, unknotted my bikini strap, and was all over me, like a sex-starved teenager. When I finally shook him off, I saw that Jack's Jaguar was parked at the top of the hill. Obviously, he had seen us together and misunderstood."

"Are you sure Jack saw you together?"

"He must have seen us."

"Why didn't he throw Kevin out, then?"

"Oh dear. How I've overestimated you. You don't understand Jack at all, do you? He's crazy. Don't you know that?"

Like a fox, possibly, Joshua thought.

"I'm sure you've often wondered why a woman as intelligent and beautiful as I am ever married Jack in the first place."

"Yes. Often. It's something I really brood about. If he's crazy, why don't you leave him?"

"And just what would I do, an older woman like me? Get a job serving at Holt's? Set up as a call girl in Cantlie House? He's got a weak heart. He won't live forever, old son. *In vino veritas*," she said, thrusting out her glass for more.

He poured her a stiff one this time. "Jane, I want to ask you something," he said earnestly.

"The answer's obvious," she said, reaching out to stroke his thigh.

"I want to know," he said, squeezing her hand, "if you

ever saw Kevin sign Coral papers for Jack without reading them?"

"No," she replied impatiently.

"Did he know what was really going on at Coral?"

"If you mean, was it all Jack's doing, I'm sorry, darling, I wish I could help, but the answer is no."

"I just don't believe Kevin would actually set out to swindle his old friends."

"How can you be so dense? Kevin, my darling, never set out to do anything in his life. But there was all that money there and he helped himself to some. Like candy in a jar. And then Jack wanted to look over the accounts and he tried to cover by making risky investments. They didn't jell. He panicked. He reached into the jar again. He made even riskier investments. But he didn't set out to actually do anybody harm. He never did. Neither could he ever face the music," she said, holding out her glass again.

"One more," he said, "and then I'm driving you home."

"Aren't you gallant?"

"Oh, go to hell, will you."

She blew him a kiss. "I've only fucked once with a Jew, and what he liked best was going down on me. Oy vey, trying to make an impression, even in bed. For the rest, it was thirty seconds of action and an hour of apology. Are you all like that?"

"We're a bad lot."

"If you stopped being so superior, I'd stop being so coarse. *Give me my blouse, please.*"

Startled, he fetched it for her.

"I don't want to sit here like this. Not with you. I'm cold. Oh, I'm so cold. I'm beginning to grow little hairs on my upper lip. Have you noticed?"

"No," he said, as she stood up and he helped her into her blouse.

"But don't you even think I have beautiful skin? I don't mean my neck, my neck's going. But oh my arms. And my shoulders were always better than Pauline's. Touch me, Joshua."

He kissed her perfunctorily on the shoulder.

"Stop! Don't do any more, you wild Jewman, you satyr, or I'll come in my panties."

He had to laugh. She giggled, and then all at once her mood soured again. "I think you're full of shit," she said, retrieving her coat from the hall floor, "you and Pauline."

"I'll drive you home," he said.

"I wouldn't dream of putting you out. Call me a taxi, please."

"I'll drive you."

"I want a taxi. Do you understand?"

Diamond said they would be there in ten minutes.

"I'll wait outside," she said.

"Now come on, it's freezing out there."

"And here."

"And here," he agreed.

"I would have thought," she said with a sudden smile, "that you would have enjoyed having me strip for you, just like your mother used to."

"Who told you that?" he demanded, outraged.

"Why, I could tell you things about your precious Pauline that would make your hair stand on end."

"Out," he said, whacking the door open.

"Do you know why the senator really drove poor Kevin out of the house?"

Which was when he struck her with the back of his hand, sending her sprawling.

8

Five weeks. She had been in the hospital for five weeks. And from the day of his return from Ibiza, he had not missed an afternoon visit. Appealing to an unresponsive, mute Pauline. Once he had reminded her of their first dinner together: L'Etoile on Charlotte Street. A decidedly horny Joshua determined to get it over with nicely, but as quickly as possible. Then bed. Pauline in his bed.

Imagine.

"I don't think," she said, after he had apprehensively ordered what he devoutly hoped was a good wine, "that we ought to have a Bordeaux with our veal."

"I ordered it," he said, flaring. "We'll drink it."

"You're being stubborn. It isn't proper."

"Neither am I."

"It's gauche."

"So am I."

"I'm not marrying you."

"Yes, you are."

"And if I don't?"

"Eat fast."

"I beg your pardon," she said, fiddling with her marinated trout, her lips parted.

Pauline's lips.

"We can have our coffee and cognac back at my place."

"And what makes you think," she asked, her smile maddeningly mysterious, "that I'm going back to your place?" But he shrank so visibly that she immediately relented. "Can't you wait?"

"No. Can you?"

"Why don't we leave right now?"

"Really?" he asked, astonished, as under the table her bare foot was already riding up between his legs.

"Yes, please," she said.

Pauline's first retreat to her bed—a breakdown, Dr. Hamilton said, although Joshua bridled at such a clinical description—had come some six months after Susy's birth.

Alex had the measles. Susy had colic and had to be walked through the night. The newly installed oil heating furnace conked out—the plumber blamed the heating engineer, the heating engineer blamed the electrician. The contractor, standing in the kitchen, flicking cigarette ash into the palm of his hand—a reproach—would not accept any responsibility. Pauline paced, her eyes heated, Susy struggling and squealing in her arms.

"Put more sugar in her bottle, ma'am."

"Don't tell me how to bring up my babies. Fix my furnace."

He appealed to Joshua over her shoulder: We're men. We understand.

"I'm in the middle of work," Joshua said, retreating. "I've got a deadline to meet."

Lists began to accumulate. Lists and lists of lists. Overwhelming her. Broken dishes in the dinner service had to be replaced. But John Barnes no longer carried the line. Imported. Discontinued, madam. But you promised I could always get replacements. Would you like to see the manager?

"Look, darling," he said, "I really don't give a damn about the dinner service, or whether or not the plates match."

"But I do."

He shrugged.

"You have a way of diminishing everything I do for you."

"Should I pretend to care, then?"

"No."

"What, then?"

"Oh, help me, Josh. Please."

346

Reuben helped.

She came to adore him, though at first she was fearful. "He doesn't approve of me. He thinks I'm too prim. I don't shoplift."

He reminded her of the time, maybe a year after their return to Montreal, when Alex had complained to Reuben about his teacher at Selwyn House.

"He picks on me," Alex wailed.

"Well, yeah, right. Now, what's his name?"

Pauline, chopping vegetables, froze. "Don't you dare give him your teacher's name," she called out instinctively.

Reuben hooted with laughter. Pauline broke up. A kinship was forged.

Now she lay in her hospital bed, wasting, and Joshua came by every afternoon to sit with her.

The worms must be crawling in his mouth now. The flesh putrefying.

Then one afternoon, after she had been there for five weeks, he managed to provoke her into a conversation by insisting, "I'm bringing the children here tomorrow."

"I don't want to see them."

"Why not?"

"I'm not their mother any more. Or your wife. I don't want to see anybody."

"The house isn't the same. They need you. So do I."

"Get a housekeeper."

He stared at her, astonished.

"The children can survive very well without me. So can you. And I don't need anybody any more."

Joshua hastily lighted a cigarette.

"Surprised?" she asked.

"Yes."

"Is your sweet Pauline being ugly?" she taunted.

"I didn't say that."

"The truth is, you never say very much, but you expect a good deal."

"I see."

"I can find fault with all of you. That's what I do here. I lie in bed and make lists of your failings. My family's failings. Especially yours. You're not what you once were."

Don't I know it.

"You never should have married me or had a family," she said, her voice rising. "You might have written more instead of frittering away your time at The King's Arms. Joshua Shapiro. Regular guy."

347

"Possibly I needed you more than I ever cared about writing."

"Or, more likely, you were less afraid of having us than of testing your limits. You use us, Josh. You resent us. You tell yourself that if not for them, you would be able to live on a pittance and write what you wanted. You think you're one fine fellow. You're a coward."

"That's simply not true."

"Once I thought you had sufficient appetite for both of us. You were such a grabber. Charging into any roomful of people, determined to make an impression. 'Look at me. See what I made of myself.' Now you've learned to sit back and wait. Strangers will bring you drinks at any party. Others will attend to your needs. Obeisance must be paid to Joshua Shapiro, television's fool."

Biting back his anger, he protested, "But I love you."

"So what?" she shrieked back.

"Pauline, please."

"Will your loving bring back the dead?"

Do you know why the senator really drove poor Kevin out of the house?

"There are people who say you married me because you're a climber."

I could tell you things about your precious Pauline that would make your hair stand on end.

"Why wasn't a Jewish girl good enough for you?"

"That's enough. Really, Pauline. You don't know what you're saying."

"I do. I do. Something in you called out for a prize. A golden shiksa. And what if they had to cut off my breast? Like Barbara. Snip, snip. Would you find somebody younger?"

"I'm going to find out exactly what drugs they've got you on. I want you taken off everything."

"You wanted Seymour and your cousin—what's his name? —to envy you. *Dress classy. I want your breeding to show.* Do you remember saying that to me?"

"Did Kevin mean that much to you?" he demanded.

"Yes. Yes. Kevin meant that much to me. And I betrayed him."

"Or, more likely, he betrayed you."

"You don't understand. How can I make you understand? I don't care about the money. The hell with the money. He was my brother. I should have helped him. I should have lied for him. But I couldn't, because I didn't want Joshua to think badly of me. Well, the hell with you. Who do you think you are? Even my father's frightened of you. He turned down that dreadful Izzy Singer, those directorships. He wanted the money for his grandchildren, but he turned it down because he didn't want to offend you. He never cared about his son. His own son. But he didn't want you to think badly of him."

"Sometimes," he said, his voice subdued, "I think you married me in the first place only because you wanted to shock your father."

"Well, in the end, we were both shocked, weren't we?"

"How come?"

"You turned out to be more moral than we were. Possibly because you're new to it. Me, I come from an old family. Well established. Rotten to the core."

"What is it you want, Pauline?"

"I want to be complete unto myself. I want to live alone. I don't want to need anybody."

"But we're so right together."

"We were. But not any more. We're on a new standard now."

He tried to take her in his arms, but she slid away from him, trembling. "What would I do if anything happened to you? Or Alex? Or Susy? Or Teddy? Don't you understand? Look at me. Take a good look. How could I survive another loss?"

"We can't live without risks."

"I can. I will. Our kind of loving is madness. Harden yourself, my darling. I have. I'm going to live alone. I'm going to become my mother. I'm going to go to bed with other women's husbands and I'm not going to feel a thing when they're fucking me. Neither am I ever going to be left for a younger woman or be denied by my children. Look," she cried, sweeping up her nail scissors from her bedside table and driving them into the palm of her hand, "I can hurt myself more than anybody else can possibly hurt me."

He leaped up to yank the scissors out and took her raw bleeding hand in his own. A shaking Pauline yielded to sobs. The nurse came running. Pauline required five stitches, a sedative. Joshua sat up with her through the night.

A moaning Pauline.

Her legs curled up, with her knees all but touching her chin. Her hands locked between her thighs.

Joshua slept in for most of the next day, and the following morning he went to Morty Zipper's office. He had meant to talk to him about Pauline, but once he got there he found that he just couldn't trust himself to mention her. So he asked Morty about Seymour instead. Morty said that Seymour was going to be all right.

"When you guys say 'all right,' I get the shivers. What exactly do you mean, Morty?"

"His second attack was very minor. It was to be expected. His chances are good. What more can I say? Now roll up your sleeve. I'm going to take your blood pressure."

"Well?" Joshua asked afterwards.

"Two months ago, Seymour's was normal too. Have you been to North Africa yet?"

"No. Why?"

"Last year we went to Yugoslavia. This year we're going to North Africa. I don't postpone things any more. Neither should you."

Seymour, Seymour.

Seymour, who had suffered his initial coronary while Joshua was in Spain, had been back in circulation as soon as he was sprung from the hospital two weeks later. One evening he had barged into The King's Arms, flushed with excitement, not even stopping to introduce the plump giggly young girl on his arm, but pulling Joshua abruptly away from the bar and hurrying him into the toilet.

"Seymour, you ought to be taking it easy. What in the hell's the matter with you?"

"Quick," he had said, dropping his trousers, "we've got to change. I need your underwear."

"You're out of your mind. Nothing will get me into those goddamn lace panties."

"Put them into your pocket, then. But I need your shorts," he had said, tugging at Joshua's belt.

"It's late-night closing. Try Simpson's."

"Come on," he had said, unzipping him.

"What if somebody found us here like this, dear?"

"No jokes, please."

So they had exchanged underwear, and Joshua had lingered at the bar until closing time, forgetting all about his car parked outside. And the next morning Stuart Donald McMaster had come to the house.

Now Seymour was back in the hospital, the Jewish General, and Joshua went there directly from Morty's office. A minor attack, Morty had said, but Seymour had aged, leaping a generation in ten days. His face seemed drawn, his eyes without heat. He had already lost twelve pounds and had been ordered to shed another ten. He had given up smoking and had been put on a salt-free diet. Seymour diminished. All the same, Joshua should have known better than to enter his room without knocking. A shapely black nurse leaped away from his bed.

"Hi," Seymour said. "I'd like you to meet Ms. Brenda Hopkinson. What a mind! Honestly, she's one of the most intelligent women I've ever met. Brenda's a Seventh Day Adventist. It's fascinating. She's given me a book to read on it. I'll lend it to you."

"Excuse me," Brenda said, leaving the room.

"Pour yourself a drink," Seymour said, indicating the bottles on his bedside table. "You'll find ice cubes floating in the sink."

"You're looking better."

"And you're looking worse. If you've come here to depress me, go now. Your visit is untimely, to say the least."

"You know where I'm going from here?" Joshua asked, helping himself to a Scotch. "I'm going to the Royal Vic. I'm going to take Pauline off all that stupefying shit they've been feeding her in there. I'm going to bring her home."

"You mean she's better?"

"I'm taking her home. The hell with them. Do you think I'm crazy?"

"On the contrary. I think it's about time. Wait," he said, pulling back his blanket and swinging his legs over the side of the bed. "You could need help. I'm coming too."

"No, Seymour. I'm going alone."

"Come here." Seymour hugged him, his eyes welling with tears. "Hey, you know what we are?"

"What?"

"We are the boys of Room forty-two. I'm going to cry. Go. Get out. No, wait. If you can drop by tomorrow, would you please bring me my black bag? I've got something in there for Brenda. And send her in on the way out, will you? Hey, Josh."

"Yeah."

"We are the boys of Room forty-two."

Nurse MacGregor was not surprised to see Joshua at the Royal Vic. Bristling, she said, "Dr. Grant wishes to see you immediately. He will take no responsibility."

"I haven't come to see Dr. Grant, but I have come to take responsibility. I'm taking my wife home."

"But Mr. Shapiro," she said, the color drained from her face, "your wife left this morning. Isn't she with you?"

"My wife what?"

"Oh, heavens! Oh my God! Come with me. Quickly."

Outside, Joshua dashed into the street, grabbing the first taxi to come along, and shouting out his address without even bothering to look at the driver.

"Well, well, if it isn't Denny Dimwit himself. I'm honored. I won't have the back seat washed out for a month."

"I'm sorry," Joshua offered in a failing voice, "that you have to drive a taxi at your age."

Uncle Oscar was sixty-nine.

"What do you mean, sorry, I'm my own boss, aren't I? My friends ask me what I do now, I tell them I go out at night, cruise around, pick up girls, and drive them home."

Joshua tried to light a cigarette, but couldn't manage it, his hands were shaking so badly.

"Aren't you going to laugh?"

He managed a laugh.

"I pick up fares, you know, they see my name on the license plate there, and they ask if we're related. I say, sure we are. They've read your stuff. Or they've seen you on TV. Once or twice they've given me big tips. More often they're angry. They say, 'You know, I think that guy is full of shit most of the time.' "

"They may just happen to be right. Could you drive faster, please?"

"Faster. Slower. We're all heading for the same place. Six feet under. But you're earning some living, I hear."

"Thousands."

"You know, Dimwit, that's what I should of done. Become a TV personality."

"What you should have done, you old fart, was to hold on to your junk instead of breaking it up for scrap. You were sitting on a fortune all those years. Ha, ha, ha."

"Ha, ha, ha, yourself. Prick. I wasn't going to become some faggola antique dealer, that's your department in our family, isn't it? Or haven't you been listening to the radio today?"

Joshua didn't know what he was talking about and he

didn't care. They were on Wood Avenue. Home. Fumbling, dropping his money on the floor, an embarrassed Joshua managed to settle the fare and hurry into the house.

"Pauline," he called. "Pauline."

She wasn't there, of course. But a troubled Susy told him the phone hadn't stopped ringing since he left. The *Star*, the *Gazette*, the New York correspondent of the *Daily Express*. CBC, BBC. Reporters from Toronto. *News of the World*.

10

In a statement read to British reporters and later repeated for the benefit of CBC-TV cameras, the young but as-yet-untested film-maker Ralph Murdoch declared that when he had sold his father's correspondence with Joshua Shapiro to Rocky Mountain University, he had in fact been aware of its scurrilous nature. He felt that he could not destroy the letters because of their literary importance, and what they had to say about the nature of a love that once dared not speak its name. He did regret the many, possibly unsubstantiated references to the sexual predilections of literary figures who were still alive. He sympathized with their protests. But—and on this point he was most emphatic—the curator of the rare manuscripts collection at Rocky Mountain University had assured him, at the time of the purchase, that the correspondence would not be made available to scholars for at least twenty-five years. In response to a question that had initially been put forward by his stepsister, young Murdoch allowed that according to the terms of his father's will he did share, with the other surviving children, in royalties from all future editions of his novels. However, he emphatically denied that he had leaked the letters himself in order to profit now. He also refused to speculate on how his father's stifled passion for Shapiro had affected his subsequent life and work. As for the still-living Shapiro, or "Uncle Josh," as he called him, he wished him no ill. On the contrary, he remembered him fondly.

Dr. Colin Fraser, curator of the rare manuscript collection at Rocky Mountain University, could not understand who might have slipped into the library and surreptitiously photographed pages from the correspondence. To Alberta's outraged minister of culture he justified the large fee paid for its purchase by saying that it was, after all, of some fifty percent Canadian content, and he had been unwilling to see it pass, like so many other national treasures, into eager American hands. Although Shapiro, he continued, could not be reckoned a writer of the first rank, he had written a book of some significance on the Spanish Civil War and was considered by many to be a sporting journalist of note. When asked if there had been many competing American offers for the correspondence, he refused to either confirm or deny this. "We are nobody's cultural colony any more," he said.

Margaret Robinson, Murdoch's first wife and Ralph's mother, and a well-known literary agent who still represented Shapiro, forthrightly claimed she was in a position to say that neither man was homosexual. The letters, she insisted, were no more than a bad joke, written by two young men for fun and profit. "Wherever he is, Sidney must be roaring with laughter. But in Joshua's case, there's his family to consider. I'm afraid my son has behaved very badly indeed."

Dr. Fraser, apprised of Ms. Robinson's comments, observed, "What else can she say? And, in any event, she has certainly not questioned the authenticity of the correspondence."

Reuben phoned Joshua the morning after the story broke. "Hey, Oscar says he picked you up in his taxi, yesterday I think it was, and you were too cheap to tip him."

"He's right."

"And what's this shit I'm reading in the *Gazette?* I buy it for the sports, not to read my son's a pig."

Joshua explained. Then he phoned the senator in Ottawa, explaining again.

"Sue them, my boy," the senator said.

"I'd rather not."

"I'm afraid you'll have to."

Which turned out to be bad advice.

Joshua, shoving past TV crews and reporters gathered outside his door, went to see Dickie Abbott. He had him issue a denial, as well as send a letter to Rocky Mountain University threatening to sue for slander and invasion of privacy. The considered statement Joshua typed out and handed to reporters won him some support. Then the roof fell in.

Out in California, over the wires, there floated a photograph (slightly out of focus, copyright Ellen Markham Studios) which showed Joshua and Murdoch kissing at a Beverly Hills poolside. It was supported by a story that an enterprising *Daily Express* reporter had bought from a black chambermaid at the Century Plaza Hotel. Blessed with a retentive memory, she recalled that Murdoch and Shapiro had shared a room there one night. "I do hope I'm not getting anybody into trouble," Mrs. Cartwright said, "because I sure know what prejudice is."

Esther's photograph appeared in newspapers from coast to fabled coast. Standing in front of her Winnipeg massage parlor, she wore a sandwich board that proclaimed: MY SON'S GAY, BUT THAT'S O.K.

The phone never stopped ringing, but Joshua didn't dare switch to an unlisted number in case Pauline was trying to get through to him. Pauline, Pauline. Alex, who had begun to screen all calls for him, let Seymour through.

"Hey, is that you, honey poo?"

"It's no joke, Seymour."

"I want my panties back. I want them right now."

The photograph of Joshua and Murdoch kissing had made page one of both the *Star* and the *Gazette*. There was another story on the sports pages. Players' representatives from three NHL teams had announced that Joshua Shapiro was no longer welcome in their dressing rooms. "Hell," one player was quoted as saying, "I'm still too ashamed to get undressed in front of my wife. How can we allow *him* in here any more?"

A spokesman for the Canadian League of Homophiles declared that this was a clear case of sexual discrimination and proposed to lodge an immediate complaint with the Canadian Civil Rights Commission. Then a television producer, a friend, managed to get Joshua on the phone.

"Come on, Josh. Give us a break. We won't cut or edit. We'll run your statement in full."

"Sorry. I'd love to appear on your show, but I'm washing my hair tonight."

"Do you want me to say that on the air?"

"Say anything you like, love."

Early the next morning, he managed to slip out the back door without being seen. The snows were melting everywhere. Buds were fattening on the trees. Tomorrow afternoon all the regulars at The King's Arms were going to the opening ball game at The Big O. Joshua made it downtown, where he wanted to speak to a detective he trusted about Pauline. Unfortunately, he ran into Eli Seligson outside his Guy Street office, Eli hurrying to catch a plane for Zurich.

"I want to tell you something," Eli said. "They've included one of your so-called essays in a book on my son's reading list at school. I've written a letter of protest to the principal."

Joshua grabbed him, driving him against a mailbox. "Eli, your father was a black-marketeer and you are a shit. I hear your desk drawers at home are crammed with hot banknotes."

"Whatever I am," he said, struggling free, "thank God I'm not what you are. Feh!" And he ran for a taxi.

And right there, heaving with anger, Joshua decided to fix him. He would plant some vintage banknotes of his own in Eli's desk. The police would find them after the break-in, obliging Eli to answer some embarrassing questions. Har, har, har.

11

Stuart Donald McMaster was speaking, seated opposite a watchful Reuben in a booth at El Ponderosa on the Decarie Strip. McMaster digging into his turf 'n' surf, Reuben sipping his V.O. slowly. "I remember the day exactly, a Tuesday, pissing with rain. I had tickets for the opener—my luck—laid on by that fuck Ginsberg of Upper Belmont. Rogers was supposed to pitch. You know how many games he'd win if he was with L.A. or Boston? Plenty. Shit, that's some arm, and I remember Don Newcombe when he was with the Royals. Couldn't take the pressure, that boy. El Foldo in the series every time. Rogers was supposed to throw, and there I was with Ginsberg's box seats. So it rained. It was really pissing out there."

"Your luck. Yeah. Right."

"It was a couple of days after Pauline clean disappeared from the Royal Vic. There one minute, gone the next. Everybody jumping. Joshua hollering. Hoo boy!"

Reuben nodded.

"His wife taking off like that into the wild blue yonder. I don't mean to pry, but have you any idea of her whereabouts yet?"

"No."

"Geez, do you think she knows what kind of shit he's in now?"

"If she reads the newspapers, she does."

"Would you like us to try to find her?"

"No."

"Look, Reuben, I hate to even think this, and sure as shit I wouldn't say it to him. But we've been around. We know the score. What if she's committed suicide?"

"That's possible."

"Hey, you're some cool cucumber."

"Yeah. Right," Reuben said, ordering another V.O. "You were saying there was no game."

"Yeah. No game. I mean, they weren't going to cancel until the last minute, those boys. Oy vey, rain checks. Refunds, yet. And I couldn't take my grandchildren to a movie instead, because there wasn't one playing in all of Montreal where they weren't showing fucking, between men and women if you were lucky, but more likely between women and women or men and men. But I don't have to tell you about faggolas. You've got your plate full now, you and him. I've seen the pictures in the newspapers, you know. Who hasn't? But I don't believe a word of it," he said, probing, unable to forget the black satin panties with the lace trim.

"Good. Right. It was a Tuesday."

"Two days after Pauline had skedaddled. Anyhoo, I took the kids back to my daughter's place. NDG. Benny's Farm. Then I noticed one of our cars parked outside of Ma Heller's, and I can do with a burger and a beer, so I pull over. And what do you know, but it's Henri Lupien sitting there. Detective from my station. One of the best."

"Is that the one you had out following Josh all those nights?"

"Nobody was following Josh. He imagined it. Anyhoo, I joined Lupien and I don't know what started it, but suddenly we were talking about the break-ins in Westmount. The kinky ones. Somebody taking the trouble to soak the labels off Pinsky's vino bottles. Somebody diddling with the bathroom scales in Dr. Cole's house and altering the signature on his A. Y. Jackson. Etc., etc. We both agree that we are dealing with a real joker. Maybe even a psycho."

"Or maybe my son."

"And we decide, as neither of us has anything special to do, we will go back to the station and run through the files one more time, just because it's such a puzzle, and we are genuinely intrigued. We're sitting there—mulling over the files, bouncing theories around, laughing a lot—when the call comes in. Ring ring. If it hadn't been pissing. If I had been able to go to the ball game. Shit. There's a prowler reported in the Seligson house on Edgehill. Eli Seligson, he's one of your Jewish heavies. Very active in community affairs. Anti-Defamation League. Etc., etc. We bust a Jewish kid peddling

357

pot in the Alexis Nihon Plaza and we hear from Seligson, you bet. The kid lost an uncle eight times removed in the Holocaust. He suffers from allergies. Don't ruin the pecker's life. Boo hoo. We catch a *yenta* shoplifting—we get a lot of that now, you'd be surprised—and Seligson's on the line. Let my people go, blah blah blah. He's an accountant, the big stuff, and the night the call comes in he's in Geneva or Liechtenstein, registering kosher companies. The call comes in and I've got this gut feeling. My balls are tingling. My mouth is dry. I've been a cop for thirty years now, and your balls are tingling, you don't ignore it.

"Anyhoo, we take off for Edgehill and of course I still have no idea it's him, and like a horse's ass I don't even notice the car down below, on the Boulevard, or I would have recognized it and so help me, we never would've gone in with our guns drawn. I mean, I would have known he wasn't armed. I wouldn't have been scared. But you take a prowler and you never know what you're going to run into. Maybe he's a psycho. Or stoned out of his mind. *Stop smiling at me like that. I didn't know it was him.*"

"You're an honest cop, Stu. I know that."

"The rain's belting down. Some pisser. Henri takes the back door, me the front, and we don't know there's another door in the dining room, leading onto a small balcony, and that he could jump from there. We count to ten, me in front, him in back, and in we charge. Gang-busters. He hears us. He takes off like he was shot out of a cannon. Through the dining room—onto the balcony—into the garden. Down the stone steps to the Boulevard and into his car. Vroom, vroom. We still don't know it's him. I swear we don't. So we run for our own car and take off after him, the sirens going, me with my gun ready. We are gaining on him as he turns into Lansdowne, hitting maybe seventy going down that hill, never mind the rain, the damn fool, and as we are approaching Sherbrooke I can see it coming like I'm already watching a replay. He's going to charge through the red light and cars are already beginning to move across Sherbrooke. Wham. Crash. Bang. Dead bodies everywhere."

"He tried to slow down, you know, but his brakes weren't working."

"He was born with a horseshoe up his ass. I still can't get over the fact that nobody is killed and that he swerves just in time, avoiding the other cars, but bouncing off a hydrant and piling on right through Steinberg's window. Holy shit. Plate glass everywhere. Cans. Broken bottles. And the car totaled.

We send for the firemen. An ambulance. And it's only after they've cut him out of the car that I get a good look at his face. A bloody pulp. And I'm not so much surprised as kicking myself for not thinking of it before. It had to be him."

"Yeah. Right."

"And now he's bleeding all over the place and you can actually see the bones sticking out. I figure he's one dead cookie. I still can't get over the fact it looks like he's going to make it."

"What do you want, Stu?"

"I want you to tell him I need help with my memoirs. Look at that Wambaugh joker. We could make a fortune."

"Yeah. Right."

"It isn't much to ask. Like, I'm really sticking my neck out for your son."

"What about Lupien?"

"He's all right. He owes me. He won't say a word about who was responsible for the break-ins. Neither will he say anything about the furniture."

"What furniture?"

"Most of those antiques in Joshua's house were stolen. A lot of it is listed with us."

"No shit?"

"Don't take me for a fool, Ruby. That would be one big mistake."

"I can see that."

"Will you tell him what I asked?"

"Not yet."

"When?"

"After we move him out of the hospital, not before. But he won't do it, Stu."

"Maybe he'll do it for your sake," McMaster said.

"The furniture?"

"You said it, not me."

"Yeah. Right. Say, Stu, was there any money lying about?"

"Where?"

"Seligson's desk. Or maybe in Josh's car."

"Geez, he wasn't there to rob the place. That was never his bag."

"Yeah. Right. But Seligson's father made bundles on the black market during the war—"

"Figures."

"—and the story is, Eli still has some of it stashed in the house, and I was just wondering, that's all."

359

"There was no money in the car or lying around the house."

"Good. That's a relief to me, Stu. I'd hate to think my son was a crook."

And now that Reuben was sure McMaster had stolen the money Joshua had strewn about Seligson's desk, he knew exactly what to do.

FIVE

1

"... so we break down the door," McMaster continued as the Sony whirled, "and this little Pepsi runt . . . Scrub that. This disadvantaged habitant—he's a holy terror with a gun, but he hasn't got it now—he's cowering in the corner. A rat at bay. Trembling from head to foot. And Sweeney, he was my partner in those bygone days, he's moving in, ready to pistol-whip him. I step right in there, stopping him. I say to Sweeney, quote, We are not vigilantes, but officers of the law. I cannot, in conscience, acquiesce to violence. It does not behoove me. We should endeavor to dig to the roots of this miasmic problem. Social injustice, unquote. And that little punk, he's still shit-scared, he trips and falls down all the stairs, head first. And how's this for irony? Afterwards, his lawyer claims it was us who marked him up so badly. Well, I tell ya. That's when I became cognizant of the veracity to be found in the works of that well-known French writer Albert Camus. Our lives are absurd. Hoo boy, are they ever."

Reuben came in to say that was it, more than enough for one day, and then he led McMaster into the kitchen.

"I've got me a problem, Stu. Maybe you can help."

"Shoot."

"Seligson still doesn't know it was Josh in his house that day. We appreciate that. But the son of a bitch is letting it out in certain circles that a heap of old banknotes was lifted from one of his desk drawers."

"If there was any money stolen, why didn't he register an insurance claim?"

"Because I figure those old banknotes were what was left of his old man's black market money. It was never legit. He doesn't dare claim it now."

"What's he been doing with the money until now, then?"

"Well, he certainly hasn't been unloading it at his bank, because they would have to report such notes coming into the mint. Especially if there was a real wad."

"Yeah. Right."

"I figure Seligson has been unloading it all these years with a coin dealer in New York. Cassidy's on Lexington, who isn't too fussy."

"Gee, those guys. Fucking clever."

"Hey, Stu," Reuben asked, nudging him, "you know why Jews have such big noses?"

"I'll bite. Why?"

"Because the air is free."

McMaster didn't drive out the following morning, but phoned to say he had a more important matter to handle in Montreal. He would resume the tapings on Monday. Meanwhile, he certainly expected Joshua to work on the material.

The senator was relieved for Joshua's sake, but suspicious. Seated before the fireplace with Reuben that night, he said, "I don't understand what could be more important to that boor than his odious memoirs."

"He's in New York."

"What's he doing there?"

"Looking up Cassidy's on Lex. He's a coin dealer. Hey, Senator, aren't you something at the Royal Bank?"

"Board of directors, for my sins."

"Well, there's one of your branches that is on the main street in Ste. Agathe, which is in the Laurentian Mountains. It was robbed on the afternoon of October nineteenth, nineteen thirty-six. Bastards got away with a lot of mint notes, all in sequence."

"Good grief, Reuben, if you also robbed banks you mustn't tell me. I don't want to hear."

"I never got mixed up in anything like that. But I hear on the street that those notes have been buried in somebody's garden all these long years. Only now that somebody has dug them up and taken them down to a coin dealer in New York called Cassidy's which is on Lex."

"You're not suggesting McMaster?"

"As a director, it is surely your duty to inform the Royal Bank, and for them to check out what must be a federal offense."

362

"You're incredible, Reuben, you really are. But, much as I detest the man, I can't be a party to a frame-up."

"Joshua left the money on Seligson's desk. His idea of a joke. McMaster swiped it. That makes him a crook. He should be brought to justice."

The senator got up to poke the fire.

"Cassidy will cooperate. He doesn't want any trouble."

2

He left out snares, like a trapper. Lures for his absent gardener. Bales of peat. The rose bushes she had wanted. Flats of leeks and lettuce and green peppers that had to be brought in every night because of frost. A bag of seed potatoes. A bag of onions. Sacks of leaf mold. Her garden tools sharpened. Everything stacked in readiness at the bottom of the hill. But Pauline didn't come. Instead, Trimble finally turned up.

Jowly Jack Trimble, mooring his Grew 212 at their dock. Strutting a little as he entered the living room. Wearing a fisherman's sweater and paint-stained chinos and scuffed running shoes. His manner overbearingly masculine, which amused Joshua.

"Well, old son," he said, accepting a drink, "I can't pretend that I haven't been reading about your troubles."

Aha.

"Anything in it?"

"In what?"

"In what they say," he replied, smirking.

"And what, exactly, are they saying?"

"Look here, I'm not prejudiced."

"Do you mean, did I love Sidney Murdoch?"

"Well, O.K."

"Yes, I did."

Joshua beamed invitingly and patted down a place beside him on the sofa, but Trimble chose to sink into an armchair on the far side of the room, propping his feet up on the coffee table. Big man. Big country.

"But you're not still . . . well . . . like that?"

"Like what?"

"Oh, you know."

"What a prick you are, Jack!"

Hard little eyes glittering, he asked, "Is that why poor Pauline took off?"

"I'm awfully good with this cane, Jack. And fast. Now tell me what it is you want here."

"I came here to show you that, no matter what, you still have friends."

"I'm touched. Now, tell me, have *you* any friends left?"

"There's nobody on this lake I give a shit about," he said, "except for Pauline. Now there's a real lady."

"What about your wife?"

"You heard me right the first time."

"Does she realize that you were born right here, and that all that tiresome British bit of yours is just a pathetic act?"

"Well now, let me ask *you* a question. Does Pauline know that while she was in the hospital, you entertained Jane at home?"

"Hey, you're a real sweetie."

Trimble reached for the Scotch bottle. "You fucked my wife, you bastard."

"Did I now?"

"I'm not the only one who knows, either. She also told the Abbotts."

Now Joshua reached for the Scotch.

"I'm willing to keep quiet about your humping my wife—after all, it's not the most exclusive club in town, is it?—if you drop all that codswallop about my not being British."

"Did you happen to notice the old man in the straw hat sitting out on the balcony?"

"Your father. I saw him. Yes."

"Well, he's very well connected in surprising places. You were born right here, Jack. In the Point. My father dug up your birth certificate. Do you want to see the photostat?"

"So the two of you are into blackmail as well now?"

"You know, I could call that old man in right now and he could break your fingers. Just like that."

"How much do you want?"

"You really don't understand. I don't want anything. I won't even say anything. I just don't understand why you give a shit. Why you ever bothered. You never had to come on with that lot, Jack."

"Tell me," Trimble asked, reaching for the bottle of Scotch again, "did you ever read the society pages when you were a kid in the ghetto?"

"We only read the financial pages there."

"Well, I read them. I kept a scrapbook, I still have it some-

364

where. 'Mrs. Angus Mitchell of Westmount and Georgeville entertained the chief justice of piddly little P.E.I. at home yesterday.' 'Mrs. Angus fucking Mitchell's daughter Jane was among the twats presented at St. Andrew's Ball last night. She wore a gown of white chiffon, but no panties, I'll bet.' All they used to go in for in those days was finger-fucking.''

A contagion seemed to fill the living room. Pestilence. But there was no stopping Trimble.

"You should have known Angus. Her chinless wonder of a father. Staggering about in his kilts on New Year's Eve. Went through the family fortune easy as shit through a goose. And you're looking at the yahoo who stepped in and salvaged what was left of his holdings and built on it. If not for me, it would have been good-bye fake Tudor manse with the coat of arms in the entry hall. So long golfing hols in Bermuda. Ta ta Murray Bay. I saved that old drunk's ass. Then one day I walk into his study—it's only eleven a.m. and he's already stewed to the eyeballs—and I ask him for his daughter Jane's hand in marriage. And do you know what? He looks me in the eye and says, 'And who might your father be, Mr. Trimble?'

"Yes, I was born in the Point and my little mouse of a father was a barber. Shave and a haircut, two bits. 'Hey, Jack, do you know who I got to shave today? McAndrew of the Bank of Montreal.' 'Hey, son, this morning I shampooed the president of Dominion Steel. He told me to buy Algonia Mines right now.' *Yeah, with what? His cheesy little tips?* Then the war came. World War I. Pack up your troubles in your old kitbag and smile, smile, smile. My father is one of the first to enlist and they take one look at that skinny groveler and of course they make him a batman. Jimmy Trimble now not only gives shaves and haircuts, but he also shines the shoes of his betters. Only he comes marching home minus a lung, the other one filled with stringy green slime. Back to the barbershop on St. James Street. 'Welcome home, Jimmy. I told you your job would be waiting.' 'Thank you very much, Mr. Selby.' The big brokers and bank presidents who come in there, they tell my father how glad they are to see him back, but the truth is, they're not happy for long. Mr. Selby takes my father aside. 'Jimmy,' he says, 'I've got to let you go.' 'Why?' 'Well, you're always hawking your lungs out in the sink, and it makes my customers feel bad. They're big men, under constant pressure. Some of them didn't fight. They feel guilty here, and they go get their hair cut somewhere else.' My father not only understands, he apologizes for himself. But all he knows is cutting hair. So he begins to cut hair for sick people at home, and he learns to swallow his slime rather than hawk it. He comes home and he races for the toilet and he's in there for an hour, retching. Only one fine day the little groveler goes too far. He swallows too much on the job. My father, far too polite to upset a rich customer, finally drowns in his own snot. That's it. That's how he went, drowning in his slime.

"Well now, time for Jack to quit school. Right? I worked as an office boy. I took correspondence courses. I worked here. I worked there. And, in 1942, I got a job as a curb-service waiter at Miss Montreal. Remember it? The first drive-in on the strip. The Jewish kids used to drive out there in Daddy's black-market Buick. Outremont punks. Big tippers, though. Then the real McGill crowd. The quality. McTeer. Tim Hickey. Dickie Abbott and Wendy. The beautiful Pauline Hornby. Kevin in that MG. The outrageous Jane Mitchell. Yeah, that's right. I knew them back then. Not to speak to, mind you, but to serve. Two Michigan Red Hots and fries? Yes, sir. Four burgers dressed and coffees? Coming right up, sir. I'm nothing. I'm nobody. Once I caught Kevin and Jane doing some heavy necking in the MG. They were loaded, both of them, and he had one hand on her bare tit and the other under her dress. I came up with the order and they didn't even bother to stop. Me, I blushed. I was terribly embarrassed. But they didn't stop. I was no better than a nigger for them," he cried, tears rolling down his cheeks. "Who had to be ashamed? They didn't see me. I didn't exist."

Trimble wiped his nose on his sleeve and reached for the bottle again.

"Fuck it. It was the army and off to war for Jack Trimble. Only I wasn't going to be anybody's batman. I joined the ordnance corps and it was up through the ranks and even into officer's training school once they began to run short of properly born second lieutenants after Normandy. I found out that in class-ridden England, I was not only acceptable to middle-class girls, they found me attractive. I had money. I wore two bars on my shoulder. Then three. Captain Trimble. When we were demobbed, I didn't go home. No more Point for me, thank you very much. I took up my DVA education grant and entered the University of Leeds. Redbrick. Just my style. From there it was Lloyd's and then Warburg's. I learned German. I studied French. I was a hotshot, I had the touch. Money stuck to me. But those *Gazette* society pages were still burning holes in my head. 'Mrs. Angus Mitchell of Westmount and Georgeville . . .'

"I figured out that if I was going to have everything, it would only have meaning for me in provincial fucking Montreal, where I had never had anything. I didn't get a charge out of having my hair cut at Simpson's. I didn't give a shit about eating at the Savoy Grill. I wanted to send the wine back in our very own Ritz-Carlton. I dreamed of it. I could taste it. I was leading a good life. I had lots of girls. South Ken pussy, Belgravia pussy. I had it all. But damn it to hell," he shouted, "you are looking at the man who was going to get his dirty fingernails under Jane Mitchell's skirts. She would see me. I existed. I was going to ram it up her ass and make her howl for more. She was going to take my barber boy's Point St. Charles cock into that well-bred mouth and choke on it."

"Obviously," Joshua said, "you were in love."

"O.K., I pretended to be British. *Why not?* In those days if you were a tea boy at Barclay's over there, you could come to Canada and get to be president of the Royal. If it was British, we were impressed; if it was Canadian, it was shit. I got myself established here easily enough, and one day I was invited to a cocktail party at the British Trade Commissioner's residence and there she was, Jane Mitchell, the family fortune exhausted, her long romance with Kevin Hornby kaput. I wined her. I dined her. Café Martin. Drury's. The Ritz. You name it. But there's something I want to make clear. If she had a bun in the oven when we were married—and it's true enough—nobody was taking me for a sucker. Charlie's my son," he said, beginning to weep again. "No matter what she says now. You just look at him. You look at me. He's my son."

"But I've never heard otherwise," Joshua said, surprised.

"Yeah," he said dubiously, reaching for the bottle. And his voice softer now, a spent force, he said, "I still serve, but now I exist. I manage their portfolios for them. I make those wankers pots of money so now they sure as hell know who I am. They come into my office, *they* grovel. They adore my parties. I put out a better barbecue than anybody else on the lake. I'm not going to carry the can for Kevin's fancy footwork. I'm not to blame if he turned out a coward. I didn't run his airplane into Owl's Head."

"Why did you set him up?" Joshua asked.

"I most certainly did not," Trimble protested.

Joshua had already spoken to Dickie Abbott.

"As far as I can make out," Abbott had said wearily, "and I'm telling you this 'without prejudice,' as I'm bound to say, they were screwing each other. In my opinion, they were both lying. But now Jack will come out of it clean, if not exactly smelling clean. It will take years to unravel."

Watching Trimble closely, Joshua said, "I'll tell you what happened. You were in deep trouble on the market last summer, and then you found out about Jane taking up with Kevin again in Bermuda. So you decided to have your cake and eat it too. You would cover your ass and make Kevin the patsy. Right?"

"You're out of your mind, you crazy fool!"

"Possibly it didn't occur to you until you drove back early from Montreal that day and saw them going at it together in the boathouse."

"I don't know what you're talking about."

"I don't entirely blame you, all things considered. But neither do I believe you."

"Jane may fool around. O.K., everybody's after her, she's so gorgeous, and she's a bit of a flirt. But she always comes back to me, because I'm the only one who can satisfy her. Dickie Abbott is a premature ejaculator, did you know that?"

"For God's sake, Jack, why don't you leave her? She's such a bitch."

"Now you watch it there. You watch what you're saying. I'm not leaving her, she's not leaving me. We're going to open the house for the summer. We're going to have our regular Sunday barbecues. Everybody will come, you'll see. And we're going to have dinner parties again. I've made Jane the leading hostess on this lake. We were in the *Gazette*, the social pages. You must have seen the story. And I'm more of a man than anybody here, including you. She told me that night at your house that she found out you were thirty seconds of action and an hour of apology. We have nothing to be ashamed of. Kevin ran it. The whole show."

Leaning on his cane, Joshua walked to the window, his back to the raging Trimble.

"I gave him a chance when none of his so-called friends would touch him with a barge-pole. And let me tell you something. If he had had to serve a year or two in the pokey, you are looking at the man who would have hired him again, no matter what."

But Joshua wasn't listening any more. His heart was soaring. He felt himself quivering all over. My God, but she was

368

out there, at the bottom of the hill. Pauline was in the vegetable garden. A fork in her hand.

"Coral will be wound up by the receivers and I will do my bloody best to minimize everybody's losses. Kevin wouldn't have wanted his friends to suffer financially."

"Go now. Please go, Jack."

He could see the children approaching her. Tentatively.

"What?"

"Will you please get the hell out of here, Jack. Right now." And he slipped out the side door, starting for the garden.

Joshua, leaning on his cane, met his father halfway down the hill to the vegetable garden. Joshua was descending, his step cautious; his father was coming up, the senator trailing a little behind.

"I once flinched from your kiss," Joshua said.

"Did you?" Reuben asked, startled.

"Don't you remember?"

"I guess I do. Josh, there's something you got to know."

"Isn't she here to stay?" he demanded.

"Hold it. Don't get excited. It wasn't the morphine, Josh. You didn't dream it."

"What are you talking about?"

"She came to the hospital more than once when you were there. I brought her."

"You mean to say you knew where she was all this time?"

"Yeah, well, right."

"Son of a bitch."

Reuben took off his straw boater and wiped his forehead with his handkerchief. "I promised her not to say anything. She needed time to work things out. Well, now you know."

"How could you do such a thing to me?"

"Well, you're no longer all I've got. There are the kids now. There's also Pauline. I was doing what I thought was best for everybody. What did Trimble have to say?"

"He had a stone in his shoe and he took it out himself."

"Now, look here, she's still rocky on the subject of Kevin. I want you to go careful. I want you to lie if necessary."

"Don't worry."

The senator smiled shyly. "Everything is going to be fine," he said.

Reuben was already whistling for the kids, collecting them under the cedar tree. "Well now," he said, "the senator and I are going to take you to Magog for ice creams. How about that?"

The two old men continued down the road, the kids

trailing after, and everybody piled into the Jeep. Reuben could see Joshua and Pauline in the vegetable garden. They weren't embracing. He was touching her hair. Then, watching from the rear window of the moving Jeep, Reuben saw them start back for the house. Joshua wasn't leaning on his cane. Pauline was supporting him. Well, yeah, right, he thought.

ABOUT THE AUTHOR

MORDECAI RICHLER, as prolific as he is gifted, is the author of eight novels, including the present one, writer of many screenplays (among them the film version of his own *The Apprenticeship of Duddy Kravitz*) and observer of curious societies—from the Klondike to Hollywood—in articles that have appeared in leading English, Canadian and American periodicals. He lives in Montreal, where he was born and brought up and to which he returned a few years ago after two decades in London, with his wife and their two daughters and three sons.

SEAL BOOKS

Offers you a list of outstanding fiction, non-fiction and classics of Canadian literature in paperback by Canadian authors, available at all good bookstores throughout Canada.

The Canadian Establishment	Peter C. Newman
A Jest of God	Margaret Laurence
Lady Oracle	Margaret Atwood
The Fire-Dwellers	Margaret Laurence
The Snow Walker	Farley Mowat
The Dionne Years	Pierre Berton
St. Urbain's Horseman	Mordecai Richler
Act of God	Charles Templeton
The Stone Angel	Margaret Laurence
Love Affair With a Cougar	Lyn Hancock
Judith	Aritha van Herk
My Country	Pierre Berton
When Lovers Are Friends	Merle Shain
The Diviners	Margaret Laurence
Lunar Attractions	Clark Blaise
Bronfman Dynasty	Peter C. Newman
The Edible Woman	Margaret Atwood
Men for the Mountains	Sid Marty
Needles	William Deverell
A Bird in the House	Margaret Laurence
Never Cry Wolf	Farley Mowat
Children of My Heart	Gabrielle Roy
People of the Deer	Farley Mowat
Life Before Man	Margaret Atwood

The Mark of Canadian Bestsellers

SB-5